AS 101541

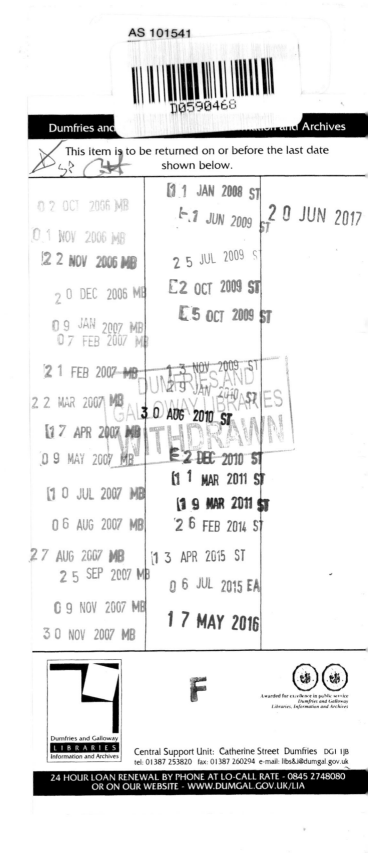

Also by Moira Forsyth

Waiting For Lindsay

What the Negative Reveals
(ArtTM)

David's
Sisters

MOIRA FORSYTH

SCEPTRE

First published in 2000 by Hodder and Stoughton
A division of Hodder Headline
A Sceptre book

10 9 8 7 6 5 4 3 2 1

A CIP Catalogue record for this title
is available from the British Library

ISBN 0 340 75002 2

Typeset by Palimpsest Book Production Limited,
Polmont, Stirlingshire

Printed and bound in Great Britain by
Clays Ltd, St Ives plc

Hodder and Stoughton
A division of Hodder Headline
338 Euston Road
London NW1 3BH

For Dorothy

Prologue ∫

'See this photograph? There, that's my mother, Faith, coming up the path between the lilac trees. It's not a good photograph – the sun is behind her, so you can't see her face.'

Eleanor was kneeling amongst packed cardboard boxes, with the helpless expression of someone who has meant to get through a lot today, but has instead spent the morning re-reading old letters, trawling the past.

She looked down at the photograph in her hand. 'She's so small and slender you might think she was a boy in those trousers, with her open-necked shirt. But it was how she dressed. All the other mothers wore skirts and jumpers.' She spread out the faded snaps like a fan on the floor. 'It's the garden at Pitcairn. I found this packet of photographs tucked away in an envelope at the bottom of a box of books. Look, here's one of all of us – all except my father. He must have taken it. I look about nine or ten, don't I? My fringe is too long, and I'm frowning. That's Marion just behind me, and David of course. Two well-behaved sisters, standing together staring at the camera, and David, refusing to be the right way up, trying to walk on his hands.'

Eleanor gathered up the remaining photographs, tapping them together like a bunch of cards. 'I associate that day with Aunt Alice, for some reason. And the fire – did I tell you about the fire at the Mackies'? In the barn? That was the big drama of our childhood – well, it seemed like it at the time. I must have told you. Anyway, it had been really hot, and I think this day, the day the photos were taken, it was thundery. There was a storm in the afternoon, and everyone said, if only it had happened the night before, the fire wouldn't have taken hold. Maybe it was Alice's camera, she doesn't seem to be in any of the pictures.'

She picked out another, looking at it again. 'Here we all are on the bench at the back door – Aunt Mamie too, so Aunt Alice must have been somewhere about. And David, hanging over the edge, spoiling it again.'

She sat back on her heels, dreaming, thinking how strange it was that a photograph could tell the truth about a single moment, and yet was no more than another lie in the tight weave of their lives. The false picture.

'What?' She looked up, startled out of memory. 'No, you're right. It's not a good idea, to go through old photographs at a time like this. It's only a house move or a death that makes you do it, eh? When there's more than enough disturbance already.'

Eleanor tucked the photographs back in their yellow envelope, faded with age, one corner torn.

'Right, that's that. I've had enough of stirring up the past – let's put them back in the box.'

$\int$

Old houses move in the night, attempt to flex tired muscles, creak and crack and moan a little. There is nothing in this, it does not matter; it is even, in its familiarity, reassuring.

Faith woke from a dream she could not catch as it fled. Something of it was left, a taste in the mouth, a feeling of dismay. John still slept, whistling through his teeth. In a moment, he would begin to snore, and she would nudge him over on his side. The house, the room, were very cold. She listened, wondering what had wakened her – the dream, or a child's cry? If it were one of the children, another call would come, '*Mummy,*' thin along the landing, and she would get up and go to see what was wrong. But there was nothing. Only the faint crack of a floorboard, the settling of a window frame, a draught lifting the edge of a rug. Cold, she edged nearer to her husband, but could not get back to sleep. After a moment or two, she slid out of bed and reached for her dressing gown. She would check the children, to set her mind at rest.

In the girls' room, Marion lay on her back straight as a soldier, a curly-haired doll on either side. A gap in the curtains let moonlight in, so the children were visible, but Marion was quite still and made no sound. Faith leaned over the child's bed, to hear her breathe. How often she had done this, especially in babyhood, those first terrifying nights when the new infant seemed fragile as glass, a whisper away from birth, from death.

Eleanor was curled round tightly, the bedclothes rumpled, books and teddies fallen on the floor. Faith straightened the bed, and eased Eleanor's thumb out of her mouth. A few seconds later, as her mother left, Eleanor tucked it back in, sucking vigorously in her sleep.

In David's room, the curtains were wide, as if he had got up to open them after bedtime (hoping to catch sight of the fox), and on the edges of the window panes frost glittered. Since falling asleep, David had flung off his blankets and lay at right angles to the mattress, one leg hanging over the side. He gazed at her as she settled him again, dark eyes wide but not seeing. 'It's all right,' she whispered, 'go to sleep.'

He closed his eyes, and she crossed to the window to draw the curtains. In the garden, moonlight moved among the trees and over the grass. You could imagine you were seeing things in this clear, bluish light, under the thick-starred sky. Shadows moved and separated and a thin figure seemed to float over the lawn. Faith thought of the tinker woman who had appeared a few weeks ago, standing at the back door in pouring rain. She had carried a baby, a strong, black-haired boy of a year or so, who pulled away from her arms, and kicked. Despite her thin face and bony ankles, she was clearly pregnant, her belly swelling beneath the cord tied round her coat.

Faith had taken the woman into her warm kitchen, where she had nothing to sell but a few pegs. The boy, set down on the floor, made for the cat, and then the hot oven, ignoring his mother's whine as she tried to restrain him.

'Have you somewhere to stay?' Faith asked, heart sinking as she saw them out, the woman warmed by tea, a half dozen scones wrapped in greaseproof paper tucked in her bag that was made of sacking, and already wet.

'Aye, we've gotten a van,' the woman said, and made, to

Faith's surprise, a sign of the cross in the air. 'God bless you, mam, God bless,' adding some words that were torn away by the wind howling across the yard and whipping up her coat. Underneath she wore a skirt of some thin material that clung to her bare legs. Faith made out only the word 'bairns', and nodded, glad her own had stayed in the living room where they were playing, unaware of the tinker woman or her child.

Later, John said Dan Mackie, from the Mains, had told him the woman passed this way every year. Her eldest child had died of pneumonia, and there was a man with her, who was rough, but did some labouring work on the farms.

'Dan says he doubts they're real travelling folk – they mostly stick together. This pair's on their own.'

'And she's having another bairn.'

'Aye, well, that's the way of it.'

'In the town, folk like that . . .' Faith hesitated. 'There are plenty of them, I know. But they don't come to your door, as a rule.'

'A fine easy time you had of it,' her husband teased, planting a kiss on her dark head as he went to get in more coal for the fire. 'Growing up in the fancy West End of Edinburgh.'

'Ach,' she retorted, 'it was you wanted to live in the country.'

But they did not pursue this: they had agreed to leave Aberdeen, at the same moment, and for the same reason.

'We want to bring up our family in the country,' they said to all their friends when they sold the house in the city and found Pitcairn. But it was not the real reason.

Faith sighed, and pulled David's curtains together. It was not the tinker woman who had crossed the garden, only a shadow. Or perhaps the fox was there, as David believed. Dan

Mackie had said there was one about just now. Thinking of her chickens, she was more afraid of this than any tinker, any ghost. There were no ghosts at Pitcairn. The house had lain empty for a year before they moved in. It had damp, and mice, and a pigeon nesting in the loft, but Miss Sutherland, the last of her family to live in the place, had died in a nursing home, leaving nothing of herself more sinister than a wheelbarrow and an old coat in the shed, and in the pantry a dozen stone jars her nieces had not thought worth removing. Faith and John had bought some furniture with the house, not having the means to fill such a large place at once, but everything was empty except for a button or two in a chest of drawers. So they had started afresh at Pitcairn, cleaning it all the way through, ready for their family.

Faith turned to look at David asleep, and quite still now. She tucked the blankets under him more tightly, then she went out, pulling his door to behind her.

Along the broad landing, moonlight fell from the open doors of the spare bedrooms. If you did not shut these doors firmly, the handles turned of their own accord; the doors moved across linoleum, and stood open. Empty rooms, chill and sparsely furnished with Miss Sutherland's mahogany and oak, lay behind these doors. Two years after moving, they could not fill this house, or afford to furnish it anew. Faith knew everyone thought it was she who had chosen the place, insisting on a big house. She was the one brought up in an Edinburgh suburb, sent to a private school, a lass with a talent, a future, who had stooped a little, in marrying John Cairns. But John had wanted this house, he had found and chosen it, wanted the ground that went with it, space, quiet, the distance from both their families. She would rather have stayed in the city. Aberdeen was not Edinburgh, but it meant town life; it was prosperous and busy.

She stepped across the landing, moving, as she occasionally did even now, like a dancer, placing the ball of her foot down first, turning out her leg from hip to ankle, the instep facing the ceiling, her whole body controlled. Play acting. She pulled her dressing gown round her, and went back to her own room. But as she reached the door, something caught her eye and she halted, drawing in a fine breath. The shadow again, thin and dark, moving down the stairs into the deeper darkness below, where the hall had no outside light but what slipped through the cracks in the closed doors of the downstairs rooms. It was no more than a movement of the heavy curtains over the landing window, vanished into blackness, lost. *I know who you are*, Faith told the shadow. *And you're too late.*

A decision had been made, with which everyone agreed. There was no going back, for the shadow in the garden, or the one on the stair, or for Faith herself. She closed the bedroom door, and got into bed again.

Once, when Marion was eleven and Eleanor and David nine and seven, Aunt Mamie and Aunt Alice came to look after them. Their parents were going to be away for two nights.

'Why do they always appear at the worst possible moment?' Faith cried, dusting flour from her hands when Marion came to tell her that the Ford Anglia was coming up the drive. It was a new car, but Dad said the gear box would wear out in six months, the way Mamie drove. 'Go and help them take their bags in.' Faith was making a pie for them all to have at tea-time, when she and John had left. 'I'll be through in a minute.'

Marion and Eleanor went out of the back door and ran round the side of the house. It was mid-summer, and the tubs at the front door were full of red geraniums and trailing lobelia, lavender and white. The breeze that drove thick clouds fast across the sky swept up Mamie's scarf as she emerged from the car, breathless with the effort of getting the pair of them safely all the way from Aberdeen.

'Now then, let me see you?' She stood Marion and Eleanor back to back. 'What a pair – grown six inches every time! And where's Davy?'

'Out with Stanley. Stanley's his best friend,' Marion amplified.

'In the woods I bet,' Eleanor added.

Mamie had a cream leather suitcase, and several other bags, including a hat box. Alice had a brown suitcase, and that was all. But there was a pot plant still to come from the recesses of the Ford Anglia, a box of biscuits, a parcel from the butcher Mamie favoured (a little slimy, a drip of blood through the brown paper – Eleanor would not carry this), a Dundee cake in a tin and a box of chocolates.

'I've plenty here for them to eat,' Faith said, offended, when Marion and Eleanor deposited all this food on the kitchen table.

'Ach, I'm sure thae bairns eat you oot a house and hame.' Mamie came into the kitchen and took off her hat. Under it, her fluffy hair had gone flat, so she ruffled it up again, standing in front of the tiny mirror pinned to the wall by the back door. (This was the glass they got on a stool to glance in to see they were 'tidy' before they set off for school.) 'Dearie me, what a sicht.'

'You're fine,' Alice said. She had come in silently, unnoticed in all the commotion. She and Faith looked at each other and nodded, but did not hug or kiss. Alice was not a hugging sort of aunt. Yet the girls were drawn to her, and followed her about, watching, listening, asking questions. Davy hung around Mamie, who always had sweets in her pockets. But this time, he made off as soon as he'd got his packet of Smarties and chocolate bar, to share them with Stanley, down in their den beyond the apple trees.

Later, all three children stood at the front door with their aunts, and waved as their parents drove away. They too, had a new car, and what the children envied most of all was this journey in the blue Morris Oxford. They had not been further than Sunday School yet.

'When will they be back?' Eleanor tugged Mamie's sleeve.

'Sunday,' Alice said, 'before tea-time.' David picked up the stick that went everywhere with him, and ran along the side of the house, scraping it on the wall.

Mamie put her arm round Eleanor's shoulders and squeezed. She smelled of sweet perfume, and of the mints she sucked because of her heartburn. 'Dinna you fret. You've got your aunties to look after you – we'll hae a fine time, eh?' Eleanor wriggled away, and Mamie popped another mint in her mouth. 'Oh my, it's giein me gyp the day.'

'You eat too fast,' Alice said.

'What's heartburn anyway?' Eleanor asked, following Mamie along the hall to the kitchen. She imagined Mamie's heart bursting into flames inside her, then settling down to a deep red glow. No wonder it hurt.

'It's my auld enemy,' Mamie said. 'Now then, who's going to be a help getting these dishes done? Where does your mother keep her apron?'

But Alice had unhooked it from the back of the cupboard door, and made a start already. Marion stood by with a tea towel, Eleanor behind her to put things away. Mamie sat down at the kitchen table and took out her cigarettes.

In the afternoon, Alice weeded the front borders, showing Marion what to do, and Mamie lay on a deck chair on the lawn, reading *The People's Friend*. Eleanor sat beside her, making a daisy chain.

'This is the longest one I've ever done.'

'Right you are.' But when she held it up a little later, to show how she was getting on, Mamie had fallen asleep with her mouth open, and her knees had moved apart, revealing a pink petticoat with lace, and the tops of her fat thighs where the stockings ended. Eleanor tried not to look.

*   *   *

On the first night, Mamie told the bed-time story. David came into the girls' room and sat on Marion's bed, leaning against Mamie's comfortable bulk, rubbing his face on her angora cardigan that she said was made from the fur of white rabbits. Her stories, like her conversation, were about herself.

'Och, I canna mak things up,' she said. 'It's Alice has the imagination for a that. I'll tell you about when I was married, will I?'

'Yes,' said Marion and Eleanor, although they had heard this before. The story was full of descriptions of Mamie's wedding clothes, and Uncle Tom Marshall, whom David had never met, and Marion and Eleanor could not really remember. Mamie was soon in full flight, and did not, fortunately, hear David muttering *Not that again.'*

Marion kicked him to shut him up, but he moved too quickly. Bored, he rolled off the bed and played on the floor with the dolls' house. Aunt Mamie got to the part about Uncle Tom's terrible death (he had been a policeman who was killed in a motor accident), and recalled in detail the funeral, her black coat and skirt, and the hat with the veil. This had happened when Marion was three. It was difficult for any of them to imagine a time before Mamie moved back to Scotland to live with her Cousin Alice, so it did seem, to both girls, quite like a made-up story.

'Now then,' Mamie continued, 'Alice had a very nice flat, but there was no room for all my bits and pieces, was there? So what did we do?'

'Bought your house beside the park,' Marion and Eleanor chorused.

'That's right, so that two lassies I know, and a wee loon, can come and feed the ducks when they visit their aunties.'

As she spoke, Eleanor turned to see David rocking the dolls' house violently to and fro. 'Stop that!' she screamed, hurling herself off the bed.

David paused, bewildered. 'What for?' he asked. 'It's an

earthquake. All the furniture's going to get broke, and the people's being killed.'

'No, they're not!'

In the struggle, the house fell over between them, crashing to the floor on its side: a chimney snapped off, the front clattered open and the dolls and their possessions tumbled onto the floor. No one heard Aunt Alice come in, but in a moment, she had made everything straight again, and quiet. Mamie had set off downstairs in search of glue to fix the chimney, and the house was upright, the furniture at least indoors again, if not all in the proper places. David said he was sorry, though not with any appearance of knowing why he should be.

'Tell me a story, then,' he whined. 'I was fed up, I never got a story.' But Alice took him off to his own room.

'Tomorrow,' she promised. 'Tomorrow you can have three stories – one each.'

'Made-up ones,' he warned.

'Made up,' she agreed, tucking him in, drawing the curtains.

Alice knew how to tell stories. She looked ordinary, but her stories were not.

'We'll have the first story in David's room,' she said, 'and then he canna cause a rumpus and break abody else's toys.'

'It wasn't my fault.'

'No, it was the bad ghost's fault,' she agreed. David stopped in the act of climbing into bed.

'What bad ghost?'

'Get under the covers,' Alice ordered. 'That's right. Are you settled, girls?' Eleanor and Marion were tucked in the armchair together. It was a squash now they were so big, but they lay with their arms round each other, Eleanor's long hair tickling Marion's chin, and Marion's rabbit slippers falling with soft thuds from her feet to the floor. They waited for the stories to begin.

'You said there was a ghost,' David persisted. 'Is it in this house?'

'Everywhere,' Aunt Alice said, 'that there's naughty children. Then, when there's mischief, some other body can get the blame.'

David looked confused, but he wanted his story, so he leaned back on the pillow, hugging the blue cloth dog, whose ears he had almost chewed off.

David's was the story of the Tinder Box. This took a long time, and at the end of it, he was almost asleep. Eleanor had her thumb in her mouth, though once or twice, Marion had tried pulling it out with a 'pop'. Aunt Alice stood up and tucked David's covers round him. Then she signalled to the girls, and put her finger to her lips to warn them to be quiet. They slid off the chair and tiptoed back to their own room.

Aunt Alice did not have a smell, like Aunt Mamie, and she was bony, not soft and yielding. She stood by the window in their room, thin as a pencil in her navy skirt and jumper, while they said their prayers and got into bed.

'Now then,' she said, and drew the curtains across. 'It's getting late – what about one story tonight, and another one before Mummy and Daddy come back tomorrow?' But they wanted both of them now. Alice sighed, and began.

Eleanor's story was about the Little Mermaid. Both girls cried when they heard how her feet were cut to ribbons by the sharp stones, how she had sacrificed herself for love. Later, hearing of this, Faith said, 'For goodness sake, that horror story! Whatever possessed her?' Faith liked *What Katy Did* and *Little Women*; she thought stories should be about good behaviour, and have a moral. She had no time for fairy tales, and seemed annoyed with Alice. But then, she often seemed a bit annoyed with Alice. This was strange, because in the children's opinion, it was Aunt Mamie who could be really irritating.

By the time Marion's story was properly begun, Eleanor too was asleep. Marion sat straight up in bed, feeling special, and determined to stay awake.

'If you tell me,' she offered, 'I'll tell it to Eleanor and Davy.' She was afraid Alice would not think it worthwhile to tell a story to just one child.

There was still light outside, and the birds sang on, not knowing it was bed-time. Night-scented stocks and sweet alyssum, filling the borders next to the house wall, floated their fragrance through the open window. Aunt Alice sat in the basket chair and folded her ringless hands in her lap. Her voice was low and seemed to come from far away, from the land where the fairy tales began.

'Once upon a time,' she said, 'there was a princess who liked to get her own way. She was a very hardy wee girl, so that when her mother the Queen said, "Keep your shoes on; wear a coat or you'll catch cold," she disobeyed. She went out on the coldest days in her party frock and silver sandals. She was never ill, so she thought she must be right, and her mother wrong.' Already, Marion could feel retribution must be on the way, and she was not sure if her sympathy was with the naughty Princess or the long-suffering Queen.

'She used to sit by the river,' Alice went on, 'and put her bare feet in the water. Her mother said, "Don't do that, you'll catch your death of cold." But she never did. What happened was, the fishes came and kissed her toes, and nibbled at them, very very gently, and it was tickly, so she liked that.' Aunt Alice leaned forward suddenly, and lifting Marion's blankets, touched her toes with icy fingers. Marion drew her feet back with a squeal.

'Wheesht!' Aunt Alice nodded at the sleeping Eleanor, and smiling, sat down again.

'Then, one dreadful day, a great big fish came along, gliding through the black water, and when he saw the other fish kissing the princess's toes, he thought she must be something good to eat.' Marion felt the bad thing coming, and wanted Alice to stop. But she knew the end of the story had to be told. 'So along came this big fish, swoosh, through the water, and the wee fish swam off, scared, when they heard him. So, do you know what happened next? Do you know what he did, that great big muckle fish?'

'No,' whispered Marion. 'Don't tell me.' But Alice did.

'He nibbled and nibbled at first, gently, then he liked her so much, she was such a sweet-tasting wee lassie, that he opened his great mouth, with all its sharp teeth, and he bit off her toes, one by one, all of them, all the way along her feet. She had none left, not one.'

Marion put her hands over her ears. 'I told you not to say!'

'Wheesht, it a comes right in the end.'

Then there was the rest of the story: a search for a wise woman, a Prince appearing suddenly who could carry out the tasks that followed, an adventure, and eventually, a spell to make the princess's toes grow again. But Marion, trying later to tell all this to Eleanor and David, got confused at that part, and gave it up. Perhaps she had fallen asleep before the end. She was not sure.

'Anyway,' she finished, 'I know they grew back.'

'Poor Princess,' Eleanor sighed.

'She was naughty, though.'

'I'm a shark,' David growled, diving at Eleanor's feet, 'and I'm going to eat your big toe first!'

'Well,' Faith said, coming in, 'I wish I'd stayed away longer, if this is how you're all going to behave.'

Marion flung her arms round her mother's waist. 'No,' she cried. 'We never want you to go away again!'

Faith held Marion tightly in the circle of her arms. She

had her own reasons for being uneasy all the weekend away from home. 'We won't. Not till you're much older.'

That night, checking her children before she went to bed, Faith was relieved to see them all asleep and peaceful.

'What stories that pair have been filling their heads with,' she said to John as they got into bed.

'Well, what can you expect? They've no experience of bairns.' For a moment, they looked at each other in silence. Then John said, 'Ach, put out the light.' So she did, and they lay down to sleep.

2

Saturday afternoon: the High Street full of families. Eleanor leaned forward in her seat and tapped on the window of the café.

'There are the girls – look. On the other side of the street.' She tapped again.

'They've seen us.' Marion waved; their daughters weaved between shoppers, the bell of the café door pinged and they came up to the table.

'We're going to Woolworth's to get smelly stuff for Emma's birthday present.'

'Gimme a taste of your cake, Mum.' Claire bent her fair head, mouth open, and Eleanor fed her a spoonful of chocolate sponge. A quick pink tongue whisked away a smear of icing from her upper lip. 'Yum. It's nice.'

'Go away,' Eleanor said. 'We're trying to have a quiet cup of tea here.'

'OK.'

'Can I have a bit more money?' Eilidh tugged Marion's arm. 'I bought a magazine, and the wrapping paper cost—'

'How much? Here.'

'Thanks.'

'See ya.'

Marion and Eleanor watched the girls stride off up the High Street, leaning together and giggling.

'What long legs they have,' Marion said, 'or is it just the trousers they wear?'

So here we are, Eleanor thought, as the dark head and the fair one disappeared into Woolworth's. Here we are, eating cake in the afternoon, while our daughters plan parties, discos, presents; our daughters are fillies cantering over grass, tossing soft new manes, testing out the boundaries of the field.

'You've got a funny look on your face,' Marion said. 'Is that cake all right?'

'Fine.' Irritated, Eleanor pushed the plate away, and poured herself another cup of tea. 'I was thinking about . . . time.'

'Oh.'

'Do you remember,' Eleanor went on, adding a splash of milk, 'David and his friend Stanley Robertson having a den at the bottom of the garden at Pitcairn? They wouldn't let anyone else in. But when we did go in there was nothing there but a pile of sticks and some sweetie wrappers.'

'What on earth made you think of that?'

'I don't know. It just came into my head.' Eleanor pushed her finger along the tablecloth, making a track through some spilt sugar. 'I wonder where he is?'

'Och, let's not think about that again. We only go round in circles. He'll turn up, he always does. And Dad's all right.'

'I know. He seems to accept it now – the way Davy disappears.'

'Used to it,' Marion said. 'I think, you know, as long as he has Pitcairn, and the garden, he's happy.'

'You're probably right.'

They turned to look out of the window again, as if expecting to see Claire and Eilidh reappear. But both of them were still picturing the long garden at Pitcairn, and their father going steadily down the path with his wheelbarrow, more slowly, and with a less heavy load now that he had angina. They watched him, in the clear space imagination makes for a real place, a real person.

Then Marion began to gather her things together, and Eleanor turned to pick up her bag.

'Whose turn is it to pay?'

'Mine, I think.' Marion opened her purse and poked among the coins. 'I'm sure it is. And I've got change for once.'

Eleanor waited by the door while Marion talked to Joan at the till about the weather, and Joan's mother's operation. Then they were out in the High Street, and a keen wind flapped open Eleanor's mac.

'I'm teaching all week,' Marion said, 'so I'll ring you on Friday.'

'All right. I'll be going up to town – but I'll do it early.'

'Right. I think it's turning colder, don't you?'

'Yes. Freezing.'

Do I feel the cold more than Marion? Eleanor wondered as she walked up the High Street towards the car park. We should be hardy, we both grew up in that cold house, no central heating. We wore liberty bodices, and thick grey socks and navy nap coats in winter, with a wide scarf tied round like a shawl, and pinned at the back. What little barrels we must have looked, wrapped up against the East wind, the snow, the long winters.

Outside the newsagent, Claire and Eilidh were in a huddle of girls. Around the fringes, two or three boys showed off, balancing on the back wheels of their bikes, shoving each other, calling out. The girls said, 'Hi,' as Eleanor passed; the boys stared, embarrassed.

'Tea at six, remember,' Eleanor said. 'I'm going out tonight. How are you getting home – you want to come with me now?'

Claire hesitated. 'No, it's OK. Sarah's mum's picking her up. She'll let me off at the farm road.'

'That's fine.'

*   *   *

When Eleanor bought the cottage, Claire was nine, and taken everywhere by car: school, Brownie night, swimming club, ballet lessons . . . Eleanor was scarcely able to remember that different life. Even the names of the other women, and the little girls Claire played with, eluded her. Apart from Barbara, who had been her own close friend, and her daughter Hannah, who was Claire's, they merged, undifferentiated in memory. Now Claire was almost fifteen, and they were living in a very different world. When she chose her country cottage, Eleanor had been imagining quiet mornings and silent nights, the wind in the trees, and having room to breathe. She had not foreseen Claire's impatience with its remoteness, or that she herself might one day no longer want to be separate and alone.

She and Claire lived at the far end of a row of three farm cottages. The farm had changed hands before she moved back North, and the cottages were sold off separately. The middle one was bought by Jim and Edie, who had always lived there. Jim had worked on the farm until he retired. The other house had been bought by someone who rented it out as a summer let, then put it up for sale. It had lain empty all the previous winter. In the summer, a couple had bought it, moving in at the end of August, but Eleanor had not seen much of them. Sometimes there were two cars by the door at night, sometimes one, but during the day there was no one at home.

Eleanor had the biggest piece of garden. She spent a lot of time there, but her efforts did not seem to have made much difference to the ragged grass or overgrown borders. Next door, Jim and Edie had flowers and vegetables in neat rows, and a patch of lawn smooth as green felt.

Indoors the cottage felt cold. Eleanor hung up her coat and hurried to the kitchen, which the Rayburn kept warm. She stood with her back to the stove, letting the heat flow up to her neck, resting her hands on the metal bar where the tea-towels were hung. After a moment, she turned and got her apron from the hook behind the back door. Then she began to prepare the meal.

Just before six, Claire came in, banging the door and kicking off her trainers in the narrow hall.

'Hi, what's for tea? Sarah's coming for me at quarter past seven, I've to be at the end of the road. Can I have a shower?'

They had just begun to eat when the telephone rang. Claire scraped back her chair. 'I'll get it – it might be Eilidh.'

'Tell her you'll ring back.' But Claire reappeared in a moment.

'It's Grandpa John.'

'Oh, right.' Eleanor put her plate in the bottom oven to keep warm.

'Dad?'

'Marion's engaged, and she's an awful bletherer, so I thought I'd try you now.'

'Dad, can I ring you back, we're having our tea.'

'It's all right, I've not phoned to take up your time. I thought you'd want to know David's home.'

'When?'

'Arrived this afternoon, out of the blue. As well it wasn't my golf day.'

'On his own?'

'Aye.'

'So – how is he? Where's he been all this time?'

'You'd better come and ask him yourself.'

'How long's he staying?'

'Och, you know him, never says. A wee while.'

'I suppose Claire could go to Marion's. Marion is teaching this week, so she wouldn't be able to come.'

'You away to your tea then, don't let it get cold.'

'Are you OK?'

'I'm fine, lass, I'm just the same.'

'Right, well, I'll ring you. See you Wednesday, maybe.'

Claire was reading a magazine while she ate. She looked up as her mother sat down again. 'Is Grandpa all right?'

'Yes, but your Uncle David's turned up.'

'I haven't seen him for ages – not since I was wee. He came and stayed with us when Dad was alive, didn't he?'

'Yes, often. He worked in London then.'

'Where's he live now?'

'Oh, I think – maybe Edinburgh.'

'Mum! He's your brother, you must know that.'

Eleanor laughed. 'He moves around a lot.'

'Is he coming to see us this time?'

'I don't know. Grandpa wants me to go down to Aberdeen and see him.'

'Can I come?'

'You'll be at school.'

'I could easy miss it, it's boring just now. We don't learn anything anyway.'

'Don't be daft, Claire.'

'I liked him – Uncle David. He used to bring presents every time, those play people, remember? I've still got them, in the loft.'

'Did David give you those?' Eleanor thought back to that other world in Berkshire, the new house, and Ian coming home at seven off the London train in a swarm of commuters. The hot car, Claire bouncing on the back seat, and the other women standing with toddlers and dogs in the treeless car park, July sun merciless on tarmac, flashing off the cars' metallic sheen. Then Ian, amongst the other men, jacket hooked over his shoulder, tie loose, rumpled and sweaty from London, carrying the *Evening Standard* and his briefcase.

'I don't think it's fair. You can go off any time you like, and I'm stuck with boring school.' Claire pushed her plate away, and Eleanor was back in the cottage kitchen, dark enough for the light to be on, October rain spattering against the window.

'What rubbish. I hardly go anywhere.' Eleanor stacked plates and cleared the table.

'I'm having a shower, right?'

'Don't use all the hot—' But Claire had gone. Eleanor fell into a dream, a clutch of cutlery in one hand, thinking of the years when she was married, and her brother David.

But by seven she was driving Claire down the farm road to meet Sarah's mother at the gate. It was raining hard, and they sat in the dark, water streaming down the windows, engine running and lights on so that they kept warm, and Sarah's mother would see the car.

'We're getting all steamed up,' Clare said, rubbing her window with a sleeve, peering out into oblivion.

'I'm picking you up from Emma's tomorrow, is that right?'

'Yeah, I'll ring you. Maybe lunch-time.' She turned to Eleanor. 'Where are you going?'

'Out with Andrew. The new doctor in Fergus's practice.'

'Oh. Is he your boyfriend now?'

'I'm too old to have a boyfriend. And I've only just met him.' She hurried on before Claire could ask another question. 'We're seeing a film. He's picking me up at half-past seven, so I hope – look, there they are.' Another set of headlights, another car moving slowly along the road. Claire grabbed her things, hugging the sleeping bag under one arm.

'Careful – mind the puddles.' Eleanor tooted her horn in greeting to Sarah's mother, then began to turn the car and head back up the track.

She had a tepid shower, cursing Claire, and was ready by the time Andrew's car stopped outside the cottage.

'Good week?' he asked as she got into the car.

'Fine. Hang on – is that my phone?' Inside the cottage, ringing. 'You're not on call?'

'No, no – I'd have the bleeper, anyway.'

'I'd better get it.' Halfway out of the car, Andrew's voice following her. 'The film starts at eight-fifteen, and we're cutting it fine as it is!' But she was already unlocking the door and hurrying into the hallway.

'Thank God, I thought you'd gone out. I desperately need someone not elderly to talk to.'

'Hello, David.'

'Hi, Eleanor – are you OK? Dad said you were coming down, but he's got Alice and Mamie here and they're driving me crazy.'

'Oh, the aunts. They drive *him* crazy. David, look, I'm sorry, I was on my way out. I can't talk just now, we'll miss the beginning of the film. I only came back because the phone was ringing.'

'And telepathically, you knew it was me, and I was in dire straits.'

'Rubbish, of course you're not. Just bored.' And drunk, she thought, realising this. Or had a few at any rate. 'Look, I'll ring you tomorrow.' She was conscious of Andrew, whom she hardly knew, waiting outside. And yet, what she wanted to do was stand in the cold hall and talk to her brother. 'I'll see you on Wednesday, I told Dad I'd come down. Or – Davy, you could come here. Claire was saying she wanted to see you again.'

'Gorgeous Claire – is she still blonde and beautiful?'

'Oh yes, even more so.' She was laughing.

Andrew was in the doorway. 'Are you OK? We'll be late, they won't let us in.'

'All right, sorry. Coming. David, got to go, someone's waiting for me. No, tell you later. See you.'

'My brother,' she explained, as Andrew drove too fast down the track and leaped onto the main road through blinding rain. 'We'd sort of lost touch. But he always resurfaces,' she went on, aware that this man, whom she had met twice before, liked the look of, no more than that, was annoyed. 'Sorry,' she added. 'It was a bit of a shock, hearing his voice.'

'So where is he now?'

'At my dad's. At Pitcairn.'

'Right, your family home. Isn't that what Fergus said? Where is it?'

'Aberdeenshire.' Yes, she thought, my home, my childhood. Suddenly there was something in the car headlights. Then it was gone. 'Careful! What was that? Too big for a rabbit.' She swivelled, but saw nothing in the blackness.

'Fox, maybe.' They were on the A9 now, and he had steadied. He seemed to have stopped being annoyed.

'Sorry,' Eleanor said again. 'Didn't mean to hold you up.'

But the evening was changed, and the film, which he had wanted to see, and she had agreed to because Marion had said how nice he was, how it was time she went out with men again, floated past, leaving her unmoved. Her thoughts were busy with David, and the past. She had forgotten the sense of excitement he could generate, even on the end of a telephone line. I want to talk to him, she thought. I want to ring him up when we get home, or go straight to Aberdeen tomorrow, and see him again.

'Can I give you a coffee?' Andrew asked as they came out of the cinema and walked to the car. 'Or do you have to get straight home?'

Eleanor considered this. What did it mean? She had gone out with only two men since Ian's death, and this was one of them. The first one had not been much of a success. She had suspected he really just hoped for sex; he seemed like a man who was not sure how to find it. Worse, he had bored her. Now she thought Andrew might turn out to be boring too, and really, it was best not to give him the idea this could go on, get anywhere. David had upset her and made everything look different.

'All right,' she said, 'yes. Thank you.' Immediately, she regretted this, and worried all the way to the Tore round-about, where she gathered courage, and told him, actually, she was tired, so if it was all right with him, she would just go home. 'But,' she said, now regretting having changed her mind, 'you could have coffee with me, if you like.'

'No,' he said. 'If you're tired, we'd better leave it.' Was there a hint of sarcasm in this? Eleanor could not tell, and blushed, glad the car was too dark for him to see. What she wanted, she decided, was that he should be just a friend. But now David was coming back, so she would have that anyway, and without all the tiresome business of getting to know each other first.

The rest of the way home, they politely discussed the film.

'I still don't understand,' Eleanor said as the car drew up at the cottage, 'how the man with the gun knew they were in Switzerland. It's a mystery to me, that sort of film. Too complicated.'

'Well, here's something simple, instead,' he said, switching off the engine and turning to her, so that she knew he meant to kiss her, and that if she wanted it to, this could lead (now, or later) to sex. So she kissed him back, but without enthusiasm, not sure she liked his calm face so close to hers. Oh, I am tired, she thought, and my period's due, that's all it is. But she moved her mouth away, leaning with a sigh on his chest. It was as if she was somewhere above them both, watching indifferently as he caressed her shoulder, tried another kiss.

'I'll give you a ring,' he said after a moment or two.

'Yes,' she said, 'that would be nice.'

Through the night, she woke once, wondering where she was. She had been dreaming of Pitcairn, and David.

3

Marion came into the kitchen.

'That was Eleanor,' she said. 'David turned up out of the blue – he's at Dad's.'

Fergus disengaged himself from the sports pages. 'What?'

'David, he's at Dad's.'

'Your brother David? Where's he been, then, all this time?'

'Eleanor doesn't know, she's only spoken to Dad. But she's going down on Wednesday for the day.'

'What about you?'

'Teaching all week.' She sat down opposite her husband, and looked at him across the detritus of the Sunday breakfast table. 'I might go next Saturday, if you're not on call?'

'No, it's Andrew next weekend. But Eleanor would have the kids for you.'

'Och, I know, but it's complicated with Ross's football, and Kirsty's dancing. Eilidh's OK, she looks after herself these days.'

'Aye, I've been noticing. Where is she this time?'

'I told you – Emma Macdonald's. A birthday do last night, so they all stayed over.'

Fergus folded his paper. 'Well, then,' he said, 'I suppose if you want me to see to that shed . . .'

Marion put her boots and jacket on and followed Fergus down the garden. They stood in the crowded shed, between Ross's old bike and the shelves with Fergus's tools.

'I think the water's coming in the window somewhere.'

Fergus ran his finger along the sill. 'No, that's dry. Let's see now.'

'I'll leave you to it.' Marion turned to go. 'I'd better get on.'

But she walked the garden after she left him, looking for signs of damage after last night's wind and rain. Eilidh's sunflowers were leaning sideways, but the stems were strong and unbroken. Marion took a large flower pot and picked up fallen apples from the lawn. As she tipped them into the compost bin, the warm rank smell rose to meet her. 'Needs turning,' she murmured, 'maybe next weekend, if it's dry.'

In the house, she could hear from the kitchen as she worked, the sound of television in the living room where Ross and Kirsty lay on sofas, Kirsty wrapped in her downie, arguing about which programme should be on. Marion pushed the kitchen door shut and turned on the radio.

In the afternoon, she and Fergus were left to themselves. Ross went to a friend's house; Kirsty was collected by Fergus's mother for the weekly visit to Granny's, to take the dog along the beach and eat too many sweet things for tea. Eilidh had gone to Eleanor's house with Claire, and was not yet home. Marion meant to go into the garden; she would just read the paper first. Fergus fell into a doze by the fire, the papers slipping off his knee. In the silence, Marion felt herself drifting. The sky darkened, and it began to rain again. As it spattered on the window, Fergus woke himself with a snore, and snatched at his newspaper. 'What?'

'Nothing,' Marion said. 'You were asleep.'

'Was I? What time is it? Any chance of a cup of tea?'

So she roused herself to make it, and they sat comfortably together, while he talked about work, and the possible need for a fourth partner, and she thought about Eleanor going to Aberdeen, and what David would be like now.

'I know I should be pleased,' she said, when they had disposed, for the meantime, of the fourth partner, 'that he's home. I mean, Dad's always so pleased to see him. But David – this is an awful thing to say – David's trouble.'

'Well, he's a bit . . . never seems to settle, does he? He was in the police for a few years, wasn't he? The Met.'

'Och, that was ages ago. You know that. I think they slung him out, in the end.'

'What's he doing now? Did your father say?'

'The police, that was the last thing he should have gone in for. That or the Army. He never liked discipline of any kind. But I suppose it was the excitement. I don't know what he's doing now. I only hope he has a job, and won't be sponging off Dad for weeks on end. That has happened, you know. Remember – after Mum died.'

'Well, your father was probably glad of the company then.'

'I don't know that he was.' Marion pressed her lips together, disapproving. 'But it just seems to me that whenever David's around, something happens. Something we could well do without.'

'Like what?' Fergus helped himself to more cake, eating one by one the crumbs that showered his jersey. Marion moved the plate away.

'Don't have any more,' she said. 'I thought you wanted to lose weight.'

'You shouldn't make such a good cake, then.'

'What were we saying? Oh, David. Well, the year we got married, for a start. All that business.'

'He was only a kid,' Fergus said. 'He did get a job, didn't he? He lived in London for a while after that.'

'Yes, then when Eleanor moved down to Berkshire, he started going to stay with Ian and her. They weren't long married when she got ill, really very ill for a while. Some sort of virus – remember? He went abroad after that, or Eleanor thought he had. When he came back, that's when he joined the police. You must remember that year he came up to see Dad at Christmas, came up with Eleanor and Ian, and their car crashed at Stonehaven.'

'Oh, I remember that. Eleanor was pregnant, but they lost the baby?'

'She miscarried in the hospital, the night after the crash. How old was Ross – about five? So Eilidh and Claire must have been, what, two and a half? That was an awful Christmas.'

'I'm not sure you can blame David for the accident or the miscarriage. He wasn't driving, was he?'

'No, Ian was. But it was the van-driver's fault. At least, there was something wrong with his brakes.' Marion finished her own tea, and put the mug down. 'But he still hung around, coming to them every weekend, when he was between girlfriends. It was around then that they threw him out of the Met. He said he resigned, but I'm pretty sure . . . He kept saying he was going abroad again, the States this time, but he didn't. Then Ian had his heart attack.'

'So what you're saying is he brings poor Eleanor bad luck?'

'Not just Eleanor. Och, I don't even want to think about it.'

'I suppose every family has a black sheep, eh?'

'Well, he's never done anything really bad. That we know of.' She paused. 'I mean, he's my brother and I'm very fond of him, but—'

The door banged, Eilidh shouted, Hi,' from the hall, and Fergus rose and stretched, scattering more crumbs. 'Time I stirred myself.'

'Me too.' Marion put the mugs on the tray, and began to

straighten newspapers and shake out cushions. 'Good party?' she asked, as Eilidh came in.

'Can I have some of that cake? Yeah, it was great.'

'Use a plate. Don't – oh, well, the state your father's left the place in, I don't suppose it matters.'

'Claire says her mum's going to Aberdeen on Wednesday because Uncle David's visiting Grandpa. Can Claire come here?'

'I'm sure she can.'

'Auntie Eleanor said she'd speak to you about it later.'

Eilidh curled herself in the warm place her father had just left. He ruffled her hair as he went out.

'Mum?'

'What?' Marion paused with the tray.

'It's really queer, isn't it, Uncle David losing touch? I can't imagine that happening with us. See, if Ross went abroad or something and we didn't know where he was – I can't imagine that.'

'The way the two of you fight, I wouldn't have thought you'd mind.'

'That's different. When you were young, what was Uncle David like? I thought he was nice – remember, he came and brought us a Christmas tree one year, absolutely gi-normous, and loads of glass balls, and you said they were dangerous because Kirsty was a toddler?'

'What a memory you have, Eilidh. I'd forgotten that.' But she had not forgotten altogether, knew what was coming before her daughter spoke again.

'Was that the time Timmy was incredibly sick, so we had to get the vet out at Christmas, and then he died anyway? Timmy, not the vet.'

'Yes.' Another terrible Christmas, she thought.

'That was horrible. He was a lovely dog, wasn't he? He was Ross's special dog, really. I've never had a dog of my own. Toby's so old he hardly moves.'

'Don't start, Eilidh.'
'Where's the cats, anyhow?'
'On your bed, no doubt.'

In the kitchen, putting dishes away, Marion went on thinking about the Christmas when David had stayed with them. Eleanor and Ian had not come North that year; they had gone to Ian's parents instead. But the house had been packed on Christmas Day: Fergus's mother, her own parents, David, her father and both the aunts. Where had they all slept? The aunts with Fergus's mother, probably. Was that it? All she recalled with any clarity was the spaniel throwing up in the scullery, then collapsing in his bed, looking up at her, apologetic, helpless. All through the Christmas meal, she and Ross had kept going to check on Timmy. It was all she could do to prevent Ross abandoning the meal altogether. *I'm not hungry, Mum.* They had finally called the vet in the evening. Everyone in front of the television, Eilidh reading, the dog weaker and weaker, Ross very quiet. And David? David beside her in the kitchen: 'Get the vet, somebody's on call. Paid for it. They get paid enough. Just ring him.' So she had.

But in the end, Timmy died. He had cancer, he must have had it since long before Christmas. It could not, of course, be anything to do with David. And he had been a comfort, the one to stay with Ross and talk to him, the only one able to get the boy to come out of his room.

Marion took off her apron and went to telephone Eleanor.
'Did you have a nice time with Andrew?'
'Yes, it was fine.'
'What was the film like?'
'Oh, car chases and stuff. I didn't really understand it.'
'We'll have Claire on Wednesday. Just tell her to come home with Eilidh and bring her things for school next day.'
They talked about David, and their father, but Marion

could not bring herself to say 'He brings bad luck,' or 'Be careful,' which were the things she wanted to say. It was too fanciful. Eleanor was the imaginative one; all the more reason not to put the idea in her head. She went to draw the curtains. The hour had changed, so perhaps that was why she had felt so dull and sleepy all day. The thought of the dark months ahead filled her with gloom. I wish I was going to Pitcairn with Eleanor, she thought. They would all be there without her. But she shook this off, and resigned herself to television, and the ironing. She had no time to brood.

'Now then,' Fergus said later, as they got ready for bed, 'did you change the alarm clock?'

'They're all changed – you saw to the central heating, didn't you?'

'Aye, but I can never remember, are we going to bed an hour later or earlier?'

'Later.'

'No wonder I'm tired.'

'So am I. I've been tired all week. Longer.'

'You do too much. Leave that now.' For she was tidying up after him again, folding his trousers. 'Come away to bed.'

So she did, and they lay with their arms round each other, and talked for a while, and kissed. Eventually she turned on her side and he curved round her, his knees behind hers, his hand on her breast. But his fingers kneaded, pressed.

'Oh, Fergie, do you really . . . I'm so sleepy.' But still his fingers probed, and she realised it was not love-making (which, after a while, she would have responded to) and she moved on to her back.

'What is it?'

'I thought . . . on Friday night, when we – but I wasn't sure. Marion, can you feel a wee something, just there?'

'Oh, doctors never stop working,' she teased, but put her hand on her breast, growing cold as she did so.

'There?' he prompted.

'Yes,' she whispered. Now she sat up, put the lamp on again.

'It's sure to be nothing at all, but see Mary Mackay, anyway.'

'But you should know.'

'Aye, but I don't want to be the one to . . . I don't want – see Mary. I'll make you an appointment when I go in tomorrow. When do you get back from the school?'

Marion was pushing, using all four fingers. It had gone, it was nothing. No, there it was again. 'It seems to sort of move about.'

'It was nothing the last time. That wee scare we had, after Kirsty was born.'

'That was different. It was hard, didn't move.'

'Are you sure?'

'A blocked milk duct or something. Anyway, it went away by itself.' She was angry now, with fright. 'God, Fergus, tell me. You should know.'

'I'm sure it's nothing. I'm sorry I—'

'No, you're right, you were right to say. I'll see Mary, I'll come down after work. About five.' She lay down again. 'All right, satisfied?'

He took her in his arms again, but she lay stiff, wide awake, touching and touching her breast, chasing the tiny elusive lump. So this, she thought, is what the long, dull, ordinary day was leading up to.

'I was bored,' she said to Fergus. 'I was bored all day. But now I wish I was bored again. I wish nothing was happening.'

Fergus held her close, but eventually he slept, and slipped away. She would not tell anyone, even Eleanor. Not till there was something to tell. She would keep it to herself. Still she lay awake, seeing hospital beds, saying good-bye to her children, planning her funeral. This was useless, stupid. Pull yourself together, woman, it's a wee lump, it's nothing.

She leaned on Fergus, warmed herself on solid flesh, listened to his breathing. I won't die. I'm too busy to be ill. I have to see the children grow up anyway; Fergus would never manage the girls on his own. And I have to get Eleanor settled with Andrew, or some other nice man. Make sure Dad's all right, and there's Pitcairn. Eleanor won't know what to do about it, she needs me to talk it over with. (Her breast was sore with being prodded; the lump had gone again.) And it came to her suddenly that she had bought a bag of daffodil bulbs a month ago, to plant under the apple trees, and had forgotten all about them. The bag was still in the garage, the bulbs unplanted.

At last she slept, and dreamed of hospital waiting rooms, and searching for a space to put bulbs, in the garden at Pitcairn.

4

Sometimes, when Eleanor drove to Pitcairn, she went into Aberdeen first, parked, and shopped. But this time, she went directly there by the back road, having no money to spend in the glittering city centre with its new arcades. What she needed was a job.

Ian had left her comfortably off. She had benefited from the surge in house prices in the South of England, which happened after she and Ian had stretched themselves to buy the detached house in Berkshire. Now she had no mortgage, and there was money in trust for Claire to see her through university – if she ever wanted to go there. Eleanor sighed, partly over Claire, partly because she had to slow for a tractor which she could not pass till they were well round the next bend. No, she had enough, the pension covered the basics, and there was still a small income from the money she had invested from the sale of the house. But there was nothing to spare, no money she could really call her own. The road straightened, and she overtook the tractor, but there was a lorry ahead spraying water up from the wet road, so she resigned herself, deciding to stop at Baxters for something to eat.

If she said to her father, 'I could do with a job,' he would say, 'Aye, it's a shame you never finished your degree, like Marion.' It had not seemed to matter then, when she went against her parents for the first time, marrying Ian as soon as he graduated, and setting off with him to the far end of the country. They had wanted her to finish her three years, get a qualification. *Ian says there are plenty of jobs in London. What use is an arts degree anyway?* Pity, she thought now, putting on the wipers to clear the lorry's fine, gritty shower. Pity I was so hasty, so desperate not to lose him, so keen to believe that the only thing that mattered was his wonderful job offer, *his* career. What good did it do me in the end?

The first year had not been the glorious adventure she anticipated. Aimless and homesick, Eleanor had worked in a bookshop, then for an estate agent, giving up gladly when she was pregnant. After she and Claire moved back North, she had worked briefly in a solicitor's office in Dingwall, a job Marion found for her. She was deputising for the 'Properties Assistant'. When the real Properties Assistant recovered from her stay in hospital and returned to work, Eleanor had gone back to doing nothing. Not quite nothing, she told herself. But her poems, her water-colours, seemed trivial, and they did not earn her any money. Sometimes, she wondered if her life would have been different if she had been able to say to her mother, all those years ago, 'I'm not going to university, I'm going to Art School.' But then, the Art School might not have taken her, her portfolio was not varied enough, the teacher had said. He had meant, she thought now, that it was weak.

Fochabers. Eleanor turned off the road, and parked at Baxters, climbing the steps from the car park to the restaurant, turning up the collar of her mac. It was beginning to rain again. She bought vegetable soup and a sandwich, and sat at one of the window tables, looking out at the rain. She would get to Pitcairn by half-past two, three o'clock, at this rate.

The last part of the journey was best: the familiar road, the heavy trees gold and red, still dressed in early November, though leaves drifted in front of the car. The rain stopped:

a ragged hole appeared in the clouds and weak sunshine washed the road with light. Home, Eleanor thought, as she always did, coming round the last bend, seeing the cottages on the right (Ruby lived in the last one), the Post Office and shop, the Pitcairn Arms, and then on the left, half hidden by leaves in summer, but visible now, the sign: *Mains of Pitcairn 1; Pitcairn House 2*. She slowed, and turned into the narrow road.

There were other houses on the way up now: bungalows on both sides, with flat tidy gardens and new conservatories on the south-facing sides. Once, but years before they had bought the house, the land had belonged to Pitcairn, and so had the farm. The farmland had been broken up and sold off, though the farmhouse was still there, just visible in the lee of the hill up on her right. It too had a conservatory now, but the Scotch firs had been cut down, and the place was run as a market garden by one of the Mackies' daughters, and her husband. Not Eileen, who had been their baby-sitter, but the older girl. A middle-aged woman now, with grown-up children.

As Eleanor reached the drive, winding off to the left, she heard the crunch of conkers beneath the wheels. The great horse chestnuts at the entrance to the drive loosed their five-fingered leaves, yellowing now, shook them over Eleanor's car as she arrived.

There was the house. Square, solid, and built of that silver granite that refracts sunlight in flashes, intensifies the light around it. When the sun moved behind a cloud, the granite became cold and grey. Today's sunshine, weak, and dappled through thinning trees, was enough to bathe the house in yellow light, and make it look its best. Eleanor took her car round the back, driving into the doorless outbuilding they had always used as a garage, and taking out her bag (she was going to stay one night, after all), went into the house through the back door.

David was sitting at the kitchen table, reading the *Press and Journal*. He looked up at the sound of the door, and was on his feet as she came in.

'Hello, you got here.'

'David – look at you!' He had a beard, thick and dark as his hair. It changed him: his face was less boyish. But then, he was older. Two years since she had seen him. He spread his arms wide, enveloping her. He was bigger than she remembered, more solid, smelling of tobacco, and some herby scent, and then of himself, skin, sweat, hair, his family smell, that she knew. 'Oh, David.' Absurdly, tears in her eyes.

'Right then.' David took her jacket, sat her down. 'Tell me all – about Claire, and Marion and her brood, everybody.'

Eleanor laughed. 'You're the one who should talk. I bet Dad's told you all about us. There's nothing anyway, we have nice dull lives. Where have you been?'

'Here and there. Round and about.' He grinned, taking her cold hands in his warm ones. He and Marion had the same kind of hands: long-fingered and strong, like their father. Eleanor looked at them, watching her pale bluish fingers thaw out in his grasp, and turn pink.

'Where's Dad?'

'It's one of his golf days. I'm supposed to make the tea. Good, now you can do it.'

'Hey, you're a better cook than I am. There won't be any food, there never is. Come on, David, I want to know. I can't go back to Marion and say, "Oh, he's been here and there." She'll be down on Saturday, I think, unless you're coming back with me. Why don't you? How long are you here for?'

'Oh, a while. You're looking great – a merry widow, now?'

'Well, better, at any rate.'

'The Highland life must suit. Maybe I'll try it.'

'Are you moving again?'

'I've a flat in Edinburgh. Rented, so I'm free, really.'

'And a job – are you working?'

'In between. Moving on.'

'Oh David, can't you ever settle?'

'Seems not. But it's the new thing, mid-life change, swapping jobs. Did you know the average number of times people change career in a lifetime is five?'

'Well, I should think you've pushed the average up a bit.'

'And that's not jobs,' he went on, ignoring this, 'it's careers. Major change.'

'So you're not in insurance any more?'

'Well, the last thing was a kind of partnership with these guys – we were importing clothes.'

This sounded even less likely than insurance. But Eleanor recalled suddenly an afternoon in London's Oxford Street, when David, off duty (he was a policeman then), had met her to go shopping for something for Ross's christening. How interested he had been in the hats, and whether things matched. He had spent money on clothes for himself then, had worn silk shirts, soft leather jackets. She took in his appearance again, the beard, the jeans, the faded rugby shirt.

'What sort of clothes?' Eleanor asked.

'Teenage stuff. It changes all the time, so you have to be one jump ahead. We were selling it in warehouses, wholesale.'

'So, what happened? Wasn't it a success?' But nothing David did, she knew of old, was ever admitted not to be a success.

'Huge – terrific.' He shrugged. 'But, hell, there was nowhere to go, except into retail, and the other guys didn't have the experience, weren't interested. Then the collapse of the Asian markets finished it – that's where we got the stuff.'

'But I'd have thought that meant you'd get it cheaper – with the pound being strong and everything?'

'Doesn't work like that. They have other outlets, won't sell to us just now. It would mean we were selling for less than it cost them to make. Even with sweated labour.'

'Oh. Oh well . . .' She couldn't make sense of this. But you could never be sure, with David.

'Cup of tea?' he said, getting up to put the kettle on. 'Or coffee?'

'Tea, please.' He filled the kettle and went on talking as he got out mugs, and milk from the fridge.

'No, the internet's the thing. I've got this mate who's teaching me how to design web pages, and the point is, you can do this anywhere. I get myself the hardware – well, I've quite a nice setup already – and the right software, and I could be working in Achiltibuie if I wanted to. Ullapool, Lochcarron, Skye. It doesn't matter.'

'The way you rattle off the names,' Eleanor said, 'you'd think you'd already done a tour of the Highlands.'

'Maybe I have.'

'So, will you move?'

'I'm thinking about it.' He busied himself with tea bags, and hunted for biscuits. 'God, you're right, Dad has no food in this house. What was I supposed to make for us tonight? One tin of tomato soup, half a jar of marmalade, and that's it.'

'I know. Last time Marion was here, she went straight into Aberdeen and stocked up for him at Safeway.'

'He says there's a superstore now about five miles down the road,' David said, bringing her tea. 'I'm going to take him there tomorrow.' They both peered into their mugs. 'Do you think the milk was off?'

'Probably.' Gingerly, they sipped, made faces at each other, left the mugs on the table.

'How long are you staying? You could come shopping with us.'

'Oh, I have to go back in the morning. Look, why don't you come home with me? Dad's all right – Ruby cooks for him sometimes, and he has all these bar meals with his golfing cronies.'

'I might just do that. Scout around. I'll give Phil a ring tonight.'

'Phil – is that the friend who designs web pages?'

'Oh, he does a lot more than that. Phil Amers.'

'So you're coming?'

'Yeah, why not. For a few days.'

'Good.' She smiled at him. 'Good, I'm glad. It would be wonderful if you did move North. Then we'd all be together.'

'Persuade Dad to sell up and come too?'

But Eleanor shook her head. 'Oh no.'

David leaned back in his chair, tipping it on its hind legs. 'Now then,' he said, 'tell me about you and Marion.'

So she did, and they talked until their father came home. Then they went out to the Pitcairn Arms, and ate chicken and chips, since David and Eleanor had talked so long the shop was shut, and no food bought.

'Dad, are you eating properly?' Eleanor asked. He ate slowly, but finished his meal, relished it.

'I'm well looked after,' he said. 'Ruby makes me a pot of soup, and whiles she brings a casserole.'

'What about apple pie?' David asked, waving the menu at them. 'Ice cream?'

'Is that it, apple pie or ice cream?'

'Well, you could have Black Forest Gâteau. Straight from the supermarket freezer.'

'I bet the apple pie is as well,' Eleanor retorted. 'No, I'll just have coffee. What about you, Dad?'

'No, no, I'm fine. I'm not much of a sweet hand. Cup of coffee. And what about a whisky?' He and David discussed malts. Her father knew malt whisky. Eleanor had heard him often enough on the subject. But David, who sounded so sure of himself, what did he know, really?

'Your cupboards are bare, Dad,' Eleanor said, reverting to what was bothering her as soon as the plates were cleared away, and the coffee and drams set out.

'Ach, I'm fine. I haven't a great appetite these days.'

'Maybe not, but you need to have something in the house – milk, bread. Let's do what David suggested – go to Asda tomorrow, and get you stocked up before I go home.'

'I thought I might go back with Eleanor for a few days,' David said. 'Would that be OK?'

'Fine by me. You'll see a difference in the bairns, eh?'

Before she went to bed, Eleanor inspected the pantry, and made a list. She would speak to Ruby before she left. Her father put his head round the kitchen door. 'I'm off upstairs. An early bedder, these days, especially after my golf.'

Left alone in the cold kitchen, Eleanor began to see dust, grime round the taps, an unswept floor. What was Ruby doing these days? Not much. But she was getting on too, must be nearly seventy. Maybe it was time someone else came in to clean. But Ruby had been with them so long, had come in to clean and gossip and give Mum company, since they were all still at secondary school.

David was in the living room. He held up a bottle of whisky. 'Want one?'

'No bread and butter, but he's got drink in the house. All right, a wee one.'

David had brought in an electric fire, since the coal fire in the living room had not been lit. The room was warming up. They sat in the wing chairs on either side of the fireplace, David in his father's, Eleanor in the one that had been their mother's.

'This place is getting dirty,' she said. 'Look at the carpet. And bleak – since Mum died.'

'It's too big for him on his own.' David handed her a glass, half full.

'God, I'll never drink all that.'

'Try.'

'Oh well.' She let the first swallow burn down her throat. 'David, who paid for the meal? I went to the loo and when I came back it was all settled, and we were leaving.'

'I did.'

'D'you want my share?'

'Certainly not. My treat.' He's in the money then, she thought. So often he had nothing, or a lot of money that seemed suddenly to vanish.

The second whisky mellowed them both: Eleanor became expansive, and they talked for a long time, the room growing stuffy, but warm at least. Later, in the cold bedroom that had once belonged to the two girls, and then just to Eleanor, she hugged a hot water bottle and realised David had not told her much at all. He had encouraged her to talk about Claire, and living in Scotland, and about Andrew. How convenient it would be, if she could like him. Marion thought so, anyway.

'But what you're saying.' David had said, 'is that he's not The One. OK for now, but not what you really want.'

'Oh, how would I know? I only ever had one serious boyfriend, and I married him. I don't know any more than Claire, and she's just beginning.'

'A good place to be.'

'Is it?' She stirred in the chair, resettling herself. 'What about you? Why haven't you found some nice woman, got married?'

'You always ask me that.'

'I always wonder. Marriage, children, you'd have to settle then.'

'And that's the thing to do, is it? Settle?'

'Och, I don't know. It suited our parents. It suits Marion – she's happy.'

'Is she? With the worthy Fergus, the good doctor? He has a bad effect on me, makes me feel a real flibbertigibbet.'

Eleanor giggled. 'Men can't be . . . flibberti-things.'

'Shallow then, useless. I don't know how the human body works, I only know the effect of alcohol on stomach, head and spirit. I don't know how to put up shelves, fix a dripping tap, mend the lawn-mower. Not a real man.'

'Real enough, surely,' Eleanor said, 'to fall in love with somebody.'

'Oh, that.' But he would not be drawn. There had been someone called Sally, that much she gathered, but the affair was over. Eleanor suspected she had been married.

In bed, she turned, curled tighter, was still not warm. The room, with its familiar furniture, was plain and cleared of all their make-up, clothes, toys, but in the dark she knew the bookcase was still under the window with rows of Enid Blyton, the battered copies of *Little Women*, *A Dream of Sadler's Wells*, and the other favourites. In the wardrobe, an old dressing-gown covering her wedding dress. She realised the room smelled chilly, even damp. What if the house needed major repairs? Some of the window sills were rotten, she had noticed this time, and the outside paintwork was flaking, showing bare wood. Her father spent all his time in the garden. It was her mother who had cared for the house. And if I had a man, thought Eleanor, growing confused in the first stages of sleep, would he take care of all that for me? Electric sockets, shelves, the falling-down shed in the garden. She dreamed that Claire had a boyfriend, and he was grown-up, with a beard.

In the morning, Eleanor went out early to the shop by the Post Office and bought sliced bread (a day old), butter (very expensive), and milk (full cream). Her father needed the extra fat, she decided, he had got leaner and hollower this year. She paid what seemed far too much for these things, and drove back to the house to make breakfast for them all. Ruby pedalled up shortly afterwards on her bike with its wicker basket. She came into the kitchen still wearing her woolly hat and gloves, and a padded jacket, looking round and rosy. Under the hat her hair was a fluff of thin grey curls, sticking up like a halo.

'Aye, aye, Eleanor, fit like?'

'I'm fine, Ruby, what about you? Pretty fit, anyway, look at you, still on that bike.'

'Nae for much langer,' Ruby said, hanging up her jacket. 'My knee's giein me gyp.'

'Your knee?'

'Arthritis, the doc says.' She rolled up her trouser over one mottled leg and displayed a red knee. 'See yon. See the size o it?'

'Is it sore?'

Ruby snorted. 'Ach, I'm nae een to complain.' She rolled the trouser leg down again, and went to fetch her nylon overall. 'You'll be here to see your brither,' she stated, as she poked around in the broom cupboard, reappearing with dustpan and brush, then going back for the vacuum cleaner and a duster.

'Yes, I came down yesterday.'

'I see he's gotten a beard since last time.' Eleanor could tell what Ruby thought of this, so did not ask. 'And how's Marion, and the bairns? Yon Ross was some hicht fan she was here in the summer.'

'Nearly as tall as his dad.'

'And the doctor?'

'He's fine.'

'I speired him aboot my knee – he was very helpful. Mair nor yon Dr Cleland at the surgery. Him – he writes it a doon, but never says a word. Ye come oot wi anither prescription, and still nae idea fit's wrang wi ye.'

Ruby began to unwind the flex of the vacuum cleaner, but made no move to plug it in. Eleanor went to rinse her cup at the sink.

'An fit aboot yersel? Nae sign o a man yet?'

Eleanor laughed. 'You think I should get married again, do you?'

'It's nae natural, at your age. Ye're a bonny enough quine, fit wey have ye never taken anither man?'

'Maybe I have.'

'Hm.' Ruby narrowed her eyes and sniffed. If there was no wedding ring, it hardly counted. Seeming to lose interest, she led her vacuum cleaner out. Eleanor heard it roaring away up the hall. She shut the kitchen door and read through her shopping list. Later, she might tackle Ruby about the bare cupboards, but she did not feel up to it yet. Something she was calling a hangover made her feel irritable and headachy. What business was it of Ruby's – or David's, or anyone's – whether she had a man or not? I don't want one, she decided. I really only want someone to put up shelves in the living room, and fix the cistern in the loo. A handyman. And a bigger hot water bottle.

'Ready?' David came in from the garden, where he had been having a smoke. She could smell it on him, that and the damp November air.

'Where's Dad?'

'In the shed. He's going to get some garden stuff at Asda as well.'

'Right. I'll tell Ruby where we're going.'

In the hypermarket, David bought beer and whisky to take North with him; their father disappeared into the gardening section at the far end, and Eleanor was left to buy groceries. When she had done that, and packed them in the car, she went back to find the men, and to see if there was any cut-price designer underwear, as a present for Claire. Then they must go; she did not want to drive home in the dark.

Suddenly, going through the do-it-yourself section, still in search of her father and David, she halted. Someone behind almost ran into her with a full trolley. 'Sorry,' she said, 'sorry.'

But she still stood there, in everyone's way. *Ian*. And he was present to her again, in his suit and tie, neat, good-looking, capable. *I was safe. I was safe when you were here. Nothing's safe now.* It was the house, decaying around her father. She could see Pitcairn was going down, no one was caring for it. And if they sold up, how could her father survive? 'Your mother's still here, for me,' he had said, months after her death. Other people, well-meaning (especially the aunts), said, 'He'll have to move. He can't stay in that great barn of a place on his own.' But Marion and Eleanor and David had all said that it would break his heart to leave. He had leaned on them, relied on their understanding, so that never, never would any of them tell him it was time to sell. But I left Heatherlea, Eleanor thought, as soon as Ian was gone. She stood and stared at rows of screwdrivers and drill bits, till they were blurred by tears, and the haze of loss thickened around her.

'Here you are.' It was David, carrier bags clanking as he moved. 'Eleanor? You OK?'

'Yes.' She blinked hard, found a tissue and blew her nose. 'I was just thinking – being at Pitcairn, and you being here – I suppose that's what brought it back.'

'What?' But he knew. 'You're all right, Eleanor, you're much more all right than you ever were with him.'

'Am I?'

'Yes.'

'It wasn't my fault,' she said.

'No.' They stood and looked at each other.

'Was it?'

'No.'

Eleanor took a deep breath. 'Let's go and find Dad.'

They drove home after lunch. Ruby had made lentil soup.

'You could stand a spoon up in this,' Eleanor's father said. 'Sticks to your ribs. Keeps me going all week, Ruby's soup.'

Ruby herself had passed them on the drive, woolly hat pulled down, pedalling briskly.

When they had washed up the dishes, and David had packed, he and Eleanor left. John Cairns stood in front of the house and waved them off.

'Hist ye back,' he said to Eleanor. 'Bring Claire with you next time.'

How thin and shadowy he seemed, alone in front of his big house, in the threadbare clothes he wore for gardening – wore, Eleanor knew, almost all the time. A thin old man, beak-nosed and gaunt. She felt guilty, leaving him.

On the way home, they talked mostly about Marion and the children, and David irritated her by fussing among her music tapes, changing them round, criticising her choice.

'Leave me alone,' she said. 'I like them. Discuss it with Marion, she knows about music.'

'Does she still play?'

'Occasionally. She says she hasn't time to practise. She was teaching Eilidh, but that seems to have stopped. Eilidh lost interest.'

'But Marion's doing fine, herself?'

'Oh, you know, copes with everything, looks after everybody. The perfect doctor's wife. And she's happy, I think. I sometimes envy her. Not envy, that's wrong. But she does seem to have it all – family, teaching when she wants it, a good marriage, a lovely house.'

'Good,' David said. 'Glad one of us is sorted out.'

'You mean you're not – I'm not?' And they laughed, like children doing something behind the grown-ups' backs, guilty, but not caring.

Driving North seemed an easier journey because it was the right direction to be travelling. By Elgin David was dozing. They moved through the darkening afternoon, closer and closer to Marion, and home.

5

'The way you talk about it,' Fergus had said, when he was getting to know Marion, 'I thought your family must have lived at Pitcairn for generations.'

'No,' Marion admitted. That was what she would have preferred to be the truth. 'My father bought it when he inherited money after my grandmother died. That and becoming manager, then managing director. He was doing well.'

'At what?'

'Road haulage. He went in just to organise the schedules and do the books. He'd trained as an accountant, but he didn't like the place he worked, it was deadly dull, I think. Anyway, when he started, there were only half a dozen lorries. But it grew – Eddie Shanks was very successful – so my father got the benefit. There must be, oh, thirty, maybe fifty lorries now. And removals and storage as well.'

'Oh,' said Fergus, light dawning. 'He works for *Shanks*.'

So that was why they had Pitcairn: it reflected their new status. This was what Marion and Eleanor believed, as they grew up. They found that people assumed, because of the similarity of their name, Cairns, and the house's name, that there must be some family connection. But when they asked their mother about this, Faith answered vaguely.

'Oh well, there might be some link there, years ago. Anyway, the house suits us as we are. I feel as if I've lived here all my life.'

David came closest to this. Marion was four, and Eleanor almost two, when David was born. Neither had any memory of their mother's pregnancy, and Eleanor could not remember David not existing. Marion remembered being told she had a brother, and looking round, expecting to see a boy arrive. Later, a white-shawled infant, with a red face, was held out then put away again in a high pram.

'Odd,' Marion said, when they discussed this, as they did from time to time, trawling their childhood, comparing memories, 'when I was expecting Kirsty, I discussed the whole thing with Ross and Eilidh. Especially Eilidh – she was so interested. Wanted to feel the baby move, listen to it. She talked to the baby. It was so funny – we'd be in the Co-op and she'd pat my tummy and say, "This is the sweetie counter, but you can't have any".'

But Eleanor only nodded, since the funniness of children is only in your own. She often felt, anyway, that she could never be as much in love with any child (even Claire, perhaps) as Marion was with hers.

'But,' Marion went on, 'I suppose she was older. Well, a bit older than I was when David was born. And children are so much more aware now.'

However, when they looked back, it was not at the baby David, but the boy, and the trouble he got into, got *them* into. When he was four, they moved from their house in a granite terrace near the Westburn Park, not too far from school, to Pitcairn House, which was in the country, near nothing at all. Marion remembered the Aberdeen house and Eleanor claimed to (*we saw fireworks from our bedroom window one year. I banged my head on the gate when I fell*); David told everyone he was born at Pitcairn.

'You're a liar,' Marion scoffed. 'You're too young to know, anyhow.'

They moved in the autumn, and at first, Marion was unhappy. There were no other families within walking distance except the Mackies at the farm, and their children were teenagers. Occasionally, if their parents went out, Eileen Mackie came to baby-sit, and Eleanor was allowed to try out her red nail polish. David refused to stay in his bed, and once, roaring like a lion at the top of the stairs, slipped and tumbled all the way to the bottom.

'He's always doing that,' Marion said, watching unmoved as Eileen rocked the yelling David, and Eleanor sobbed in fright beside her. 'Will I telephone for the doctor? I know how.'

But Eileen called her mother instead, and they decided David was not hurt.

'My mum says get him checked over tomorrow,' Eileen told John and Faith when they came home. 'I'm awful sorry, Mrs Cairns, I'd put him to his bed, but he kept getting out.'

Eleanor and Marion had crept out of their room, and were peering through the banisters. Down in the hall, their father in a dark suit, their mother in a black dress with her peacock shawl, which shimmered purple and indigo in the light as she moved. She was like a tiny butterfly next to their father, and to Eileen, who was plump and fair. From here, her hair was a shining black cap, but they could see, faintly pink, a patch of their father's scalp beneath his hair, light brown and smoothly brushed. Eventually, Eileen went away and their mother turned to come upstairs. The girls scurried back to bed. But she went first to David, who was bruised but asleep, perfectly all right. Then she came to their room, bringing with her perfume, cigar smoke, the aroma of rich food: all the scents of the exotic world she had left, to come back to them.

In the morning, she was in her slacks and old jersey, cleaning out cupboards, her hair tied back in a scarf. She was irritable, so they kept out of her way.

Their first spring at Pitcairn House, Marion cheered up. It grew light in the evenings, and every day after school they explored the garden. A new henhouse was being built in one corner; they were going to have fresh eggs, Faith said. Their father walked them round on Saturday mornings, pausing to fill his pipe, and using it to point at what he wanted them to notice.

'Rasp canes – need tying up. Plenty of fruit in August, though,' or, 'Another year and you'll be able to climb that tree.'

'Not David,' Eleanor said. She was tall, and had caught up with Marion in height.

Her father laughed. 'David too, I'll be bound – I doubt you could stop him. He'll fall out a few times, though, knowing him.'

It was Marion's job to collect the eggs, as she was the eldest, and most careful. Sometimes, though, a hen would lay away, and all three would hunt. They were getting used to being in the country, but Marion still longed for company. Sometimes a girl in her class at school would come to tea. Eleanor recalled them as if they were all the same girl, but Marion claimed there were several. Violet lasted longest: she was prim, with long hair bound tightly in plaits, a clean dress and white socks. She ate very little and seemed to like only baked beans, which Faith never bought, and chips, which the Cairnses had only on Saturdays, while Dad listened to the football results, and they all had to be quiet. Marion and her friend would disappear upstairs and giggle behind the closed door of the bedroom. Eleanor would hang around her mother, girning.

'They won't let me in, and it's my bedroom too.'

'Go and find David.'

'Don't know where he is.'

'All the more reason – go and find him. He'll be in the garden.'

Eleanor had wandered about the silent summer garden: everything overgrown, because of the wet spring that went on till June, then the sudden blaze of a hot July. It was hot now, the sun fierce in a blue sky. Eleanor kicked stones, scuffing her sandals. A brown hen pecked around on the dusty path by her feet. One of the cats sat by a bush, gazing upwards, its eye on an invisible bird, ignoring Eleanor. No sign of David.

'Davy!' she called, then tried out a different voice, not liking the thinness of her own. 'Davy!' Deeper again, almost a grunt: *'Davy!'* Still nothing. He might think it was Daddy shouting, if she could make her voice really deep. She came to the wall, and climbed onto it, sitting astride a part that wasn't too mossy, and felt dry. On one side, the garden, apple trees and fruit bushes, and the path dividing, going one way to the hens' shed, the other back up to the vegetable plots, and then between the lilac trees to the house. On the other side, familiar now but still unknown, fields with cattle standing in clumps in the corners, as if they expected it to rain at last, and here and there small houses, their windows flashing in sunlight. Then hills. But further to the left, if she swung a leg over and faced the other way, there were woods, where they got brambles in October, and David often wandered on his own, or with a boy from the village. Stanley's father was a joiner, and they lived next to the Post Office and shop. Faith did not encourage Stanley at first; she thought him rough. Then his mother died suddenly, and she was full of pity. After that, he was allowed to come as often as he wanted to, and was often given his tea. His father, mourning, spent more and more time in the Pitcairn Arms.

Maybe David was in the woods now, with Stanley. Eleanor slipped down the other side of the wall, and landed in long grass. By the edge of the wood, smoke drifted. Not a bonfire – David was not allowed to light one on his own. He was not allowed to have matches at all, and there had been a big row only the week before when he and Stanley had set fire to some paper in their den down at the bottom of the garden. Faith had seen the smoke from the kitchen window, and had run down the garden. The boys stood back, curiosity and pride turning to trepidation as the fire caught hold, and dry leaves under the paper crackled, twigs snapped, suddenly alight.

Now, as Eleanor got closer, she saw the spiral of smoke was from a bonfire after all. Closer still, she saw signs of other people: clothes spread on the fence, a dog on a long rope, straining at it and barking; a small child running out, a man appearing for a moment, and shouting. Then she saw there was a cart of some kind, which they must have pulled down the lane that skirted the other side of the wood, leading to the Smiddy in one direction, the Mains of Pitcairn in the other. The bonfire had a pot suspended above it on a framework of sticks, and a meaty smell came over the field towards her. A woman in a dark blouse and skirt, a man's hat pulled down so you could not see her face, was stooping over the fire. Eleanor hesitated, afraid to go nearer. As the woman looked up and saw her, she turned and ran back across the wet grass to her safe place on the wall.

'Travellers,' her mother said, and, 'Tinks,' supplied Violet, turning her button nose up at ham and tongue salad, whispering to Marion that she did not like tomatoes, the seeds grew in your stomach.

'Where are they travelling to?' Eleanor asked.

'Oh, they just keep moving on,' her father said, as he sat down at the end of the table.

'Don't you go near them.' Faith set out glasses of water, but Violet did not drink just water.

'Have we got any ale?' Marion asked, as if she did not know her mother had told the Hay's Lemonade lorry not to stop. 'She has ale at her house.'

'There's milk,' said Faith, 'or water.'

Later, Violet made up for the deficiencies of the meal by

eating two plates of ice cream and jelly, which had been produced as a treat because Marion had a guest. Then, in the living room, she regaled the Cairns children with what she knew about travellers.

'They're dirty,' she said. 'My ma won't let me speak to the kids. They dinna even ging to the school.'

'They have to go to school.'

'The attendance mannie goes after them, but sometimes he canna catch up. They're aff somewey else.'

'How long will they be here then, in our wood?'

'Me and Stanley,' David announced, 'we went right up to them. Up to their camp.'

'They're filthy,' Violet reiterated. 'Disgustin. They never get a bath, and they've nae proper toilet.'

'Well then, how—' Eleanor broke in, but Violet shook her head, pursing her lips.

'The dog's all right,' David said. 'Dog's really friendly, it doesn't bite or anything if it likes you. And there's two boys, younger than Stanley and me. The older one's hardly ever gone to school.' He sighed.

'Can he read?' Marion asked. But David shrugged.

'I would get leathered for speakin to tinks,' Violet sniffed.

'Scaredy cat,' David grinned, leaning backwards over the sofa arm until he landed on the floor and rolled over. 'Scaredy, scaredy,' came his muffled voice as he rolled again, then got up and went out, bored with Violet.

Faith warned them again, next morning. It was Saturday, and although only breakfast-time, Stanley had appeared at the back door, asking for David.

'You two keep well away from that camp.' But David and Stanley were speeding across the yard, so David's answer might have been agreement, or it might not. Faith sighed, and turned back to the girls. 'And that goes for you as well.'

'Violet says they've got fleas,' Marion informed them,

stacking plates neatly by the sink. 'So don't worry. I wouldn't go near that camp.'

'Well, I don't know that . . .' Faith was caught.

'They're doing no harm, are they?' John had asked the night before, when Dan Mackie had come down to discuss what should be done.

'Aye, but I dinna like that bonfire down by the woodies,' Dan said. 'Grass is like tinder, it's that dry.'

'Are you moving them on?'

'Nae my land, yonder. I hinna ony right.' But Dan looked doubtful; he pushed back his flat cap, rubbing at his forehead. 'I could spik to Archie, richt enough. I doubt he wants them either.'

He and John stood outside the back door in the heat, shirt-sleeves rolled up, Dan's arms leathery brown, like his throat where the shirt opened. A little further down on his neck, you could see skin white as milk, and soft, where he did not expose it to the weather. Faith stood in the kitchen doorway, listening to them, wondering about the woman. She remembered a traveller coming several years ago, the first winter they were at Pitcairn, a woman with a baby, and pregnant. She was sure it was the same people.

'Have they a van?' she asked now. 'They were here before, weren't they? They had a van, then.'

'Aye, they've been on the go a few years,' Dan agreed. 'I let them sleep in the barn, once, but her man smokes, and I wasna very easy aboot it.' He turned to Faith. 'He's doon in the world this time – they've a cartie he pulls wi a their chattels, but nae van that I've seen.'

'Well,' John said, 'they'll need shelter. The air's heavy – I doubt we'll get a storm in the next day or so.'

'What will they do?' Faith asked. 'Her with these two wee boys, and the baby.'

Dan shrugged. 'I'm nae keen, but I suppose she could come in aboot the Mains again,' he conceded. 'Her and her bairns.

It's her man I canna abide. She'd a black eye afore she left the last time. He lifts his hand to her, it's my belief.' Dan's face, wizened already, closed further in disapproval.

Faith turned indoors, a twist of pity knotting like fear in her chest. Maybe she could find some baby clothes, she could do that at least. She had been meaning to clear out the loft. In the kitchen, she cleared up the tea things, brisk and hurried, trying not to think of the tinker woman.

Now it was Saturday morning, and still the threat of storm hung in the air. But the sky was blue yet, and cloudless. Eleanor went down the path to her place on the wall. The smoke from the camp thinned slowly, vanishing upwards without seeming to move. Two boys, smaller than her brother, ran back and forth, and the dog leaped between them, barking. She waited, looking out for David and Stanley, but they were nowhere to be seen. After a few moments, she got down and started back for the house. The boys were in the yard again, sitting side by side, cross-legged, playing jacks. Then suddenly, so suddenly it seemed as if she had simply materialised, there was the woman Eleanor had seen the day before, in her long skirt and man's hat. Close up, she was thinner, and younger. She wore short boots, tied up with twine instead of laces, and between boots and skirt, her legs were bare, and hairy. She was holding something out to the boys. In her other hand she held a wide basket. Eleanor reached the yard as David went into the house for his mother. The woman turned to Eleanor.

'Buy some lucky heather, dearie, tell your fortune?' Eleanor shook her head, backing off. Then Faith was there, and to Eleanor's astonishment, invited the woman into the kitchen.

The children stood by the back door, listening. The woman's voice was soft and coarse, with a lilt they had never heard before. It rolled on and on, a long spiel that made Faith shake her head. But in the end, she bought clothes pegs, and a piece of lace. Then the woman came out, and stopped, seeing the children.

'Two lovely bairns you've got,' the woman said. 'Two and no more, though one other has come to you. And there's one you'll lose.' She touched David lightly on the head, and he squirmed. 'A danger, this boy, and a wild one. Watch him. But never fear for him.' She turned back to Faith. 'Thanks to you, madam, you're a kind lady. Blessings.'

'All nonsense,' Faith said when she had gone. 'Lot of rubbish. They seem to feel they've got to spout all that stuff so that you'll buy something.'

Marion went off with the piece of lace. Eleanor never even touched it. David sat at the table eating bits of raw pastry from the pie Faith was making, and he and Stanley played soldiers with the clothes pegs.

After tea, when Eleanor went down to look, the travellers had gone, and all that was left of them was the blackened bit of ground where the fire had been, and a piece of rag caught on the fence.

She soon forgot about them, in the hunt for David. He and Stanley had gone out again as soon as tea was over. David was supposed to walk Stanley to the end of the lane at half-past eight, then come home to bed. But by half-past nine, he had not reappeared. John and Faith set out to look for him, in a light that, for all it was August now, was still almost clear as day, the sky fading pink on the horizon, pearly overhead.

At half-past ten they brought him back, and he was put to bed in disgrace. At eleven, the Mackies' barn, smouldering, heating up like an oven, burst into flames.

Everyone was up all night: the children forbidden to leave the house, but leaning out of their parents' bedroom window, watching the red glow in the sky, intensifying and rising, hearing the fire engines wailing, the shouts, the fearsome crackle and roar of the blaze. David ran from one window to another, trying to get the best view, white-faced, his eyes burning like coals, his breath coming fast and hard. The girls knew to ignore him; Faith often said he over-excited himself, and anyway, he was still in trouble.

Eventually, Faith came in, and made them go back to bed. Their father was still at the Mains, and would be there all night.

'What a tragedy for the Mackies,' she said. 'Their straw, the hay bales – the barn destroyed. Terrible.' But she spoke to herself, not to them. She tucked the girls in briskly, pulling the bedclothes far too tight, as if she hardly saw them, her whole mind elsewhere. They lay stiffly, pinned down by blankets, as she went to David next, and heard her hush him, her voice low.

He called after her as she hurried along the landing. 'Go to sleep,' she said, not pausing.

Downstairs, she made tea and sandwiches for the men, for all those still working at the site of the razed barn, choking in the black smoke that filled the air. The Mackie girls, Susan and Eileen, were with her, frightened and tearful, and Ruby from the village, and Mrs Masson from the Post Office. The girls could hear the women's voices rise and fall, and the clatter of dishes. Light was filling the bedroom again. At dawn, the girls slept.

Years later, they would still say to each other, when they heard of a fire, 'Remember the night the Mackies' barn went on fire?'

It was the fire they recalled, not the deaths, which were kept from them for a time, not talked about in front of children.

6

'What do you think of him, then?' Claire asked. Her voice was muffled because she was chewing her nails. She had grown them for Emma's party, but now she was going to bite them again for a little while. Then she would start growing them for the school Christmas social. She liked the satisfying crunch of her teeth through a new bit of nail, the way you could nibble all the way round a long one, and the flaky texture of it in her mouth before she spat it out.

'Who – Uncle David?' Eilidh asked. She never bit her nails. She was painting alternate fingers green and black, and her bedroom was heady with acetone. 'He's all right.'

It was cosy in Eilidh's room. The windows were steamed up with talking. Eilidh sat on a stool in front of her dressing table; Claire was on the bed, a cushion at her back and a sleeping cat over her feet.

Eilidh waved the finished hand to dry it. 'My mum says he's going to stay with you next.'

'Yeah, Mum's trying to clear the spare room. It's been full of boxes since we moved. Now she's put everything on the landing, so I have to climb over it to get to my room.'

'I don't know why he isn't just staying here,' Eilidh said, 'since our house is much bigger.'

'Well, your mum has your dad to talk to. My mum doesn't.'

'Does she still miss your dad?'

Claire shrugged. 'I suppose so.' Eilidh wanted to say 'Do you?' but sometimes Claire did not like to talk about that.

'Uncle David never brought loads of presents, did he?' Claire said. 'When he stayed with us in England he always brought stuff.'

'Yeah, he did with us, one Christmas. But Mum says he's skint just now.'

'You reckon?'

'Well, he hasn't got a job, has he?' Eilidh pointed out.

'No. He's going to do something with computers, though.'

'Is he? He's pure mad, eh? You know, like at Halloween, when he got dressed up for all the kids coming round, and instead of just opening the door and standing there like the other mothers and fathers, he leaps out with a mask on—'

They both started giggling.

'Yeah, I know, and the little Macleod girl, Rosie, she starts crying!'

'And Mum goes, "David, you're terrifying them!"'

Claire shrieked, 'And he goes, "It's Halloween, isn't it?"' She was laughing so much that the cat leapt from the bed. 'You're right,' she told Eilidh. 'Like, he's always singing these songs, and they're really rude, and Auntie Marion's making a face at him—'

'She says he's going to do it sometime when the minister's in, or Mrs Wylie, when she's collecting for the jumble sale or whatever, just start singing out loud.'

'He's got a good voice though. He's musical, like Auntie Marion.'

Eilidh laughed. 'He's nothing like my mother.' She turned back to the mirror, and began on the other hand. 'Don't make me laugh now, or I'll splodge this all over.'

There was silence, while Eilidh concentrated on keeping her hands steady, and Claire flicked over the pages of *Bliss*. She held it up to show Eilidh several photographs of a moody boy with a fringe of hair falling over one eye.

'Which d'you think is best, this one or this?'

Eilidh turned for a moment and pointed with a black-tipped finger. 'That one.'

'This or this?'

'Na, I don't like them.'

'This one?'

'Yeah.'

Claire leaned back on the cushion again, examining the photographs. 'He's gorgeous, isn't he? Mum says Uncle David was quite tidy when he was young. *Good-looking.*' Unable to imagine this, they looked at each other, screwing up their faces and giggling.

'He didn't have a beard then, of course,' Eilidh conceded.

'He's only just grown that,' Claire said. 'And he told me he was going to shave it off.'

'You know what?' Eilidh swivelled to face Claire again. 'He's more like your mum than mine.'

'He doesn't look anything like—'

'No, except they're tall. But he doesn't look like anybody in our family.'

'Grandpa?'

'We-ell . . . a bit,' Eilidh conceded. 'Not really. Their eyes are different, his whole face is different.'

'It's queer, isn't it, the way people in families sometimes look like each other and sometimes don't?'

Claire got up and came to sit on the edge of Eilidh's stool. They gazed solemnly at their own reflections in the mirror: dark-haired and fair, round-faced Eilidh and Claire with her thin oval face and long blue eyes, thick-lashed as her father's had been; Eilidh's strong hand next to Claire's narrow one. And yet they were alike, though neither of them thought so, each preferring the other's appearance to her own. They did not see (looking for imperfections), the similar set of the jaw, curve of the mouth, and the likeness they had, simply in being both young, and sharing genes.

'Know something?' Claire said.

'What?'

'See, he sings and makes jokes and all that? Well, underneath, I reckon he's really worried shout something.'

'What?'

'I don't know.'

'Actually,' Eilidh said, 'I think something's bothering my mum. She's a bit snappy.'

'PMT?'

'No, she's just had that, and she's still snappy. Then she starts apologising, and being really nice. It's not like her, usually she's sort of the same all the time.'

'Menopause?'

'She's still too young for that, isn't she?'

But they did not know. They only knew what they read in *Bliss* and *Sugar*, which concentrated on the other end of the hormone spectrum.

'Maybe,' Claire suggested, 'they're worried about the same thing.'

'I thought it was because she was getting fed up with having Uncle David staying here.'

'Oh, why, he's such a laugh?'

'Yeah, but he seems to get on her nerves a bit.'

A silence, while they remained baffled by adults. Then Claire dived back on to the bed and grabbed her magazine.

'Come on, let's do this quiz that tells you what kind of boy is most likely to be attracted to you.'

Downstairs, Eleanor had just tapped on the back door and come into the kitchen. 'Hi, it's me.'

'Claire's upstairs,' Marion said, not turning from the sink for a moment.

'What's wrong?' Eleanor looked at Marion's back, her tense shoulders. 'Something's wrong – is it David?'

'Oh, I can hardly blame him,' Marion smiled, as she faced her sister. Eleanor's heart sank, sank, as if something really moved downwards in her chest. 'It's nothing.' Marion said, 'almost certainly nothing.'

They sat down at the kitchen table, facing each other.

'Do you want a cup of tea or something?'

'No, never mind that. What's happened?'

'Nothing.'

But she told Eleanor what the nothing was, making light, telling her Mary Mackay wasn't sure, but there was going to be a biopsy soon, next week. They would know the result in a couple of weeks.

'She says eighty something per cent of them come back clear. Non-malignant.'

'So they're just checking it out, then?' Eleanor reached out a hand, as if to clasp Marion's shoulder, reassure by touch. But drew the hand back, not wanting to make too much of this. Since Marion would not. Marion was holding herself tight, smiling, getting up to put the kettle on. So Eleanor would hold on too, and not think of the worst.

'It's all right,' Marion said. 'I know what you're thinking. And I've been through it all – imagined my funeral, not that I'd be there, would I? Everything.'

'Oh, God, don't – it's curable, anyway, isn't it? People don't die or anything. And you've caught it early, that's a good thing.' Hastily, she added, 'And anyway, you said it's usually all right – it's almost certainly nothing.'

'Oh yes,' Marion said.

'Well, then . . .'

'I suppose I just don't really believe I'm one of the eighty something per cent. For once in my life.' She smiled. 'Och, it's just a wee panic I'm having. After all, no one in the family's ever had it that I know of, so it's not very likely . . . and, as you say, it's curable.'

But now Eleanor felt the thrill of it in her own body, wanted, more than anything, to put her hands on her own breasts, pat, prod, touch every inch of them, check.

'You could have a mammogram,' Marion said, 'if it does turn out to be – you know. Put your mind at rest.' Marion lightly, lightly, touched Eleanor's shoulder as she set down her mug of tea.

'But Marion, it's you—' Eleanor clasped the hot mug, anxious to do something else with her hands, which might otherwise stray, start to feel for something she knew (of course) was not there.

'Anyway,' Marion said, sitting down with her own tea, 'no sense in fretting about it till we know.'

'Except you can't help . . .'

'No. I try to think about other things, and at work, or when I'm busy, I manage fine. To tell you the truth, I think it will be easier when David's at your house.'

'Have you told him?'

'No. I don't want him talking about it in front of Fergus, somehow. Fergie's very worried, I can tell. Though he's being so sensible.' She sighed. 'And David's quite likely to say something in front of the children. There's no sense in telling anyone yet. I wasn't even going to say to you . . .'

'Oh, Marion!'

'No, well, not much hope of you not noticing something's wrong. Eilidh's suspicious, too. She's so quick, about things like this.'

'She's growing up, I suppose.'

'So's Ross, but boys live in a world of their own, don't notice anything. And Kirsty's too young.'

'What'll you tell them about the biopsy?'

'Just that I have to go into hospital for some tests. That I might have to have an operation.'

'An operation?'

'Oh yes, Eleanor. If it's malignant, they won't hang about. I haven't really any choice.'

Both women put their hands to their breasts. Marion's fluttered away again at once. 'I suppose it depends how far it's gone,' she said.

'But they won't . . . not all of it?'

'Probably.'

'Oh, Marion.' Eleanor's eyes filled with tears and she began to cry. Marion fetched her the box of tissues.

'Here, look, it's all right.'

'Sorry, sorry, I'm so pathetic. You're the one who should be crying, not me. I'm sorry.'

Marion blinked hard, smiling at her sister. 'Believe me, I have. I did. But just the once. I'm all right now. It was only self-pity anyway. And fear, I suppose. But Mary Mackay was very good, she explained the whole process.'

'Right.' Ashamed, Eleanor blew her nose again, faced Marion. 'Sorry – look, is there anything I can do?'

'I might ask you to help with the kids. Or David can come over – make himself useful.'

'Oh dear, you are fed up with him. Never mind, he'll be with me tomorrow, and I think he's planning to go back down to Pitcairn next weekend.'

'Och, I'm not fed up with him. I'm fond of David, and the kids think he's great. But I kind of resent the way he drifts in and out of the family, as if it doesn't matter that for months, even years, he doesn't bother to keep in touch, send birthday cards, anything. Besides, he and Fergus don't really get on.'

'Not soul-mates.'

'Not exactly.'

They sat in silence for a moment.

'What about telling David?' Eleanor asked. 'Are you going to?'

'I suppose so.'

'Do you want me to?'

'No, it's all right.' Marion hesitated. 'Or . . . would you mind? But don't make too much of it, please, Eleanor.'

'No, no, I won't.' She glanced up at the clock. 'I suppose I'd better take Claire home.'

'I'll give them a shout.' Marion stood up. 'Fergus has evening surgery, which is why I haven't even started the meal. But I'd better get going now.'

Upstairs, the girls were reading the magazine's Problem Page, the cat purring between them on the bed.

'See this girl?' Claire said. 'That's like me. I get so moody.' She sighed. 'You're lucky, Eilidh, you're not moody at all.'

'I get bad-tempered,' Eilidh offered. 'Especially with Ross.'

'You're lucky having a brother as well.'

'Not Ross.'

'Well, maybe not Ross,' Claire admitted and they both laughed.

'Time for *Neighbours*.' Eilidh fired the remote control at her portable television. They sang the theme tune together, exaggerating the words, and so loudly Marion had to come all the way upstairs to tell them it was time for Claire to go home.

The next afternoon, Fergus brought David over to Eleanor's cottage.

'I'll take a look at that cistern of yours while I'm here,' he said. 'Marion was saying you had a bit of trouble with it.'

'Thanks. I'll put the kettle on.'

From the kitchen, as she made tea, Eleanor could hear the flush roaring, on and on, and then clanking noises. David was in the living room, talking to Claire. His bag was blocking the hall, his jacket flung over it. Eleanor left the tea-pot on the edge of the Rayburn, and carried the bag upstairs to the boxroom where David was going to sleep. She had pulled down the sofa bed which she kept there because she had no spare bed now, and no room for it anywhere else. There was a bedside lamp, and she had put some clothes-hangers on the hook at the back of the door. The curtains were too long and wide because they had come from the old house, and she had not bothered to take them up. They were rose velvet, and had once hung in a pretty spare bedroom, with Laura Ashley wallpaper. Now they clashed sulkily with the tartan cover of the sofa bed, and the brown carpet she meant to throw out soon.

Long ago, when Claire was small, and they often had friends of Ian's to stay (or sometimes Eleanor's relatives), she had taken pleasure in her guestroom: flowers, a box of pink tissues, a glass jar with home-made biscuits. She sighed, thinking of this, and shoved a half-full box of books into the corner with her feet.

Downstairs, Fergus had helped himself to tea. 'All fixed,' he said as Eleanor came into the kitchen.

'Really? That's great – thanks.'

'Any time. Right, I'd better be off.'

Eleanor stood at the door and watched him drive down the bumpy lane. In the garden of the cottage next door, Jim was raking leaves in the dusk. He tipped his cap at Fergus driving past, and raised a hand in greeting when he saw Eleanor. She went over to the fence.

'I've got my brother staying,' she said. 'Fergus was bringing him over.'

Jim straightened up. 'Your brother, eh?'

Already, Eleanor could see Edie bobbing at her living room window, her hand fluttering in a hesitant wave. Eleanor smiled, and Edie came out.

'Eleanor's got her brother staying,' Jim said. Edie hopped a little.

'Your brother staying? That'll be nice, dear, you'll have company. A bit of company. I say to Jim, she manages awful well on her own, but lonely, all the same, for a young lass, lonely for you, dear.'

'I've got Claire.' Eleanor knew by now that Edie simply told you her thoughts: she had no filter, as most people did, between thought and speech.

'Yes, you've got Claire, a lovely lassie. I say to Jim, a comfort to have a bonny girlie like that. Mind, we never had a girlie, just the boy, and boys go away, don't they? You'll always have your girlie, though. Lovely, I say to Jim, lovely and bright she is.' Edie fluttered, hopped again. 'Now then, we're keeping you back.'

'I'd better go in. I made some tea for David.'

But Edie beckoned, and Eleanor stepped closer. It was almost dark; Edie's tiny pale face bobbed several inches below her own.

'See, next door.' Edie jerked her head in the direction of the third cottage. 'Shouting. Late at night, we hear them, don't we Jim, shouting very late. And music, but that's not so loud, I don't mind music myself. We like a good tune, we still have the gramophone. And Robbie Shepherd, I listen every day.'

'Shouting?'

Jim cleared his throat and looked away, embarrassed.

'Shouting,' Edie confirmed. 'And then she comes out, and off she drives in the car. Late at night.' She nodded at Eleanor. 'Now, it's cold, don't stand out here. We're keeping her back, Jim, tea-time anyway.'

David was just appearing at the door as Eleanor reached it.

'Did you help yourself to tea? It'll be stewed. Edie was giving me the scandal about our neighbours. I don't think I've ever had more than a glimpse of them.'

'I love your wee house.'

'Good – so do I.'

They sat at the kitchen table with mugs of tea. From the living room, they could hear the television.

'Does Claire like it?'

'The cottage?'

'Living here.'

'Oh yes. Yes, she has loads of friends, Eilidh's house to go to, Eilidh's cats and dogs, all that.'

'What about you – don't you have any cats and dogs now?'

'No. Soon after we came here, the old ginger cat – d'you remember him? – was killed, caught in a trap. Jim, Edie's husband, found him on the edge of the wood, near the burn. I really didn't feel like getting another animal after that.'

'I'm sorry.'

'Och, we were upset, of course we were. Claire asks me for a dog now and then, but I don't know. I just don't want any ties right now.'

She drank her tea, and fell into silence, thinking that she had no ties but Claire, so what did she mean, saying this? She was hardly likely to get a job.

'Where am I sleeping then?' David broke in on this.

'I'll show you.'

Upstairs, looking round, David said, 'Remember your fancy spare room in Heatherlea?'

'Heatherlea!' The very word sounded foreign to her now. Another kind of life.

'Suburbia at its best, eh? Your barrel of biscuits, the frilly thing round the bed.'

Eleanor laughed. 'You were the only visitor who ever ate those biscuits.'

'What? Are you saying it was always the same biscuits?'

'Don't be daft. Home-made and fresh every time. But nobody ate them, except you. All too polite, I suppose.'

'Slept on crumbs,' he said. 'Munched them in bed, reading.'

'Funny,' Eleanor remarked as they went back down the narrow stairs, 'I can hardly believe now I ever lived there

– in our four-bedroom detached, with its double garage and en suite bathrooms. That awful new estate, with the gardens flat and empty, just thin grass coming up from seed, and everybody shoving in Leylandi to hide their bit of garden from everybody else. As if they weren't all exactly the same.'

'So do you miss it, all that luxury?'

She stopped at the foot of the stairs and turned to him. 'Sometimes.'

'It's OK, I didn't mean—'

She brushed this aside, changed the subject. Not even you, she was thinking, will make me rake all that up again. For a moment, she wished he had stayed at Marion's, or gone straight back to Pitcairn.

Later, though, over supper, which he and Claire insisted should be by candlelight, with wine for everyone (Claire gravely drank some, called it bitter, then became giggly), she was glad he was with her. The game of *do you remember* was oddly painless when it was Claire's past that was taken out and aired.

'It's nice,' Claire said when she went in much later to say goodnight. 'Uncle David remembers Daddy and our house, and Marmalade, and my teddies, and taking me to school. He even remembers my friend Hannah. Nobody else here knows about any of that except you, and you get sad if we talk about it.'

'Oh, Claire.'

'It's OK, I don't think about it much now. But Uncle David makes me remember all the nice things again.'

'Good.' She brushed a strand of hair away from Claire's face, and bent and kissed her.

Downstairs, David was washing up dishes.

'Oh, thanks. I'd forgotten we'd left the pans.' She sighed. 'I think I'll just go to bed too. I've to be up to get Claire off in time for the school bus.'

'OK.' He dried his hands on the cloth he'd been using for the dishes, and left it crumpled by the sink. 'I'm going out for a fag. Then I'll watch TV for a while. Can't sleep much before two – I'm used to being up late. I won't have it loud, though.'

As she got ready for bed, Eleanor thought, I haven't told him about Marion. She was not sure why she was putting it off. But it was wrong that he did not know. As she drew her curtains, she heard voices in the garden, and paused. Then she realised Jim had come out too, for his last pipe of the day, and he and David were talking by the fence.

Comforted, she got into bed and read till she heard the front door close, and David come indoors. Then she switched her lamp off and lay down.

7

The last time Eleanor and Marion saw their mother was on a visit made two years earlier. They had come for Christmas shopping in Aberdeen, choosing a Tuesday which would be quiet, and meaning to go back on the Wednesday morning. Marion had two days teaching at the end of the week.

'And I can't afford to lose it, if I buy all the things the kids want,' she told Eleanor as they drove down on the Monday afternoon.

'They're really pleased we're coming, you know,' Eleanor said. 'Mum and Dad. Somehow, the fact that it's just the two of us.'

It was growing dark when they turned off the main road, and the house was shadowy, only one window lit at the front as they came up the drive. But someone had heard the car, and the front door opened as the engine died. Both their parents stood framed in the yellow hall light as they got out.

'Now then, good journey?' Faith leaned forward and kissed them in turn as they reached the top of the steps. 'Come in, come in, it's a cold night. Dad will put the car away for you.'

Inside the warm hall, the familiar smell of Pitcairn: wax polish, coal fire, and something damp and sweetish, that might be just the dish of apples on the sideboard. In a blue bowl on the brass-topped table, shaggy chrysanthemums, and across the varnished floorboards, rag rugs their grandmother had made. Then they were in the living room, where their father had built up the fire. Marion and Eleanor sank onto the Chesterfield together, and stretched out their feet. Eleanor kicked off her shoes.

'Tea? A cup of tea? I didn't want to start supper till you got here.'

They had stopped on the way, and did not need tea, but could not refuse anything here, at home, where they were the girls again, looked after.

'Lovely. Do you want a hand?'

'No, no. Dad will get the tray for me. Sit where you are.'

'Oh, it's nice to be here.' Marion leaned back and closed her eyes.

Firelight glinted on the gold rims of their grandmother's tea-set, brought out when there were no children around to put it at risk. Once, Eleanor had said, 'I love that tea-set so much,' and since then, Faith had always used it for Marion and for her. There was gingerbread too, thickly buttered, but Faith did not really want them to eat it.

'You'll spoil your supper,' she said, but they each had a piece anyway, and drank their tea, and grew hot in front of the fire their father kept piling with coal.

They talked family: children, houses, and in Marion's case, husband. Eleanor had gone out once or twice with a teacher from the Academy, but she did not mention that. She had enjoyed the concert and film, but had been bored by him, and sorry she was bored. Not worth telling.

'Mamie and Alice are coming to lunch tomorrow – so you won't have to visit,' Faith said. Marion and Eleanor groaned, and laughed. 'Oh, the aunts.'

'Good,' decided Eleanor. 'I love seeing them. They never change.'

'I thought that's why they got on your nerves.' Faith had

not forgotten an impatient remark Eleanor had made twenty years ago.

'Och, you know what I mean. I don't mind that now, it's sort of reassuring. I've had enough changes the last few years.'

'You have that, lass.' John put his hand on her shoulder as he rose to collect the cups and saucers, and take the tray out for his wife.

They ate in the kitchen.

'I suppose I'll have to use the dining room tomorrow,' Faith said. 'I hardly ever do these days – don't even heat it. I can't say I like it much now.'

'That's just because it is hardly used,' Marion told her. 'Unused rooms are uncomfortable.'

'Like my spare bedroom in the cottage,' Eleanor said. 'You'd think in such a tiny house there wouldn't be any unused rooms. But it's full of boxes.'

'Still?'

'Och, I've nowhere else to put the stuff.'

'Maybe you should throw it out,' her mother suggested.

'Mum, it's books mostly. You can't throw out books.'

Faith raised her eyes. 'Oh, books.'

'Probably,' Marion said, 'you still associate that room with the ballet classes.'

'Very likely. If your father had ever got rid of those mirrors for me . . .'

'Now then,' John broke in, 'we're not going over that again. It's a question of finding someone else who could make use of them.'

Faith shook her head, smiling. 'Well, well, tell them our news, John. Never mind the mirrors.'

'What news?' Eleanor looked from one to another, but could tell from their faces they were pleased. It was nothing bad. John got up and went to the dresser for his glasses, and picked up an envelope lying there.

'It's David,' Faith announced, before he could sit down again. 'We've heard from David.'

'At last!'

'What – not a letter?' Eleanor exclaimed. 'Good heavens, fancy him writing a letter.'

'Well, a note. On a wee card.' John took it out of the envelope. On one side, a reproduction of a Botticelli Madonna; on the other, a few scrawled words. Eleanor realised with a tiny shock that the very handwriting, large and black and looped, jolted memories. She kept still, listening as her father read.

'Moving to Edinburgh before Christmas, back to being a Scot at last. Will be in touch. Love to all.'

Silence, as they took this in.

'Well,' Marion said.

'I have no idea what he means by saying he'll be back to being a Scot. Presumably he didn't stop being Scottish just because he was living in England.' Faith started piling up dishes.

'Is there an address?' Marion took the card from her father. 'No – not even a phone number.'

'But he's going to be in touch,' John said, taking his glasses off and beaming at them. 'Back for Christmas.'

'Oh, that's what I was going to ask. Fergus wants to know – well, we all do. Are you coming up to us this year?'

Her parents looked at each other.

'Are you sure?'

'There's Alice and Mamie . . .'

'Oh them too.' Marion waved away objections. 'Fergus's mother will put them up. We'll manage. Or,' she grinned at her sister, 'Eleanor could clear out her boxroom.'

'You'll have David too,' their father prompted. 'David will be here.'

'Maybe.' Faith rose from the table. 'Poke the fire up, John. We'll take our coffee through.'

*   *   *

Later, Eleanor tapped on Marion's bedroom door. Marion was sitting up in bed with a cardigan round her shoulders, reading her way through a selection of her mother's *Woman and Home*.

'Do you want any of these?' she asked.

'No, I've got the *Scots Magazine* and the *Reader's Digest*.'

'I thought you always re-read *What Katy Did* when you came home?'

'So I do. But one night isn't quite long enough these days. I just fall asleep. Anyway, I love that page in *Reader's Digest* – what's it called – you know, "Life's Like That".'

'Why, for goodness sake?'

'Because mostly it isn't like that. Life is like . . . oh, something else. Not like anything in *Reader's Digest*.' Eleanor sat on the edge of the bed. 'It's freezing in here.'

'I know. Heating went off at nine o'clock as usual.'

They grimaced at each other.

'We grew up in this,' Eleanor said. 'How did we survive?'

'Hardy.'

'I suppose.' Eleanor flicked over the pages of a discarded magazine. 'Mum's not too chuffed about David, is she?'

'You can hardly blame her.'

'Dad's thrilled.'

'He always is. David's still the blue-eyed boy.' Marion sighed, and leaned back on the pillows. 'Mum's sharper with him, with all of us.'

'And you think that as far as David's concerned, she's quite right?'

'Yes, I do. He's so unfair to them. Why can't he write, call them up, make sure they have his address? It's not much to ask. What on earth is he doing that's so secret?'

But Eleanor only shrugged, so Marion went on, 'You ought to know, if anyone does. I mean, he was forever staying at your house at one time.'

'Yes.' Eleanor bit her lip, and leafed through pages of recipes.

Marion looked at her in silence for a moment, then said, 'Oh well, Mamie and Alice tomorrow. Lots of news and good advice.'

'The aunts. You don't really want them at Christmas as well, do you?'

Marion smiled. 'Och, where else are they going to go, if Mum and Dad come to us? They'd have a wee chicken on their own, and drive each other crazy.'

Eleanor laughed. 'So they'll come and drive all of us crazy instead? Let me help, then. I'll make a pudding.'

'No thanks. I know your pudding. You can come and make table decorations and fold napkins. I know your strengths, Eleanor Cairns, and they don't lie with pudding making.'

They gazed at each other, startled.

'Now,' Eleanor said, 'I can't imagine anyone calling you Marion Cairns.'

'Sorry, don't know why—'

'Oh, I never liked Ian's name much anyway. But women didn't keep their own names when we married. Eleanor Cooper. Hm. Doesn't suit me. But maybe I've gone back to being single. Nice to think you could go back to being young.'

'It's because we're here.'

'Being the girls. Is David still "the boy", do you think?'

'To Dad he is.'

Eleanor got up, stiffly. 'I'm frozen. Must get a hot bottle, and go to bed.'

'Up early,' Marion warned. 'I want to be in Marks by half nine.'

Eleanor groaned, but nodded, 'Aye, OK,' then went back to her own room.

At Pitcairn, they slept in the rooms they had had as teenagers, when Marion had demanded a bedroom of her own, and moved out of the one they had shared as children. It meant her room was always more grown-up than Eleanor's, for Eleanor could not bear to leave the nursery bedroom, with the beech tree at the window, and wallpaper with pink roses and blue forget-me-nots. And yet, the rooms were very alike now, with single beds and low bookcases their father had made, and empty wardrobes that held only their wedding gowns, and the dresses they had worn as each other's bridesmaids. Marion's bookcase was full of stories about girls who became air hostesses, nurses, ballerinas; on the top shelf a row of pottery rabbits alternated with china figurines, dressed in pink tutus. Eleanor's books were the old childhood classics: Enid Blyton adventures and *Little Women*, and the *School Friend* annuals. On top of hers, a row of sea shells, collected long ago, and so brittle now many were chipped and broken. But the posters of pop stars, the clothes and make-up and long playing records, had years ago been cleared out. Childhood remained; adolescence had been swept away. No wonder, Eleanor thought, huddling round the burning hot water bottle, that coming back here is like being a child again.

Not meaning to, or wanting to, she began to think of David, when he had stayed with her that last time. New Year. January. Black ice, and the funeral cars going so slowly in freezing air they seemed to move through silence. Not a sound all the way to the Crematorium. But there must have been sound, after that. A hymn, words, farewells, some sort of conversation. But Eleanor could recall only silence, and the coffin gliding away in hollow stillness. Think of other things. But she could not. In the end, she put the lamp on, and read 'Life's Like That' until her eyelids fell and she could put the light off and try again to sleep, numb and heavy, not thinking at all.

Marion woke early, as she always did. Her mother was

downstairs already. The bedroom doors at Pitcairn still sprang open in the night, and though the fitted carpets they now had stopped them moving very far, Marion could hear Radio 4 very faintly from the kitchen. She lay listening to the sober murmur of the news, lulling herself with the illusion of being young again, a daughter, someone who did not have to get up and cope with waking a household, getting everyone organised for the day. But the thought of the Christmas shopping kept her from sleep; she would have to get up.

The kitchen light was on; outside, daylight crept up the garden. Faith was making pastry. Gently, she lifted a rolled-out disc and laid it in a pie dish.

'You're an early bird,' she said, looking up.

'Ach,' Marion shrugged, 'it's years since I was able to lie in.'

'Well, you would have a family,' her mother smiled, as she began to roll out the second disc.

'What are you making?'

'Apple pie. I thought we'd have a pudding, since Mamie and Alice are coming.'

Marion filled the kettle. 'I've not much in the way of cereal,' Faith went on, watching her. 'Your dad likes his porridge.'

'I'll have toast.' Marion moved about the familiar kitchen. 'You must be relieved to hear from David,' she said as she made herself tea, and waited for the toaster.

'Oh, I've given up worrying about him.'

Marion knew this was not true. 'I suppose he's old enough to take care of himself now,' she said.

'He always thought so.' Faith pinched the edges of the pie crust, and put the dish in the pantry. Then she began to wipe up the table, clearing it. Marion sat at the other end, spreading marmalade on her toast.

'He's thoughtless, though,' she said.

Her mother paused, looking up. 'Och, Marion, people say

boys are easier – you know? I hear other women say that about their children. But it wasn't true for us. David was the difficult one.'

Marion thought of Ross, who was easy-going, quiet. 'I suppose, even as a wee boy, he was always in trouble.'

Faith sat down suddenly, the cloth still in her hand. 'I used to blame Stanley,' she said. 'You mind on that lad, Stanley?'

'Yes, of course I do. He was never away from the place when we were kids.'

'I used to blame him – no mother, and his father forever in the Pitcairn Arms.' She sighed. 'But it was David – David was the leader. I saw that when Stanley came back that time, told us what had happened to David. And years before . . .' She hesitated.

'What?'

'They had a spell of lighting fires, him and Stanley. Down in the woods, up the lane – they near set the henhouse alight one day. And it was all David's idea – he was fascinated by fire. I was terrified they'd do it sometime there was nobody to catch them.' Her face tightened.

'But they never did any real damage,' Marion protested. 'It was just a bonfire or two – wasn't it?'

Faith stood up, drawing the cloth across the table to catch the rest of the crumbs, sweeping them into her cupped hand, held at the edge. 'I hope so,' she said. 'I hope that's all it ever was.' She looked up at the clock. 'You'd better get Eleanor out of her bed, if you want to be in the town early. It's terrible trying to get parked at this time of year.'

Marion got up. 'Right,' she said. 'I'll go and see if she's awake.'

They were gone all morning, and came back in time for a late lunch, the back seat of the car full of bulging carrier bags.

'Well?' Faith asked as they came into the kitchen. 'Success?' 'Yes,' said Marion, and 'No,' said Eleanor.

'Oh come on, Eleanor, you've bought heaps of things.'

'Ach, I hate shopping.'

'I just can't do it any more,' Faith said as she turned the soup down to a simmer and put the lid back on her stockpot. 'My legs hurt. Shops don't have chairs now, so you can have a wee rest.' She went to get rolls from the bread bin. 'I'm getting old, that's my trouble.'

'No, you're not.' Eleanor squeezed her mother round the waist, her tiny mother who seemed even smaller these days, and fragile. But Faith shook her off, smiling, and put the rolls in a basket.

'I'm not so spry as I was. And neither's Dad.' Marion halted with her arms full of carrier bags, hearing something like caution, almost a warning, in her mother's voice.

'He's all right, though?'

'Well, he's got angina.'

'When – when did he get that?' Marion put her bags down, and Eleanor stopped in the middle of taking off her jacket.

'He's been breathless for months, but I couldn't persuade him to see the doctor. Then, a couple of weeks back, chest pains in the night, so I got Martin Cleland to come in, next morning.'

'You never said!'

'Nothing to say. No sense in worrying you girls.'

'But – what are they going to do about it?'

'Oh, he's down for some procedure where they put a balloon inside an artery or something. Don't ask me. He's got tablets for now, and Martin says there's nothing to worry about. But the specialist has to decide, about the balloon thing. He's seeing him in December.'

Eleanor and Marion stood there for a moment, watching their mother shave curls of butter into a flowered china dish, getting on with things, not looking at them.

'I wish you'd said,' Eleanor muttered, as she hung up her jacket.

'I'll take this lot upstairs, out of the way,' Marion said, gathering packages.

'Right, then, Eleanor, take the bread and butter through.'

The dining room fire had been lit, and the first chill just removed from the atmosphere. But the room was still bleak, and smelled of soot. Against the left-hand wall, opposite the window, stood the piano, long out of tune, where Marion had practised, and their mother, or Ruby, had played for the ballet classes. The long polished table was set with silver and glass, and the press door at the side of the fireplace stood ajar, showing on the shelves more glass, napkins and spare flower vases. It was an ordinary dining room, rarely used, a little musty, until you turned to the wall on the right of the door. All the way to the end, there were full-length mirrors fitted, and halfway up, a wooden barre. As Eleanor put the basket of rolls on the table, she caught sight of herself in the looking-glass world, the other dining table and chairs, the other fire burning silently in the grate, the other Eleanor fair and solemn, hair falling forward. Then all this dissolved, for a moment only, and she saw the row of little girls again in their leotards and pink practice shoes, heads poised, arms arched, one, two three, one two three, heads up, tummies in, and again, one two three . . .

'Now then,' Faith said behind her, 'you could get the white napkins out.'

'I wish Dad would get rid of these mirrors.'

'Oh, he's promised me that for years. And the room redecorated. This gloomy paper, it's long overdue for a change.'

'It could be a really lovely room – the fireplace, and the big window.'

'Och, it's hardly worth it now. This house is too big for us. I'm only setting the lunch in here because it keeps Mamie out of my kitchen.'

'You're not thinking of moving though?'

'No, no, I'm too old for that palaver. Pitcairn will see us out. Then you girls and David can please yourselves.'

'Don't. You and Dad are going to live for ever.'

Faith laughed. 'Oh aye.' She raised a hand. 'Hark, is that them now?' Faintly, along the drive, came the chugging of the aunts' Morris Minor.

Eleanor went through the hall to the front door, but her father was there before her. She thought how gaunt he seemed, but he still moved briskly, so he could not really be ill. Angina was common, wasn't it? You didn't die of angina. They could ask Fergus, when they got home.

Mamie and Alice eased themselves stiffly out of the Morris Minor, Mamie in purple and blue, all floating scarves and sweet scent, a plump butterfly of a woman, her rings flashing as she waved to them in the sunshine of this mild November day. Alice came more soberly behind, thin and upright as her brother, and plain, in her grey coat and hat.

Eleanor's heart, chipped with anxiety about her father, squeezed by the past, by David's careless note, relented and relaxed, and she ran down the steps to meet them, and take the flowers Mamie held out, the parcels Alice carried.

Next morning, going home, Marion said, 'They seem quite well, don't they, Mum and Dad? I'll ask Fergus about Dad's angina. I don't think there's anything to worry about, though. Do you?'

'They're both fine,' Eleanor assured her. 'Mum's never been ill, has she?'

'All that exercise when she was young, the dancing.'

'And those classes – remember? When we were at the Academy, and she wanted to make a bit of money herself.'

'Is that why she did it, do you think?' Marion sounded surprised. 'I thought it was just that she missed teaching, and we were getting older, and anyway, both of us were utterly useless at ballet. So she took in all those other would-be Fonteyns.'

'Those dreadful little girls on Saturday mornings, shrieking and laughing. How long did it go on?'

'A few years – till around the time David left school? Can't remember now. She could never have made much money at it. How many parents would bring their children all the way out there for a ballet class – the middle of nowhere.'

'Those awful mirrors,' Eleanor said.

'I know.' Marion laughed. 'If you're at the fireplace side of the table, you get a nice warm back, but you have to sit and look at yourself eating.'

'Yes, and the back of Mamie's head, nodding up and down. I try not to look.' Eleanor had been conscious all through lunch-time of her reflection, and of Mamie's plump rear view, the fluffy white hair less buoyant from the back, and showing pink scalp beneath. Even then, in the middle of the flow of reminiscence and gossip that made up family talk, she had been able to conjure them again, the row of little girls, hopping down the room, Ruby thumping on the piano, and her mother, tiny and dark, shouting instructions.

'Nearly home – thank goodness.' Marion could see the necklace of lights strung out along the Kessock Bridge, a reflected glow of Inverness like a reddish haze across the dark blue sky. She was worrying about whether she had bought the right presents, and beginning to regret asking everyone up for Christmas. But it would be all right – it always was, in the end. She closed her eyes and leaned back, while Eleanor drove them home.

Marion had no need to worry about Christmas after all. Three weeks later, their father telephoned her at eight in the morning, as she tried to get Ross out of bed and into the shower, and Fergus burned toast in the kitchen.

'Dad? What is it?' Her heart leaping up, the certainty of something wrong.

'It's your mother. I thought you'd better know, you and Eleanor. I had to get the doctor out last night, she wasn't well.'

'What's happened – is she all right?'

'Well, no. Not just yet. She's in the hospital. A wee stroke, the doctor says. Just a wee one, but she's not awake yet, not speaking or anything.'

'Oh God.'

'I'm away up to the hospital again in a while,' he went on. 'But I thought you'd want to know where she is.'

'But how bad is it? Look, Dad – we'll come down. I'll ring Eleanor – we'll come down.' And then she thought, *I'm in Dingwall today, they're relying on me, I'll have to leave it till after school. Drive down in the dark.* She knew from her father's voice that it was bad, that he was shaken. No question, they should go at once.

'No, no, she'll be fine. The doctor said the first twenty-four hours were what mattered. They can't tell yet what the damage is, but if she pulls round out of this – they tell me folks make a good recovery.' He cleared his throat. 'Anyway, she's in the best place. The nurses are awful kind. I'll phone you again when I've seen her.'

'Look, Dad, I'm teaching today. Phone Eleanor, or phone the surgery and they'll put you through to Fergus. Can I ring the hospital – is that where you'll be?'

'I couldn't say. Probably. Aye, I'll bide at the hospital. See how she gets on.'

Marion found her pulse was racing. The day was growing dark and confused, and when she put the phone down, she did not know what to do first.

But their mother died that morning. Eleanor called her at school, and she came out of her classroom in a rush, to pick up the telephone in the school office, knowing what the news must be, but not believing it.

'I didn't know what to do,' Eleanor said, her voice full of tears held back. 'I'm sorry, Marion, I should have left it till you got home, but I felt you had to know.'

Marion went back to the classroom, and taught for the rest of the day. She and Eleanor would go to Aberdeen next morning, when they had made all their arrangements.

Claire was to go to Marion's house after school, and stay the night. Marion took a casserole out of the freezer; made a list for Fergus; found someone to take Kirsty to Highland dancing; reminded Ross about his football kit; brought the ironing up to date; made sure someone would give the old cat her tablet, feed all the animals, and leave the *Betterwear* catalogue at the front door. When Eleanor said, 'I'll drive if you like,' she could only sigh with relief.

As they drove down the A96, a faint haze of snow drifted through the air towards them. Pitcairn House seemed bitterly cold, the fires unlit, newspapers spread on the kitchen table, unwashed dishes in the sink. Both sisters, bleakly facing how it was going to be at Pitcairn without their mother, set to work.

'Ach, don't worry about cleaning,' her father said, finding Eleanor with a brush and dustpan, about to sweep down the stair carpet.

'We want to leave everything tidy for you.'

'I've Ruby,' he said. 'She'll come in an extra day or so, now, maybe.' Eleanor realised he had thought of this already. 'Your mother would have done without Ruby, you know. She said there was no need, with just the two of us. But I persuaded her. She was company, anyway, Ruby's a cheery soul.'

'But she's getting on, Dad. You think she'll want more work? Maybe Susan Mackie – what's her married name, I always forget – maybe she knows somebody.'

'We'll see,' he said, which meant he would not. 'Anyway, what I came to tell you – where's Marion?'

'In the kitchen, I think. She was going to make us something to eat.'

'Well, I've had Alice on the phone. They're coming in past. Would there be something for them as well?'

'Oh, I'm sure we can manage.' Eleanor went to find Marion. 'The aunts are on their way. Can we feed them?'

'You should see the freezer, Eleanor. Mum has everything labelled – soup, casseroles – you'd think she knew. There's enough to feed Dad for months.'

'But she didn't know. Marion, it *was* right out of the blue, wasn't it?'

'Yes, yes. Of course it was. She was organised all the time – always plenty to eat. Too much for just the two of them, really.'

'She was like you.' Eleanor saw this as if for the first time. 'You are like Mum – not to look at, or only a bit. But you're methodical, the way she is . . . was. Oh Marion.'

'I know.'

They stood looking at each other, and Eleanor fought back tears.

'Right,' Marion said, turning away. 'I'll get more soup out.'

Mamie was tearful; Alice seemed as usual, if a little more grave. Mamie embraced them, *Oh dearie me, we saw her a week syne, and naethin wrang ava.* Alice touched Marion on the shoulder, and said what a shock it had been. Sitting down to eat seemed pointless, but the organising of it (*you sit there, no that's fine. I can manage – who's for soup?*) a relief. Mamie, protesting that they didn't need more than a bite, nobody had an appetite at such a time, had a bowl of soup and several sandwiches. Alice, to Eleanor's surprise, also ate well, and seemed almost cheerful by the time Marion filled the coffee cups. Their father hardly touched his food, and got up before everyone else had finished, to go out and 'see to something in the garden'.

'Go and look for him,' Marion murmured to Eleanor as Mamie and Alice vied to wash up and clear away. 'See he's OK.'

Eleanor put on her coat and boots and walked down the garden. Her father was standing by the wall near the henhouse now dilapidated, looking out over the fields towards the woods. Eleanor had a sudden memory of herself, seated astride the wall, watching the tinker family, hearing their dog bark.

'You all right, Dad?' She slipped her arm through his.

'Aye, lass.' He patted her hand, but did not move, and they stood there together for a moment in silence. Oh, why did she die? Eleanor thought. He's going to be so lonely.

'Dad, do you remember that family – two wee boys – the woman came to the back door and told our fortunes. I think she came every year round this way, with her family, but I can only recall the one time. They were tinkers, I suppose, and they had a sort of camp – over there.' She pointed towards the woods. Her father did not answer at once. Thinking he did not remember, Eleanor went on, 'There was something else. For some reason, they're connected in my mind with that terrible fire at the Mackies. The barn – did their hayloft not go on fire?'

'It did.'

She saw that he did remember. He shook his head. 'Poor souls,' he said. 'Aye, I mind on them. Her and her bairns. They appeared every summer for a few years. Her man took work on the farms, but he was a shiftless cratur. Folk employed him because they felt sorry for her. What made you think of them just now?'

'I don't know. Standing here – this is where I was when I saw them first.' Eleanor called up the memory again, herself balanced on the wall, then running inside for some reason. 'She had a baby too, didn't she? As well as the boys.'

'It was a terrible thing to happen,' her father said, and there was a note in his voice of something more than regret for people he had scarcely known, more than thirty years ago. Eleanor looked at him.

'What?' she asked, but as she spoke, memory unlocked.

'They died in the Mackies' fire.'

'Oh – oh, that was it. I remember the fire.'

'Dan was in two minds about letting them take shelter there for a night or two. I think in the end he said no, he didn't like her man at all. But the weather was heavy, and a storm forecast. They must have gone in after all, when the Mackies were in bed.'

'They all died?' Eleanor saw herself and Marion, up at the window, a fierce glow in the sky.

'No, just the woman and her baby. Somehow the boys got out, or maybe they weren't in the barn. I canna mind now but the man had been out drinking, and he wasn't back. They found him in a ditch the next morning, still fu', and knowing nothing about it.'

John Cairns turned to go back up the garden to the house, and Eleanor followed him. 'What happened to the children?'

'Oh, the Welfare must have taken care of them. What's it now, Social Services? I dinna ken what happened to the fellow. Never saw him again.'

Eleanor paused by the bench at the back door, and turned to look down the garden again. Her father stopped with her, waiting. The lilac trees were bare, the garden brown and grey in weak November light.

'What an awful thing to happen,' Eleanor said. 'How did – I mean, did they ever find out how the fire started?'

'The man smoked. Could have been one of his fag ends. Dan wasn't keen on having them at all for that very reason.'

'But his wife and baby burned to death.'

'A tragedy. You know, Eleanor, some folk say they see her whiles, going round the doors, carrying her bairn.'

'Her ghost?'

'Ach, I've nae time for stories like that. Neither had your mother. But Ruby swears she's seen her here. Though why the poor soul should haunt this house, when she died up at the Mains, goodness knows.'

'But he was *out,*' Eleanor said. 'How could it have been *his* fault?'

'A cigarette end can smoulder away a good long time.' He hesitated. 'Did your mother speak to you about it?'

'Mum? No, why? I have a sort of memory of the fire – well, the excitement of it. And was that not the night David went missing? Out late with Stanley.'

'Oh, we got him home well before the fire started.' Her father was emphatic. 'No, no, your mother always had a fear he'd something to do with it – him and Stanley, with their matches. They were terrible lads for lighting bonfires. But there was no question – he was home before it started. I don't know that he was even up at the Mains that night. They denied it, anyway.'

Eleanor thought of heat smouldering beneath straw, the smoke threading through, the first tiny lick of flame.

'They played with those boys, him and Stanley,' she said.

'What boys?'

'The tinkers' kids.'

Before her father could reply, Alice opened the back door.

'We're away,' she said. 'But we'll be back the morn, just to see you're managing, see if there's anything wanted.'

'There's no need,' John Cairns said, as he and Eleanor stepped into the kitchen, shutting the door behind them. 'Chisholms are coming out this afternoon. I phoned them and we decided yesterday – the funeral's to be on Friday. So I'm fine.'

Alice seemed to hesitate. She spoke directly to her brother, as if Eleanor were not there. 'I'd like a word,' she said, 'afore we go.'

Mamie was in the living room with Marion; Eleanor could hear her voice, querulous, rambling. She looked from her father to Alice, saw the likeness between them, and how, for once, her father looked as old as his sister, for all the seven years between. There was some tension she could not understand, and she wanted to protect her father.

'It could wait,' he said, passing a hand across his eyes.

'Just as you like.' But she did not move. Then she turned to Eleanor. 'Ask Mamie if she's ready, would you, Eleanor?'

'All right.' Eleanor went out, and Alice shut the kitchen door behind her. For a moment, she thought of waiting, of standing there to listen. But of course, you couldn't do that sort of thing. She heard her mother's voice suddenly, its warning, advising note. And hurried down the hall to Marion.

In the afternoon, they saw the minister and the undertaker. At six, Marion cooked a meal none of them had appetite to eat. On the Friday, they would come to Pitcairn with their families, and stay on, just the two of them, over the weekend. Something had to be done about Faith's things.

'Only,' Marion said, as they made a pot of tea before they went to bed, 'I don't know if I can face it.'

'Let's put it off, then, if Dad doesn't mind,' Eleanor suggested. 'It doesn't seem true, anyway, that she's dead, that she's not coming home.' She sighed. 'I wish she'd been brought here, not taken to the funeral place. She should be here.'

Marion poured tea into mugs, and set the tea-pot down. 'It doesn't matter, really. I mean, she's not here any more, at all.'

'But that's what I'm saying. I can't believe it.'

'Well, we're going to have to.'

'Not yet,' Eleanor said, her eyes filling with tears. 'Not yet.'

Their father seemed very calm, as if he had managed better than Eleanor could, to believe what had happened. And yet, he talked about Faith as if she still had an opinion which must be taken into consideration.

'She would want you lassies to sort out her clothes, and take her bits of jewellery away with you. Take whatever you want. It's no use to me.'

'Let's not do anything in a hurry,' Eleanor said.

'Well, well.' He seemed to accept this, and looked down into the fire Eleanor had lit, cradling his mug of tea. After a moment, he said, 'But there's one thing exercises my mind, lasses. One thing there *is* a hurry for.'

Marion and Eleanor looked at each other. They had talked of this on the way here, unable to decide what to do about it.

'David,' Marion said.

'We need to speak to him. He'll have no idea at all.'

'Well, how could he,' Eleanor burst out, 'if he never gets in touch?' She felt, under all the new grief, anger with herself, guilt again. *It was because of me he lost touch, kept away.*

Their father went to find David's card, and the envelope it had come in. But the postmark was blurred.

'It's London, at any rate,' Marion decided. 'WC something.'

'But that just means he posted it in the centre,' Eleanor pointed out. 'Maybe he's been working there. Look, I have phone numbers somewhere, in the old address book, for one or two of his friends. I'll look them out.'

'Och, I'm sure if we put our minds to it, we can find him,' Marion said, patting her father's knee.

'Aye, that's the ticket. I wouldn't want him not to be at the funeral. Terrible for him not to be at the funeral.'

Eleanor felt something almost like jealousy, as she watched her father sink back in his chair, looking not at them, but at something in the past or future, at David.

In the morning, he stood at the front door to see them off. Beside him, as they turned for a last wave, the ghost of their mother, small and straight next to her husband's stooped figure, the light in the hall behind them, and on either side the stone urns, yellow-leafed ivy trailing down from them over the top step. Upstairs, a curtain seemed to move in their parents' bedroom window, a trick of light, a shimmer of winter sunlight on the glass.

'I feel so bad leaving him,' Eleanor said. She blinked away tears, swallowing hard.

'We'll be back,' Marion promised. 'Only a couple of days.'

For a long while they drove in silence. On either side, the landscape lay bleak and bare, the sky stone grey, heavy. Then, when they were beyond Inverurie, Marion said, 'Do you remember my friend Violet?'

'Was she the one with incredibly long pigtails?'

'Yes, and lovely frocks. Well, I thought they were lovely then.'

'I remember Violet. She was there when the gypsy came. Or just after – she said they were dirty.'

'What?'

'Tinks. You must remember her.'

Eleanor was about to begin on the story her father had told her, when Marion said, 'You know, Violet didn't believe me when I said my mother used to be a dancer – on stage. We had quite an argument about it. She accused me of making up stories and I got really upset.'

'Violet had a narrow view of life, as I recall.'

'I suppose she did. She wouldn't go to the Academy – she wanted to work in Esslemont and Mackintosh in Aberdeen, and sell ladies' outfits. So she did. Anyway, we went out to the back door, Mum was there doing something, and I said to her, "Violet doesn't believe me about you being a ballet dancer. She says I'm telling lies".' Marion paused, remembering the angry, hurt feeling, the belief that her mother would put things right.

'What did Mum say?'

'Nothing. She just picked up her skirt – it was summer, she had a dress on for once, and she whirled across the yard – entrechats, well, some sort of jump, and then she twirled round and round. It was so amazing.'

Then Marion, and Eleanor (who had not witnessed this, but saw it now), watched her again, transformed, their tiny, unyielding mother, spinning across the yard and out onto the grass, brown hens squawking and fleeing, as she pirouetted past them, skirts flying, head flicking a second behind her shoulders, face composed and aloof. Suddenly, it was over, she was straight and still by the coal bunker, holding her skirts with curved fingers, then swooping down in a deep, deep curtsey.

'Oh Marion.' Eleanor was blinded by tears, and had to slow down, come off the main road, stop the car.

'What a disappointment we must have been,' Marion said, gulping down a sob, trying to laugh. 'Two great lumps of girls, far too big for ballet.'

'Kirsty,' Eleanor blew her nose. 'Kirsty can dance.'

'Well, she has the ability, I suppose. Even if it's for Highland dancing.'

The car grew cold, but they sat on, unable to move further, caught by the past.

'We'd better get on,' Marion said at last. Eleanor, who was no longer thinking of the tinker woman, turned the key, and started the engine. Then they drove on, the space between themselves and Pitcairn lengthening behind them.

8

When she knew for certain that she had cancer, Marion came home and fetched her waterproof jacket and boots, took the car out the old Evanton road and headed for Cnoc Fyrish. She would climb the hill, sit under the monument for a while, and then walk back down and go home to talk to other people.

The hill itself was only just over a thousand feet; a good hour's walk to the summit. They had done it many times with the children, and she had gone up with Eleanor too, just after she had moved here. At the top, great stone arches had been built by the hard labour of local men, given employment by Hector Munro when he came back in glory from the Siege of Serangapatum. The arches represented the gates of the Indian city. Marion had explained all this to Eleanor, on that first walk they had made together up the hill, when Eleanor was newly widowed and you had to talk to her all the time, tell her things, keep her from brooding. Or so other people advised. Marion had not been so sure.

'So it was to give men work,' Eleanor asked as they set off through the trees at the foot of the hill.

'That was his idea.'

Then, at the top, standing with her hand on one of the stone pillars, Eleanor turned and said, 'It was all pointless, wasn't it? All that lugging great muckle stones up the hill

. . . it wasn't work with any dignity, or that would help their families in the future, was it?'

And Marion had agreed. The sisters sat in silence, drinking tea from the flask Marion had brought, their backs leaning on hard stone. They looked along the firth to the Sutors at Cromarty, the rigs by Invergordon tiny at this distance. In May sunshine, the landscape, blue and green, ochre and brown, was rich with fertility, new growth. 'How beautiful it all is,' Eleanor said. 'I'm glad I came.'

'So am I,' Marion answered, and that was the last time she tried to distract Eleanor with talking. The land, the shining water, the Cairngorms far and misty away to the south – all that was what rested the spirit, not talking.

Now, wrapped up against November cold, Marion remembered that climb with Eleanor. She was so new in the place, she had had to be told all the local stories. But now she belonged. Marion felt she should have brought her sister with her this time. But she had not yet called Eleanor. Only the hospital knew, and Fergus.

At the top, the wind was fierce, and she zipped up her Goretex jacket, pulling the hood forward. The light was going already, so she should set off down again as soon as possible. She would just get her breath. The hills were dark today, obscure, and there was no view. You could not even see the Sutors. But in the firth, two or three rigs were lit up like Christmas trees, winking and glittering in the bleak afternoon. Marion touched one of the stone pillars, and it struck cold even through her glove. So much wasted effort, just so that succeeding generations could tell Munro's story. But she was glad she had come. Soon she might not be fit enough for the climb. Another year could pass before she did it again.

She must go down now, go home and see Eleanor, and talk to her children, her father. This was when you wanted your mother still to be there, to tell you it would be all right. But it might not be all right. Cancer. Cancer. She said the word over and over to herself, till it had no meaning left, was two syllables like a mantric chant, no more. *Can-cer, can-cer.*

Still she stood in the fading light, unmoving, afraid.

Late in November, Marion went into hospital, and the operation to remove her left breast, and thus excise the cancer, was successfully carried out. Afterwards, she seemed to recover quickly, and was quite cheerful when they went in to see her.

'The good news,' she told Eleanor and David, who sat on hard chairs beside her bed, 'did Fergus say? They're not going to start my treatment before the New Year – I've to have a scan and some tests or something first. So I'll have Christmas more or less in peace, without having to worry about the side effects.'

'Side effects?' David, who had slumped, and was flicking through a magazine, drew himself up.

'From the chemotherapy.'

'So . . . they're definitely going ahead with that?'

Marion made a face. 'Not looking forward to it, I have to say. Six months, they think. Maybe I won't be able to work much.'

'Och, you're not to bother about that,' Eleanor said. 'Just get well.'

Marion sighed. 'The way things happen – it's ironic. There's a full-time post coming up at Easter, and before all this started, I was thinking of applying for it. Kirsty's in Primary 7 next year, and it's the same school; it would be so convenient. I was beginning to feel I was ready to go full-time.' She took a deep breath. 'Till this happened.'

Eleanor murmured reassurance, and meant it, but she was thinking that if Marion worked full-time, they would not meet so often, and really, she should be the one to find a job. *I've only one child, and not even a husband,* she scolded herself, but felt weak even contemplating work, having to be out of the house every morning, tied to some routine she could not even imagine, let alone wish for. Anyway, for now, she decided, she was needed at home, to support Marion and Fergus, and see them through this.

David was restless in the ward. Since Eleanor had told him about Marion, he had behaved like someone trapped, who wants to leave, but knows he must not. He had alternated between this sullenness, suffering but not talking, and talking too much, suggesting alternative therapies he had heard or read about, each sillier than the last, it seemed to Eleanor. Now he got up and strolled about, then stood looking out of the window at the spread of parked cars opposite the hospital, gleaming in winter sunshine.

'Look at it,' Marion grumbled, her gaze following David. 'The dreariest autumn for years, and then as soon as I'm in hospital, the sun shines.'

'But you'll be home by the end of the week,' Eleanor soothed.

David turned and came back to the bed. 'I'm going out for a fag. OK?'

Marion shook her head, smiling. 'You don't like hospitals.'

'Well, who would?' He sounded defensive. 'Be glad to see you out of here.' He bent and kissed her. On her hot cheek, briefly, the roughness of his beard, and the smell of tobacco and garlic. Then he was off, moving easily down the corridor now, on his way out.

'He's restless,' Marion said. 'Not just in the hospital. Isn't he?'

'Och, he never settles anywhere.' Eleanor was annoyed with David. Somehow, when you needed him, he thinned out, grew insubstantial. There was nothing to lean on. She thought of Fergus, his devoted attention to Marion, the crease of anxiety on his forehead deepened in the last weeks. Then she looked at her sister, taking in what David did not like, what filled Fergus with concern, what she herself was afraid of: Marion flushed and weary, her hair flat, damp-looking, not springing up glossy with copper lights as it usually did. The pink nightdress, and beneath it, a white bra with broad straps, that held one living breast, and on the other side, some sort of padding, that looked (at first) just the same. But was not. Eleanor's heart beat fast. How often would she sit here in the future, by Marion's hospital bed, growing sick of the sight of the ward: too familiar, the cluttered locker, the swivel table holding get-well cards, a bottle of lemon barley, tissues, paperbacks . . . And above the bed, the hothouse roses, tight furled, never to open, that Fergus had brought that first day.

Marion leaned back and closed her eyes. 'Ah me,' she said. 'I'll be glad to get home.' After a moment, she sat up again. 'It's what I can't understand about David, how he doesn't seem to want that. To go home.'

'Yes, well, he never has one to go to.'

'Except Pitcairn.'

'Which is probably why he turns up there now and again.' Eleanor glanced at her watch 'I suppose I'd better make a move, collect him on the way to the car.' She began to put her jacket on and stood up. 'I do hate leaving you, though.'

'It's all right. Fergus will be in later.'

'I know.' They looked at each other. 'Maybe it won't be so bad.'

'The chemo? We'll just have to wait and see.'

Eleanor still did not go. 'Marion, I was thinking – about Christmas.'

'Oh God, don't. I'm so glad I got the kids' presents before I came in here.'

'It's more than I've done. Look, why don't we go to Pitcairn? All of us? David will stay on with Dad – it was his idea, actually. I'll cook – David and I will cook. And I'll go down a day or two earlier to sort the house out. Then you don't need to have anybody to stay, and the aunts will still be included, so all you have to do is sit in the car till you get there. And leave the rest to everyone else.'

Marion looked doubtful. 'Oh, I don't know, Eleanor, the kids like to be at home.'

Eleanor pulled on her gloves. 'Think about it. The kids could cope for once. And Fergus is quite keen. I didn't think he would be, but he said he was in favour of it, as long as you were happy. It would just be for the two days – down for Christmas Eve, back Boxing Day morning. You'd be home in time for Fergus's mother's Boxing Day do if she's still having it. Or you could use it as an excuse not to go . . . whatever.'

Marion smiled, and leaned back on her pillows. 'Oh well,' she said, 'I'll see what the family say. I'll think about it.'

Eleanor patted her arm. 'I'm off. See you tomorrow.'

Outside the sliding doors, David stood with his hands in the pockets of his Barbour jacket (bought when he had intended to live in the country and rear rare-breed chickens), waiting for her.

'Did you ask about Christmas?'

'She's going to think about it.'

'Good, we'll work on Fergus.'

'Why are you so keen? We could just scale the whole thing down, try to stop her making pies and puddings, not invite anyone else.'

'Wouldn't work,' he said as they made for the car park. 'Anyway, I'm all for big family Christmases, I'm good at them.'

Eleanor thought of the Christmases he had spent with Marion or with her in their grown-up, married lives. Spectacular and festive, and ending in tragedy. No, that wasn't fair, it was only twice that happened, and . . . She put her key in the car door, looking at David over the roof.

'As long as you do intend to stay and help,' she said.

'Well, I can't promise to last out till Hogmanay,' he shrugged. 'Got friends who want to go skiing, might go with them. But I do promise to stay for Christmas.'

'Skiing? I thought you hadn't any money?'

'Come on, it's freezing out here, let's get home.'

Once they were on the road, pausing at traffic lights, Eleanor said again, 'Skiing? I didn't know you *could* ski.'

'There's a lot you don't know about me.' He was looking out of the window; she could not see his face.

'But that's expensive, isn't it? All the equipment and stuff?'

'Lights have changed,' he said. She put the car in gear and moved forward. David folded his arms; glancing sideways she saw his profile was severe, secretive. Then he seemed to relax.

'Got a business deal coming off,' he said. 'Should net me a few thousand. Enough for a holiday anyhow, before I get started on the internet thing.'

'So . . . are you really doing that?' She did not believe in the business deal. Sometimes she thought he did not tell the truth about anything, as if, a long time ago, he had lost himself in his own maze of lies.

'Looks like it. But Phil's based in Perth just now, so I'll be going down there for a while.'

A fortnight ago, she would have ached with disappointment. Now, she was almost relieved. Somehow, whether he was there or not, mattered less. What mattered was Marion, and that she got better. Marion must not die. All their lives would change too much, if Marion died. There was no point in thinking like that. But she could not help her mind turning again and again to this one terrible fear. Marion was the centre they all clung to. By the time their mother had died, she was no longer the centre; her children had grown up and created their own families. That was how it should be, with death. Eleanor thought of her mother's funeral, and it struck her with such force that she slowed for the Tore roundabout only just in time, that if David drifted off again, he might not be there should Marion die. Eleanor pictured Marion's funeral, the white-faced children, the packed church, the flowers banked up. But no David.

He had come at the last minute, when Faith died. He had walked into the house as they stood in the hall, the aunts and John, Fergus and Marion and Eleanor. The children were in the living room, watching television in subdued silence, while they waited for the funeral cars. But when a car sounded on the drive, it was with a squeal of brakes, the gravel skidding beneath wheels, not the stately crunch over stones, the quiet engines of the Daimlers they were listening for. Eleanor and Marion and Fergus looked at each other, and their father suddenly headed for the front door.

'I got the message,' David said. 'I'm sorry, I'm sorry, Dad.' Taking in the black ties, the sombre coats. He stood in the rain in an old sweatshirt and jeans, looking thin and young and unshaven.

'Come in, son,' his father said. 'I'm glad you're here.'

Later, Marion said to Eleanor that she had smelled drink on David as he embraced her, but Eleanor thought she must be mistaken.

'He drove all the way,' she protested. 'From Birmingham, he said. Overnight. It couldn't be drink, surely not.'

But Marion pursed her lips, knowing she was right.

He had stayed on after the funeral, after the others had gone home, apparently with no job to go back to, and soon no money. For several weeks he seemed to do little but sleep and watch television. Then he and John took down the old henhouse, and he started talking about putting up another, and breeding rare fowl at Pitcairn. Somewhere, he must have had some money, Eleanor realised, to buy that Barbour jacket, and the green rubber boots.

She had gone down to spend a weekend with her father, primed by Marion to find out what David was doing, and afterwards was glad she had not taken Claire with her. She left again on the Sunday morning, just as her father was getting ready for church, and managed to say to him, both of them awkwardly standing in the kitchen, 'Does David drink as much as that . . . well, often?'

John had hesitated. 'He'd a good drop last night, right enough.' He picked up his Bible and car keys. 'He's young, he needs company. I think he's going to bide with a couple of friends until he finds a job. Somewhere about Edinburgh, he says.'

'Time he did find a job.'

'He's a sponger,' Marion had said. 'It's an awful thing to say about your own brother, but I hate the thought of him there with Dad all that time. And Dad so vulnerable.'

'What?'

'Well, where is he getting money from? He's none of his own.'

'He can't need to spend much, at Pitcairn.'

But now Eleanor knew about the new waxed jacket, the empty bottles standing by the kitchen bin. She kissed her father and saw him off to church. She would be on her way North again by the time he got back at lunch-time. David had not appeared, and she did not want to go to his room to say good-bye. Later, she was sorry, since two days after that he had left Pitcairn, telling his father he would be working in Edinburgh. Since then, he had not contacted any of them until he had turned up at Pitcairn this October.

So here he was, in the car beside her as she drove the last mile into Dingwall.

'I want to stop at the supermarket,' Eleanor said.

'We could have a drink.'

'No, we couldn't. I have to get back for Claire.'

'She's fifteen – she won't bother if we're a bit late.'

'Fourteen. Her birthday's not till April. You should know that – it's the day after yours. You used to be so good at remembering, when she was wee.'

'Why can't we just stop at the Queen Mary and have a quick pint?'

'It's nearly five already. There's not time. Anyway, I don't want to sit in the Queen Mary.'

'You're right. Place is a prize dump. Time I went back to Edinburgh – to drink in a decent pub.'

'Oh well, if that's what counts.'

'It helps.'

Eleanor drove into the supermarket car park, and switched off the engine. David said, 'I'll nip round to the old Queen M while you do the shopping, eh? Just for one pint. You can pick me up.'

'But I'm only going to buy a bit of chicken and some milk—'

He got out and banged on the roof twice like a drumbeat before he slammed the door. 'Good girl. See you soon.'

When she went to collect him, he was deep in conversation with a group of men she vaguely recognised, but did not know. Football, the amazing things computers could do, the state of the world – conversation she had no wish to join.

'Hi.' He was cheerful now. 'What do you want? A wee dram?'

'I'm driving, David, and I've got to get home.'

'Right. Fine. Just finish this pint.' But he had hardly begun; he must be on his second already. Eleanor perched on a bar stool beside him and waited. Again she refused a drink, feeling conspicuous. The men eyed her, and one said 'how are ye the day?' but they soon turned back to their drinks and their talk. Eleanor sat glazed with boredom for a few minutes, then slipped off the stool.

'Look,' she said, tugging David's arm. He had his back to her by now. 'I really do have to go.' She half expected him to protest again, or even refuse to move. And then what would she do? It was familiar, this getting David out of a bar. But she had never minded before, when they had been in the Red Lion near their new suburb in Berkshire, she and Ian and David. She had been willing to stay on then, having no children to go home to. It was Ian who always got up first, wanting to leave.

But David came peaceably enough. In the car, he was contrite. 'Sorry, sorry. Guy insisted on buying me a pint. What could I do?' He ruffled her hair. 'You're not mad at me, are you?'

'Don't do that.'

'You *are* mad. Sorry.' He slumped in the seat, and gazed out of the window at darkness, like a scolded child. She smoothed her hair with one hand, relenting.

'I just don't like being late for Claire.'

'Of course not. You're quite right. I'm a bastard.'

Eleanor laughed. 'No, you're not. You're just too fond of bars. And drinking.'

'My hobby,' he admitted, cheering up.

At home he carried the shopping in. Claire was in her room, and had not lit the fire. The cottage was cold and dark. Eleanor ran upstairs to see Claire, and when she came back down, David had unpacked. But since he seemed, even after several weeks, not to know where anything was stored, this was not much help. He leaned against the Rayburn, watching Eleanor put things in cupboards, and eating the heel of a new loaf.

'I was thinking,' he said, 'of going down to Pitcairn on Friday. I could start sorting things out for Christmas.'

'You could clean the bathrooms,' Eleanor suggested. 'Marion's always saying how awful they are since Mum died. And light a fire in the dining room for a while every day. That would help.'

'I was thinking about getting a tree – a really massive one, like when we were kids. And that box of decorations – is it still in the loft?'

'Goodness, they'll all be dusty, and probably broken.'

'I'll get new ones.'

'I thought—'

'Make the house really festive.' He caught Eleanor's eye. 'I'll light fires, promise.'

'Well, I'll come down the day before Christmas Eve,' Eleanor offered.

'You can do the bathrooms then.'

Eleanor swiped at him with a tea towel. 'Ha! Just wait – I'll make you work, when I get there. Seriously, David, we must make sure everything's warm and comfortable for Marion.'

'Yeah, sure. I know.' He rubbed his hands. 'Right. What's for tea?'

'Oh . . . chicken pieces.'

'Let me at them. Stir fry? You got a red pepper, onions?'

Eleanor left him to it, and went to light her own fire. Soon, she could smell frying, and a hot spicy smell floated out of the kitchen.

'What's David cooking?' Claire came into the living room, where Eleanor had discovered three empty beer cans behind the sofa, and a full ash tray.

'God, I hate him smoking in here – he knows that. I knew I could smell it.' She looked round. 'He's being creative with chicken and red peppers, I think.'

Claire watched her mother tip the ash tray into the fire. 'He doesn't smoke in here, really, Mum. He just brings the ash tray in after he's been smoking at the front door. I told him he shouldn't drop fag ends in the garden.'

'Did you? Good for you.'

'How long's he staying?'

'He's going down to Pitcairn on Friday to help Grandpa. We were thinking – it depends how Auntie Marion is – but we were thinking of going to Pitcairn for Christmas.'

'I don't want to. I want to go to Eilidh's, like we did last year.'

'No, I mean – we'll *all* go. Whole family.'

'Will Auntie Marion be out of hospital?'

'Oh yes, in a day or two. So we could go down a bit earlier, just you and me. Make sure the house is warm and everything. So Marion is comfortable.'

'Yeah. If you like. I can't miss the school social, though.'

'No, no. You won't miss anything.'

'Mum?'

'What?'

'There's something weird going on at the end house.'

'How do you mean, weird?'

'Well, you know Edie says there's shouting and that?'

'Oh, Edie exaggerates. She's nervous, and she hasn't much else to take up her attention.'

'Yeah, but she's right. There's a mad guy lives there. Well, I think he looks mad. He's got red curly hair, ginger. I could never fancy somebody with ginger hair, could you?'

'What? I don't know.'

'You couldn't!'

'All right, I couldn't.'

'Anyway, he comes rushing out today—'

'What? When?'

'I'm coming up the lane, right, and it's not totally dark, but it's kind of nearly, you know, so I can see it's him, and he's yelling at somebody. Looking back at the house and yelling – at his wife, right, but I never saw her. Then he sees me coming up the lane and he stops, and you'd think he'd be embarrassed, wouldn't you, but he just says, "Hi, how ya doing?" and—'

'So did you speak to him?'

'Well, I just go "fine" or something. That's all, I never stopped. Then this woman comes out behind him – she's mad as well, I think. She's got her coat on, a long black coat and a hat, so I can't see her face, right, and it's nearly dark like I said. So she yells at him, and—'

Eleanor shook her head, smiling. 'They sound a dramatic pair. What were they yelling about?'

'Oh I don't know – *you wouldn't*, and *Oh yes, I would*, and stuff like that.'

'Some couples do fight a lot, it doesn't mean much.'

Claire shrugged this off. 'You and Dad didn't. Eilidh's mum and dad don't.'

'No, but—'

'Anyway, she never saw me, I don't think. I'm going past Jim and Edie's by this time, I mean, I wasn't going to stop, was I? And suddenly she goes "By the time you get back, I'll have gone, cleared out".'

'Goodness, is there a car there now? I didn't notice.'

'No, that's what I was doing upstairs. Well, for a while. Then I did my biology homework.'

'What – you were watching them?'

'There wasn't really anything to see after that. And it was dark. But he drove away, he never even had a jacket on. Then she comes out right after, and she puts a lot of suitcases and stuff in the other car, the red one.'

Eleanor went to the front door and looked along the lane. The only light came from Jim and Edie's living room window. Then Edie must have drawn the curtains, for that went dim.

'No cars,' Eleanor said, stepping backwards onto Claire, who had followed her.

'See? She's left him. Exciting, eh?'

'Well.'

'I wonder if she'll come back?'

'Oh probably. Just a quarrel.'

'Did you quarrel with Dad? Not like that, did you, I don't remember that. Shouting and stuff.'

'No. We argued of course. Everyone does.'

Eleanor went back to stoke up the fire, now it had caught. Claire followed, as if wanting to go on talking about this. But instead, she pulled her magazine from between the sofa cushions, and took it upstairs to read. Eleanor sat down. She was remembering Ian's cold silence, her own frustrated sobs. No quarrelling, though. You couldn't quarrel with someone who remained silent and disapproving, who made it clear you were wrong and he was right.

'Well, he was,' she said aloud. He was always right. Stop it, she told herself. Stop thinking about it. It would be Hogmanay soon, and she always thought about it at this time of year. But what was the sense in brooding about it now. There were more important things to think about – Marion, and what David was going to do, and Pitcairn. And Christmas.

From the kitchen, David called: 'Grub's up!' So she rose and went to call Claire.

9

'At Pitcairn,' Marion said, 'if we were ill, we had a fire lit in our room. It was so cosy, watching the embers at night.'

'Sorry,' Fergus said, 'you'll have to make do with gas central heating in this house.' Marion watched him attempt to hang up her skirt. Twice it slipped off, and he swore under his breath.

'I wish you'd just let me get up,' she said. Fergus shoved the hanger deep into the wardrobe, in the hope that he'd got it right this time. Then he turned to Marion where she lay propped up in bed.

'People always underestimate how tired they'll be, coming home from hospital. You can get up tomorrow.'

'What a bully,' Marion grumbled, but leaned back on the pillows with a sigh of relief. 'It's wonderful to be home.'

'Good.' He bent and kissed her, and she caught his arm.

'Thank you,' she said.

'Good heavens, what for?'

'Coming to see me every day, keeping the house in order, doing everything.'

'Eleanor was here a lot, and Eilidh's been a grand help.'

'I know.'

'Now then. Will I send Eilidh up with a cup of tea?'

'In a wee while. Stay a minute, Fergie.'

He sat on the edge of the bed, and took her hand.

'I'm sorry,' she said.

'Sorry?'

'You've not got the same wife back. I'm different now.'

'You're the same to me,' he said, and got up, squeezing her hand before he let go.

'Fergie—'

'No, you have a rest. Plenty of time to talk.'

But he did not want to talk. She knew that. She let him go this time, and waited for Eilidh.

'Does it feel funny?' Eilidh asked. Released from hospital visiting, she seemed able to ask questions. In the ward she and Ross had sat immobile, uncomfortable, then found something to squabble about, so that Fergus had to check them, and they fell silent and sullen. Kirsty climbed on the bed, and read all the get-well cards. Soon, Fergus had sent the children away, giving them money to spend in the café by the hospital entrance. Then he had sat with Marion on his own, talking of work, going over the local news, complaining about David.

'Does what feel funny?' Marion asked, sipping her tea.

'Having only one – you know.'

'Well, yes.'

'It doesn't show,' Eilidh reassured.

'I'll get better bras later. This is just a temporary one.'

'Is it sore?'

'A bit. The scar's tightening as the flesh heals underneath. That's all.'

'Oh.'

Marion hesitated. 'Do you want to see it?'

Eilidh drew back. 'No, it's all right.'

'It's not horrible to look at – a bit red and sore yet. Don't worry. I'll show you when it's healed up, and there's just a neat white scar.'

'Yeah . . . if you want.'

Marion set down her tea. 'They've been very careful, very thoughtful. It doesn't look nearly as bad as . . . well.'

'That's good.' But Eilidh was standing by the end of the bed now, looking nervous. 'Mum?'

'What?'

'Have you got to go back to hospital?'

'Yes, you know that.'

'But they've got rid of all the cancer, haven't they?'

'I hope so. But I'll only be there for a few hours at a time. Maybe overnight.'

'So, is there more cancer?'

'Well, a little. They just want to be sure it's all treated.'

'Oh.'

Marion reached out a hand. 'It's all right,' she said. 'I'm going to be fine.'

After her Highland dancing lesson, Kirsty came in and curled up at the bottom of her mother's bed.

'You could have one of the cats, since you're ill.'

'Oh, that's the rule, is it?'

'Well, Snooker was allowed on my bed when I had chicken pox.'

'I'm not ill. I'll be up tomorrow. It was just a wee operation.'

Ross appeared in the doorway, but Kirsty, not seeing him, exclaimed, 'Oh, I know. Dad told us about it – he said one of your boobs went sort of bad and they had to cut it off.'

'He never said that, you total moron!' Ross flushed dark red. 'You OK, Mum?'

'I'm fine. This is your Dad's idea, me being in bed. I'll be up and about tomorrow.'

'Good.' He went out again.

'He's embarrassed,' Eilidh said. She was sitting at her mother's dressing table, taking the lids off jars, poking her little finger in cream, spraying tiny spurts of perfume on her wrists and neck. This was forbidden, usually, but in the scale of things, Marion felt, hardly worth bothering about now.

Kirsty moved up the bed towards her mother. 'Mummy,' she said, 'will it grow back?'

Beneath the water the fishes nibble and nibble, and the princess begins to be eaten away. Marion closed her eyes, counted one, two, three, then opened them again and smoothed the child's hair away from her face.

'No, of course not, Kirsty,' she said. Kirsty's eyes opened wide with horror.

'Here,' said Eilidh, 'you can have a wee bit of perfume as well.'

Willing to be distracted, Kirsty got off the bed and went to see what Eilidh was doing. Marion lay back, exhausted.

Next morning, when Eleanor came round, Marion was writing Christmas cards at the kitchen table.

'Put the kettle on,' she said. 'I could do with a coffee.'

'I'm sure it wouldn't matter if you didn't send any cards this year.'

'No, probably not. But next year I might feel even less like doing it. You never know. And you can't leave it two years.'

'I did.'

'That was different.' She got to her feet, the cards left in three neat piles at the end of the table, the unused ones back in the box.

'Why are there three separate lots?'

Marion started making coffee. 'Waiting for letters or parcels,' she said, 'local ones, and ready for the post.'

'You're so organised.'

'I don't feel it, this year.'

'Never mind, you won't have to do anything else.'

'Won't I?'

They sat down together with mugs of coffee.

'Fergus thinks it's a good idea,' Eleanor said. 'We wouldn't have gone ahead if he wasn't keen.'

I want to stay at home, Marion thought. Every Christmas that David had to do with ended in disaster. Something bad happened. Right now, Marion could not face anything greater than the anxiety she already carried, like a load that gets heavier, the further you go. But she could not say so; Eleanor was full of her plans.

'The house will be really warm – don't worry about that. I promised Fergus. David and I are going to make sure—'

'Yes, I know.'

Eleanor put her mug down. 'You do want to come to Pitcairn, don't you? I thought it would be like when we were children. The kids will love it, and I really mean it about doing all the cooking and everything.'

'I believe you.'

'Dad's ordered a turkey – free-range, from the organic farm that bought the land that used to belong to the Mains.'

'Good.' No going back, then. And maybe she would be fine by then, maybe she would feel different.

'You look tired,' Eleanor said. 'Can I do something – hang washing out, Hoover, whatever?'

'No, no, it's all done.'

'Oh, Marion.'

'Fergus's mother beat you to it. Nan was in at nine this morning.'

'Is she still here?'

'No, off to her coffee morning at the church.'

'Maybe we should ask her to come to Pitcairn too?'

Marion laughed. 'No, that would be overdoing it. She's going to Dundee, to Stuart and Cathy's.'

'Oh. Right.'

Marion got up. 'You want some more coffee? We'll take it through – Nan lit the fire this morning for me, so if it hasn't gone out, we'll be nice and cosy.'

It felt strange to Marion, sitting around drinking coffee on a weekday morning.

'Everyone's been very kind,' she said. 'There's really nothing for me to do.' Would it go on like this, she wondered, all through the chemotherapy treatment? The thought of the treatment terrified her, but she did not say so to Eleanor, who was telling her some story about the man in the next cottage, who had been abandoned by his wife.

'Watch yourself, then. They're the most dangerous kind,' she warned, smiling, thinking it was time Eleanor found a man. But not a married one, no one complicated. It was a pity nothing seemed to be coming of the date with Andrew, who was nice, and unattached.

'Oh you needn't worry,' Eleanor said. 'He's skinny with bright red curly hair, and Clare tells me it's impossible to fancy anybody with ginger hair.'

They passed an hour together, and planned the Christmas dinner. Later, when Eleanor had gone, Marion meant to get up and make soup, but she dozed off in her chair, and was wakened by Eilidh coming in from school at one o'clock. Kirsty had lunch at the primary, as it was too far for her to walk. Ross was already in the kitchen, making himself a pile of sandwiches.

'Oh dear, what on earth's the time?'

'It's OK, Mum. We can manage.'

They could. She watched them, trying not to mind the crumbs on the floor, the sink full of dishes, the spilt orange squash.

'Do you want a sandwich, Mum?'

'No, Eilidh, no I'm fine. I dozed off, I'm not hungry yet.'

It was Fergus's day for the Strath, where he took a surgery in the village once a week, so he would not be back until late in the afternoon. Marion sat at the table and listened to her children argue mildly with each other, and eat.

'See you, Mum.'

They were off, the door banging, bags shouldered, talking as they went down the drive together. Marion went through to the living-room window, and watched them go. At the gate, two girls from a house nearby waited for Eilidh, and a boy from Ross's year joined him as they headed up the road. As long as she got better, Marion told herself, this would not harm them, it would not even affect them much. She smoothed a hand over the place where her breast had been, touching the odd flatness of the padding material, that had no give in it, and yet no resistance, as living flesh has. *Pull yourself together, woman.*

In a week, the anaesthetic out of her system, healthy flesh healing, she was doing everything just as usual. 'She's marvellous,' her friends said to Eleanor, to Fergus, and 'yes,' they answered 'she's coping so well,' Marion did really feel fit; she had put off thinking about the treatment, would face that in the New Year.

'I could manage Christmas fine,' she said to Fergus, 'but Eleanor has set her heart on all of us going to Pitcairn. What do you think?'

'I'm easy either way. But there's no sense in your overdoing things. It'll make a change, eh? And Mother's all set for Dundee now.'

'Right. Let's just do it then.'

She threw herself into preparations for Christmas. David, now at Pitcairn, phoned regularly. He had discovered the 'conference call', and he and Marion and Eleanor were all on the line together, whenever he wanted to discuss anything with them.

'Now then,' he said, a week before Christmas, 'the tree's up, but I thought the kids might want to decorate it. So I've bought masses of those bauble things, and stuff.'

'Do you want my decorations?' Eleanor asked.

'Not unless they're silver or white. I'm having a white and silver theme.'

Eleanor laughed; Marion snorted. Neither knew whether to believe this. Was he kidding?

'Wait till you see it.'

'I'm not bothered,' Eilidh said, when Marion asked her about the tree. 'I'll help decorate it if you like.'

'Decorate the tree?' Ross echoed, as Marion ticked off her list of things to do. 'What tree?'

'David's. At Pitcairn.'

'It's a bit far to go to decorate a Christmas tree, isn't it? What about our own one?'

'Ross, for goodness sake, you know we're all going to Pitcairn for Christmas.'

'Are we? No one told me.' He shuffled off to the kitchen, in search of more food. 'Can I have a bit of Christmas cake?' he asked, as his mother came in after him.

'Certainly not. We're taking it with us.' Marion looked round the kitchen, and spotted the Wellington boots in the porch. 'No wonder it's freezing in here – someone's left the porch door open. Now, Ross, get a carrier bag from the cupboard and put everybody's wellies in.'

'Why?'

'We'd better take them with us.'

'What for?'

'Walks. It can be very muddy round the lanes.'

'I don't go for walks.'

Kirsty came in on her mother's heels. 'We've still got to have our own tree. Mum! I said, we've still got to have our own tree, haven't we?'

The whole thing, Marion and Eleanor realised, as they counted down the days, was turning into an expedition.

'It will be like the Christmases we used to have at Pitcairn when we were children,' Marion told her family. 'But better.'

'What was good about them?' Eilidh asked.

'Am I still getting to decorate Uncle David's tree?' Kirsty wanted to know.

At home, Eleanor watered her plants and turned down the Rayburn. Then she went next door to give Jim and Edie a bottle of port and tell them where she would be for the next few days.

'Oh lovely, a family Christmas.' Edie hugged the port. 'You shouldn't have bothered, no need. Very kind, isn't she kind, Jim? But we'll keep an eye, Jim will keep an eye, quiet here, but you never know, and next door—' here Edie jerked her head in the general direction of the other cottage – 'seems to be on his own. One car, just the one car now. Not that he's at home a great deal. Works on the rigs, Betty at the Post Office tells me, works away.' She dived for their Christmas tree, with its winking lights. The curtains were kept half-open, so that you could see it from outside. 'Now then, a wee thing for Claire, she likes a parcel, eh? They all like a parcel to open.'

'Oh, you didn't need to—'

'Now dear, you drive safely, have a lovely time. We'll keep an eye, Jim will check for you.'

Eleanor backed out, thanking them, and Jim nodded, to show all was well, before they disappeared indoors. The other cottage was dark, and there was no car outside.

On the morning before Christmas Eve, Eleanor and Claire set off, Marion, with all her family, would follow next day. When she knew that Eleanor had gone, Marion had a sudden lapse in all her new enthusiasm and energy. She thought she would make brandy butter, but found herself with the ingredients marshalled before her, unable to decide how much to make. In the end, she put everything away again. There might be time tomorrow, and if not, well, she did not care any more.

'All set?' Fergus asked when he came in after his last surgery.

'I think so.'

'Who's feeding the troops?'

Marion had arranged for a neighbour to feed the cats, and take care of the dog while they were away. 'Sue's doing it. I must remember to leave a bottle of wine for her.'

'I must say, I'm beginning to think this has turned out to be even more work for you than staying here would have been.'

Marion smiled. 'You noticed.'

'Oh dearie me. I hope it's all worth it.' He put his arms round her, and she leaned on his chest. 'You would have thought this week you and Eleanor were setting off for the North Pole. I've never seen so much food.'

'We'll need it, we're feeding . . . oh God, nearly a dozen folk. And Dad never has a thing in the house.'

'I thought David was seeing to all that?'

'All what? You can't rely on David.'

This was what Fergus was afraid of. 'Don't worry,' Eleanor had reassured him, 'it's all right. I'm going to make sure the house is warm, and everything's organised.' But Marion was the one who was organised. Eleanor, certainly, was a better bet than David, but she was airy-fairy, Fergus thought, lived inside her imagination. It came, he had decided, of being widowed so young. She needed steadying; it was as if she had never really settled down. No use saying any of this now. All he could do was get them there in one piece, and bring them home again afterwards.

But he sighed, coming up to bed that night, and wished they were staying at home.

'You're not happy, are you?' Marion asked, as he got into bed.

'Ach, ignore me. I'm a boring old so and so. I like my ain fireside.'

'I wish you'd said. I thought you wanted me to go.'

'I wanted you not to wear yourself out, woman!'

'Och, it's not for long. We'll have Hogmanay at home.'

'Good thing too.' He took her in his arms and they lay in the lamplight together, her face on his breast, her breath warm on his skin, hair tickling his neck. She thought how strange it was that the thing other people (his mother, Eleanor) considered a flaw in her husband – his predictability, his steady sameness, was what she loved most.

'Don't worry,' she said. 'I don't mind how boring you are. That's what I like.'

'Just as well, eh?' He switched off the lamp, and they settled. After a moment or two, Marion turned round with a little sigh, and nestled herself into the curve of his body.

This was how they went to sleep, like spoons in a drawer, he had said to her, years ago, and still said it, never seeing any need to change the simile, since it had served him well. Only – it was different now, changed for ever. That first night she had come home from hospital, she'd turned like this in his arms, and tucked her bottom into the crook of his body, against his pelvis, his chin resting on her head, his right arm coming round to cup her left breast. But the breast had not been there, round and full in his palm. Only the cotton pad of the dressing, and beneath it a flat place, a healing wound. Neither of them, for all their talk beforehand, had truly anticipated this moment. Marion's eyes had filled with tears, and she had turned to face him again, to find, in pity and distress, that he too was crying.

She had never seen her husband cry before. In the dark, they comforted each other, and though she wanted to say something, to ask for reassurance that he did not mind, the finer part of her knew there was no question of his minding for himself, only for her. And he knew the same of Marion. There was no help for it. After so many years of marriage, you cannot change sides, make yourself sleep facing the other way, in the other half of the bed.

Later, Marion thought that was the moment the change became real to her, permanent. Not all the discomfort to come, the nausea, the thinning of her beautiful hair, the weariness, the terrible uncertainty, gave her a pain as sharp and final as that one moment in bed with Fergus, the night she came home.

10

The dolls' house had come the Christmas Marion was nine.
No one even pretended that Santa Claus had brought it down
the chimney; the whole family knew it had been given to the
girls jointly by their parents, and that it had been made by a
friend of Aunt Alice's, who was good with his hands. No one
had attempted to wrap it either. It stood by the Christmas tree
in the hall, with a piece of gold tinsel tied in a bow round
one of its chimneys.

At first, waking in the dark, and fumbling among the
parcels at the bottom of their beds, hearing paper crackle,
feeling the lumpy woollen sock full of tiny things, and at
the end the round solidity of a tangerine – they thought
there was no dolls' house at all.

'Where is it?' Eleanor whispered.

On Christmas Eve, David was allowed to sleep in their
room, on Daddy's army camp bed. Usually, he fell off some
time in the night, and lay like a green chrysalis in the sleeping
bag. He woke now, hearing their voices, saying as he wriggled
out, 'Where's the dolls' house?' They all knew about it. There
had been too many hints and whispers for them to doubt.
Until now.

Then Eleanor said, 'You know you said a girl in your
class told you about having all their presents under the
tree?'

'Yes, they don't get to open them until *after breakfast*.' None of them could imagine such cruelty.

'Come on then,' David urged them. 'Look under the tree.'

So they crept downstairs in single file, Marion first, and hung over the banister, and looked. There was no light in the hall. Then David, not caring (it was Christmas, you didn't get into trouble at Christmas, and he wasn't five yet, couldn't be blamed) ran down ahead and jumped up to reach the switch, flooding the hall with light. They blinked and staggered, and then, getting used to the brightness, they saw it.

It was perfect. Most presents, Eleanor discovered as she grew older, were a disappointment. They could not live up to the promise of anticipation, hope, the mysterious shape under the wrapping, the electric rustle of tearing paper. But the dolls' house was perfect – better than Marion or Eleanor had imagined it could be. Marion unhooked the front and it swung gently open. Furniture, curtains, tiny rugs, a whole life waiting to be lived in miniature. There was even a family to live it: father, mother and daughter. These little figures were made of wire, covered with cotton padding, and they had painted faces which faded in time, and had to be re-done with biro. It was hard to keep their expressions the same: mother quietly resigned; father brisk, with a moustache; child rosy and cheerful. But Eleanor, whose job this became, did her best. The family was a little stiff, and would not sit properly in the chairs, so they went to bed a lot, or stood around. David took the father for his person, Marion the mother, and Eleanor the daughter.

As he got older, David rarely played with them when the dolls' house was used. He had better things to do, and he was, anyway, too rough. Something always got broken, and the girls did not really want their father doll to lead a life so full of risk and terror as David made him have. But still, when they were feeling dull, and short of ideas, David did brighten things up.

When Marion was ill, that long winter she was twelve, she played with the dolls' house while she was convalescing. After that, she seemed to outgrow the house, and it fell more to Eleanor. For Eleanor it was always there, waiting, and it was always worth opening up the front to see what the family was doing. Sometimes she made them a newspaper, or a cardboard swing for their imaginary garden, or took them out in one of David's cars, when he wasn't around to argue. When she was well, Marion wanted company, and Eleanor, who did not care for Violet or the other friends very much, often played on her own.

Eleanor could not remember much else about that perfect Christmas, or separate it out completely from all the others at Pitcairn. They merged in memory. Perhaps that was why Marion was unable to explain to Eilidh and Kirsty what was special about Christmas at Pitcairn.

As Eleanor came slowly up the drive she saw that David had been watching for them. He opened the front door as they got out of the car, and stood there in the glow from the light behind, a whiter glow than usual. He stopped them on the steps.

'Wait. Shut your eyes, both of you.'

'Why?' Claire asked, but they did it, allowing David to lead them in.

'Now!'

All they could say was 'Oh!' and gasp, and gaze. The tree must have been nine feet high. It shimmered, silver and white with a thousand lights, a cascade of silky threads, pouring from the top where a silver fairy glimmered, a long way off.

'Wow,' said Claire. 'Cool.'

'Oh David, it's lovely, it really is – shut the door, Claire, keep the heat in – oh David, how on earth did you get it here?'

Her brother touched the side of his nose. 'Trust me,' he said. 'Man with a trailer, slipped him a fiver.'

'Cool,' Claire said again, looking more closely, slowly circling as much of the tree as she could. It stood in the stairwell, behind it the dark varnished panelling. 'Oh hey, Mum – see the wee animals and that.'

Eleanor went to look. Amongst the branches where the silver trails of ribbon wound in and out, hung tiny crystal animals, winking in the lights, and glass baubles, and twists of green and silvery mesh in the shape of candles, parcels and bells.

'David,' she gasped, 'this tree must have cost a fortune! Where did you get all this?'

'London. Flew down last week for the day.'

'What? You're joking.'

'No, I'm not.' He stood there looking pleased.

'But I thought . . .' She had thought he had no money. She remembered Marion saying 'he's a sponger,' and she began to worry.

'Sold my car.'

'What car?'

'Phil – sold my car in Edinburgh for me. Got a nice fat cheque. So I thought we'd do something special with it – for the whole family.'

'I didn't know you had a car.'

'An MG. I usually have an MG when I'm in funds.'

'Years ago – that little red car . . .' A twoseater. Just Eleanor and David, off for a spin. Ian standing by the front door with a tiny Claire in his arms, watching them go. And before that, Ian studying for his professional exams, Eleanor and David off for the Sunday afternoon, leaving him to get on with it, having sandwiches and beer in a pub way out of town. David driving very fast through country lanes.

'An MG,' Eleanor said again, shaking herself free of the past.

'No more, alas. And don't worry – I got a cheap fare to London, and I do actually have some cash left over. The tree stuff didn't cost that much. Anyway, I needed to see a guy in London. A bit of leftover business.'

'Where's Grandpa?' Claire asked. She had finished inspecting the tree.

'In the garden somewhere. Getting veg for tomorrow.'

'I'll go and tell him we're here. OK, Mum?'

'Yes, you do that. David, give me a hand, we've masses of stuff to get in from the car.'

Much later, when they were all home again, Claire said to her mother, 'That was when Christmas began, wasn't it? When we saw the tree.' But Kirsty, arriving on Christmas Eve, burst into tears when she saw it.

'You promised I could decorate it!'

Stricken with remorse, David took her into the garden to cut a large branch from a tree there.

'This is yours,' he said. 'We'll find the old decorations, and you can have this one in your room.' Kirsty looked at him with contempt.

'I want lights,' she said. 'I want a proper tree. This one is a branch.'

David came into the kitchen, where Marion was setting out everything she needed for the turkey.

'What can I do?' he asked. 'I'm finished with Kirsty. She hates and reviles me.'

'Don't be silly,' Marion scoffed. 'Pass me those onions.'

'You could buy her one of those wee artificial trees,' his father suggested. 'They've got them in Asda.'

'Brilliant. Right, Kirsty, where are you?'

Fergus and Ross had gone out to split logs. As Marion began work on the turkey, and Eleanor checked dishes and cutlery, Fergus came in with a full basket.

'Where do you want these?'

'Dining room,' Eleanor said, taking the basket from him.

Fergus took off his boots by the back door. 'I thought you were supposed to be sitting about, letting everyone else do all the work?' he said to Marion.

'Ach, I'm fine. It turns Eleanor's stomach to do the turkey.'

'This is the same Eleanor who was going to do everything?'

'I don't mind. I'm no good at sitting about.'

'Well, be sure and have a rest after you've finished with that bird.'

'Don't fuss me, I'm fine.'

So he left her, pushing stuffing into a bald unwieldy fowl that looked to him obscene. He could see Eleanor's point. Would they actually *eat* it?

Eleanor had borrowed a portable gas heater from the Mackies' daughter, and it stood in the hall, blazing.

'I've never known the front of the house so warm before,' John said, standing over it, his hands held out to the heat. 'This is a great thing. Expensive to run, I doubt. What is it, calor gas? I hope you've a spare canister.'

'David's getting it from Asda – he's taken Kirsty there.'

Ross was bored, and for once Eilidh and Claire did not seem to want to spend every minute in each other's company. But Marion and Eleanor ignored this as best they could, giving the children jobs to do (which they did not want, preferring to be bored), and allowing them to watch endless television.

David, coming back with Kirsty and a small Christmas tree, was stopped in the hall by Eleanor.

'Has anyone been to see Ruby? When was she in?'

'Oh, I forgot to tell you. She's had flu. Dad hasn't had her here for over a week.'

'For goodness sake. Someone might have told us. I'll go

and see her,' she said to Marion. 'As long as one of us does. She might want to come tomorrow, do you think?'

'She's sure to be invited somewhere else,' Marion said, 'if she's well enough. But Dad always gives her a bottle of sherry and chocolates. Ask him if he's been along yet.'

Eleanor found her father in the garden in front of the house, far down the drive, being made to cut holly by Claire.

'Look, all this stuff with berries,' Claire called to her mother. 'I saw it on the way in yesterday. Grandpa didn't even notice.'

'You'll be wanting ivy to go with it next,' he grumbled, throwing another branch into the wheelbarrow. Claire looked at him blankly.

'Oh,' she said at last. 'The holly and the ivy.'

'They sound like two elderly spinsters, I always think,' Eleanor said, pulling on her gloves. It was cold out here. 'Anyway, I'm going down to see Ruby. Have you given her her Christmas yet?'

John folded the small set of steps he had been using, and tucked them under his arm. Claire picked up the wheelbarrow handles, ready to go.

'Now, that's well minded. There's a bottle of sherry for her, in the pantry. And maybe you'd buy some sweeties – the shop'll be open the day, surely.'

'Right. Anyone coming with me?'

Claire was setting off with the wheelbarrow. 'I'm helping Grandpa put up the holly. You could ask Ross,' she added. 'He's only watching TV.'

In the kitchen, there seemed to be a lot going on. Eilidh was helping her mother wrap tiny sausages in strips of bacon. The turkey was ready: it too was spread with bacon slices and flattened lumps of butter and stood in a roasting tin on a shelf in the pantry. Eleanor tried not to look at it as she picked up the bottle of sherry.

'Should I wrap this up? Have you any paper?'

'Somewhere.' Marion had a smear of suet on her cheek, and she was flushed.

Fergus put his head round the door. 'Any chance of a cup of tea?'

'What are you doing?' she asked him.

'Watching TV with Ross. Anything you need?' He came in and filled the kettle. 'You sit down in a minute, you hear me? I'll make the tea.' He tapped Eilidh on the shoulder. 'Don't let your mother get too tired. It's not even Christmas Day yet.'

'I know.' Eleanor halted with the bottle of Bristol Cream. 'This is awful – the whole idea was that we'd do everything. Marion's supposed to rest.'

'Aye well, fat chance of that,' Fergus sighed, giving Marion a hug with one arm, then turning to get mugs from the cupboard behind him.

'I was going down to see Ruby,' Eleanor explained. 'David says she's had flu.'

'Well, let me get Marion in a chair with her feet up and a cup of tea,' Fergus offered, 'and then I'll come with you.'

'Oh good. Ruby will love that. You're her favourite – she can tell you about her bad leg.'

'God, on second thoughts . . .' But he grinned, not meaning it.

It was dark by the time Fergus drove them down the lane to the main road, and the Post Office and shop, where Eleanor stood dithering between Quality Street and Black Magic, and wished she could have bought something more interesting for Ruby this year.

Ruby had been dozing by her fire, and looked flushed and flustered when she came to the door. But she was delighted to see them.

'Come awa in – oh, and the doctor. My, you're lookin well. How's the family?' She stopped by the entrance to her tiny living room, and coughed harshly, banging her chest with a fist, as if this might help. 'Ach, fit a dose of the flu I've had. Terrible. My legs wis awa tae jelly, ye've nae idea. Come in, come in. Sit yersels doon.'

A yellow-eyed cat slunk off the sofa and disappeared. Ruby lived alone now, her son grown up and gone, her husband dead for many years. The room was crowded with furniture, and every surface covered with crocheted mats, china dogs and horses, framed photographs. The fire blazed, so the room was stifling. Eleanor took off her jacket at once, and tried to sit away from the fire.

'Now then, you'll be for a fly cup? I've a lovely bit of Christmas cake. Susan Mackie, well, her that was Susan Mackie, I forget her married name, she was in yesterday, and brought me a bit of cake. Marks and Spencer, very nice.'

There was no getting out of the tea and cake. Fergus looked at Eleanor and winked.

It was soon ready: china cups and saucers decorated with forget-me-nots on a tray covered with an embroidered cloth; the bought Christmas cake and shortbread.

'I never bake now,' Ruby told them as she poured tea. 'Nae worth bothering, just for mysel. But now and again, I maks a scone. Your dad likes that.'

Eleanor saw how her hand trembled as she handed out the cups and saucers, realised the wiry grey hair was thin at the front, and that illness had made Ruby look smaller and almost frail. She is old, Eleanor thought. She can't keep taking care of Pitcairn, and Dad.

They asked after everyone they could think of: the Mackies, retired now to Ellon, and Eileen living in Glasgow with her family; Ruby's son and his wife, in New Zealand with their children; the people who used to have the Post Office, but who had also retired. Eleanor felt sleepy and comfortable, and the cat crept back to make a nest of her lap.

'Ach, pit him doon,' Ruby said. 'He's an affa cratur. I

used to keep him ootside, but he's getting auld, like me. He likes the fireside.' She handed round the cake again, but this time they said no, it was lovely, but they would have to stir themselves.

'Now then,' Ruby went on, not wanting to let them go just yet, 'how's that brother of yours? He's back again, I see.'

'He's fine. He's actually going to be working in Edinburgh.'

'Ye ken, I aye thocht he was on anither planet, that loon. You and Marion were that weel-mannered, nice behaved quines, but Davy – he had the licht o mischief in his een – like a wee devil wis lookin through him.' She shook her head, remembering. 'You'll min on that Stanley Robertson he was sae pally wi?'

'Oh yes, Stanley. What happened to him?'

'I can tell ye that. He was a set to follow his Dad – apprentice joiner.'

'Oh yes.' Eleanor was remembering now.

'But Jimmy was a terrible man for the drink. He lost a good bit a business that wey. An affa pity – a'body said fit a good workman. But. Well, well, Stanley couldna manage the business himsel, when his da was yon wey. And his mother dead when Stanley was – fit? Nine? A man canna be father and mother baith. Well, Jimmy Robertson couldna.' She shook her head.

'But – what happened to Stanley? Did he not get married, really young?'

'Oh, Irene Walker. A richt wee—' Ruby checked herself. 'Stanley, he went for a soldier, when his da got so he wisna workin ava. Irene liked that fine at first – the uniform, ken, and a steady wage. But he was posted to Germany, and she wouldna ging wi him. Too far frae her mother.'

'Great support to him, then?' Eleanor put in, sarcastic. She did remember a blonde girl with a skirling laugh and black eye make-up, shoving a push-chair with a pasty baby slumped in it. Was that Stanley's baby?

'So where's Stanley now?'

'There was some bother in Germany, I dinna ken aboot that. But he came oot of the Army.'

'Maybe he missed Irene and the baby.'

Ruby snorted. 'Oh, by that time she had another man. Bidin in Aberdeen wi him. He was in the fish, as I recall.'

A step down, then, Eleanor thought, knowing how Ruby's social ladder went.

'But poor Stanley,' Ruby went on, 'he was a changed lad – intae the drink like his father. He was fechtin in a bar in Aberdeen, and another lad wis hurt bad.' She paused for the climax of her story, and looked from Eleanor to Fergus and back again. 'He's in the jail.'

'Jail!'

'Craiginches, three years. I read it in the *P&J*, but it was Doreen at the Post Office telt me first.'

As they left, Ruby thanked them for the sherry and chocolates.

'You know,' Fergus said as they drove away, 'I have an awful feeling there's about twenty bottles of Harvey's Bristol Cream in her sideboard.'

Eleanor laughed. 'Oh dear, you could be right. But, Fergus, fancy poor Stanley in prison. I wonder if David knows.'

'It's no good, Eleanor, your father's going to have to find someone else to look after the house.'

'I know.'

'How old's Ruby? His age, anyway.'

'I suppose so.'

'And going by the state of Pitcairn any time we come here – she doesn't do much these days.'

'No. I know.' But she felt curiously irritated by Fergus saying what she believed herself. He did not remember Ruby as she did, could not see her in the kitchen with Faith, or turning out the living room on a fine spring day, the windows wide open, the furniture moved back, the rugs beaten over the washing line. And Stanley. Fergus did not care about Stanley. She could hardly wait to tell David and Marion, who would care.

But all this went out of her head as soon as they got back to the house. Putting the step-ladder away, her father had slipped going into the shed and sprained his ankle. He was in an armchair in the living room, his trouser leg rolled up, the foot turning black and blue and swelling up.

'Oh thank goodness – you've been hours down there,' Marion greeted them. 'Dad's fallen and done something to his ankle. It's just a sprain, I think. Come and look at it, Fergus.'

Fergus thought it was a bad sprain, but he would never make a decision about someone else's patient. So there was nothing else for it but to go into the Royal Infirmary in Aberdeen to get it X-rayed.

'Oh God,' Marion sighed, 'on Christmas Eve. The traffic. We'll have our tea first, Dad, and Fergus will bandage it up for now.'

'Ach, I'm fine. I've nae need to go to the hospital.'

'David could take him,' Fergus said, putting his father-in-law's foot down gently and standing up. 'He's not doing anything else.'

'No, but,' Marion pulled Fergus aside, 'he's been drinking all afternoon, since he came back with Kirsty. He couldn't take a car.'

'What?' Eleanor had heard this.

'Well, it's Christmas. I'm sure he doesn't drink in the afternoon usually.' Marion looked harassed. 'But, no, I wouldn't want him driving Dad anywhere.'

In the end, John refused to go. If his ankle got worse, he said, David would take him into the infirmary on Boxing Day. It would be quiet on the roads, an easy journey. Fergus gave in, and did his best with an elastic bandage.

There had been, intermittently throughout the day, an

ongoing discussion amongst the children about where the presents should be left. Kirsty still wanted to believe in Santa Claus, and her family kept up the fiction because she was the youngest, and allowed to go on believing as long as she liked, because they had been able to. But the compromise they had reached by tea-time was that Santa came only for children, and everyone else got presents from Mum and Dad. 'It's daft,' Eilidh said to Claire, 'because she knows perfectly well, really.' But they decided that all the adults' and family presents were to be put under the tree, while Kirsty's offering from Father Christmas, and everyone else's filled stockings, would appear miraculously at the end of the beds, as usual. Eleanor and David volunteered to stay up late, and sort all this out.

By midnight, the house was silent, and everyone else in bed. Eleanor and David sat on in the living room, feeding the fire a little, and David drank the wine that was left from their evening meal. Eleanor could tell by the way his eyes were slightly unfocused when he looked at her, and by the easy expansive way he talked, that he was very drunk. But he was perfectly lucid. It was the first time Eleanor had had a chance to tell him about the visit to Ruby.

'I nearly forgot. Remember that boy you played with – Stanley?'

David poked a log further into the fire, sending up a shower of sparks. He looked up, flushed. 'Aye, I remember Stanley. Of course I do. My old mate.'

'He's in prison. Ruby told us.'

David stared. 'You're kidding?'

'No, Ruby told us the whole story.'

'My God. Well, I suppose one of us was bound to end up there.'

'I was really shocked.'

'You would be. Doesn't take much to shock Eleanor.'

'Don't be rude. You're out of your head. Poor Stanley.'

'What did he do? Bust a bank?'

'A fight in a pub. Assault and battery or something.'

'Jesus.'

'He never seemed in the least aggressive to me.' Eleanor could see the skinny child with cropped fair hair, the boy who was David's shadow, his follower. Because it was David who led, wasn't it, David who organised. She remembered the last time Stanley had come to Pitcairn, standing awkwardly at the back door, asking to see their mother, more than twenty years ago.

'She's not well,' Marion had said, not letting him in. 'What is it?'

'I thought I better tell Mrs Cairns about Davy.' He shifted uncomfortably. 'Tell your Ma and Da he's a right.'

Now Marion let him in. 'Where is he?'

'He'll likely be in London e'er now.'

'London?' Marion grabbed Stanley's arm, bone beneath the skin. He winced, trapped.

'We was hitch-hiking,' he said. Eleanor saw the dark marks under his eyes, saw how tired he was, tired to death.

'I'll get Mum,' Marion said.

Faith was there in a moment. 'How are you, Stanley?' she said. 'I'll put the kettle on. Sit yourself down.'

'No, I better nae bide.' He moved backwards. 'I'm sorry, Mrs Cairns, he wanted me to go to London as well. But – I couldna leave my Da.'

'So you came home then?' Faith was perfectly calm, the only one of the four people in the kitchen not agitated and upset.

'Aye. I've to go home now, my Da took me up here, he's waitin in the van.'

'Where did you leave David?'

'Somewey about Newcastle. He'd gotten another lift – in a Jaguar. Big car, ken.'

'Good for him.' Marion was bitterly angry.

'Thank you for coming – don't keep your father waiting.'
White, expressionless, Faith saw him out.

Had they talked outside? Eleanor wondered now. Had their
mother questioned him more? All she could remember was
Marion going out of the kitchen, banging the door, a thing
she had never done in her life before.

She pulled herself back to the present. 'Davy,' she began.
He was slumped in his chair, not seeing or hearing her. Then
he stirred.

'We had this den,' he said. 'Stan and me. Nobody else was
allowed in.'

Eleanor sighed. 'There *wasn't* anyone else except Marion
and me.'

'Once, one year, there were those kids – the tinker kids.
For a week or so.'

'I know. The woman came to the door – Mum gave her
money, bought stuff.'

'She told fortunes, didn't she?' David interrupted. 'She said
something to Mum about us – Mum said it was rubbish.'

'That's right. I don't actually remember what she said, but
Marion might. She got the piece of lace – I fancied it, but
Marion took it away. I never saw it again.'

'Poor bloody Stanley – she never told his fortune, anyway.'

'No, but she—'

'Where's he in clink?'

'Craiginches, Aberdeen.'

'Maybe I'll go and see him, take him a file in a cake or
something.'

Eleanor knew he would not go. He seemed suddenly
morose, dejected, and stared into the fire.

'I'm sure Stanley will be all right,' she said. 'At least he's
got a trade to go back to. And he's shot of that awful
Irene. It wasn't a long sentence, and Ruby didn't say when
it happened. He could be out by now.'

David looked up. 'It wasn't my fault,' he said.

'Of *course* not – how could it be? You hadn't even seen him for years.'

'I did see him.' David drew himself up in his chair, and reached for the bottle to pour himself another dram. 'Once, when I was in Aberdeen about – what? Five years ago. He was working as a joiner again. Not for his father of course, for some big firm. They did a lot of council work, he said. He seemed OK. We went for a pint.'

'There you are. It probably wasn't even his fault, the fight in the pub.'

'He was easily led, was old Stan.'

'You were always in trouble, the pair of you.'

'You don't know the half of it, Eleanor.'

'Don't I?'

He shrugged. 'I'm not a *good* person, you know. I never was.'

'What are you on about?'

'Guilt,' he said, swallowing whisky, picking up the bottle again. 'The fires of hell will consume me in the end, dear sister. A fitting end.'

What did he mean? She had stood with her father in the garden here, talking about the night the Mackies' barn went on fire. *No question. He was home before it started. A cigarette end can smoulder a long time.* She looked across at her brother, his heavy-lidded eyes, the twist of self-disgust in his mouth. And did not want to know what might not be true, or even possible.

'You're drunk,' she said. 'Come on, you've had enough of that.' She stood up, taking the bottle from him. 'Let's do the presents. Surely to goodness Kirsty's asleep by now.' She glanced up at the clock on the mantelpiece. 'I've missed the watchnight service. I've been able to go to that the last few years. Edie's kept an eye on Claire for me. Next year, who knows, she'll maybe come with me.'

'You go to church?' He seemed to come to himself again, and looked up at her, surprised.

'Sometimes. Now and again, I think maybe, there's some way of being . . . forgiven. You know?'

He looked away, and kicked at a log on the edge of the grate. It collapsed into the red glow at the heart of the fire, and sparks flew up. 'Not for me,' he said. 'Not for me.'

'Come on Davy.' She reached out a hand to pull him to his feet. 'Time for bed.'

In the morning, it would be Christmas again. All the Christmases of her childhood crowded in on Eleanor, as she stood by her bedroom window, looking out into the garden. The sky had cleared, and moonlight moved shadows across the grass and through the trees. For a few seconds, she fancied she saw the tinker woman, come to tell their fortunes. *As if we'd want to know now*, she thought, and drew the curtains across.

11

'It worked out fine,' Marion admitted to Eleanor on the way home. Claire and Eilidh, friends again, sat on the back seat, fallen silent as the journey went on, dozing by the time they passed through Keith. Fergus was ahead, with Ross and Kirsty.

'It did, didn't it?' Eleanor agreed. 'I think everyone enjoyed it.'

We've escaped, Marion thought, nothing happened. 'It was long enough, though,' she said aloud. 'I'm glad to be going home.'

'I hope Dad's OK. David's promised to take him for an X-ray before he leaves for Edinburgh.'

'Well, he *says* he's going to Edinburgh. No sign of packing or anything, was there?'

'He'll be waiting till we've all gone.'

'I'm relieved, you know,' Marion went on, 'we're not bringing our children up in such a lonely place. You're in the country, right enough, but it's only ten minutes from Dingwall, and we all dot about in cars these days.'

Eleanor stopped on the narrow village street behind a parked car, to let a lorry manoeuvre past going the other way. Marion glanced behind her at the sleeping girls, leaning sideways, soft mouths just open, Claire's head on Eilidh's lap.

'You see,' she went on, 'I feel really strongly about the kind of childhood we give our family. I've never said this before, but I suppose I can now, you won't mind.' She glanced at Eleanor, who was still concentrating on traffic. 'When Ian died, it made everything so precarious. I thought, what on earth would *I* do? I couldn't imagine – I shut my eyes to it, persuaded myself one tragedy in a family was surely all, and I nagged and nagged Fergus for our house. We were in the bungalow out at Muir of Ord then, remember? It was too small anyway, especially once Kirsty came along, so I was right, we did need a bigger house. But it was more than that. I wanted a house, oh not like Pitcairn, you couldn't have that now, it would be ridiculous.'

'But Dunvegan is a big house, Marion,' Eleanor broke in.

'It's a family house,' Marion said, 'and that's what I longed for. I wanted my children to have this wonderful safe childhood, space and freedom, but more *people* than we had. Company. We were very isolated, at Pitcairn.'

I'm isolated now, Eleanor wanted to say, but held her peace. She knew Marion was afraid that the family structure she had built so firmly was at risk. An earthquake shook the house: none of them was safe, after all.

'Are we going to stop?' she asked.

'Let's not bother, if the girls are sleeping. Unless you want a break from driving.'

'No, I just want to get home now. I thought you might like to.'

How careful they were of each other, finding themselves alone and quiet after the crowded Christmas. But they *had* all enjoyed it, Eleanor thought, even though Marion had done far too much. Presently, she said. 'Did you think Alice was a bit odd, yesterday?'

'Odd – how?'

'I think she's getting . . . narrow. I flinched every time Claire opened her mouth. Alice can be so disapproving.'

'I didn't notice. It's Mamie who seems to get exaggerated

with age. She eats too much, complains of indigestion, thinks the Queen's speech is actually worth listening to, and then falls asleep in front of it.'

Eleanor laughed. 'Oh dear, I know. But she's kind, and she thinks all the children are wonderful. Alice is different – she always was. And when we were little, do you remember those weird stories? I used to have bad dreams afterwards.'

'And yet she's not the sort of person you'd think would like fantasy,' Marion wondered. 'As you say, she seems narrow sometimes. But very practical, and independent. She's always had to be – she earned her own living for years.'

'What did she do – some sort of office job?'

'She was a legal secretary, you must know that. Dad always said she should have been a lawyer, she had that sort of brain. But girls didn't have careers then. He was the one who got qualifications.'

'Girls were supposed to get married. I wonder why she never did. She was nice-looking when she was young. A bit severe, maybe, but handsome. Not that black and white snaps tell you much.'

'Well, Mamie turning up and moving in couldn't have helped her chances.'

'Oh, she was getting on for forty then,' Eleanor said. 'She's what, seven, eight years older than Dad?'

'And Mamie's about the same.'

'Except she seems perpetually youthful. In a way,' Eleanor added.

'You mean childish,' Marion said, but smiled.

'I'm not like that, am I?' Eleanor exclaimed. 'Turning up to live with you because I can't manage on my own?'

'Don't be daft. You live in your own place, completely independent. And you have Claire. I think having children matures you, it can't help but do that. Mamie never had children. She doesn't seem able to do a thing without Alice, does she?'

But Alice had shaken Mamie off, after Christmas dinner, Eleanor noticed. Mamie was in front of the television, Kirsty cuddled up beside her. Alice was still in the kitchen, which had been cleared, the dishes put away. On the table, the turkey carcass, the remains of Christmas pudding, the toys from the crackers. Mamie had taken the chocolates to the living room where the children were, John was dozing in his chair, and Marion had been made to sit by the fire. Only David and Eleanor remained in the kitchen with Alice. David was pouring himself a whisky.

'Anybody else?' He held up the bottle.

'Oh no.' Alice shuddered. 'Dear goodness, I couldn't touch a drop. I can't take whisky anyway, it's like medicine.'

'Exactly,' David said with a grin.

Eleanor shook her head. 'No thanks.'

Alice took off her apron and hung it on the back of the pantry door. 'Now then, who's for a spot of fresh air?' She looked at David as he raised his glass.

'Nasty stuff,' he said, 'fresh air. No, think I'll fall asleep in front of some terrible TV programme. That's what you're supposed to do on Christmas Day.'

Eleanor thought Alice was disappointed. In the bright kitchen light she looked older, her skin whitened, her hair almost completely grey now. For years (and when did it go?) there had still been dark brown streaks in it.

'I'll come, if you like,' she offered.

Alice's grey eyes rested on Eleanor, but did not seem to see her. 'If you like, dear,' she said. 'I don't want to take you away from the television if . . .'

'No, it's all right. I wouldn't mind some fresh air myself.'

As she and Alice left for their walk, David was pouring himself another drink.

'He drinks too much,' she said to Alice, as they set off down the drive. 'It's time he had a job.'

'He tells me he's got one now,' Alice sounded satisfied

with this. 'Off to Edinburgh soon – and a flat all lined up, it seems.'

'What sort of job?' Eleanor did not believe it. He had said nothing to Marion or her.

'Insurance.' David had told his aunts this because it sounded safe and respectable. There was no guarantee it was anything near the truth.

'He's like himself again,' Alice went on, 'now he's taken off that terrible beard.'

'Well, he looks younger,' Eleanor conceded.

The light was fading already as they reached the gates and turned into the lane.

'Which way will we go?' Eleanor asked, seeing that Alice hesitated. 'I suppose we could take the road to the Mains, and come round the back way to the Post Office. But I don't think there's time for all that. It'll be dark soon.'

But Alice wanted only to walk along the lane a little way, and back again. She seemed suddenly tired, and her pace, which had been brisk, slowed. At the bend in the lane, where it branched off up to the Mains, she paused and put her hand on a fence post.

'Are you all right, Aunt Alice?'

For a moment Alice did not answer. She caught her breath in a gasp. Alarmed, Eleanor reached out to steady her, taking her arm.

'Aye, lass.' She patted Eleanor's hand, and took a step or two. 'We'd maybe best turn now, eh?'

'Are you sure you're all right to walk?' What if she's not, Eleanor thought in fright. What will I do?

But Alice was walking steadily and her breathing had quietened again. 'I'm fine, dinna you fret. I have a wee turn now and again.' She looked sharply at Eleanor. 'I don't want a word to Mamie, mind. She's an awful worrier, I'd never hear the end of it.'

'Maybe you should see the doctor though?'

'I have.'

'Oh.'

'Nothing to worry about.' Alice was dismissive. After a moment, she said, 'And what about Ruby – have you seen her?'

'Yesterday. I was going to ask her to come for her dinner, but she was invited to the people who have the Post Office now. She seems very friendly with them.'

'Oh Ruby wouldn't expect her Christmas dinner,' Alice said. 'Time she retired a thegither.'

They had reached the gates, and were going slowly up the drive again. In the dusk, Pitcairn glowed from within: every window seemed to be lit. That's how it should be, Eleanor thought, full of people, full of life.

'What'n a lights are on – young folk never think of electricity bills.' Alice shook her head. 'Mind, your father should gie this place up. He should have done it when your mother went. Plenty of room with Mamie and me – not that I'm suggesting that. But he could get a nice wee flat in the town, near at hand so we could keep an eye.'

'Oh, Alice!' Eleanor could not help herself. 'You know fine he'd hate it – he loves this place.' And anyway, she thought, who was to keep an eye on whom?

'Ach well.' Alice stopped, and they both gazed at the house. 'It was a fine retreat, for the pair of them.' There was something in her voice that might have been anger. Eleanor waited, wondering. Then Alice went on into the house, so she followed.

On the journey home, Eleanor wanted to tell Marion about this, but by the time she had gone over it in her mind, Marion too was dozing. So she turned her thoughts to home, and Hogmanay.

'What are you going to do?' she had asked David.

'Go to a party,' he said. 'Phil and his partner are having a bash in Perth. Then I'll go on down to Edinburgh.'

'I thought you were going to be Phil's partner?'

'His girlfriend, bidey-in, whatever.'

'Oh, that sort of partner.'

'What about you – going to Marion's? Out with a fellow?'

'Stop fishing. There is no fellow.'

'What about this Andrew?'

'He's OK, but I keep thinking, why is he a bachelor in his late thirties?'

'Mysterious, that.'

Eleanor shook her head. 'Ach, I wonder about you as well. But you've . . . well, you seem to have lived with women at least. Not that you ever admit to it. But Andrew's different. He's sort of solid and dependable. Husband material.'

'Perfect.'

'You're being sarcastic.'

'Well, I can just see you – doing the same thing all over again.'

'What?'

'Never mind.'

'*What?*'

'Leave it – sorry. And sorry for asking about Hogmanay. I know you hate it.'

'Well, I do, David. And you also know why.'

'Yes, but maybe you should be like me – pack it away. Move on.'

Of course, this was exactly what he did. Move on. David did not carry the past with him, as she did. He shrugged it off. Things hadn't worked out; someone had let him down; the bank wouldn't put up the cash; he was ahead of his time, no one was ready for what he had to offer. Nothing was ever his fault: no blame, no shred of responsibility ever clung to David. Even with Ian's death, Eleanor had not thought to blame David, her own sense of guilt so overwhelming it left no room for other ideas. It was Marion who said, 'He brings disaster with him, haven't you noticed?'

Now, when Marion yawned, stretched, began talking again, she said, as if she had overheard Eleanor's thoughts, 'I'm glad David's going away for Hogmanay. Let him take his bad luck somewhere else. Not infect our New Year.'

'Marion!'

'Sorry. I was dozing. I had a sort of dream about the year Timmy died.' In the back of the car, the girls also stirred and woke. Marion leaned towards Eleanor and said in a low voice, 'Sorry. I'm getting nervous about the hospital next week. Making me grumpy.'

Eleanor put out a hand and touched Marion's knee. 'I know. It's OK.'

'Where are we?' Claire's sleepy voice rose plaintively. 'I hope we're nearly there.'

'Yes,' Marion told her, reassuring. 'Nearly home.'

12 ∫

Claire was no sooner home than she wanted to go off out again, this time to Sarah's house.

'I'll just ring her, Mum. I said I'd ring as soon as I got back.'

Eleanor was standing in the narrow hallway of the cottage, opening the Christmas Eve post, before she got down to the dreary business of unpacking. 'All right,' she said, not listening. There was a card from a former neighbour in Heatherlea, the only friend who still kept in touch, with a note inside about her children, her job, a holiday in Cornwall. It was a typed note; everyone had been sent the same message. But at the bottom, scrawled in pen: *Joe and I split up in the Spring. It's been a hard year, but I've managed to keep the house, because I was promoted in October. Hope all's well with you. Barbara.*

Behind the words, between the lines, Eleanor knew, heart sinking, there were shouts and long silences, quarrels and bitterness, a story she had not been told. Joe and Barbara. After all this time, she was hardly able to picture them, though they had been close for all of the first years of Claire's and Hannah's lives. She had always thought Barbara much stronger and more capable than Joe, but they had seemed secure together, and happy. Other people's marriages, she thought, so many secrets. She put down the letters, not having the heart to open the rest.

She would not tell Claire, there was no need. And yet, she longed to do that. In what she now thought of as their old life, Claire had been inseparable from Hannah, had played with her every day after school, gone to ballet lessons on Saturdays, swimming on Thursday nights. There was only Claire she could talk this over with. But Claire was deep in conversation, huddled over the telephone in Eleanor's bedroom. Irritated by the turned back, Claire's complete absorption, Eleanor left her case on the floor and went downstairs to turn up the Rayburn and light the living room fire.

'We should have had our own tree,' Claire said, coming down at last as Eleanor struggled with a smoking chimney. 'The house looks really *bare*. Why's there an awful smell of soot in here?'

'Oh shut up, Claire, and get me that newspaper – quick. God, I hope there's nothing stuck in the chimney. Why is it doing this?' She held up a sheet of newspaper in front of the grate, choking in smoke, angry and defeated.

'Mum, can I . . .' Claire hesitated, realising this was not the right moment. 'I'll go and unpack, shall I?'

'Yes, yes, go on.' The fire was drawing at last. Eleanor took the sheet of newspaper away, crumpled it up and stuffed it into the fire, where it blazed up. Then she went upstairs to empty her own case.

By evening she was as restless as Claire, and agreed to drive her to Sarah's house. Invited in for coffee, she was glad to accept. Claire and Sarah disappeared to Sarah's room, and she sat in the comfortable living room with Andrea. Two Golden Labradors lay steaming by the fire, giving off the stink of dog drying after a walk. There was a Christmas tree in the bay window, boxes of chocolates lay on the coffee table, and nearby she could hear the sounds (shouts and beeps), of two younger children playing a computer game.

Andrea talked about Christmas, elderly relatives, what to

do with all the food. Eleanor had coffee and two pieces
of cake. Andrea had reminded her in the past of Barbara:
good taste, enough money, and all the bits and pieces
on the window sills carefully chosen, unusual. Andrea's
husband was doing something in the garage, working with
Sarah's older brother. Now and again he came in, asked a
question, and went out again. There was throughout the
house, reflected in Andrea's calm, plaintive voice, a sense
of everything being all right, unchangeable.

Eleanor was seized with a longing to go home, to be back
in the cottage (where the fire had probably gone out) and
on her own with Claire. Claire sulked when she was called,
not wanting to leave.

'We're having a party at Hogmanay,' Andrea said, as they
put on their jackets at the front door. 'You're both very
welcome to come – Sarah has a few girls staying over.'

'Oh please, Mum. Sarah wants me to – I can, can't I?'

'We'll see. Oh, probably.'

'You'll come too, won't you?' Andrea patted her arm.

'I might be at Marion's. But it's nice of you to ask me.'

'Just turn up if you feel like it – no need to let me know.
About eight.'

'I don't have to go to Auntie Marion's, do I?' Claire
persisted, as they drove down the lane.

'No, it's all right. You can go to Sarah's.'

'You come, too – her mum wants you to. So do I. Why
can't you come?'

'I might.' An uneasy silence.

'I know you don't like Hogmanay. I'll stay at home, Mum,
if you want me to.'

Ashamed, Eleanor said, much more warmly, 'I'll be *fine*. I
might come – it doesn't matter. You can stay with Sarah.'

'Are you sure?'

'Yes.'

*   *   *

She could not face a party, of course. In a little bottle in a drawer, tucked under knickers and tights, she had two sleeping tablets left. This was what she had done, every Hogmanay since Ian's death: she had taken a sleeping tablet, and gone to bed. In the morning, it was next year, and the bleakest night was over. Claire had been too young to care about staying up. Last year, Fergus and Marion had had people round, and she and Claire had gone there. It had been, just, bearable. But she had still wanted to be home before midnight, so she left Claire with Eilidh, and drove back to her cottage, to the bottle of tablets, and sleep. She did not have a drink before or after. She had drunk no more than one glass of wine, or one whisky, on any occasion, for five years. David, of course, had taken the other option, and drunk more as each year passed. But both of them still sought oblivion, a way of not thinking.

This year, she said to Marion, 'I might go along to Andrea's party.' To herself she said, *I'll go to bed.* In the end, she did not even drive Claire to the party: another mother was taking her daughter, and they called at the cottage on their way. Claire hesitated by the door with her sleeping bag and rucksack.

'Are you coming later? Michelle's mum and dad are.'

'I don't think so.'

'Are you going to Auntie Marion's then? You're not going to be *by yourself*?'

'No, no I won't. You have a lovely time – ring me tomorrow if you want to be collected.'

'It'll be late. We're going to stay up for hours.' She leaned forward, kissing Eleanor quickly. 'Happy New Year, Mum.'

Eleanor held her for a moment, tasting the sweetness of hair and skin, then Claire was gone, the car disappearing down the lane.

Jim and Edie's house was dark, the Christmas tree lights off. They had gone to Jim's sister in Aviemore, and would be back in a couple of days. Eleanor was 'keeping an eye' for them. Outside the end cottage the old Saab was sitting, and there was a light on in the front window. The ginger-haired man, abandoned by his wife, must be spending Hogmanay on his own. For a moment, Eleanor was curious, then did not care. She turned indoors.

But the evening was long, and the book she had been saving to read, a disappointment. In the end, she thought she would walk up the lane, as far as the farm gate and back. She stood at her open front door, trying to make up her mind whether to do this. It was a clear, starry night, with a three-quarters moon, bright and full. In front of the end cottage, the blue Saab had its lights on. Was he going out then? He wouldn't be on his own after all – he had a party to go to, friends or family to be with. Then, stepping outside, she saw the car was empty, and the cottage door closed. He must have gone out and come back, leaving his lights on by mistake. Eleanor put on her jacket, and went out.

She paused at the end cottage. If he meant to see the New Year in, as she did, alone, he would not go out till late in the morning, and his battery would have run down by then. Eleanor put her hand on the gate, pushed it open, and went up the path. From inside the cottage came music, but no voices. She rapped the knocker three times. After a moment, the man with the ginger hair opened the door.

'Hi!' he said. 'Come in.' He stepped back, inviting her.

'No, sorry – I just came to say you've left your car lights on.'

He peered out. 'So I did. Thanks.' He came past her down the path, and opening the car door, switched off the headlights. He's local, Eleanor thought, or he's lived here a while – the car wasn't locked. He was Scots, but she could not guess where he came from.

'Can I give you a drink? Or are you on your way out?'

'No. I was just going for a walk.'

'A walk?'

'It's a lovely night,' she said, defensive.

'So it is.' He stood on the path beside her, and they looked up at the sky. 'Think I'll come with you, if that's all right.' He unhooked a jacket from the row of pegs in the hall. His house, a copy of hers, looked bright, with a crimson hall and stair carpet, and rows of small pictures on the walls. 'You don't mind?'

'No, of course not.' But she was taken aback, and felt shy.

He pulled his door shut and they began to walk up the lane side by side. 'I'm Gavin Soutar,' he said. 'You're Eleanor, aren't you? Edie calls you Eleanor.'

Something flew close above her head, so close she stopped and cried out. 'What was that?'

His hand held her arm. 'Wait – it was a bat, I think. Probably be some more.' So she waited with him, and two or three tiny bats flew out of the trees and wheeled above them. Then they were gone.

'You're not frightened?'

'Oh no. I was just taken by surprise, that's all.' She thought of the bats in the loft at Pitcairn, and David yelling when one skimmed his hair.

'How long have you lived here?' he asked, as they went on down the lane.

'More than four and a half years. I came up from Berkshire.'

'What made you choose the Highlands – is it home?'

'Now it is. My sister lives here, so it seemed the best place to come with Claire, my daughter. She was only nine then, and Eilidh, her cousin, was the same age.'

'Claire's the long-legged blonde?'

'Yes.'

'The *other* long-legged blonde.'

Was he flirting with her? Eleanor was not sure. They had reached the farm gate, and had it been daylight, would have been looking over the firth. In the clear moonlight, Eleanor could just make out the gleam of water.

'Do you want to go on?' he asked.

'I was just thinking I could see the firth. But maybe not. This is my favourite walk, up here, and along this path—' She indicated the way the track took, away from the farm, along the ridge of the hill. 'The view is wonderful, and you can go all the way along to the Neil Gunn Viewpoint.'

'I know,' he said. 'You're right – it is lovely.' They stood for a moment in silence, gazing at the hidden view. 'Come on,' he said, 'it's freezing out here. Come back with me and share my bottle of wine.'

'Well . . .'

'I could do with some company.' He was looking at her, she could feel that he was. But she did not look up to meet his eyes, beginning instead to walk back down the track to the cottages. 'Maybe you could too,' he went on, keeping pace with her. 'Or were you going out later? Where's the lovely Claire?'

'At a party. A friend's house.'

'The worst night of the year, this,' he suggested, 'or the best. Depends where you are at the time, or who you're with.'

Eleanor did not reply, unable to say anything that would not be an admission of some kind. She followed him into his house. In the living room, the same size and shape as hers, but quite, quite different, she stopped on the threshold. The room was full of quivering light, flickering shadows, cast by a dozen or more candles set out on the mantelpiece, on the bureau, the bookcases, and round the edges of the floor, between rug and skirting board.

'You left all these candles burning!'

'You think I was stupid – it's dangerous?'

'What if one had fallen over onto the floorboards?'

'You're quite right.' He looked crestfallen.

'They're beautiful – it's just – but so many of them . . . What made you think of it?'

'Oh,' he shrugged, 'you know. Defying the dark.' He picked up a bottle half-full of red wine, which had been standing near the fire. 'Let's sit down, eh?'

In the firelight, candlelight, face to face, she looked at him properly for the first time. He was thin and fit-looking, taller than she was by a head. He brought her a glass of wine.

'Now then, let's see this terrible year out, drink its dregs.' He sat on the floor cross-legged, near the fire, raising his glass.

'Has it been a bad year then?'

'Well, the last few weeks haven't been so . . .' He shrugged again, grinning, not seeming to care, so that after swallowing some of the dark buttery wine, she managed to say, 'You're on your own now? Has your wife – is she away?'

'Oh come on,' he laughed, 'I'm sure Edie's told you. I was abandoned. Kate's gone – flown the coop.'

'Oh, I'm sorry.'

'It's OK. Everyone should be on their own at Hogmanay at least once, don't you think? Just for the experience.' He topped up her glass.

'No, it's all right. I don't really drink at all now.'

'Except, of course,' he said, ignoring this, 'I won't be alone after all. You're not rushing off, are you? You'll see the New Year in with me?'

'Yes, all right.' How could she leave him? He might not be as cheerful as he pretended, might be miserable left on his own. He seemed anxious for her to stay. So perhaps she could do it after all, get through these last bleak hours conscious, watching them go by. She tried to relax, and leaned back on the sofa cushions.

'It's very nice wine,' she said.

'My father likes a good Burgundy.'

'Your father?'

'It's what he gives me every Christmas. Case of wine.'

'Wow. A case.'

'He knows it'll be appreciated.' He leaned over. 'Have some more.'

'No, really, I've hardly touched—'

'Went to my old dad's for the festive dinner,' he said. 'What about you?'

'I went to my father's house too,' she told him. 'We all did – my sister, her family, my aunts, Claire, me, and my brother.'

'Quite a party.'

'It was. Was yours—'

'Just Dad and me.'

'Is your mother—'

'Left years ago. Tired of his shenanigans. She's married to someone else now.'

Eleanor was not sure what to make of this. It seemed an odd way to speak about your parents.

'I suppose all families are different,' she said. 'So your wife – she . . .'

'We're not married.'

'Sorry, I thought . . .'

'Nope. We never got that far. In fact, we've only actually lived together for a year.'

'I've got a brother like you,' Eleanor scoffed. 'David. He drifts along, won't commit himself to anything. Anyone.'

'Modern male disease, is that what you think?'

'Oh well, not my business. You and . . . Kate. You must have loved her though,' she went on, growing warm with good wine, not thinking how big the glasses were he had poured it into, not noticing that he was topping hers up again.

'Oh yes. For a while.' He emptied the wine bottle, dividing the small amount that was left between their glasses. 'But what about you?'

'What about me?'

'Your life, your loves, your grief. Come on, it's Hogmanay. Talk about the past, then throw it off. That's what I mean to do.'

'Do you?' She thought about this, or tried to. Everything seemed to be growing distant and free, as if the world had loosened at the edges. 'Yes, right, I'll get rid of the past too.'

'Good. We've got—' here he glanced at his watch – an hour or so to do it.'

Eleanor stopped worrying about time, about drinking or not drinking; it was too much effort. Surely here, nothing could happen, no harm would come of a couple of glasses of wine. So they grew warm in front of his fire, and she listened to him talking, taking most of it in, laughing when he amused her. Then it was almost midnight, and she stirred a little, conscious of the hour, the moment.

'We have to go outside,' he said, getting up. He took her hand, to raise her from the sofa, and steadied her as she swayed a little, feeling the effect of the wine.

They stood on the little path in the garden, still holding their glasses, waiting for the last few minutes to tick away.

'We might hear the bells,' Eleanor said, growing cooler and clearer in the icy air. 'We'll hear the bells in Dingwall, it's so still tonight.' Then they heard them, faint on the breathless air, and he bent and kissed her, first on her cold cheek, then, tilting up her chin with one finger, on her mouth, his mouth still warm, tasting of wine, soft and slow, till she broke away, and said loudly, her voice thin and high, 'That's it then – Happy New Year!'

Indoors again, he said, 'Right – I'll open the first bottle of the year, now.'

'I'll have to go home.' She hovered, uncertain.

'You're joking? Night's young. Don't leave me yet. I'll get morose, and start thinking about Kate.'

'Well, all right – but just for a little while.'

This time, he sat next to her on the sofa. Some of the candles had burned right down, and gone out. The rest flickered faintly, but most of the light came from the fire, as he banked it up with dry logs.

'There's a reason, isn't there,' he said, refilling her glass. 'I mean, a particular reason, you don't like tonight?'

'Oh well.' She could not answer, or even think.

'Relax,' he said. 'I don't believe I've ever kissed such a *tense* woman in my life.'

'I'm not – I –' His eyes were hazel; fine lines made them seem humorous, quizzical. His face seemed very near and very kind. *I'll say it,* she thought, not caring.

'My husband died on Hogmanay. I do hate it, you're right. I don't know why I'm sitting here, how I can bear it. I must be . . . I must be drunk.'

'Do you want to tell me about it?'

'No. No, I don't want to think about it ever again.' Her eyes filled with tears, and he became blurred, he and the firelight a prism of radiant colour, meaningless.

'You know what I'd like?'

'No, what?' She blinked hard, and the tears spilled over, but she could see again, see him against the glow of the fire, dark.

'I'd like to have sex with you. Now.'

Eleanor said nothing. She seemed unable to have a coherent thought, and could not have uttered any she did have. She gazed back at him, but he seemed to be someone a long way off, perceived through a tunnel. Immobilised, she felt that somewhere at the back of her mind there must be words, a phrase, a way to respond. And in this whirring conscious part, she realised she was very drunk.

'Sorry,' Gavin said. 'I'm being completely crass. Sorry about that.'

As he moved towards her, firelight glinted on his hair,

flushed his skin: he shimmered and sparkled for her, ochre and gold. On his throat, where the shirt neck was open, a tiny pulse beat, and there were curling hairs like copper wire. She smelled the red wine on his breath, and the heat of him so strong it seemed as if what she warmed herself on was his skin, and not the fire at all. She closed her eyes, giddy.

When she woke, she was stiff and cold, and the fire had fallen into a heap of grey cinders. Outside it was still dark, and so dark indoors too, she could see through the uncurtained window a spray of stars, a sliver of moon. She moved a little, testing to see whether her legs were still there. Icily, one foot slid against the other. She raised her head.

She was on the sofa, covered by what felt like a travelling rug, hairy and rough, but so light her breathing shifted it. She was very cold, all the way up to her chin. But her head was burning, her throat parched, and her bladder painfully swollen and hot. Slowly, she eased herself up, trying to think where she was, where the bathroom might be. She had been dreaming about searching along a huge empty hall for a lavatory that worked, with a door that would close. Was she still dreaming? Or was she, this time, really padding along a narrow hallway, in size and shape exactly like her own, but not her own, to a bathroom even chillier than hers, but dark blue instead of pink, with a pile of *National Geographic* in the corner, dirty towels slung over the bath, and shaving things along the shelf. All this she saw, as she sat down heavily on the pan, and peed copiously, the warm ammonia smell rising like steam. She stood up and pulled up her jeans. Nothing had happened. She must have passed out, and he put her on the sofa.

Sitting down again in the living room, while she tried to work out, in darkness, where her shoes might be, she pondered whether this was a mark for or against him – that he had put her on the sofa, and taken the bed himself. If that's where he was. I must still be drunk, she thought.

Why don't I put on the light? She paused, listening, heard nothing but an owl hoot. Then one of her feet encountered a shoe. There. And the other one. Jacket. She had a jacket. But she could not think where it was.

Giving this up, she let herself out of the front door and made for her own cottage. In front of Jim and Edie's, she stopped. The owl again, and suddenly a beating of wings. It had flown almost directly above her. But she had not seen it, and now it was gone. Too late, she looked up. How clear the sky was, how *many* stars. The air was so cold her eyes hurt, and breathing was difficult. But she went on standing for another minute, testing the cold, aching but awake. It is next year, she thought. I have got through Hogmanay, I am in next year. It was all right now to go home and be alone. She moved then, and went back to her own house. There she pushed open the door she had left on the latch, going to tell Gavin his car lights were on, last year, a long time ago.

In the kitchen she made tea but did not drink much of it; heated a kettle for hot water bottles, filled them and went to bed with paracetamol. How icy the pillow, and her feet and her back burning where she had tucked the bottles. Something of the evening came back to her: the walk in the dark, the candles, the fruity wine. Of all he had said to her, just this one thing: *I want to have sex with you.* Had he really said that? Not *I want to make love/go to bed/sleep with you* – all the expressions she knew. Was this what people said now? Well, I wouldn't know, Eleanor thought. How would I know? Was sex, then, something you had, like dinner, or a night out? Perhaps, after all, she had dreamed it. And yet, a tiny spurt of something that might have been lust was released in her. Not that she would know about that either, after all this time. Ashamed, she turned over, trying to sleep.

She had desired her husband, of course, had longed for him, especially in his absence, and surprised (perhaps dismayed) him on his return with arms flung round his neck, an enthusiasm he did not often see in her. But what had she longed for? Something that was never found, she knew now, in their love-making, however considerate and patient he was. Eventually, she had learned not to trust this vague ache, the warmth spreading through her thighs, the treacherous quickening of lust. It ended in such disappointment.

I got through it, she told herself now, curling up tighter in the bed, turning her thoughts away from Ian and the dangerous past. She was drifting in half-sleep, losing control of where her imagination travelled. She shuddered a little, but grew warm at last, and slept.

13

'He's an interesting sort of man, he's done lots of different things. He has all these opinions, on subjects I've never even thought about.'

Eleanor was explaining Gavin. She had gone to see Marion after her first chemotherapy treatment. That had been bad, Marion admitted, but not so bad as she had feared. She felt fine.

'If it goes on like this,' she had said to Fergus, 'it will be all right.' But Fergus had squeezed her shoulders, saying only, 'We'll see. See how you go.'

The sisters were in Marion's living room. The frost had not thawed on the grass all day, and it was beginning to grow dark and icy again outside. Marion got up to draw the curtains.

'So, where did you say his wife had gone?' She sat down again, and took up Ross's school shirt, to sew on a button.

'They're not married. She's his girlfriend. I don't really know where she's gone. Living with a friend, he said, or maybe a cousin. I'm not sure. The cottage is his – she had a flat in Inverness, but it's rented out just now.'

'Complicated,' Marion observed, bitting off a thread.

'He doesn't seem to expect her to come back.' Eleanor sounded doubtful. Gavin was behaving like someone single and unfettered, but she would have liked to be sure about this.

'So – are you . . . have you been out with him?' Marion asked. Being in hospital was like being out of the world altogether; even after an overnight stay you felt a lot must have happened in your absence.

'Well, not out. I mean, he lives practically next door, and he's onshore till the end of the week, so I see him every day. He comes in for coffee, and he's asked Claire and me round for a meal.'

'Can he cook?'

'Well, I suppose so. We'll find out on Friday. After that he's offshore for a couple of weeks.'

'What does he do, on the rigs?'

Eleanor was vague about this. 'Something to do with drilling, and chemicals,' she said. 'It's technical – he doesn't wear a hard hat and climb about the rig.' But Eleanor had not asked him. They had talked books, politics, hill-walking, not about his job.

'So,' Marion said, winding thread round the new button and putting in a final securing stitch, 'you've got over your horror of red-headed men?'

'That was Claire!' Eleanor smiled. 'Och, no, I don't fancy him or anything. But it is lovely to have somebody look in and chat for a while. He's easy to have around, you just get on with the ironing or whatever. And he fixed the sash rope in the kitchen window the other day.'

'You've been lonely,' Marion said.

'No, how could I be, with Claire, and all of you so near?'

'Yes, but lonely for – I don't know. Eleanor, do you not sometimes regret moving here, leaving your friends, the life you had in England?'

Eleanor looked at her in astonishment. 'Why, are you sorry I came?'

'Of course not. But I sometimes feel it was selfish of me to want it, that I maybe tried to influence you when I shouldn't have done.'

'No, never think that. This is my home, and my friends are here now, anyway.'

Marion, seeing her off, wondered about Eleanor's solitary life. Friends, but not many of them. She needed something useful to do, or a job. A greater purpose in her life.

Eilidh's bag dropped in the hall with a thud and she came into the kitchen. 'Hi, Mum, you all right?'

'Yes, fine.'

'Sorry I'm late – we went down the street. Ross is playing football, did he tell you?'

'Yes. And Dad's in evening surgery, so we'll have a late tea.'

'I'm starving – what can I have now?'

Kirsty, who had come in earlier from the primary school, slid downstairs by leaning across the banister and skimming her legs over the treads. 'I get a packet of crisps?'

This is how I want it to be, Marion thought, as the girls sprawled in front of the television, scattering crisp crumbs, squabbling over what to watch. I want everything to be ordinary, I don't want to be ill. She hated the interruption to her life, and had felt angry and resentful all week. Now nausea rose in her chest, her throat, but she swallowed hard, ignoring it. A cup of tea, she thought, that's what I need.

Eleanor had no wish any longer to keep everything the same. Keeping everything steady had been done for Claire's sake these last few years, and the great changes, (Ian's death, the move back to Scotland) had been enough to sicken her of uncertainty for a long time. But now everything had been the same for too long. She had discovered, too, what she could not easily say to anyone else, that life was simpler with just the two of them. She even preferred it. Other people had observed (after a decent interval) that she would find someone else, and marry again, but she had never believed this herself, having been surprised at getting married in the first place. You could not, anyway, expect to be chosen by someone like Ian twice in your life, someone attractive and successful, who always knew the answers. Fergus was the only other sort of husband Eleanor understood. He was not quick or ambitious like Ian, he was dependable and unimaginative, but he was like Ian in this: he was the kind of man who knew what to do, however sudden the crisis, or serious the problem. Marion said Fergus was worried, but Eleanor saw only calm reassurance. He seemed concerned, but not afraid, and that was a relief. If Fergus expected everything to come right in the end, it was bound to be that way.

This was not the impression Eleanor had of Gavin Soutar, who confessed often to being unreliable, and cheerfully admitted his failures. But the cottage seemed to brighten when he came in, and Eleanor had more energy, and a sense that things were happening. She was self-conscious with Claire, though.

'Where'd you get those flowers?'

'Gavin brought them.'

'Ooh, ooh – givin' you flowers. Watch out, Mum, he fancies you.'

'Don't be silly. They were reduced in Tesco, so he bought a bunch for himself and one for me.'

'A man, buying himself flowers? Weird.'

'There's nothing weird about it. His house is so nice, Claire, full of books and CDs and lovely coloured rugs.' She cleared a space on the kitchen table where Claire had spread her homework. 'I need a bit of table, sorry.'

'I'm nearly finished.'

Eleanor began breaking eggs into a bowl. 'Anyway,' she said, 'you'll see his house on Friday.'

'How will I?'

'We're going there for dinner at night, remember?'

'Oh. Friday. I can't, Mum – Sarah's dad's taking us into

Inverness to go to the new cinema and we're having chips and that at Harry Ramsden's after. I've got to go – I promised Sarah I'd stay over.'

'Oh, Claire.'

'Anyway, what would I do there? You and him just talk about stuff I'm not interested in.'

'Thanks.'

'Well, you do. I mean, he's nice and everything, but . . .'

'All right.' Eleanor left the half-beaten eggs, and put on her shoes.

'Where are you going?'

'To tell Gavin you won't be there. I don't suppose you want to do it.'

'Thanks, Mum, you're brilliant.'

'We could make it another night,' Gavin suggested, 'but it would have to be a couple of weeks away – I'm off on Saturday.'

'I know. I'm sorry.'

'No problem – you'll still come, won't you?'

Eleanor hesitated in the doorway. She had refused to come indoors, and now she hugged her arms round herself in the cold wind. 'Yes, if that's . . . if you're sure.'

'I imagine Claire would rather be with her pals anyway?'

She smiled at him, relieved. 'Yes.'

'See you Friday, then. Seven o'clock?'

Going home again, Eleanor was conscious that something had shifted between them. She thought of Hogmanay, which they had not spoken about, except to joke that they had both been so drunk they scarcely remembered it. *But I remember the walk,* he had said. She remembered more, heard him saying, *I'd like to have sex with you, now.* Did *he* remember that?

'You can have a romantic dinner eh,' Claire said when Eleanor started cooking again.

'Away you go!' Eleanor raised the lid of the Rayburn and

put the omelette pan down to heat. 'Get a lettuce out, Claire, and wash it, will you?'

Together, they prepared the meal, not talking about Gavin. But Claire said later, 'He's not your boyfriend, is he, Mum? I thought Andrew was your boyfriend.'

'I'm too old for a boyfriend.'

'No, you're not. Amy's mum's divorced, and she's got a boyfriend.' Claire was lying on the sofa, her feet propped up on the arm at the end. Eleanor had her coffee and the *Scotsman*.

'Good for her,' she said, turning a page.

Claire was gazing at the piece of flat, smooth stomach between her cotton top and the waistband of her hipster trousers. 'Know what? My belly button's different from everyone else's.'

'Is it?'

'Deeper, and a sort of longer shape.' She poked at it, then pushed it out. 'See, everybody else's is like this—'

Eleanor looked up. 'Stop doing that – it looks obscene.'

'Do you think I'm fat?'

'No.'

'I think my bum's too big. If I stand at the mirror, with my back to it, right, and turn my head round and—'

'Och, don't be daft. You've a lovely figure.'

Claire abandoned this line of thought, and picked up her magazine. 'At least Andrew's quite nice-looking,' she pointed out. 'Gavin's, like, well, he's ugly, don't you think? I mean, he's got freckles all over his arms.'

But Eleanor did not think he was ugly. Perhaps behind the way he was by day, lean but ordinary in a checked shirt and jeans, she still saw the halo of firelight glittering round him, felt his warmth as he came near. She was nervous about Friday night.

Claire disappeared at four with her friends, and the hours

between then and seven yawned vacantly ahead. Had it been light, she could have gone walking down by the firth. In the dark, what was there to do but finish the ironing, read, get changed? She had gone up to Inverness early in the day, and wandered round the shops in the town centre, looking for something to wear. She had plenty of clothes; buying something new was what she did when she was bored. Marion bought in conservative department stores, and looked neat and well-groomed. But Eleanor had become clever at finding things second-hand, or in sales, now that she did not have to dress for anyone but herself. Sometimes even Claire said, 'that's really nice,' though she was firm about never wearing anything from Oxfam herself.

In the end, Eleanor went into an off-licence and chose a bottle of wine instead. She gazed at the rows of bottles, wondering if paying a lot was a guarantee the wine would be good. The salesman, appealed to, shrugged, and pointed out the special offers. Eleanor chose at last, but regretted it as soon as she left the shop. She should have spent more.

At six, she ran a bath, then lay in it too long, so that she was late, and arrived at Gavin's door flushed and apologetic.

'You're dead on time,' he said. 'Come in.'

'Oh, something smells good.' She held out the bottle. 'I hope this is all right.'

'Great, thanks. Give me your jacket.'

There were not so many candles this time, but several stood on the mantelpiece and the table, so that the light in the room flickered, throwing shadows on the walls. *He does remember.* She would not drink much tonight, just one glass of wine, or at the most, two, and keep the resolution made years ago.

A bottle of red wine, already open, waited by the fire. He poured a glass for her. 'Food's nearly ready,' he said. In the kitchen, there seemed to be several pots on the stove, all of them bubbling, and the air was rich with tomato and spices. He tipped rice into the largest uncovered pan.

'Ten minutes or so,' he said. Eleanor looked round the kitchen, which was the same size as hers, but otherwise quite different: the old Rayburn had been taken out, and there were fitted pine cupboards and marble work surfaces. But everything was cluttered and untidy, and the windowsill crowded with pot plants.

'We'll eat next door – there's only this stupid breakfast bar in here.'

'Don't you like it?'

'Would you design a kitchen like this?'

'I used to have a kitchen like this,' Eleanor said, smiling, 'only bigger, and tidier.'

'Tidier wouldn't be difficult, eh?'

Later, she would tell Marion, 'Yes, he can cook, much better than I can.' But were men supposed to cook as well as this? Eleanor felt awkward, being waited on, exclaiming over how good everything tasted. But the wine did help; she was warmed through.

She would not have more. 'No, I'm fine. I don't usually drink.'

'Why not?'

'I just don't.'

'You're not Wee Free, you're not ill, you don't have to drive home – have some more.'

Eleanor gave in, meaning to leave most of it. Yet somehow, the glass emptied, and was refilled. She told herself she had come to no harm last time.

'What is it?' he asked, when he had cleared the table and brought coffee.

'Sorry?'

'What is it you're scared of, if you have a drink? Being out of control?'

'No, no, it's just something that happened. That wouldn't have happened if I'd been sober.'

'Guilt,' he said. 'That great Scots quality.'

Eleanor flushed. 'You don't know.'

'No,' he agreed. 'So tell me.'

'I can't.'

He seemed to lose interest. 'OK. Let's get down by the fire, eh?'

'Where do you come from?' Eleanor asked when they were settled. Her glass was full again. Had she drunk some of the third glass? She had not meant to. 'I can't place your accent.'

'Oh, I lived in England for years. I was probably in London around the time you were there. But I was born in Perth. I'm almost a Highlander.' He grinned, and raised the bottle. There was quite a lot left; they could not have had very much. But perhaps this was the second bottle – it looked like the one she had brought. They were on the rug by the fire, Gavin cross-legged, Eleanor leaning on an armchair.

'My mother left my father, when I was fourteen,' he said. 'I was at boarding school then. I came home one summer and was told I could spend the second half of the holiday with my mother in her new house. First I'd heard of it.'

'That's terrible!'

'Oh, I don't know. We'd moved to Edinburgh by that time, but my mother went to live in the Borders. There was a guy she knew who took me hill-walking with his own sons. They were older than I was. I learned a lot, that year.'

'So, who did you live with?'

'Mostly the old Dad. Felt he needed the company, and it wasn't a good time to change schools. My mother married the hill-walker eventually. Nice chap. Reliable, unlike my father. He went on having his love affairs, but he didn't seem to enjoy them so much without the secrecy.'

'You're joking, aren't you?'

'A bit.'

'And what about you? You said you and Kate weren't married.' What about Kate, she wondered, who had vanished such a short time ago. A woman with short dark hair getting into a car. That was all Eleanor knew about her. The rest was what Gavin had said, and so perhaps not to be relied on.

'No,' he admitted, 'but I was married once. It didn't work out, didn't last long.'

Eleanor was reminded of David, who had often discovered that *things didn't work out.*

'So you didn't have any children with her either?' Eleanor said this casually, a question expecting the answer no, as she had once learned in Latin class. But he said, 'Yes, yes, we did have a kid. A boy. It was difficult to kind of keep up with him after we split, though. She thought it was best if I didn't see him, less disruptive. He was – what? – about two. I was away a lot, anyway, with the job. But I should have done more, I know that. She was ill, in and out of psychiatric care – her mother brought the boy up, really. And her mother wasn't so keen on me.' He smiled at her, shrugging, as if none of this really mattered. 'He's grownup, of course. Twenty-four. I do see him occasionally, when I'm in Glasgow.'

Eleanor, dismayed, felt the weight of someone else's tragedy, dismissed in a few sentences.

'That's so sad,' she said, but her words seemed to hold no sympathy. His story, baldly told, had removed him from her, sealed him apart with his separate past. She did not want to know more, did not want it to matter now. A young man of twenty-four, grown up, not needing a father. But he hovered, spectral, reminding her of how impossible it was that she and Gavin could start something new together. She wondered how people could do that, at this stage of their lives, when so much had happened already to harden them into sorrow before they even met.

She leaned back, closing her eyes. 'I'd better go home soon.'

In the silence that followed, she sensed before he did it, that he would touch her. His hand was warm and heavy on her thigh. 'Eleanor.' She opened her eyes. There he was, tawny in firelight, his shirt open at the neck, so that the red-gold hairs sprang up curling on his throat and chest. His hand curved gently round the back of her head, and drew her face close.

'Relax,' he whispered, 'it's all right.'

All he did was kiss her, over and over, longer and longer, his beard brushing her face, his hand caressing her cheek and chin, his tongue probing first softly, then insistently, till she was boneless in his arms, her hands coming up to his chest to say *stop*, but fluttering away, then coming up again to hold onto him, round neck and waist, the roughness of beard and hair, the soft cotton of his shirt. 'Come on,' he said, and pulled her up, till they were somehow standing, though she did not know how her legs could hold her – too much wine, too much – her head filled with something that might have been music, a drumbeat.

The bedroom was cold, but not cold enough to rouse her. She was so hot, and he was so hot, the coolness of the sheet soothed. They were both half-undressed, helping each other to tug and peel off clothes. 'All right?' he kept asking. 'All right?' and 'Yes,' she said, or sometimes, 'I shouldn't, oh, I shouldn't,' while at the back of this, a tiny clear voice said *why not?*

Then he stopped, propping himself on one elbow to look at her.

'You're stunning,' he said, smiling. 'So, so beautiful, Eleanor. But you must know, you must, I can't help wondering why there's not a man, why you're on your own still?' Then he laughed, and kissed her throat, and held her close to him: 'My good luck,' he said. Eleanor moved away, struggling to come to herself, awake and anxious.

'Gavin, I haven't, I'm not – it's been such an awful long time—'

'Hey, I'll take care of you.' He waved his hand inches from

her skin, that shivered goose-fleshed at his almost-touch. 'Look at you, how lovely you are.'

So she looked. As if for the first time. White moonlight lay across the room, luminescent on skin. Eleanor saw her body as young, unblemished. She had been married and borne a child, but it seemed now as if none of this had left a mark. Renewed virginity sealed her, permanently young and perfect. Now his warm hand on her ribcage travelled up and onto one of her breasts. The nipple, raised with the coldness of the air, hardened, and as she turned to him, her flesh shimmered white, moved to meet his, and she became aware of the blue-white of his skin shading into reddish brown where the sun had darkened it. She trembled, to find herself so naked with a stranger. But it was too late, now, to change her mind, for he was making himself ready, moving over her.

'I can't—'

'Sorry,' he murmured, pushing hard and far inside her. 'I should wait, I can't – oh, God, Eleanor.' She gasped, raising her knees to make it easier, let him in, move with him.

It was the same, and not the same. Afterwards, he held her tight, tight in his arms, then rolled onto his back, keeping her close along the length of him, hugging her, one arm still round her shoulders.

'Sorry,' he said again. 'You were miles off, weren't you?' He turned to her. 'You want to come?'

'What?'

'You didn't, did you?'

'No, but . . .' She was going to say, 'I never do,' but could not, as if it would still be too much of a betrayal. 'It's all right,' she ended.

'No, it's not. Come here.'

But after a moment, she pushed his hand away. 'I can't.'

If it had never worked before, why would it now? She did

not want to reach that pitch of frustration again. Ian had tried, of course he had, but she had decided, eventually, that it was something not to be tried for. But perhaps they had both given up. 'I'm fine,' she used to tell him. 'I don't mind.' And yet now she did.

Gavin raised himself up and drew the covers over her. 'Keep warm,' he said, 'and sleep a while. We've got all night.'

'Oh no, I must go home!' She struggled up, but he pushed her back.

'I know what you're afraid of.'

'I'm not, I—'

'You think Edie will spot you sneaking past her door, and then she'll know you're not such a virtuous widow after all.'

Eleanor could not help laughing. 'You're right,' she said. 'And she gets up so early.'

'Well, then. Stay for breakfast, stay till you can wander back as if you've just been in to borrow a cup of sugar.' He lay back with his hands behind his head. 'Why would anyone want to borrow a cup of sugar, do you think?'

Eleanor too lay back. 'I don't know,' she said.

'Cuddle up,' he ordered, tucking the covers round them. *I will never sleep*, she thought, and slept.

She woke in the night suddenly, clear-headed and amazed to find herself here, and with him. He woke with her, moving already for sex, wanting her. Grateful, astonished at his tenderness, she let him touch and stroke and tickle her, giggling a little, clutching at him, knowing of course that none of it would work, but wanting to please him. Then, unwilled, and at last, wave after wave of tremulous pleasure, as she drew him in, warm and wet, moving in a rhythm not his or hers, but belonging to them both, faster and harder, deeper and stronger. Helpless within this, she was unable to tell any longer where she ended and he began. Over and over he pushed inside, withdrew, touched her again, till pleasure thickened along her thighs, with a great heat that welled and welled and thrust her suddenly up and over the high cliff at last, and she fell like a diving bird, a stone, tumbling and tumbling, plummeting down the other side.

Powerfully, she pushed him off, curled away from him, whimpering with relief and fear.

'There now,' he said, turning her towards him again. 'That's better, isn't it?' As if she were a child, to be soothed out of fretfulness. Her face was wet with tears, and he dabbed them away with the sheet, holding her, triumphant.

Later, going home boldly in front of Edie's house at eleven in the morning, she realised what it was she had learned. What she had always believed to be her lack, her fault, might after all have been Ian's. Or at any rate shared, something they lacked together.

And now – she was changed!

She phoned Marion when Gavin had left, and was driving down to Aberdeen. But at once heard something unfamiliar in her sister's voice, before Marion could discern what was different in hers.

'Oh, I've been sick,' Marion said. 'I feel a bit rough.'

Eleanor's heart sank. How could she be happy, when Marion was ill?

14

All the way to Marion's house, along the Dingwall road, slowing for the railway bridge on the bend, faster down the last straight stretch into the town, joy rose in Eleanor like a bubble of laughter.

I am all right, the words drummed in her head. *There is nothing wrong with me.*

All those years, had she really thought there was? All those years – was that happening to other women, regularly, often? To Marion? They knew everything about each other except this. They had lived apart for the first years of their marriages, and you do not write in letters, say on the phone, *I'm having wonderful orgasms,* or, in Eleanor's case, *I never manage to get there, no I never have* ... Eleanor laughed aloud, unable to help herself.

She could not remember driving the last of the road to Marion's house, the traffic lights, the corner, the street dividing. I'm a crazy woman, she thought. I've never been like this, ever. Still that tingling all the way through, a teasing echo.

Marion was white-faced and looked tired, but not ill. Eleanor, torn between guilt and relief, said, 'Are you all right? I'll make us tea, shall I?'

'If you like. But I probably won't drink it.'

They went into the living room, which was scattered with newspapers, mugs and glasses.

'I haven't even tidied in here since last night,' Marion said, half-heartedly gathering things up, and trying not to bend too low or too sharply.

'I'll do it.' Eleanor had the energy of half a dozen women. In a moment the room was straight.

'What's happened?' Marion asked, when Eleanor finally sat down with her.

'Nothing!'

'Eleanor, you look – well, I have to say, you look great.'

'I'm sorry, I feel so mean when you're not well.'

'For goodness sake, why should you? It's only this nausea. It's a side-effect, Fergus says it's common. Mary Mackay warned me, and the consultant. It's past now, I'm all right.' She leaned back in her chair. 'Anyway, tell me what's happened.'

Eleanor flushed. 'Oh, I don't know. I mean it, I hardly know myself what's going on.'

'It's this man, isn't it? I thought he was going away soon?'

'Today.'

'Oh, you were having dinner with him, you and Claire, weren't you?'

'Claire didn't go. She was at the cinema with Sarah – then sleeping over at the Pattersons'.'

'I see.' Eleanor was still glowing. My goodness, thought Marion, about time. 'Well, well,' she said aloud. 'I hope you're being . . . careful.'

'Oh, he was.' And blushed again, laughing, her head dipping so that the heavy hair fell over her face, hiding the joy. 'This is crazy,' she murmured. 'Like I was fifteen again.'

'I thought men with red hair were impossible?' Marion was laughing with her.

'I know, I know – I'm not – I don't *know*, Marion. I feel stunned.'

'I can see that.'

Marion thought she was in love with Gavin. Perhaps I am, Eleanor wondered, it's so long since – and I know so little about it. Love.

'I'll phone you,' he had promised.

'From an oil rig?'

'We do have telephones,' he said, amused. 'Sure, ring you in a few days.'

By Sunday night, one day later, she was listening for this, longing for the call to come. But when it did, it was her father.

'You tell me,' he said, 'how Marion is. She just says she's fine.'

'She feels sick a lot,' Eleanor explained, 'and she's tired. That's all. Don't worry, it's common.'

'This chemotherapy,' he said. 'How long is she to go on getting it?'

'Every three weeks, just for a day or so. She's in overnight, then home.' They had gone over this already with their father, but he did not seem to hold onto the information. Marion had said to Eleanor, 'it's like me not taking in what the doctor says – fear, anxiety – something gets in the way.' 'It'll be for about three, four months,' she explained again. 'Six treatments, then they'll do a scan. After that, maybe a bit of radio-therapy. But we don't know that yet.'

'But she's keeping all right, so far?'

'Yes,' Eleanor said, not wanting to tell him about the sickness again. Better he did not know, really. If her mother had still been there, it would have been different. No way of protecting her from the truth, who always knew it before they did. 'What about David?' she went on. 'Any word? I haven't heard a thing since New Year.'

'Oh, he rang, now, when was it? Monday – I forget. Sometime in the week.'

'Is he working?'

'Oh aye. Something to do with computers.'

A few minutes later, there was another call. This time she picked it up in the kitchen. Claire was in her room with Sarah and two or three other girls. It would be for her. They seemed to spend hours ringing each other at the weekend: three girls in one house, four in another, shrieking and giggling. Since the conference call David had arranged before Christmas, Claire had been begging her mother to let them all have one too. *It would be brilliant, Mum.*

But it was David.

'Dad's just been on. How are you?'

'Great – couldn't be better. This thing with Phil's really taking off. I'm out and about all the time.'

'What are you doing?'

'Seeing clients, fixing stuff up for them. You know.'

But of course, Eleanor did not. This was David at his worst, full of himself, expansive with plans and great connections, unreachable.

'Oh well, good. I'm glad it's going well.'

'How about you? Marion? Is she having her chemo yet?'

'What? Yes, of course she is. She's due for the second lot next week.'

'How's she coping? Phil's partner was married before, you know. He died of cancer. Different kind, obviously, but she's been through the mill with it. I was telling her about Marion, she's totally sympathetic, Sophie. Understanding.'

'This is really what we want to hear, David,' Eleanor sighed. 'For goodness sake don't go telling Marion about your friends dying of cancer.'

'What do you take me for?' He was offended, but not enough to shut up. 'I only meant, you know, Sophie was the sort who understands all that stuff. Pity Marion can't speak to her. Does she have anyone like that?'

Eleanor had been longing to say to David, 'Look, my life's changed, changing.' But why hadn't he picked it up at once, tuning into her mood. Once he would have done. Marion always could.

'Marion's being very sick,' she said now. 'It's hard on her. Fergus says she won't be able to work.'

'Doesn't have to though, does she? With the good doctor to provide.'

'Oh, for goodness sake.' She had wanted him to be in touch, had missed him. But this was hopeless. 'I have to go,' she lied. 'Claire's wanting me.'

A pause, where he said nothing, then suddenly, 'Sorry. Had a couple before I rang you. Give my love to Marion, right?'

'Yes, of course I—' A click, then silence. He had gone. That was it, of course; he had been drinking.

The phone rang three times after that. Claire's friends. Prolonged conversations, much whispering and giggling, Eleanor's bed rumpled by the girls sprawling across it.

Eleanor sat in the living room with a cup of cooling coffee, and tried, and failed, to write a poem about sex. She looked at the flat words on the page, which did not seem to reflect in any way what they had done, what she had felt. How could she live for the next three weeks not seeing him, forgetting day by day how he looked, the way his voice lowered when he spoke to her, the touch of him.

Later, in a row on the sofa bed in the boxroom, the girls talked late into the night, cosily tucked up together. Eleanor lay alone, and could not sleep.

For the next chemotherapy session, Eleanor drove Marion to the hospital. It was a fine February day, sudden and deceptive, mild as spring. The sun lay yellow on the calm waters of the firth. The trees were still bare, but everywhere, if you looked closely, were the tight black embryos of new buds, and in the wet winter earth, green shoots breaking through.

'What a lovely day,' Eleanor said, opening the car door for Marion to get in. Her sister made a face.

'What a day to be going into hospital.'

'I know – but it's only overnight. This weather might last a few days.'

They drove in silence for a while.

'Your friend, Gavin – he's away, is he?'

'Yes, he said he'd phone sometime.'

'I'm sure he will.' Marion had heard despair in Eleanor's voice. Already, she thought. This man's only been gone a week or so. Perhaps it was serious. Well, you could tell Eleanor was serious, that was to be expected. Marion hoped it was serious for Gavin Soutar too. If only Eleanor did not expect too much.

Marion pursued this line of thought, glad of anything that would distract her from the hospital bed, the doctor coming round, the drip feeding into her arm, the long hours till tomorrow, when she could go home again.

'Why can't they just give you tablets to take at home?' Eilidh had wanted to know.

'It's not tablets, it's an injection, and this drip thing, it goes in slowly, so you have to lie down while it does.' But Marion did not feel she could explain any further.

One or two of her friends had said to her (perhaps not knowing what other comfort to offer) that at least, being married to a doctor, she would have someone to answer all the questions. But of course, it was not like that. Fergus did his best, but his reluctance to commit himself to advice in an area where he had only general knowledge, his fear of worrying Marion, had kept them from much talk of her treatment or symptoms. Marion found it hard to remember what any of the hospital doctors had told her, and she had failed to ask sensible questions, even when she had the opportunity. This, as much as anything, alarmed her. Illness made you childish, she thought, her mind running on this after all, as Eleanor negotiated the Maryburgh roundabout, and they soared off up the hill to Inverness.

'Have you heard from David again?' she asked Eleanor, making an effort to get her mind on something else.

'No. I told you he phoned, didn't I, and he was asking for you?' Eleanor sighed. 'He was awful though, it was a dreadful conversation.'

'What sort of awful? You did say he'd been drinking.'

'Oh, you know. Boasting about his job, which I still don't really believe in. On a high. You couldn't talk to him at all.'

'Sometimes, he doesn't seem to belong to our family,' Marion said.

'Oh, of course he does. He's just different. But I don't know why.' Now Eleanor wanted to defend him.

Marion knew there was something linking David and Eleanor that she did not understand. Something about Ian, more than Eleanor had told her after the funeral. Marion had liked Ian well enough, without feeling she really knew him. They had moved South so soon after the wedding, there was hardly time. He was not the sort of man you could easily feel close to in weekend visits, short holidays. Marion remembered him as fit, looking always slightly tanned, with blue eyes and thick fair lashes. An attractive, impatient man. Well, impatient with Eleanor, and Claire too, even when she was little. But the last man in the world to have a heart-attack at thirty-seven. Just as I am the last woman in the world to have cancer, she thought now, a breast missing, a world split open. It was no good, all she could think about was the day and night to come.

'I hate to leave you,' Eleanor said, hesitating in the hospital foyer. She had walked across the car park with Marion, and insisted on coming in.

'I'm fine.'

'Ring tomorrow when you want me to come.'

'I will.' Marion smiled, reassuring Eleanor, since it could not be the other way round.

Eleanor thought how small her sister looked in the wide, pale-painted corridor. Like a fleeting shadow over the sun, the image of their mother appeared, then vanished. Eleanor turned away, and walked back to the car.

Afterwards, this time, Marion felt much worse.

'It's getting to me,' she admitted to Fergus, when she was home.

'It'll wear off,' he said. 'If it doesn't soon, we'll get you some anti-nausea tablets. In fact, you should really have them now.'

'More drugs,' she said. 'Then back into hospital, for it to start all over again.'

'Count down the days, the weeks,' he said, 'if you think that would help. Make a chart – some patients do that.'

'I'm not some patients,' she snapped. 'I'm your wife.' Then she burst into tears, feeling guilty. 'I'm sorry, I'm sorry – I don't cry in front of anyone else, really I don't.'

Marion's friends said to each other, and to Fergus and Eleanor, how wonderful she was, how brave, how cheerful.

'It's a matter of pride,' Marion told Eleanor. 'You can't afford to let other people see. But I get angry sometimes. I know that's not fair, but I can see them thinking. Which one is it? I want to put my hand up, point, say, "You'd never know, would you?" And if it's not that, they're looking at me and thinking. Is her hair getting thinner, would you say?'

'Oh, Marion, they mean well, everyone is so anxious for you to be all right.' Eleanor herself had wondered about Marion's hair.

'I know.' Marion sighed. 'Sorry, I know all that. Look at the cards and notes I'm still getting, the way everyone keeps popping in. I just wish sometimes they wouldn't, that's all. I'm too tired even to talk.' She leaned back in her chair, and closed her eyes.

Eleanor waited, not knowing what to say. *I'm useless, I*

can't help her at all. Then Marion opened her eyes and smiled.

'Sorry. It's awful I'm grumpy and miserable with the people I love most. You and Fergus come in for all my moans.'

'Well, that's what we're here for, there has to be someone you can say it all to.' *Is that what I do for her? It's not much.* But she was glad Marion had said this. 'Anyway,' she went on, 'you must stop doing things. Look at you today – making soup when I came in. Buy tins, no one will suffer.'

Eleanor knew Marion would ignore this. She was struggling to be normal and to look after everyone, just as usual.

Then one day Eleanor came into the house to find Marion white-faced, her cheeks streaked with tears. She was coming downstairs as Eleanor called from the kitchen door, *It's me.*

'What's wrong?' she cried. 'Has something happened?'

'Just been throwing up, that's all.' Marion leaned on the banister. 'It's not glamorous, cancer.'

'Lie down then, go to bed. Oh, Marion.'

'Sorry, no, I'm all right now. Better.'

Eleanor had driven over from the cottage thinking about Gavin. *What a fool I was,* she had decided. *It meant nothing to him.* He had grown ugly in her imagination, and she found she could not even summon his face, his presence. He had not called her. She was obsessed with this silence, reading into it meanings that changed hourly, but came down in the end to this: she had made a terrible mistake.

Now, helping Marion to a comfortable chair, bringing her water to sip, sitting by her, smelling on her (for the first time) sickness, disease, she was ashamed and guilty. They sat in silence, Marion coming to herself again.

'Oh dear,' she murmured, 'at least this happens when the children are at school. And at least – I was working it out – half-term will be my best week, before I go in again.' She sat up straighter, less white now. 'Just before I'm due to go in again, something changes. I wake up and that awful *feeling* has lifted. I can't explain it. For a few days I'm almost back to normal. Then, well, then the treatment knocks me back. It's the pattern, Fergus says, so when it's over, I will get back to normal. I have a glimpse of it, normality, and I tell myself it will be all right in the end.'

'Of course it will. As long as this kills off the cancer. That's what matters.'

'I watch the bottle, you know, think about that stuff dripping into me, and I wonder what is it killing in me that's healthy? I try and look after myself – eat well, they say, get fresh air. But oh, some days all I want to do is sleep.'

'I know, I know,' Eleanor said, not knowing, but sitting close by Marion, wanting her to go on explaining.

'The worst thing . . .' Marion knew it was years since she had spoken so frankly about herself to Eleanor. But who else could she say these things to? Perhaps Eleanor would not really understand (no one could) but she would always be there, she would always want to listen.

'What? What's the worst thing?' Eleanor prompted.

'Oh, I have these dreams. That my breast is still there. I touch it, and I'm the same on both sides.'

'Oh God.' Eleanor felt tears coming. Don't cry, she scolded herself, you fool, don't cry. And she swallowed.

Marion, dry-eyed, went on, 'I wish I was. I wish I was the same. Maybe I shouldn't have been so hasty. I keep thinking that now.'

'Hasty? But you didn't have any choice – you said the surgeon recommended it.'

'Oh yes, it's what he does. Operate first. That's why he recommends it. But Fergus wanted me to go to Aberdeen, to the oncology unit there. They could have given me some chemotherapy, to shrink the tumour. In the end, they might have saved . . . not operated, I mean.'

'What? You didn't have to – you could have gone some-where else and they might – why didn't you do that? Why didn't you *say*?'

'Och, I just made up my mind.' Marion sighed. 'I couldn't face it, Eleanor, I couldn't face going all that way. Leaving home. And in the end, it might have been the same anyway. Get it over with, I thought.'

While Eleanor wept, and she comforted her, Marion thought of how she had imagined worse things than losing her breast – keeping it, being wrong to do so, dying anyway, for the vanity (it seemed to her) of a nipple preserved, a body staying, more or less, the same. However close Eleanor seemed just now, she did not say, could not say even to her, *I miss my breast, that part of my body. I wake crying from the dream, and I long to have it back.*

'Oh,' Eleanor gasped, 'what a pathetic creature I am. Why am I crying?'

'Because you always did, when I hurt myself, or David did. You're too soft-hearted.'

They laughed then, shakily, and began to talk of other things.

That night, Gavin called. When she heard his voice, she was so utterly unprepared, despite all the longing and waiting, that for a moment she could not speak.

'Hi – Eleanor?' He did sound far away; she pictured him on the high sea, gales blowing round him. But it would not be like that; he said they had TV lounges, comfortable rooms, good food.

'Hi. I – you sound – I thought—'

'How's things? Claire fine?' He was starting again, not assuming intimacy. She too, grew distant.

'Yes, we're both fine.'

'Soon be home,' he said. 'For nearly three weeks.'

'Right.' But she did not believe in this any more.

'Would you look in on the cottage?' he said. 'I meant to ask you – just to check if there's post, everything's OK. I'll ring you again tomorrow.'

'Yes, yes, all right.'

'Seems to be ages since I saw you,' he said, and his voice became lower, closer. 'I'm looking forward to coming home, for once.'

'Yes,' she said, struggling to put some warmth in her own voice, failing. 'See you soon.'

But afterwards, her heart beat fast and hard. It was real, she told herself, going to find his key under a stone by the front door. Something will come of this.

15

The snow was so deep at Pitcairn the winter Marion was twelve that one morning they had to dig their way out of the back door, and carve a trench as far as the henhouse. Marion, convalescing after glandular fever, had been moved to a bedroom at the back of the house, with a bed made up near the window, so that she could see what was going on in the garden, and would not disturb Eleanor during the night. By this time, she was beginning to want to do something, though she had scarcely energy to do more than watch, or now and then read.

In the smothered garden, where only the trees and tallest shrubs poked bare branches through the snow, David and Eleanor helped their parents and Ruby dig the trench. The day before David and Stanley had begun work on an igloo. Stanley had not managed to get through to their house this morning, so their father helped David to finish it, since there was no possibility of getting as far as the end of the drive, let alone into Aberdeen for work. The world was paralysed by snow. The Post Office opened briefly, then shut again, because no one could reach it. The schools were closed for a whole glorious week.

But on the second day, Stanley got as far as Pitcairn by means of dogged persistence. He was so wet when he arrived he had to be changed into some of David's clothes.

Then the two of them went outside and got wet all over again. Marion heard the noise in the garden, as they flung great wads of snow at each other. Eleanor, attempting to join in, ran inside shrieking when she was hit, complaining to her mother. Marion sat up on high pillows, and looked out at endless whiteness, the landscape transformed, all the familiar landmarks invisible. And although all she could do was watch, she was still too weak to mind very much.

Her temperature was still rising in the evening, making her hot and uncomfortable again. She shifted about in bed, the sheets twisted beneath her, hearing voices from the landing, or in her head, rising and falling. But it was not so bad now. In the worst of the fever, she had scrambled out of bed, calling loudly for her mother. It seemed always to be the middle of the night, the sort of night when time slows and stops. Marion had been falling into a long tunnel, then a great ball had come after her, a huge lead ball, rolling and rolling, heavier and faster, a taste like iron in her mouth, so that she cried out and stuffed the corner of her pyjama jacket in her mouth, to get rid of the terrible taste, the sensation of that ball, rolling round and round.

Then she was in the armchair, with a dressing gown round her, suddenly cold instead of hot, and in the light from the landing she could see her mother remaking her bed with fresh sheets, the sweat-soaked ones lying on the floor in a heap. *Now then* ... She was helped back into bed, her legs like rubber beneath her, and then she was lying down again, on cool cotton, with a new hot water bottle making a warm patch for her feet. She lay still, grateful for the smoothness of those sheets, then the damp cloth on her face, and a dry towel, soft and smelling cold, like fresh air.

Then the fever passed, and Marion was better, though not strong for a long time. She reached the lovely part of being ill: the fire in her bedroom, its glow lighting the room long after the lamp had been put out; the paper dolls Eleanor helped cut out, with all their clothes that you fastened on with tabs at the shoulders; the new comics and library books.

Then the snow came. Marion was awake when it first fell, and knew by the light behind the curtains (thinner in this spare room, showing moonlight through) that something was happening. She sat up, reaching, and managed to tug the edge of one of the curtains, so that it jerked open a little. She watched through the thin panel of exposed window, the snow falling and falling, all night. In the morning, she was able to say she knew, she had seen it first, when they came in to tell her.

The snow went on falling. Then came the igloo-making day, then the next, when no one could go anywhere at all. Marion lay in bed reading *Shirley Flight, Air Hostess*, and thought that was what she might do, when she grew up. But it was hard to imagine being dressed and walking about again, never mind being grown up and getting on an aeroplane.

'You wouldn't like it,' Eleanor said. 'You'd get homesick.'

'I know,' Marion sighed. So that was that. She would never be like Shirley Flight. Eleanor was sitting on the bed with a sketch pad, a box of coloured pencils and scissors. They were going to make their own cut-out dolls, with specially designed dresses and accessories.

'We'll be dress designers instead,' Marion suggested. 'You can do that at home.'

'Daddy says we'll have to go back to school tomorrow,' Eleanor said, colouring in a blue skirt. 'The snow plough managed to get along the lane this morning.'

'I wish you didn't have to. I'll be on my own again.'

'Auntie Alice and Auntie Mamie are coming out as soon as the roads are clear. Mummy says they were worrying about you.'

'It's not the same as you being here, is it?'

'They always bring stuff. Sweets and that.'

'I don't feel like eating sweets.'

'Comics as well.'

'I'm bored reading.'

'They could read to you, or tell stories.'

'For goodness sake, I'm not a baby.'

'Well, I was only making suggestions,' Eleanor pointed out. 'I can't help going back to school, can I?'

Marion subsided, fretful. 'I know. I just feel all cross and miserable.'

'That's because you're not well yet,' Eleanor soothed. 'Look, I'll get your tray to lean on, and you can draw both the wedding dresses if you like – one for my doll and one for yours.'

This sacrifice was too much for Marion, who burst into tears. Bewildered, Eleanor too began to cry.

'I'm sorry,' Marion said, blowing her nose. 'I'm sorry. It's horrible being ill. I don't feel like me.'

Eleanor had privately hoped to catch glandular fever too, so that she could lie in bed with a fire in her room, cosy and warm. All she had to heat her room was the smelly paraffin heater on the landing which made hardly any difference at all. Then she could read and read, and draw pictures all day, as Marion was allowed to do.

By the time Marion was downstairs dressed, no longer for just half an hour in a dressing gown, the snow had begun to thaw, and everywhere people were complaining about burst pipes and flooded land. For weeks after the roads and paths were clear, snow could still be found in ditches, or heaped up underneath trees. The igloo collapsed into a greyish, pock-marked heap, smaller each day.

On her own again, Marion played with the dolls' house. Really, she had outgrown it, but when there was no one else around, you could read the baby books again, and play with the old toys. The father doll was the worse for wear: the wire beneath the padding of his legs poked through, and he had lost his smart blue jacket a long time ago. He had a slightly dissolute appearance, his face had been rubbed off and replaced so many times, and his woollen hair was all but gone. But the mother and daughter were in better shape. Faith had made them new dresses, and Eleanor had taken great care with the inking in of their blue eyes and red lips and cheeks. Sometimes Marion played that they were not mother and daughter but sisters, and the father was their older brother, who was usually away exploring Africa. Since David was at school, and could not object, she was able to use his train set. Then all three dolls, propped up in the goods wagon, could take long journeys round the living-room floor, to the land behind the sofa, or to the sea, which was the blue rug by the fire.

But when Marion wearied of this, she was too tired to put everything away again, and Faith, scolding her upstairs to rest, threw furniture and dolls back higgledy piggledy, spoiling the game. Marion decided she would do something else next day; she was too old for the dolls' house now, and playing with it on your own was boring. She cast around for what she might do instead, but listlessly, unable to think much about it.

She discovered that being ill had changed her: she was thinner, and her legs, even when they stopped shaking, were spindly and long.

'You've grown,' Faith said, swirling warm water in the bath with one hand, and looking up at Marion in her vest and pants. Left alone, Marion got cautiously into the bath. Here the paraffin heater made the room at least lukewarm, but the bits of her under the water were the only parts that did not soon feel cold. Something else had happened too: her breasts, which had only just begun to swell, were fatter. The nipples looked big and had turned a deeper pink. When she touched them, they were tender, as if all this growing hurt a bit. Other things were happening too: she could feel, under the water, downy hairs on the pad of flesh between her legs that seemed to have no name. 'Remember to wash down below,' Faith said, and this covered everything that you did not mention.

Marion was half proud, half fearful of what was happening to her body. She had no sense of foreboding about any of it, till Faith sat on her bed one evening, while Eleanor was still downstairs playing Ludo with Dad and David. Warm and sleepy from the bath, Marion lay eating toast and sipping hot milk, trying not to spill crumbs, knowing she would soon be well enough not to be allowed this any more.

'Now then,' Faith began, 'I think it's time I explained something to you.' Marion's heart jumped. Her mother seemed not embarrassed, but conscious, solemn, as she began to speak. She finished by saying. 'Eleanor's too young yet, don't talk to her about this. Time enough when she gets to your stage.'

But Marion was not going to keep this awful news to herself, however privileged. When her mother was out of the way, and David not likely to burst in, she would explain the horror of menstruation to Eleanor. After all, Eleanor was as tall as Marion had been before glandular fever, so she was catching up anyway.

'Mummy said not to tell you,' she warned, 'so if you breathe a single word to her, I'll never tell you anything again.'

'Don't tell me then,' Eleanor said, not wanting this responsibility. Marion stopped, thwarted.

'Oh well then, if you want to be a baby.'

'No, I'm not – all right, tell me then.'

The trouble was, neither of them believed it.

'Not every month,' Eleanor said. 'Not everybody.'

'Everybody, she said. But you can't imagine Auntie Alice . . .'

'I can imagine Auntie Mamie,' Eleanor said candidly. 'What a fuss she must make.'

'You can't tell when it's happening to somebody, it's secret. Nobody else could tell, Mum says.' But to herself Marion said, *I'm not going to school on those days.*

'Well,' Eleanor sighed, for once relieved to be the younger sister, 'at least it won't happen to me for ages and ages. Maybe,' she added, 'it won't happen at all.'

'It has to,' Marion confirmed, 'or you can't have babies.'

'I don't care, I don't want any babies anyway.'

'I do,' Marion said. Even if it meant going through all this, she meant to have children. Five of them: three boys and two girls. She had names for them, which changed depending on the books she was reading. The girls were called Shirley and Caroline at the moment.

'I'm going to be an artist,' Eleanor said. 'So it would be better if I didn't have children.' She was designing an evening dress for Stephanie, her cut-out doll. It had sequins round the hem and a low neck.

Faith had looked out Marion's school clothes, for going back on Monday. Now Marion stood looking in the wardrobe mirror, holding her skirt in front of her.

'It's miles too short. I've grown about a foot.'

Eleanor went on drawing. She was jealous of the Academy uniform, and could hardly wait to wear it herself, next year.

'The aunts are coming tomorrow,' she said.

Alice and Mamie had put off their visit because of the bad weather, but still arrived with all the flurry and drama of people who have struggled over trackless wastes to reach the house.

'Well, Faith,' Alice said, as they took off layers of outdoor clothes, littering the hall with coats, scarves and galoshes. 'Are you not thinking of moving back into the town? You've been fair stranded out here.'

'The Duthie Park was like the North Pole,' Mamie told them, coming to get warm at the living room fire.

• Moira Forsyth

'Have you *been* to the North Pole?' David asked. Mamie stood with her back to the fire, raising her skirt so that the heat would flow up under it. Marion was embarrassed and looked away. Alice took her shoulders and held her still.

'You've grown a wheen,' she announced. 'And you've fair got thin.'

'I know,' Marion said, freeing herself, backing out of the door.

Upstairs, her new bedroom was cold, and the grate empty. She was better now, there was no need for a fire. But she did not really feel better. She felt different, and a lot of the time she wanted to cry. Faith, coming in to see where she had got to, found her sitting on the edge of her bed, gazing down at her newly long legs.

'Come away downstairs – it's far too cold in here.'

'Can I stay in this bedroom?'

'It's too cold, I said. What, you mean not move back with Eleanor?'

'Yes.'

Faith weighed this up. 'We'll see,' she said.

'Please. I like the wardrobe and dressing table in here – I like the curly patterns on the wood, so you wouldn't have to get new furniture or anything.'

'Oh good,' said Faith, sarcastic, but smiling.

'Marion got off the bed and crossed to the dressing table. She had spent hours in this room, and had explored every corner of the unfamiliar furniture. 'It was all in the house before we came, wasn't it?'

'Some of it, yes. Not the bed.'

'Well, look, Mum, there's this wee drawer in the dressing table – it's locked. Have you got the key?'

'Oh no, Marion – this room's scarcely been used except when your aunties are staying. Alice had it last, once when Daddy and I were away.'

'I remember that.' Marion open the tiny cupboard in the

centre of the dressing table, beneath the mirror. Inside were two drawers, one which opened and was empty, the other, below it, locked.

'Well, fancy that,' Faith said. 'I never even noticed.'

'Maybe there's jewels hidden in there. A treasure map, or an old will – do you think there could be?'

'You read too many stories.' But Faith paused, thinking. 'I tell you what – there's a thing your granny did – Granny Cairns. Once she told me . . .' Faith reached round behind the mirror and felt down the back. 'Well, well.' There was a ripping sound, and she pulled away a piece of sticky tape with a tiny key attached.

'Oh, Mum!'

'We'll try it.' The key fitted. Faith turned to Marion. 'There you are – you open it, see if there's a diamond necklace inside.'

Marion's fingers trembled. But it was all for nothing: there was only a hairpin inside, and a silver sixpence. Her face fell.

'Never mind,' her mother said. 'You've got a secret drawer for your own jewels now. And maybe it's a lucky sixpence.'

'Don't tell anyone,' Marion said.

'Our secret,' Faith promised. 'Now then, come downstairs to the warm. I don't want you moping up here.'

'I *can* have this bedroom, can't I?' Marion wanted her mother to stay, so that they could go on talking, sharing secrets. But Faith seemed all at once to lose interest. She turned away. 'Don't pester me. I said, we'll see.'

Marion followed her mother downstairs. In her head, she was decorating her new room.

Alice was helping David with homework. Mamie was knitting, and Eleanor, sitting beside her, had two thick wooden needles and a ball of pink wool. Their father had said more than once that Eleanor and Mamie were alike, and Marion thought she saw what he meant: both were fair-haired (the only fair people in the family), with that white, powdery skin that fires up red with heat or excitement, and both had very blue eyes. Marion's eyes were hazel like her mother's, David's grey like Aunt Alice. We are all like somebody, Marion thought. Perhaps Eleanor wasn't very like Mamie after all, since Mamie's hair was fluffy and dry with being permed over and over, while Eleanor's was waving and shiny. And Mamie was plump and middle-aged, while Eleanor was a slim child. Eleanor hated to be compared to anyone, especially Mamie. 'How can I be like her?' She's quite old and I'm young. And she's fat, and all her clothes are frilly and fussy.'

Marion liked Mamie's frills, her lacy jumpers, her jingling bracelets and coloured scarves. She glanced up at the sideboard, where all the family photographs were crowded together at the back. One had been taken at Mamie's wedding: there was Uncle Tom, whom they did not remember, looking serious in his Air Force uniform; there were Mamie and Alice (who was bridesmaid) in 1940s suits, with hats at an angle. Mamie's blouse had a ruffle at the neck, Alice's was plain. 'A pink silk blouse,' Mamie had told the girls, 'I chose the pattern and material myself. But she wouldn't have so much as a fancy button on it. Not her.'

Marion looked down at Eleanor, who frowned hard over her knitting, concentrating. She tugged the tight loop with difficulty over the point of the needle. 'In, over, through, off,' Mamie was saying. 'Can ye mind that?'

'In, over, through, *off*,' Eleanor was muttering through gritted teeth, and the loop did fly off, but too fast, the stitch was lost. Eleanor, seeing her inch of pink knitting unravel in the middle, burst into tears.

'Here, gie it ower,' Mamie said, putting down her own cloud of white jumper sleeve. 'Dinna pull at it, Eleanor, you'll mak it worse.'

'It's in a mess,' Eleanor moaned. 'I can't do it.'

'Well,' Faith said, coming in, 'I hope *you're* not coming down with something.'

Eleanor stopped crying and looked up at her mother. 'Maybe I am,' she said hopefully.

'I'll do that,' Marion said, coming down beside Eleanor on the floor. 'See, Auntie Mamie, I know how to pick up dropped stitches.'

'Ye've good hands on ye,' Mamie agreed, guiding Marion as she picked up the loop, row by row.

Eleanor lost interest, and followed her mother to the kitchen. David, giving up the page of sums, flung down his book and went after her. Marion was left with Alice and Mamie, comfortable by the fire.

'We'd better think about getting home,' Alice said. She took the poker to the fire, which did not need it, and a shower of sparks flew up. 'Afore it's dark.'

'Are you not staying for tea?' Marion looked up.

'The roads is still bad, here and there,' Mamie said, folding up her knitting and tucking it into her tapestry bag.

'Remember when we were little,' Marion said, 'we used to tidy your work bag?'

'*Un*tidy it, mair like!' Mamie laughed. Marion fastened the bag for her, tracing with her fingers all the little pockets along the side, that held packets of needles and pins, reels of thread, scissors and scraps of wool.

The children watched from the living-room window as the aunts drove slowly through the trees towards the gates.

'They'll take hours and hours to get home,' David said, 'driving at two miles an hour.'

'I wish they'd stayed,' Marion said.

'I don't. Auntie Alice keeps wanting to talk about schoolwork.' David flung himself into a handstand, held it for a moment, moved a step, collapsed. 'See!' he shouted, red-faced. 'I nearly walked!'

*   *   *

Marion had slept too much in the day-time. Now she could not manage to fall asleep at night. And though she did not want to admit it, she missed talking to Eleanor, who was still in the old bedroom, the light switched off at half-past eight. Marion had put on her new bedside lamp and read for a while, but she tired of this too, and lay down in the dark again. The thaw had turned to rain; it spattered on the window, an irritable bluster of wind and water, fretfully knocking round the house and garden.

At last, between dozing and waking, she heard her parents come upstairs, and the line of light under the door grew wider, as Faith looked in.

'I'm not asleep,' Marion said firmly, but her mother only tucked the covers round, and said, 'You soon will be,' before going out again. Eventually, after some to-ing and fro-ing, the sound of water running, the lavatory flushing, doors closing, the hall light went out, and all was still and dark. Outside, the wind vented its temper among the trees and against the windows, but indoors, the house had settled for the night.

Perhaps she did sleep. At any rate, she thought something had wakened her, was conscious of a dream vanishing, colours fading. Marion opened her eyes in the dark. The wind had dropped; she could not tell if it was still raining. She could just make out the shapes of the furniture, so the sky must have cleared, since the gap in the curtains let in a shaft of moonlight, enough for her to see by, see all the familiar things, and know what they were.

She listened to silence, and then a sound, very faint. It might have been the wind again, sighing among the trees. But then it came again, thinner and higher, and a little less faint. Marion sat up in bed, eyes wide open. Somewhere in the house, a baby was crying. She swung her legs over the side of the bed, and felt around for her slippers. Maybe I'm in a dream, she thought, going to the door and opening it cautiously. The sound had stopped. Then it came again, that thin, despairing sound of a newborn baby, that scarcely knows yet what to cry for.

Marion was on the long landing, among shadows. Her room was at one end, her parents' at the other, the black depths of the stairwell halfway between. Slowly, she moved towards the crying. She would get her mother, her mother would know what to do. Maybe it was not a baby but a kitten, shut in somewhere. Marion hoped it was a kitten. But as she neared her mother's room, the cry was suddenly behind her, so she turned, turned only for a second, and saw the dark figure at the head of the stairs, with a bundle in her arms, and the crying rose, urgent and unearthly, in the dark.

Marion shrieked, and flung herself through the open doorway of her mother's room, diving headlong onto the bed. Faith was out of bed, heart pounding, by the time Marion reached her.

'What's wrong – what is it?' Faith held her tightly, smoothed her hair. 'Hush, hush. Was it a bad dream?' Felt her forehead. 'Are you feverish again, is that it? Hush, hush, it's all right.'

By this time, David and Eleanor were calling, so John went to settle them again. But somehow, in a moment, they were all in their parents' bed, David bouncing with excitement, Eleanor crying with fright, Marion still leaning on her mother, feeling Faith's heart thud in tune with her own, as their pulses began to slow again.

'Is it a burglar, did Marion see a burglar?'

'Don't be silly, David.'

'I saw a ghost,' Marion told him.

'Nonsense!' But it was too late. Eleanor and David believed in the ghost; their house was haunted. David pulled the sheet over his head.

'Did it go like this – *whoo . . . whoo*?' His father hauled the sheet away.

'Stop that all of you,' Faith scolded. 'There are no such things as ghosts.'

There was no going straight back to sleep. They had to have warm milk, and the hot water bottles reheated, as if they were being put to bed all over again. David stayed with their parents, falling asleep quickly, but kicking and wriggling so much they got no rest. Marion went back to her old room with Eleanor, and to her old bed. As soon as the girls were alone, Eleanor climbed in beside her. They weren't afraid any more: the landing light was on, and they could hear the murmur of their mother's voice, the low rumble of their father's reply.

'Tell me about it again,' Eleanor whispered. 'What did the lady look like?' Marion had said, over and over, *I saw a lady, I saw a lady holding something, I thought it was her baby.* Now she said thoughtfully, 'A bit like Auntie Alice.'

Eleanor was reassured by this. 'Oh, not scary then.'

'No, Eleanor,' Marion insisted, 'it *was* scary. I never saw her face, it was just she had dark hair, and she was tall.'

'She's gone now, though.' Eleanor turned round, nestling her bottom against Marion, sighing as she closed her eyes. 'Mummy says you were dreaming. Maybe you dreamed her.'

'The crying wasn't a dream. I heard the crying.'

'Yes, but you said it could be a kitten.'

Marion did not reply. *I saw her,* she thought. *I heard the crying.* Then she realised that Eleanor had fallen asleep, because she could hear sucking noises, and Eleanor never put her thumb in her mouth now except in sleep. Marion cuddled up to Eleanor's turned back, and rested her cheek on the softness of Winceyette, and listened. But the baby had stopped crying, the woman (if there had been a woman) was gone.

In their parents' bedroom, John fell asleep too, turned away like Eleanor, tugging the covers round him. Faith lay with her arms round David's hot, restless body, trying to keep him still, and waited for morning. *I know who you are,* she told Marion's ghostly lady. *Will you never let go?*

16

Gavin came back onshore at the end of February, just at the time Marion was having her third chemotherapy session. Eleanor heard the Saab coming up the lane, and knew it was his car. When the engine had stopped, she went to the window to make sure. She was thankful he had already disappeared into his house; she could look at his car, heart thumping, but not yet at him. So she waited, feverish with uncertainty. Then she made herself turn away from the window and go into the kitchen, feeling she must do something to keep her mind occupied. Something. What? Anything.

But Claire, coming past his house on her way home from school a few minutes later, saw him first. He was carrying a box of groceries in from the car.

'Hi,' he greeted her. 'How are you?'

'Fine,' Claire answered, not stopping. Gavin, wanting to say more, had to call after her.

She dumped her school rucksack in the hallway at home, 'That man Gavin's back,' she said as she came into the kitchen and opened the fridge door. 'What can I have to eat that's not fattening, but stops you feeling hungry?'

'An apple?'

Claire made a face. 'Mm. He said he'd look in and see you later.' She spread two slices of bread with butter and sandwiched them with cheese slices. 'Is this your evening class night?'

'No, tomorrow.'

'Cheese and bread are good for you, aren't they?'

'Well, real cheese is.'

'This *is* real cheese. Anyway, I don't like that stuff you eat. It smells disgusting.'

I want someone to sit down with me, Eleanor thought, and eat real food, and like the things I like. I want another adult to be here. Now.

But when Gavin opened his door to her and she said, 'Hi, I put your post in the kitchen, did you find it?' her voice emerged high and strained, and she was trembling.

He was the same. He looked tired and bit rough, unshaven, but he smiled with real pleasure to see her, ignored the post, took her (as soon as she had stepped inside) in his arms.

'A long time, eh?' he murmured, his mouth on her neck, sending shivers through her, stubble grazing tender skin, firing her up.

'Oh,' she gasped, 'it was real.'

'Real? This is real enough – I missed you.'

'Yes.' She could say it now. 'Yes, I missed you.' Then his hands were under her jersey, icy on hot skin, fingers hooked under her bra, pushing it up, then travelling down, down, a moment later, unzipping jeans, finding the secret places so soon she gasped again, tried to stop him, but felt, despite her protests, the betraying wetness seeping onto his fingers.

'I mustn't, not here. I have to get back – Claire . . .'

People did not do this, not in real life, seizing each other so hungrily, the door barely closed, the hallway too narrow, the carpet too hard so that it burned her spine as he moved inside, as she moved with him, unable now to do a thing about it.

'You want to come upstairs?' he asked, when he was spent, and had recovered a little, holding her tight, his mouth on her throat again, kissing gently.

'No, no, I have to get back.' She was up and hauling on clothes, coming to her senses. What if Claire had followed her, come to say someone was on the phone, some trivial message? 'Oh God, I've got to get a grip.' She was flushed, alarmed, and yet still trembling with the pleasure of it, wanting to stay, to reach again the place he'd taken her to last time.

He sat naked in the narrow hallway, leaning against the coats on their hooks, watching her, amused.

'Come back,' he said, 'come back later.'

'I'll try.'

She would, of course. He knew that, as he let her go.

Marion had come to hate the hospital. Till now, she had thought of hospitals as good places, where problems were solved, pain eased, sick people made well. Now, as she approached the rectangular buildings, the acre of car park, the sick feeling in her stomach intensified. This was fear. She was afraid of the hospital. Everywhere, she heard stories of people who came out more ill than they had gone in, or crippled with some new symptom or disability. Why had she never heard these stories before? They could not all be true.

It was not just being ill that made her afraid. The nurses, the staff who had once been so friendly and sympathetic, did not always seem so now. The first shock was when she went, in the New Year, to have a prosthesis fitted to replace the temporary one. She had to wait a long time, and everyone was very brisk. Except us, the poor Amazon women, Marion thought. We were not brisk. The oddly shaped, soft rubbery moulds she slipped inside her bra cup, trying for size and shape, were comically awkward. When she finally decided on one, the nurse advised her to walk around, to bend down, reach up. 'All the normal things,' she said. 'See how it feels then, dear.'

Marion resented the 'dear', the advice, the door swinging behind the nurse as she left. She wished she had brought Eleanor with her. At least there would be someone to help her make a joke of it. She leaned forward, but perhaps too suddenly, for the prosthesis slid out and bumped softly on the floor.

'Shit!' Marion said aloud, Marion who never swore, or lost her temper. 'Oh, *shit!*'

'What you should do,' Eleanor said, when Marion told her about this, 'is get some new bras. See a proper fitter. You must still get fitters in the old-fashioned dress shops, the expensive ones. There are special bras for people like you, aren't there? Well, get some of these – really pretty ones.'

'That's the first sensible suggestion I've heard,' Marion said. 'That's what I'll do.' And Eleanor glowed, knowing that for once she had said something useful.

Marion had bought a book on women's health, and another on coping with cancer. The first was feminist, cheerful, and very keen on women examining their own vaginas. The other was more clinical and explained everything in greater detail than Marion really wanted, or indeed could take in. However, neither of them, as she pointed out to Eleanor, mentioned how sticky the prosthesis felt next to skin, when you got hot. 'You sweat behind it, you know. I can't imagine a whole summer like this.'

She and Eleanor read through both books, comparing. The one on women's health had a chapter called 'Looking after your Breasts'. As if, Eleanor remarked, they were puppies, or house plants. At the end of the encouraging part about self-examination and good diet, a few statistics were lined up.

'One in twelve women contract breast cancer,' Marion read aloud to Eleanor. 'Then it says this should put it in perspective.' They looked at each other in dismay.

'God,' Eleanor exclaimed, 'that's thousands of us, millions.'

Eleanor, flinging herself from Claire, to Gavin, to Marion, back to Gavin again, veering between excitement and terror, seemed to move through a narrow pass among rocky hills that rose so high on either side they closed off every route except back (which was impossible) or straight ahead (which was dangerous). Every now and then, an avalanche of rocks came tumbling down, with a great roar. And yet, so far, not one of them had hit her. This could not last.

'One in twelve,' she said again, aloud.

Marion went on reading. 'Eighty per cent of these women don't die,' she told Eleanor.

'Well, I should hope not,' Eleanor said crossly, 'with all this bloody treatment they give you.'

'But,' Marion looked doubtful, 'it says only seventy per cent will be alive and well five years later. Shouldn't that be eighty per cent? What happened to the other ten per cent?' She flicked back a few pages, then gave up and flung the book on the floor. 'Och, I can't take it in. I'm so stupid these days.'

'No, you're not.' Eleanor wanted to pick the book up and look for herself, but knew Marion had had enough of it. 'You'll be fine as soon as the chemotherapy's over. Halfway through, now, nearly.'

Marion picked up the book again. 'The lymph nodes,' she murmured. 'I'm lucky about that. Mine don't seem to be affected.'

Eleanor had no idea what lymph nodes were, did not really want to know. 'Don't read about it any more,' she advised. 'I think these books just make it seem worse.'

'You're right,' Marion said. 'Oh, it is nice of you to come and keep me company. I can't cope with other people just now, and Fergus doesn't want me to talk about it at all. I mean, he tries to listen, but after a minute or so, he finds something to do. *I'll just check that light you said was flickering*

. . . *get the coal in* . . .. So I leave it. But it's not much fun for you, discussing this sort of thing.'

'Don't be silly – I *care* about you. I *want* to be the one you talk to about it.' She half-rose. 'Are you tired, though? D'you want me to go now?'

'No, not unless you want to.' Marion sighed. 'At least you don't keep leaning forward the way Lynn does, and Sue and the rest of them.'

'Leaning forward?'

'Like this.' Marion made an effort, moved in her chair, and leaned towards Eleanor, looking into her eyes intently. 'Tell me, how are you *really*?' she breathed.

Eleanor laughed. 'They mean to be sympathetic.'

'I know, that's what's so awful. But they can see how I am. Ugly. My hair's coming out in handfuls – I can't believe it. Look at me, I'll be bald, like somebody on *Star Trek* . . . from another galaxy.'

'You still look bonny to me,' Eleanor said. 'Just too thin.'

'That's what Fergus says,' Marion smiled.

'Well, we both love you . . . even if you had no hair at all, we'd love you.' But Eleanor felt the touch of fear, of relief, that she did not have to face this herself.

Going home, she kept pushing her fingers through her own thick bell of dark blonde hair, as if to reassure herself it was still there. I just couldn't cope with that, she thought. How does she manage? Would Gavin still want her, in that fierce shameless way, if she had thinning hair, was becoming gaunt, listless, as Marion was? Marion, who had been on and off diets for years, always wanting to be thinner than her metabolism dictated. Now her skirts and trousers were loose, and her collar bone pronounced.

None of this made a difference to Fergus. Eleanor longed to be loved like that. Only Claire loved her so unconditionally, and Claire couldn't help it; children loved without willing it, loved the most terrible parents. Look at Gavin, still admiring his hopeless father, excusing him even while he joked. In the two weeks since he had come back, they had achieved an intimacy that was surely not just to do with sex. We are in love with each other, that must be what it is, she told herself, looking for signs in him that showed he cared for her, was interested, wanted to have her around. Yes, this was what being in love was like. It had not been exaggerated, after all, as she used to think, by poets and songwriters.

She tried not to let Claire see too much of this.

'Oh well,' Claire sighed, when Eleanor kept disappearing to his house, saying she'd only be half an hour, staying almost two. 'As long as you like him. He's quite nice, I suppose.'

Then one evening, hanging round after tea long enough to have to help with the washing up, she said, 'Mum – know what?'

'What?'

'I'm going out with somebody.'

Eleanor stood still for a moment, then carried on scrubbing a casserole dish. 'Oh, who's that?'

'Just this boy at school. His name's Stephen.'

'He's nice, is he?'

'Really tidy, Mum. Loads of girls fancy him.'

'So . . . when are you going out with him?'

'Well, you know. I got off with him at the Maryburgh disco. And we're all going to the Sporty on Friday night. I'm getting the bus with Sarah.'

'To the Sports Centre?'

'Yeah.'

'You know, Claire, it might be an idea if you asked me first.'

'But you'd say yes, wouldn't you? I wish we didn't live in the country. Stephen lives in Dingwall, all the rest do except Sarah and me. We're the only ones who have to get the school bus.'

'Pretty empty bus, then.'

'Mum – you know what I mean. Everybody else goes down the street after school, and I've got to get on the boring school bus. Can I go to Auntie Marion's, and then you could collect me later?'

'No. Marion's too ill. She's got enough to cope with at the moment.'

'I wouldn't be a nuisance or anything. She's not, like, really ill, is she?'

What should Eleanor say? 'It's the treatment. It's making her feel pretty sick.'

'Oh. Right.' Claire turned away and went out.

Later, Eleanor sat on Gavin's sofa, curled up beside him, and worried aloud.

'She's had all the talks at school, and I've spoken to her about . . . boys, you know. But she seems keen on this one. That's never happened before. There was always just a crowd . . . they go around together.'

'You think she's going to have sex, is that it?'

'No! God, I hope not. She's fourteen, for heaven's sake.'

'Sauce for the goose,' he teased, grinning, kissing her ear. 'They start young, these days.'

What sort of example am I? Eleanor wondered, lying in Gavin's bed, knowing she would have to go in a minute, that Claire would be home from Sarah's, or school, or the disco, or that she'd have to get up and drive to fetch her. She was always leaving Gavin in the flush of warm vulnerability that comes after sex, tender and even a bit sore, with the ache of good love-making. Then she had to be dressed, and sensible, a mother, a good woman.

Everything they did together had an edge of danger to it, like something about to end, that must be made the most of, intense and temporary and full of wishing. Soon he would leave again, and she would be alone for at least two weeks. She would go back to her evening class, spend more time with Marion, keep a closer eye on Claire. It was time, anyway, they drew back a bit. He left it later and later to put the condom on, had moved inside her once or twice before he did. And she had let him. The risk was hers as much as his. How could she advise Claire, when she was so foolish herself? No, a break would be all right this time. It was needed. She would relax, start eating properly again. And she would not wait, long for him, think about him all the time. It was exhausting.

But when she went to see Marion the next afternoon, it was not to comfort and cheer her sister, it was to stop herself fretting that Gavin would be gone in a couple of days. She despised herself, knowing this, knowing what she wanted was to have Marion comfort *her*.

From an upstairs window, Marion saw Eleanor's car turn into the drive. She was in Ross's bedroom, sorting out old clothes, some of which were not even fit for the jumble sale. Her friend Lynn had called in the morning, going the rounds for the school Spring Fair.

'They've given me the jumble stall,' she had said, drinking Marion's coffee and scattering shortbread crumbs.

'I'll have a look—' Marion began.

'It's OK – I didn't want you to think I'd missed you out, you know, not bothered telling you about it. But nobody expects you to do anything this time.' She got up, brushing the last of the crumbs from her skirt. 'Righty oh. I'll get on to Sue's – she said she had masses of Shona's old things.'

'I'll go through my wardrobe,' Marion promised. 'It's time I had a clearout. And Ross's chest of drawers – I haven't tackled that for ages.'

So this was what she was doing, when she heard Eleanor's car. But she had not got very far, and had had to sit on the bed anyway, unable to stand for very long. She would save her own wardrobe for later, when she felt better. This was not a good day. For the last twenty minutes, she had done nothing but stare into space, not even listening to the Radio 4 play murmuring on beside her. She had been thinking about her body, and how it seemed less and less familiar, her own.

She went down with relief to greet her sister.

'You're not well,' Eleanor said.

'I'm all right.'

Eleanor followed her upstairs. 'What are you doing?'

'Oh, Lynn was here, about the school fair. She's organising the jumble stall. You can help me sort through Ross's stuff – I don't seem to be getting on very fast.'

But all they did was sit in the bedroom together, surrounded by football and rock star posters, amid a litter of school books, computer disks and chewed pens. And Eleanor talked. Marion, though unable to care very much about anything external just now, was glad to be distracted from herself.

'I wouldn't worry about Claire having a boyfriend,' she said. 'It doesn't seem to amount to much, at that age.'

'I think it's more myself I'm worried about, really,' Eleanor said. 'Having a boyfriend at my age.'

'Is that what he is?'

'Well, I don't know what else you could call him.'

'Is it getting serious then?'

Eleanor reddened. 'It's quite . . . intense.'

Marion thought with relief of Fergus, and how easy it was when you had been together for years. I would not have the energy, she thought, for all that emotion and uncertainty. Even if I felt well. And yet Eleanor had an edgy beauty just now that Marion could not help but admire, and would have envied, had it been possible to feel something so negative for her sister.

'Oh well,' Eleanor said, 'we'll see how things go.' She looked at Marion's tired, sad face, Marion who was trying so hard to be helpful, and normal. 'Come on,' she said, 'let's go downstairs and have a cup of tea. I've got an idea.'

'What's that?'

'I'll take the girls to Aberdeen at Easter. Gavin will be offshore till the second week of the holidays, so I'll take them to Pitcairn, and we'll visit the aunts, and shop, and go to the pictures. That would give you a break, wouldn't it? With just Fergus and Ross here? I'd take Ross too, if he'd come. What do you think?'

'They'd like it,' Marion said, considering. 'I think Ross is going to have to work though, with Highers coming up.'

'Would *you* like it? Would you like to have the house to yourself for a few days?'

'Oh . . .' Marion could not make decisions like this any longer. She was afraid to let the children out of her sight, wanted them all at home. And yet, when they were, she was exhausted, and longed for peace. 'All right,' she said at last. 'We'll ask them.'

That evening, lying in Gavin's arms, conscious that soon he would be gone again, Eleanor thought of how going to Pitcairn would help to fill the empty days before he came back. She was doing this for herself, not Marion, and was ashamed to admit it.

'What are you thinking about?' he asked. 'You've got tense again.'

'Have I?'

'Relax, cuddle in. Claire's at her friend's, you said, and we've got at least another hour.'

'It's not that.'

'What then?' He held her tighter. 'Not sex?'

'What?'

'You didn't come.'

'Well, sometimes I don't. I thought, after that first time, you know, that was it. I'd made it, made the switch, it would always happen. But it seems to depend on other things too.' Eleanor nestled closer, tucked one leg between his, stroked his belly, feeling him quiver beneath her touch.

'Want to try again?'

'To tell you the truth, I don't mind. It doesn't matter now. It mattered much more when I thought I couldn't. Now, loving is so . . . varied, isn't it? Not just orgasms, big waves. It's what you give, take from each other, the surprise of it. That's what makes it so . . .'

'Wonderful?'

'Well, yes.'

'You do great things for my ego,' he said, and laughed.

On the day before he left, a blustery March afternoon, they walked down by the side of the firth together, and watched a pair of swans lead their cygnets in file through grey, glistening water. Where the path was wide enough, he took her hand and walked beside her. At the ruined salmon bothies, they paused and sat on the broad step in front of one of them, turning their collars up against the wind. Above them, a bird of prey hovered, then flapped slowly away.

'Look!' He showed her. 'A red kite, I do believe. Amazing. Yes, it is.'

'How can you tell?'

'It had a forked tail. That's how you tell a kite, even at a distance.'

'Forked?'

'Yes.'

She buried her face in his jacket, slid her arms round him, pulled tight. 'You're my red kite,' she said, foolish with love.

'One more night,' he said, 'then I fly off.'

Eleanor had often been lonely when Claire stayed away overnight with friends. Now she was glad when it happened. This time, on his last night, Gavin came to her house, something he rarely did, and Eleanor thought of how the smell of him, his imprint and warmth, would remain in her sheets after he had gone.

'Tell me,' he said, as they lay close after love-making, ready to talk again.

'Tell you what?'

'What happened.'

'I don't know what you mean.'

'When your husband died.'

'No. It doesn't matter. I don't think about it any more.'

This was a lie. Gavin, guessing as much, did not persist.

'Let me make you come,' he murmured, his mouth coming down on her breast. 'I love it when you come, all that moaning.'

'Stop – I have already. I couldn't possibly again – oh, Gavin.'

'Yes, you could.'

Am I a kind of test for him? she wondered. Is he proving how good he is in bed? He was always so pleased with himself.

'No,' she said. 'Really.' And pushed him away, her mood changing, her body tensing again.

'What's wrong?'

'Nothing.'

It was because he was leaving. Can I bear this, she thought, the leaving and coming back, the empty gaps between, all this intense glorious sex when he's here . . . the uncertainty when he's not? He moved over her and came inside again, lazily, without urgency, and she let him, but not moving much.

'Don't you ever get tired of it,' she asked, 'sex?'

'Never tired of you,' he told her, and she gave way again, longing for this to be true, yielding, moving with him.

'I wish you didn't have to go.'

'Me too,' he said. 'Got to do something about this.' He slid away, and they lay side by side.

Later in the night, she realised they were both awake, and

she was part of him before she had time to think, was with him half in and half out of sleep. Suddenly, in the dark, it was easy to say what had seemed impossible an hour before.

'Just don't hate me,' she said. 'If I tell you.'

'Tell me what?'

'You might hate me. But if I don't say it now, I'll never have the courage again. And if you don't hate me, then—'

'Then things are OK, is that what you mean? We're OK?'

'Well . . .'

'I won't hate you, of course I won't, whatever you say. But I can't make promises about the future, if that's what you want. How could I, with my history? I'm not a man to rely on. You know that.'

The world gave way, and she lost courage. 'I know.'

'But—' He got up on one elbow, and switched on the bedside lamp. 'Look, if it's any good to you, I want to get a job onshore. I want to see you more. I don't want this to end.'

That was enough. In relief, she turned to him, and told him what no one but David knew, what even Marion had been left to guess at, the only thing Marion did not know.

'It was my fault Ian died,' she said. She saw him again, coming down the stairs in their four-bedroom detached house, their house with the big windows and square of garden, its gleaming bathrooms, pine fitted kitchen. Our model house, our model marriage, she thought. Ian, white as paper, holding on to the door as he appeared in the living room; David, making her laugh so much she was weak with it. Music playing. She and David were both drunk, had been fooling about all evening. Ian, irritable and remote, disliking David, had not wanted him there for Hogmanay. Ian, in the doorway, said he was going to bed.

'Stay up and see the New Year in,' Eleanor had urged him.

'Have a drink – after all, it's your whisky.' David in high good humour, at his worst. Now she thought of this as being his worst. Then, all she had thought was that David made her laugh, and she was comfortable with him; he was funny and good to be with. After Ian's silences, his distant absorption in work.

But he had reappeared just before midnight, still dressed, his shirt collar open, holding on to the door.

'Good!' David had cried. 'Good man – changed your mind – see the New Year in – have a dram.'

Silence. As if they all held their breath. Then Ian had turned away, saying nothing, had gone back upstairs. Much later, going up to bed herself, Eleanor found him lying fully dressed on their bed. It was cold in the room. His eyes were open, but there was something strange about his breathing.

'I was so drunk,' she said to Gavin. 'I didn't realise – I thought he must have had a bottle upstairs, had a drink himself. I could smell gin. And I thought he was annoyed with me, and I was fed up. After all, I'd only been having a drink with my brother.'

Ian turning to her, saying, 'Do you think I should call the doctor?'

'At Hogmanay?' Her own careless, incredulous voice.

'In the end,' she said to Gavin, 'I think I dozed off. We both did. When I woke again, Ian was gasping, he could hardly breathe, he couldn't speak to me. I flew to the phone, called an ambulance right away. I was panicking. There was this pain in my own chest, this terrible pain, as if my heart was hurting too – I still get that pain. And he was lying there, and I kept running back and speaking to him, telling him the doctor was coming, he'd be all right.'

She was crying now, sobbing into her hands. 'I did something as soon as I realised, I did.'

Gavin took her hands away from her face, held them. 'What happened?'

'He died. He died in the ambulance, on the way to hospital. I was there, but the medics, they were in the way, I couldn't see him properly – he died.' She went on crying, the tears pouring down her face, soaking into the sheet. 'Claire was with David, I'd left her in the house, she was just little. She was just a little girl, she hadn't even wakened.'

'Stop crying, it's over, you're all right, Eleanor.' He held her tight, but she went on crying, shaking in his arms, sobbing. He held her, waited.

When he thought she could speak to him, he said, 'When was this? When did it happen?'

'Five . . . more than five years ago.'

He did not reply at once. When she was still, exhausted, leaning against him, he said, 'It's long enough. You should stop now.'

Eleanor moved away a little, reaching for the box of tissues, and blew her nose. She felt cold, out of his embrace.

'Don't look at me,' she said. 'My face – all that crying.'

'You look at me,' he ordered her. 'Come on. Look at me.' But she could not. So he sat up with her, and took her hand. The other hand squeezed the paper tissue, soaked with tears.

'It's long enough,' he repeated. 'Five years. You should stop now. Stop hanging on to all that pointless guilt.'

Easy enough for him to say, who seemed to carry no guilt at all. But still, something had eased, though she hardly knew what. Just the relief, the emptiness, after such a bout of crying, was something.

'You don't hate me?'

'I said let it go. All that guilt – what does it do, except mess up the life you've got now?'

Eleanor lay back, cold tears sliding over her cheeks. 'Oh, I don't know. I don't deserve to be happy.'

'Crap,' he scoffed. 'Even if you'd been stone cold sober he'd have had the heart attack, and it must have been a pretty massive one. Something like that – if the guy was going to cop it, he'd have done it anyway.'

'But that's not the point! I should—'

'For Christ's sake, Eleanor, we've all got things we *should* have done.'

She saw, her heart beating fast and hard, that he really did not take the view she did. He did not think her to blame. He had not been there, of course, and so could not share the horror, as David had. But still, it was a relief, that he looked at it so differently. He was wrong. Even Eleanor, so used to being in the wrong herself, knew that. But she would not argue with him. It was enough to know that someone else did not think her to blame.

It would not last, this thing with Gavin. How could it? Why should she be happy? She did not deserve it. And yet, for the first time, she did begin to think it possible.

In the early hours, she woke and felt the weight on her again, of the grievous past. Then, like a cloud from the moon, it lifted, and she moved closer to him, sharing his warmth. Unconscious, he murmured, changed position, laid one heavy arm across her body, pinning her to him. Outside, a shadow seemed to pass across the window, fleeting and black.

17

Faith came at once, on the first train there was after New Year.

'Who will I get, who do you want?' David had asked Eleanor when she called him from the hospital.

'You'll have to give Claire her breakfast,' she said. 'She likes banana on toast.'

'I know that,' he told her. 'It was my idea.'

'Yes. Yes, right.'

'Eleanor, will I come to the hospital? I don't want you to be on your own. I'll ring Barbara, she'll take Claire, she won't mind it being early. I'll come to the hospital, will I?' His voice rose, trembling.

'It's all right. I'm all right.'

She was very calm, standing in the sister's office in Accident and Emergency, looking through glass at the rows of plastic chairs filled with the waiting injured, casualties of other New Year celebrations gone wrong, with their black eyes and possible fractures. They sat brooding, vacant, looking the way people must in Purgatory, if such a place exists, Eleanor thought, hardly aware yet that she had entered its gates herself.

Ian was still in one of the cubicles, covered by a sheet. They had given up trying to resuscitate him, so the noise and panic were over, the cubicle empty, the trolleys and equipment removed. In a little while, they would take him down to the hospital mortuary. But Eleanor was very calm. Soon, she would wake to find herself in bed at home, Ian still breathing beside her, the nightmare over. When it happens, she told her mother later, you do not believe it. It cannot be true, so you do not believe it.

'Mum,' she said to David on the telephone. 'Get Mum.'

'Oh *God.*'

'What?'

'No, you're right, you're right. It's the thought of telling them, telling everybody.'

'I'll do it then,' Eleanor said. 'Don't worry about it.'

'No – Christ, it's the least – I'll ring Mum and Dad.'

Eleanor longed for her mother. If anyone could put things right now, it would be Faith.

In the days between Ian's death and the funeral, Eleanor went on being calm, letting her mother guide her through the registration, funeral arrangements, dealing with the bank, the solicitor, the business of death. She sat with Claire on her knee, or close by her, holding her daughter, neither of them weeping. Then Faith arranged to take Claire to Barbara's house every afternoon. Barbara gave her tea, and she played with Hannah, not thinking of death, or her father.

'Children are protected by being young,' Faith said. 'Let her play – keep things as normal as possible for her.'

'I will. I am trying.'

The funeral director had asked Eleanor to bring some clothes for Ian – whatever she liked. Some people, he said, wore suits, others casual clothes. This was the only thing which brought Eleanor to the edge of hysteria.

'What will I do?' she asked David. Their mother was in the kitchen, preparing a meal; Claire was helping her. David and Eleanor sat in the living room in front of the gas fire, he with a tumbler of whisky in his hand.

'Well, it doesn't matter, does it?' David shrugged. 'I mean, if he's going to be cremated, who the hell cares what he's wearing?' He laughed. 'It's bizarre – dressing up the guy in his best suit in a bloody coffin.'

Eleanor started to laugh too. 'But it's what he wore,' she said. 'He was happy wearing a suit. Work, that's what he liked best. Work. Not me, not Claire. Oh God.'

She was shaking, her hands were shaking as if with some terrible palsy. David was off his chair and on the floor next to her, his hands gripping hers, his hands warm and strong on her cold ones, making her still again.

'Don't talk about it,' she warned, her hand touching his face, his mouth. 'I don't want to talk about it.'

So they did not talk.

Later, it was to her mother that Eleanor said, 'I could not have managed without you. I could not have got through it.'

'It was a terrible thing,' Faith said. 'A terrible thing to happen.' She did not say, then or ever, you are young, you will recover, knowing better than to offer this cheap comfort. But Eleanor knew her mother believed she would marry again, and indeed ought to. And though they were so close in the weeks after Ian's death, Eleanor did not once confide the reason why this was impossible. She wanted her mother to think well of her. Once, longing for a reassurance she knew she could not have, she said, 'I feel it's my fault. I should have known something was wrong, realised sooner.'

Her mother had scotched this swiftly, looking up at her tall daughter, smoothing her hair back as she had done when Eleanor was a child, ill or fretful. 'Now,' she said, 'don't torture yourself with that. Sudden death always makes us think of the things we should have done. No one's perfect, but you were a good wife to him, Eleanor.'

Eleanor accepted the comfort, submitted to the falsehood, for her mother's sake, her mother's good opinion. She and David, not talking about it, shared the truth, and the guilt.

At Ian's funeral, the crematorium was packed. He was local; his parents were still active in the community; he worked for a large company. And he was young.

'Did Daddy know all these people?' Claire asked, her hand held tight in her mother's, feeling the slippery stuff of the glove next to her own woollen one.

'Yes,' Eleanor said.

'Do *you* know them all?'

'Some.' But not all that many, she realised. This was Ian's home – his place, not hers. Soon, they were coming out of the crematorium, without the coffin now, without Ian, to stand by Ian's parents and sister, shake everyone by the hand, and thank these strangers for coming. Suddenly, it occurred to Eleanor that she did not have to stay on in the house she now owned outright, but did not love. She did not even have to stay in England.

After everyone had gone home, Marion and Fergus first, then eventually her mother, David offered to stay on, but she did not want him. They were edgy with each other, he irritated her. The guilt she had been able to keep at bay (because her mother was there), invaded further each day, and David's presence made it worse. 'I'll go,' he said, and she thought he meant back to London. But it was months before she heard from him again. Eventually, meeting a friend of his at Victoria Station, quite by chance, she heard that he was somewhere in the Middle East, working for a multi-national company. The friend did not know what he was doing, and had no address.

Eleanor was in limbo. The friends and family who had surrounded her before and after the funeral no longer telephoned or called round every day. They all went back to their own unchanged lives. She had gone on rearranging and tidying the flowers, but now the last vase, the last florist's basket, had been emptied. Pale and modest after the extravagance of lilies and carnations, a few early daffodils were coming into bud in the garden. Eleanor did not cut them. Ian's parents, stiff with grief through the early weeks, had their routines to return to: bridge, golf, the brisk and undemanding tasks of the newly retired. These kept them going. Eleanor, who had liked Ian's family without ever feeling connected to them, was increasingly reluctant to visit, even to ring them up. They had nothing now to talk about together except Ian. There was Claire of course, it helped that there was Claire. They showered her with presents, gifts of money. Then, in March, they went on a long-planned visit to their other son, James, who lived in Australia with his family.

I will never see James again, Eleanor thought, remembering the breezy man at her wedding, eight years older than Ian, coarser-featured, but with the same blue eyes, thick-lashed. Ian had often said they would go to Melbourne one day, on a long visit. Eleanor, who had not much cared whether they ever did, now felt cheated of the trip.

She was full of irrational, contradictory emotions. They beat about inside her like trapped birds, uncomfortable and frightening. She had no defence against them, since she had not even a routine to go back to, as everyone else had. When the other women got in their cars and drove to the station to meet their husbands, Eleanor and Claire stayed at home. Their days did not begin and end in the same way now.

In early spring, the lightening and lengthening of the days, the thin daffodils, and the orange specks of opening crocuses along the edge of the garden path, did not give her hope, as she knew they were supposed to do. *It will never end*, she thought. Spring after spring without him, and no chance, ever, to put things right, to make him love her as she had longed to be loved, no chance to love him back.

Then, at Easter, Marion came down again, to stay for a few days with the children. 'I wish we lived closer to each other,' she said. 'Phone calls aren't enough – especially now.'

'I've been thinking of moving back north.' Eleanor spoke tentatively, wondering what Marion would think about this. But her sister's face lit up at once.

'Aberdeen? Or were you thinking maybe the Highlands?'

'Well, yes. Near you. What do you think?'

'I would love it,' Marion said. She turned her head to look out of the French windows. In Eleanor's suburban garden, gay with daffodils, Claire was pushing Eilidh on her swing.

'Yes,' Eleanor said, 'I was thinking of them.'

She was thinking too, that in another place, it might not matter that she was single. Here, in the spreading housing estate, lived complete families, with working men and young mothers. In the summer, she would be the only woman who did not have a husband out washing the car on Sundays, or trimming the hedge.

'Well then,' Marion said, 'I'd better start looking for a house for you.'

'A small one,' Eleanor suggested. 'I want to keep as much money spare as I can, to live on until Claire doesn't need me to be at home.'

Already, Marion was moving through streets and villages in her mind, finding somewhere suitable for Eleanor and Claire.

The next day, Eleanor put her house on the market. I will go home, she decided, and although she had never lived in the Highlands, and stayed with Marion only for brief holidays and over Christmas, she knew where she wanted to be. She pictured the little market town where Marion lived, with its Victorian houses, and the new estates spreading up the hill behind. On the other side, dividing the town from the Black Isle, was the Cromarty Firth. I will have a home with a view of the Firth, she thought. I can look out at the water every day, and hear the wild geese talking and talking, as they gather overhead, telling each other the story of their own homecoming.

18

In the first week of the Easter holidays, Eleanor took Claire and Eilidh to Pitcairn. Kirsty went to stay with Fergus's mother. Lambing had begun, and the Macleods at the farm were having grandchildren to stay. Marion would be driven to the hospital for her fifth treatment by her friend Sue.

'I feel bad leaving you,' Eleanor said.

'It's time Eilidh had a break,' Marion told her. 'I'll be all right. Fergus is taking some time off next week when you're back, so the holidays are all taken care of.'

'I'll ring you from Pitcairn.' She hugged Marion, and her sister, who had always been glossy with health, felt fragile in her arms, skin dry, hair thin and brittle, bones sharp beneath the skin. Eleanor drew back, afraid of hurting her. *I ache all over*, Marion had confessed. *My bones seem to ache.*

At Pitcairn, Eleanor cleaned the kitchen, vacuumed the hall and stairs, and stocked up the store cupboards. The weather was fine, and she worked with her father in the garden. She wanted the days to be full and busy, so that she would not fret about Marion, or long for Gavin too much. Claire and Eilidh lay in bed till noon, ran baths that used all the hot water, watched videos, and painted their nails. All the time, they talked in low voices, and giggled, stopping at once when they thought anyone else could hear them.

On the Wednesday, Eleanor drove up to town, taking

them with her. They were to go round clothes shops, spend saved-up birthday and Christmas money, and buy their lunch in McDonald's. Eleanor impressed upon them several times the importance of being at the arranged meeting place at three o'clock. 'Mum – we know.' Claire exclaimed, 'Stop going on about it.' They clambered out of the car and waved goodbye. In the rearview mirror Eleanor watched them disappear into the crowd. Then the lights changed, and she drove on, making her way up Union Street, the broad, traffic-laden road through the centre of the city, heading for the part of town where Mamie and Alice still lived, near the Duthie Park.

She went in with apologies for being without the girls. Mamie was out, but Alice was busy in the kitchen. She looked white and tired, and seemed thinner. Eleanor briefly laid her smooth cheek against her aunt's dry one. Alice began to get out the cutlery for their meal.

'Now then,' she said, 'I'd maybe best say a word.'

'Is something wrong?'

'Nothing wrong.'

'Are you ill?'

'Me? I'm fine.' Alice was annoyed; she banged the soup spoons down on the tray.

'I'm sorry. I thought—'

'Mamie's just away to the shop for a packet of crackers to go with the cheese. She forgot them yesterday.' She looked directly at Eleanor. 'Her memory's not so good, these days.'

'Oh well, I suppose . . .' Eleanor wanted to say, 'she's getting old,' but Alice was even older. How could you put it, without offending them? Alice was straight-backed, independent; she finished her crossword every day, read history and biography, attended the Women's Guild, sang in the church choir. But Mamie?

'It's getting to the point when she doesn't keep a thing in her head for five minutes together. But ask her about what

she wore to the kirk on Easter Sunday twenty year ago!'
Alice sounded more irritated than concerned. 'I just hope
this is not the beginning of something. You know what I
mean. It's nae easy to live with.'

The front door opened and closed: Mamie was back. She
greeted Eleanor with exclamations of delight, and began
emptying her basket onto the table. There was a smell of
soup now, hot and savoury, as it came to the boil. Alice
stirred, turning down the gas, watching Mamie.

'Where's the crackers?'

A loaf of bread, a packet of butter and several boxes of
matches lay on the table. Mamie looked up, flustered. 'Would
you credit it? I've forgotten the very thing I went out for.'

'It doesn't matter,' Eleanor broke in. 'I'm always doing
that – going upstairs, then having to come back down to
remember what it was I went for.'

'Ach, I'm getting old.'

'I'll serve up the soup,' Alice said. 'Eleanor, the plates are
just beside you.'

Eleanor handed them one at a time, then carried them
through to the chilly dining room on a tray. Mamie had
disappeared to take off her hat and coat.

'She'll be upstairs,' Alice said. 'I'll cry her.'

Mamie appeared at the top of the stairs. 'Oh, is it dinner-
time? You should have telt me.'

The soup was good; Alice had made it. Eleanor wondered
what Mamie did with herself now, apart from knitting. They
had oatcakes with the cheese, and Eleanor explained (for
the third time) where the girls were, and when she was
meeting them.

'Now then,' Mamie said, 'I'll clear away, and make a cuppie
coffee – would you like that, Eleanor?'

'Lovely. Can I help?'

'No, no, I can manage fine. You away through to the living
room – the fire's on.'

It was sunny in the room at the front of the house. Eleanor, despite the soup, had got chilled in the north-facing dining room, and walked about, looking at all the familiar things: the Hummel figures, the faded watercolours. She could hear Alice and Mamie in the kitchen, going through the business of making coffee, opening biscuit tins. Water ran, and the dishes were washed, since it was best to get them cleared. And yet, Eleanor thought, they have nothing to do for the rest of the day. Why don't they leave them? I'll have to go soon.

She lingered by the sideboard, which was crowded with family photographs. David, Marion and herself, through several stages of childhood; their graduation photographs, holding rolls of cardboard to represent degree certificates, and wearing gowns that looked silly and false now, to Eleanor. Marion's wedding photograph (how plump and young she looked, and Fergus's hair quite long, his fringe shaggy), and then her own. Ian handsome and stern, herself flushed and excited. What an adventure I thought it would be, she realised, marrying him, moving to England, a new life. She picked up the photograph and studied it. *I am so different now.* She set it down next to one of David on his first two-wheeler bicycle, which he and Stanley had taken turns riding down the lane, the other one running beside it. One of them (neither would say who) had quite soon ridden it into the ditch, twisting the handlebars and scratching the chrome.

Mamie came in with the tray of coffee cups and biscuits.

'Now dear,' she said, when she had established again whether Eleanor took sugar and milk, 'you haven't told us about Marion. How's she getting on with this treatment? Is it going to last much longer?'

But Eleanor had told them about Marion when they sat down to eat. Alice, coming in and hearing this, caught Eleanor's eye, and shook her head slightly. Eleanor sat down with her cup of milky coffee, accepted a biscuit, and carefully, told Mamie again about Marion.

'Dear me, poor lass.' Mamie began brushing crumbs busily from her cardigan, to hide her distress. She is old, Eleanor thought, and she's failing a bit, I can see that. A surge of pity for Mamie, who was growing vaguer and more muddled as Alice grew harder and sharper, obliterated everything for a moment.

As she drove back into town to collect Eilidh and Claire, Eleanor was newly aware of her own vigour, electric and powerful. She was on the threshold of something. She felt strong, ready for whatever it was. It would happen, the new life to come. Before he had left, Gavin had said again that he was thinking of applying for a job onshore. 'There are two or three coming up. And to tell the truth, I've about had it with living like this.' This meant he wanted to be with her. Thinking of this, she grew warm with love and relief.

'Are we going to see Auntie Mamie and Auntie Alice?' Claire wanted to know as Eleanor walked with them to the car park.

'No, back to Pitcairn.'

'Aw – I wanted to see them as well.'

'I thought you wanted to shop.'

'We did, but I wish we'd gone with you now.'

'What about you, Eilidh?' Eleanor asked. 'We'd planned to go home tomorrow, though.'

Eilidh shrugged. 'I don't mind.'

She looked tired, Eleanor thought. 'Are you all right?'

'I feel a bit sick.'

'Back to Grandpa's then, eh?'

As soon as they reached Pitcairn, Eilidh said, 'Can I ring Mum?'

'Of course you can.'

Marion said she was fine, resting a lot, but Eilidh went on being quiet.

Later, alone with her father in the garden, Eleanor said, 'Probably just as well we're heading back tomorrow. Eilidh seems a bit peaky – I think she's sickening for home. For Marion.'

'Aye, maybe.' John held a branch of forsythia in one hand, and clipped it with his secateurs. In the wheelbarrow behind him was a pile of prunings. Eleanor took the rake and hauled it over the herbaceous border they were tackling, gathering up plant debris, dead leaves. The air smelt of spring, and was shrill with birdsong.

Everything is coming to life again, Eleanor thought, and Marion will soon start to get better. She must. Then she thought of Mamie and Alice, and stopped, looking round at her father.

'Mamie's getting forgetful,' she said. 'I think it annoys Alice.'

'Old age. She's just absent-minded. And Alice never had much patience. By God, d'ye see that?' Something hopped away suddenly through the shrubs, and he was after it. 'Bloody rabbits! Ye canna keep them out.'

Eleanor picked up the handles of the wheelbarrow and went to empty it into the bonfire they were making. When her father joined her, having lost the rabbit, she said, 'Will I make us a cup of tea?'

'Aye lass, grand.' He grasped the wheelbarrow. 'I'll be in in a minute.'

Eleanor went slowly up the garden. At the back door she turned to take off her muddy boots and leave them outside. Holding on to the lintel with one hand, she eased off first one, then the other. Straightening up, she looked back down the garden to see where her father was. The evening sun was low in the sky, and at first she was dazzled, giddy with bending, seeing only the translucent pink-edged blue of the sky, and the black silhouettes of the two lilac trees on either side of the path, branches just touching overhead. Then, as her vision cleared, between the trees, just coming into bud, a figure moved. But it was not her father, it was someone slight, stooping a little, carrying a heavy bundle. Eleanor clutched the lintel of the door, her nails digging into flaking paint, and shut her eyes. When she opened them again, there was nothing moving by the lilac trees but a blackbird, flying up between.

The following morning, they drove home, going over to the Black Isle before returning to Dingwall, so that they could collect Kirsty from her grandmother's house. As they went through Munlochy, they saw the first of the spring tourist coaches stopped by the spreading tree they knew as the Clootie Well.

'Look,' Claire said, 'there's people at the tree. Do they know about making a wish?'

'I expect the bus driver has told them the story.'

The place was familiar. Water from an underground spring gushed through a pipe onto mossy stone. Above, every branch and twig of the spreading tree was hung with hundreds of strips of cloth, fastened there over several generations, each one attached with a wish, a prayer. Over the years, the rags had grown dirty and matted, packed layer upon layer until time and weather had stiffened them into permanency. The sight disgusted Eleanor; she could not imagine wanting to hang there any shred of material she had once held dear.

'Do the wishes come true?' Claire persisted. 'Do you know anyone it worked for?' Eilidh did; she had a fund of stories.

When the girls had gone up to the farm with Kirsty, to inspect new lambs, Nan Munro and Eleanor had tea, and talked about Marion. Nan was as old as Alice, but she seemed younger, still brisk and motherly. Eleanor could see she was disturbed about Marion, though she spoke calmly enough.

'We'll see how she goes when all this treatment's finished.'

She stood with Eleanor in sunshine at her back door, watching the girls as they came down the track from the farm, Kirsty skipping from one side to the other, a long way behind the others.

'Right,' Eleanor said as they reached her, 'let's get you all home.'

Kirsty was breathless with running to catch up. She flung her arms round her grandmother, who stood still, submitting to this, and smoothing Kirsty's hair away from her face.

'Now mind,' she said, 'you're to be a good girl for Mummy when you get home.'

'Claire says we can make a wish at the Clootie Well,' Kirsty announced. 'To make Mummy better.'

Eleanor and Nan Munro looked at each other.

'Ah well,' the grandmother said, easing the child's arms away from her. 'Anything's worth a try.'

On the way back, Kirsty wanted to stop by the tree.

'I've got nothing with me that we could use,' Eleanor told her. 'It has to be something . . . a piece of material, whatever, that has a meaning, a value for you.'

'Can we do it though?' Claire asked. 'Get something, and tie it on next time we come past?'

'Yes, if you like.'

Eilidh looked out of the window, saying nothing.

At home, Marion had found the days long on her own, and though she had tried to be grateful for the rest, was almost tearful with relief when she saw Eleanor's car turn into the drive.

'How was Dad?' she asked, when she and Eleanor eventually sat down to talk.

'Fine. Pretty good. But I saw Mamie and Alice yesterday. Alice looks tired, quite unwell. And Mamie doesn't remember anything for two minutes together.'

'They're getting old.'

'They *are* old, Marion. Like an old married couple, in some ways. Get on each other's nerves, but devoted really.'

'Do you think so?' Marion was doubtful. 'I always thought what a pity it was Mamie never married again. She should have had children, a life of her own. Not just stuck with Alice, like a kind of glorified housekeeper.'

'Perhaps. But what about you – how have you been?'

Marion managed a smile. 'One more night in hospital,' she said. 'Then the scan a few weeks after that. So if it's all right then . . . maybe they won't do any more.'

'You mean no radiotherapy?'

'I hope not.'

'You've had enough, haven't you?'

'I'm OK.'

But she was not, Eleanor could see that, could see how far she had travelled without her even in the few days she had been at Pitcairn.

'I'm sorry. I'm sorry I went away now.'

'No, you were right. You mustn't feel you have to hang round me all the time. I'm not much company, anyway.' Marion did not want to talk about symptoms and aches. 'Tell me about Gavin,' she said. 'Have you spoken to him?'

'Not since I went to Aberdeen But I told him I'd be back tonight. He'll probably call.' Eleanor flushed, warm with the thought of this, but could not talk about it till she had been home and spoken to him again.

'You know what the girls want to do?' she asked, turning the subject. 'That awful tree at Munlochy with all the rags hanging on it – the Clootie Well. Claire calls it the Wishing Tree. It's a tinkers' place, isn't it?'

'What about it?'

'Kirsty wants to hang a piece of cloth on it and wish for you to get better.'

'Oh, I suppose every little helps,' Marion said, smiling.

'I told her it had to be something you were sort of attached to. Not any old dish cloth.'

'Well, now.' Marion was thinking about this. Then, with more energy than Eleanor had seen her muster for weeks, she got up out of her chair. 'Oh – oh. I did that too quickly.'

'What is it? Do you want me to get something?'

'Well, all right. Upstairs, in my chest of drawers, top left. Where my bras and knickers are – underneath at the back, in a piece of tissue paper.' She sank back into her chair. 'Would you mind?'

'No, of course not. What is it?'

'Wait and see. I wonder if you'll recognise it.'

Eleanor went up to Marion's bedroom. Fergus's cord trousers over a chair, books on the floor, the window open to spring air, flowered curtains fluttering a little in the breeze. No sign that anything was different, or that anyone was ill, threatened. But on the bedside cabinet, on her side of the bed, Marion's bottles of tablets. Eleanor looked away, and went to hunt in the drawer.

Under the cotton and silk, the pretty, sensible underwear, the special brassieres with their pocket for the prosthesis she knew Marion disliked and resented, Eleanor's fingers found the rustle of tissue paper, and she drew out a small flat packet. When she opened it up, twelve inches or so of lace ribbon, creamy and a little brittle with age, slipped out and lay across her hand. Why had Marion kept it – from her wedding dress, a christening robe? Then Eleanor remembered, and knew. It was the tinker's piece of ribbon, sold to their mother years ago, when they were children. Marion had taken it away; the boys had played soldiers with the clothes pegs.

And the tinker woman had come back, to walk in their garden. Was she warning or reassuring, a prophet or just a hapless ghost? Eleanor's hand closed round the lace, rough against her skin.

'It's the bit of lace Mum got from that tinker woman,

isn't it?' she asked Marion, coming back into the living room.

'You did remember.'

'Oh yes.'

'I wonder what happened to her. She had a baby, didn't she?'

Eleanor's face darkened, and Marion said, with a spurt of fear that had no reason in it, 'What is it? Is something wrong? You don't mind giving it away, do you?'

'No, of course not. Get rid of it. Pity you hung on to it so long.'

She was not sure if Marion knew how the woman had died. At any rate, she would not talk to her about it just now, or tell her how she had come back, and walked in the garden at Pitcairn.

'Are you all right, Eleanor?'

'It's nothing, I'm just tired. All that driving. We'd better get home.'

'Poor you. Sorry, it was selfish of me to keep you.'

'I wanted to stay. I've missed you, Marion.'

'Well, it's not because I'm sparkling company at the moment, eh?' Marion smiled, coming to the door with Eleanor.

The hour had changed, so when Eleanor and Claire reached the cottage it was still daylight. They exclaimed over the tulips that had blossomed in front of the cottage in their absence, then they went in to unpack and have supper. In the evening, John Cairns telephoned.

'I've had a call from Mamie,' he said. 'Alice isn't too well. You don't like to bother the doctor at night, but maybe I should get Mamie to ring for him, eh?'

'What's wrong – what did Mamie say?'

'Just that Alice felt a bit faint, and went away to her bed.'

'Do you want me to phone them?'

'No, no. Mamie gets worked up about things these days. Probably just a cold coming on or something.'

'I don't know, Dad. I thought Alice didn't look well when I saw her the other day.'

'Och, I'm sorry I troubled you, lass. You've enough to worry about with Marion.'

'Look – get Mamie to ring the doctor just to ask his advice, if she's worried. She could do that, at least.'

'Aye, that's an idea. Maybe he'll tell her nae to be so daft.'

'I'll speak to you tomorrow,' Eleanor promised. 'See how she is.'

But when she called Pitcairn in the morning, around eleven, there was no reply. He'll be in the garden, she told herself, he won't hear the phone.

In the afternoon, her father called her. Alice had had a heart attack, and was in hospital. It's not the same thing, Eleanor told herself, I wasn't there. I told him to call the doctor. It wasn't up to me, it was up to Mamie. Mamie who had looked so vague and lost, and who for almost forty years, had let Alice make all the decisions. I told Dad to get the doctor. What else could I do? But the old sick feeling rose again, overwhelming, and the drum-beat in her head, my fault, my fault.

19

'Alice will be all right,' Marion said, when Eleanor called round later in the afternoon. 'She's tough.'

'I'll drive down and see her when Claire goes back to school,' Eleanor said. 'Just for the day.'

But Alice was not so tough, in the end. Who is, when it's the heart that fails, Eleanor wondered, realising she would have to pack for a funeral on the day Gavin was due onshore.

Claire, coming in from school on Tuesday afternoon to hear that Alice had died, cried a little, then said, 'Auntie Mamie will miss her, won't she?'

'Yes, she will.' Eleanor turned to the stove to check that her casserole was ready. 'It's on Friday at two, the funeral. We'll drive down in the morning, and come back the same day, so that Grandpa doesn't have to make up beds or anything.'

'Is Auntie Marion going?'

'Yes, we all are.'

'Eilidh and me came to Granny's funeral, didn't we? But Kirsty was too wee – is she coming this time?'

'Yes, she is.' Kirsty was the age Claire had been at her first funeral. Eleanor closed her eyes for a moment: the cold January day, Claire in her red coat and hat, because that was all she had to wear that was warm and smart. Like a jewel among all the black.

'Set the table, Claire.'

'What about Uncle David – is he coming?'

'I haven't managed to speak to him yet,' Eleanor admitted. 'Left a message on his answerphone. I'll try tonight.'

'At least you've got his phone number now,' Claire remarked, sitting down to eat.

In the evening, Eleanor called David again. It rang for a long time, but the answering service did not cut in, so she waited. Finally, David's voice.

'Hello?'

'David, it's me. I've got some bad news.'

'Marion—'

'No, no, she's all right. It's Aunt Alice.' A pause. The echo was there again, she heard it, heard David's voice in the light blue hall of her English house, saying to Marion, *Ian's dead*, saying it, letting people know, because she could not. And her father, much later, *It's your mother, Eleanor*. How do you tell people this?

'I'm sorry, David, I don't know how to – she had another heart attack. She died this morning.'

He would say something sympathetic, regretful, but that was all. He was so distant from them now; what could it mean to him that his eighty-year-old aunt was dead? But there was silence.

'She was still in hospital,' Eleanor went on. 'Poor Mamie's very upset, Dad says. I thought last time I was down that Alice—'

'Alice is dead?'

'Yes, her heart – you know she had a heart attack last week. Dad said he told you.'

'Yes, but he said she was all right, she was getting better.'

'Well, she was over eighty. I suppose her heart just couldn't take it. I'm sorry. Davy, are you all right?'

'Yes, of course I'm all right.' But his voice was hard.

'The funeral's on Friday at two. Their church near Holborn,

and then the crematorium. You could stay at Dad's if you like. We're all going back the same day to save making up beds. There'll be seven of us – no, eight – I think Fergus's mother is coming too.'

'I can't.'

'What?'

'Things are difficult here. Friday – I don't think so, Eleanor. Sorry.'

'But—'

'Sorry. Look, I'd better go. I've got someone here as it happens.'

'Davy—'

'I'll call you later. If I can get away.'

Marion, when Eleanor relayed all this to her, was impatient and annoyed.

'That's just typical. I mean, he wasn't particularly close to Alice, but for Dad's sake, he really should be there.'

'He did sound upset.'

'Not upset enough to put himself out, obviously.'

Eleanor, wanting to defend David, knew she could not. If Marion made the effort, exhausted as she was, surely he could be there? *Things are difficult here.* But they always were. Eleanor, with a flash of perception, realised the 'someone' with David had been a woman.

Gavin telephoned on the Thursday evening.

'My replacement's sick,' he said. 'I might not be able to come in till Saturday.'

'That's all right – I'm away tomorrow.' She explained what had happened. He sympathised, kindly but impersonally. An aunt who had lived over eighty years – you were sorry, but not shocked.

Eleanor kept thinking of Mamie, and how lost she would be without Alice. But perhaps she would get a new lease of life, blossom on her own. Once, she would have done, Eleanor realised, but it was probably too late now.

At the funeral, Mamie in navy blue with matching hat, was tearful, her face reddened and puckered in April sunshine. But she was composed, leaning on her cousin's arm, shaking hands at the door of the kirk. A small funeral, but not so small as Eleanor and Marion had expected. Alice had still had a busy life and there were several rows of people they did not know, most of them elderly women. A stooped old man, greeting John and Mamie as he went out, told them he had worked with Alice for thirty years. He looked round, his tortoise head and neck rising from black coat and stiff white shirt.

'Where's the boy?' he asked. 'Is the boy here?' John and Mamie looked at each other, and John said, 'No, he's working away.' The boy, Eleanor thought, going down the steps to the car, holding Claire's hand (the first time for years, Claire solemn and overawed), the boy is David.

Later, her father told her, 'That was Peter Simpson. He was the senior partner when Alice joined Simpson and Dalgarno. He must be well over ninety by now.'

'What about Dalgarno?' Eleanor asked, wondering about Alice's working life. An independent woman, at home in an office, efficient and indispensable. She could imagine that.

'Oh, he's been dead for years. Retired not long after Alice went there, I think. It was Fraser who was the other partner, Alex Fraser. And there was somebody else for a few years, another partner. Now that caused a bit of a furore. He left with more money than he was entitled to, went south.'

'What – he stole it?' Eleanor laughed. These old people, solicitors, respectable and dull. But one of them a rogue. Alice would have seen through him, though.

'Something a bit shady, anyway. But no action was taken, as I remember. Alice went on working there – it was nothing to do with Peter Simpson.'

'You mean they just sort of overlooked it? Embezzlement?'

Her father looked startled. 'What? Oh, it wasn't as bad as that.'

'But you said—'

'See if Mamie wants a hand, there's a good lass.' Her father got to his feet. They were back at Pitcairn by this time, and had been sitting, the two of them, on the bench at the back door. But it was getting chilly now the sun had gone in.

Mamie had waved them out of the kitchen, saying she would make tea. She had a fruit cake, she told them. They weren't to go off on that long journey home without a bit of cake. But when they went back into the house she was sitting by the table, still wearing her hat and coat, doing nothing.

'Are you all right?' Eleanor asked.

'Aye, I'm fine. A bittie tired, Eleanor. Still, no more traipsing up and down to the hospital.'

John left them to it, as Eleanor had known he would. She helped Mamie set out cups and saucers, and cut the cake.

'Are you going to be all right on your own?' Eleanor had noticed how Mamie's hands, plump and blue-veined, trembled as she poured milk into a jug.

'Mercy aye, lass.' She looked up and smiled. 'I'll miss her, Eleanor, but I can manage fine.'

'You could come and stay with me for a while, if you like.' Eleanor, moved by an impulse of pity, regretted the offer as soon as she had made it. Her tiny spare room, Gavin, the impossibility of concealing from Mamie what she was trying to keep from Claire. Suddenly, Eleanor was swept by fatigue, and sat down, overwhelmed. Mamie was rummaging in a drawer for teaspoons.

'No, I hinna the memory these days, but Alice was aye impatient. If I'm left to myself, I manage fine. You don't want an old wifie like me getting in your road.'

'You're not an old wifie,' Eleanor protested, trying to smile.

'Whiles I dinna feel like it, but that's what I am.' Mamie patted Eleanor's shoulder. 'You're affa white-faced, Eleanor. What's ado?'

'Nothing. I just feel a bit sick. Probably the early start. Cup of tea will help.'

'Just waiting for the kettle.' But Mamie had forgotten to switch it on. 'Dear me, nae wonder it's takin a lang time. There, that's it now.' She sat down on the chair opposite Eleanor. 'And how's Marion doing? She's gotten affa thin, puir lass.'

'Last treatment coming up. Then maybe she'll be able to pull round a bit.'

'Aye, we'll hope so. She's had a sad time of it.'

Eleanor still felt strange. Slowly, making an effort, she got up and made as if to lift the tray. Mamie stopped her.

'That's far ower heavy for you. Get David.'

They looked at each other. 'Now then, what am I saying? Ross. Marion's laddie. Ross will carry it for us.'

'I'll get him.' As she made for the door, Mamie said, 'A pity he couldna come to his own mother's funeral.'

Eleanor hesitated, began to say, 'But he did,' then changed her mind, and went to ask Ross to fetch the tray.

When Ross had disappeared into the kitchen, in his borrowed black tie and his father's jacket (too wide at the shoulders), Eleanor sat by Marion and murmured, 'I don't think Mamie is quite right. She seems fine, then she says something way off beam.'

'Well, no wonder, today. It's awful for her. I think she's coping really well.'

But Ross and Mamie were coming into the living room, so Eleanor said nothing more.

* * *

The sisters drove the first part of the journey together, as they usually did, Claire and Eilidh in the back.

'They're stoics, that generation,' Marion observed, when they began talking again about the funeral. 'How long have Alice and Mamie lived together? A lifetime. But although Mamie had obviously had a few tears before she arrived, she didn't show anything all the rest of the day. Neither did Dad. His own sister.'

'They've been together,' Eleanor said, working it out, 'since the year before David was born. It's his birthday at the end of the month.'

'Well, at least we know where to send the card this year.'

'Marion, Mamie said something really weird this afternoon. It shook me.'

'What?'

'It's not just forgetfulness, she's actually a bit confused.' Eleanor lowered her voice, though the girls were oblivious in the back, Claire reading her magazine, Eilidh deep in a book. 'She threw me completely. She said what a pity it was David didn't come to Mum's funeral. I don't know whether she's just forgotten he did – at the last minute, right enough – or if she thought it was Mum's funeral today. It was really disconcerting. I didn't know what to say, so I just sort of ignored it.'

'I wouldn't worry,' Marion reassured her. 'She seemed fine to me. She might actually get on all right by herself. She's been bossed around by Alice for years.'

But Eleanor remembered the tremor of Mamie's hands, and her unfocused gaze as she sat at the kitchen table, doing nothing.

'David might have come,' she said aloud.

'Ach, Eleanor, you shouldn't be surprised. He never thinks about anyone but himself.'

Marion leaned back and closed her eyes. Eleanor, glancing

sideways, said no more. Let Marion sleep; two journeys along the A96 in one day were too much for her just now. But she had come, so why couldn't David? She had missed him, wanting him there. He had been with her, she realised, in all the other crises of her life. Was this a crisis, Alice dying? Eleanor had a pang of pity for her aunt, recalling their last walk in winter cold at Christmas, Alice pausing, breathless for a moment. Not yet, thought Eleanor, the ready tears springing up, this crisis is not happening yet.

As they neared home, she began to think about Gavin instead. Tomorrow. She would see him tomorrow.

Before she did, David telephoned. It was Saturday morning. The sun shone, and a stiff breeze flapped Eleanor's washing high in the air, white against blue, and bent the tulips sideways at the front door. She pinched off a sprig of rosemary from the bush by the front doorstep, as she stood watching the post van coming up the lane, the wind catching her hair. Edie had come out too, and was hurrying over to the fence.

'Now then, you've had a sad time, how was your poor father? A lovely man, your father, always a smile.'

'Dad's fine.'

They took in the post, exchanging comments on the weather with the postman, and went on talking together as he drove back down the lane, not stopping at Gavin's cottage.

'Him—' Edie nodded at the third house. 'He's offshore again, is he? You'll know better than I would. His comings and goings.' Eleanor flushed, but there was no malice in Edie, only curiosity. She had noticed, though; nothing had escaped her.

'He's due back tonight.'

'Company for you dear, and I suppose he's all alone now.' Edie patted Eleanor's arm. 'Take care though, don't you rush into anything. You're awful pale, eh. I says to Jim, "She's not looking well, it'll be her auntie dying, and all the worry about Marion." How is she, poor lass?'

Going indoors a few minutes later, Eleanor thought how there were no secrets here. Your life was laid bare, known. But the love-making, that was secret – not that it happened (Eleanor flushed with annoyance), but how, and what you did together.

She was in the kitchen when the phone rang. Claire picked it up in the bedroom and yelled downstairs a moment later. 'Mum! Uncle David.'

'Why didn't you come?'

'Sorry, sorry. How was it? Is Dad all right?'

'Dad was fine. Mamie's upset, and she was upset you didn't turn up.'

'I meant to.'

'Well then?'

'God, Eleanor, you wouldn't – I can't go into it. Sorry. I was thinking about you all. You'd be surprised how much.'

'Yes, I would.'

'Aw, come on. Makes no difference to Alice, does it?'

Eleanor sighed. 'No, I suppose. But that's not the point.'

'Anyway,' David went on, 'what's happening about the house and everything?'

'The house?'

'Alice's house.'

'Mamie's living in it, of course. It belongs to both of them, doesn't it?'

'No, I think it just belongs to Alice. Did she leave it to Mamie?'

'Leave it to her? God, David, I don't know. I suppose Dad's next of kin, but I'm sure you're wrong anyway. They used to tell us this story, well, Mamie did – you know, about buying the house when Alice's flat was too small?'

'She'll have a will.'

'What?'

'Alice worked in a lawyer's office all her life. Must be a will.'

What on earth was he getting at? Two old ladies, living on pensions – there couldn't be any money to speak of. Just the house. David wanted money. Her heart sank.

'Look, Dad will be sorting it out. I'm sure he'll tell us.'

'Yeah, right. Look, I've got to go. I'll be home at the end of the month, staying with Dad. Maybe I could come up and see you and Marion for a couple of days.'

'Come for your birthday,' she said, hearing the plaintive note in his voice that meant things were not going well for him, he was losing out again.

'What's there to celebrate?' he muttered.

'Oh, the end of Marion's chemo – surviving, you know.'

'Sure, that'll do. Maybe have some news by then.'

'What news?'

But he would not say, and the conversation ended unsatisfactorily after all. There was someone at the door of his flat. He had to go.

'I'll be in touch,' he promised. 'Give Marion my love.'

'Why didn't he come to the funeral?' Claire asked.

'Oh, work, I think.'

'Yeah, but Uncle Fergus came, and it wasn't even his aunt.' Claire had picked up Eleanor's irritation with David. Now she worried at it, aware there were things the adults knew that she did not.

Eleanor sat down. 'I'm very fond of David, there are lots of good things about him,' she began. 'But – he lives a different life.'

'How?'

'Never settles in one place, or one job. Never married, or even had a girlfriend for long.'

'Has he got a girlfriend now then?'

And then Eleanor knew. 'Yes,' she said, 'I suspect he has. And I suspect it's somebody he shouldn't be with.'

'Why not?'

But Eleanor had said too much. 'I don't know. I'm only guessing.'

'Aw, you reckon she's married to somebody else.'

'No, of course not.' But this was exactly what Eleanor did think. Look what happened when you had no other adult to confide in; you told your fourteen-year-old daughter things she should not hear. Eleanor did not know whether to be angry with herself or with Claire, who was so knowing.

But Claire had started on another tack. 'What about Auntie Mamie – will she go and live with Grandpa?'

Eleanor was startled. 'What on earth makes you think she'd do that?'

'Well, for company. They're cousins, aren't they?'

'Grandpa wouldn't like that much. When people get old, they have their own ways. Habits.'

Claire switched on the television. 'I'm fed up,' she said, as the noise started, and the blare of a game show filled the room. Eleanor realised the conversation had moved on again.

'Are you?' she asked. She must go; she had no interest in television these days. And yet, after almost six hours of driving, the uncomfortable call from David, all she seemed able to do was lie back on the sofa, glazed, unmoving. After a moment, she said, 'Are you still going out with that boy – what was his name?'

'Stephen.'

'Yes. Stephen.'

'No, I'm not.'

'Oh dear.'

Claire went on watching television. Then she said, 'It's OK, I'm not bothered.'

'Oh good. I thought that was maybe why you were a bit fed up.'

'Naw.' Claire sounded scornful. 'I'm due to come on in

two days, that's all. It's a pain – it'll be the worst day when Nicky's party's on.'

'When's that?'

'Tuesday, of course. She's having it on her actual birthday because it's the holidays.'

'What a lot of parties you go to,' Eleanor murmured, thinking, A whole night with Gavin, and blushing, as if Claire could read her thoughts. But Claire was flicking between channels with the remote control.

'What about you?' she asked. 'We usually come on at the same time, don't we? Nicky's mum says nuns living together all come on at the same time, isn't that weird?'

Eleanor herself had that twinge in her belly that meant a period was due. But she had had it for a week now. 'Yes,' she agreed. 'Something to do with the moon, they used to say.'

She got up and left the room. For a moment she stood in the kitchen by the Rayburn, kettle in her hand, but without moving to fill it, not wanting anyway the cup of tea she had intended to make. What if . . .

Fear dropped like a stone in a pool, plummeted through her heart, something physical, cold, sudden. What if . . .

She set the kettle down again and sat on a kitchen chair. You're being stupid, she told herself, there is nothing to worry about. You are forty years old. She touched her breasts gently. They were tender. In a few days it would be here, the familiar flow of blood, the cycle completed. The clock ticked, the Rayburn puttered, and she sat on in the quiet room, unmoving.

She had been pregnant only twice: first with Claire, and then with the baby she had lost. She thought that an odd expression, but people did not like it if you said you had a baby that died. But it did die, Eleanor thought, it was alive and growing inside me, then after the crash, it died. However unformed, little more than an amoeba, a collection of cells transmuting, it did die. To say she had 'lost' a baby made it sound as if she had mislaid an infant somewhere, left it on a park bench, gone home without it.

Eleanor did not remember the crash, perhaps because she had been knocked unconscious at the moment of impact. At any rate, she had no picture in her head to fill the gap between the terrifying, heart-stopping squeal of brakes and the van veering across the road in front of them, and everyone standing by the side of the road, while she was carried into an ambulance on a stretcher. She had felt foolish, horizontal in broad daylight, and yet she had not cared, being in too much pain to want anything except to get to the hospital, where someone who knew what to do would make everything all right again.

For a long time, they were all so glad to be alive at all, Ian and David and she, so overwhelmingly relieved to have Claire still safe and well with them, that the miscarriage was talked of almost as if it were a small price to pay. But Eleanor had been the one to pay it, she realised later. When she married Ian, she had not much cared whether she had children or not, but everyone else they knew did, and Claire was a docile, pretty baby, easy to love. Marion had always been different; even at ten, she was planning her family.

'I'm going to have four children, two boys and two girls. First the boys, called James and Edward, and then the girls, called Shirley and Caroline.' The names varied, but the ages and sexes were fixed. Marion knew what she wanted.

Eleanor had offended her once by saying dreamily, after these elaborate plans had been aired yet again, 'When I grow up I'm going to have six cats, and I'm calling them Eeny, Meeny, Miny and Mo—' (a pause for thought here, as she counted) – and Jonathan and Linda.'

Marion stumped off in a huff, but Eleanor had not meant to upset her.

Once Claire was born, they had of course intended to have

another child. That was what everyone else did. Then Ian was promoted, and they moved to Heatherlea. Next year, they said. Next year, we'll have another baby. David came back, and began spending his free days with them. Doing well, and keen for the next step up, Ian worked long hours, so that he fell into bed at ten soon after he got home. Eleanor sat up late, talking to David. At the weekends, Ian played golf, pleased to have been sponsored for the local club. It was a wonder, Eleanor thought now, I got pregnant again at all.

But she had. Afterwards, recovering with her broken arm, getting over the accident, the miscarriage, Eleanor knew that if she could not have another child at once, soon, it might never happen. Soon after that, Claire went to nursery; Ian was promoted again; David left the police, and was unemployed, hanging around even more. Their lives moved on a little. Everyone said to her, 'Leave it, don't rush things. There's plenty of time. Get yourself well first.'

Now, she knew that they had all been wrong. 'I was too easily influenced,' she said aloud in her quiet kitchen. But to have another baby at forty, unmarried, and to a man like Gavin – that would not be any good at all – for Claire, for her. 'You fool,' she said, as if she were two Eleanors, one sensible and disapproving, the other foolish and weak.

And yet, for the first time in her life, she felt a tug of longing, something that seemed to be the other half of sexual desire: a wish that she might be pregnant anyway, in defiance of all commonsense. It is because I feel different about Gavin, she thought, it is because the sex is different. She had not thought fear and hope could co-exist in one mind, at the same moment, with equal intensity.

Then the moment passed, and she was afraid.

20

At the end of April, Marion and Eleanor sent David cards for his birthday and promised him presents when he came to see them. But he did not come.

Their father was Alice's executor. He helped Mamie deal with the will, life insurance, the business of clearing up after death. But he was cagey about it. If Marion had not been about to go into hospital for her last chemotherapy session, if Eleanor had not been with Gavin every day, they might have asked him more questions. Marion suspected that there was something he had not told them. But Alice had left them £6,000 each. She had saved all her working life, and there was quite a bit of money, their father said. 'Shares as well, so it'll take some sorting out,' he told them.

'Mamie will be all right, then,' Marion said, but her father did not answer this directly.

'I'm assuming,' she said to Eleanor, as they drove into Inverness, 'that David's getting the same. I still can't get over it – *six thousand*. It'll be welcome, no doubt. Well, it's welcome to us, I have to say.'

'Me too,' Eleanor agreed, feeling guilty about being glad to have the money.

'Is he still in that job, whatever it is?' Marion asked.

'David? I think so.'

'He should have come to the funeral,' Marion said yet

again. There were not many things she had the energy to bother about these days, but family mattered.

'You know what I want?' she asked Eleanor, as they turned into the car park.

'No more treatment.'

'Oh that. Of course. But I meant – what normal things do you think I really miss?'

'Teaching?'

'Um. Not as much as I thought I would. I'm a domestic person, you know that.'

'Gardening, then.'

'Yes, that's one of them. Gardening, baking . . . I didn't bother about the garden till the weather turned warm. Now I see all the weeds springing up, and it's so frustrating not to have the energy to do anything about them. I sit on that low stool I've got, and lean into the borders, and poke about with a trowel. But it's pointless – I should be turning over the earth, getting seeds in.'

Eleanor moved into a parking space and switched off the engine. 'You'll get back to it. The garden will survive one spring without you. Get Ross to dig. Or I'll come over and have a go, if you like.'

'If I died,' Marion said suddenly, 'my daffodils, my tulips, the double-headed narcissi I put in last year under the apple trees – they would still come up the next spring, wouldn't they?'

Eleanor did not know what to say. Was this a good or bad thing? She thought of the garden Mamie and Alice kept tidy, the roses they fed and pruned and dead-headed, the pink one by the gate Mamie had said was called *Maiden's Blush*. They would be starting into new growth already. Without Alice.

'Sorry,' Marion went on, 'I didn't mean to be morbid. Time I got going.'

'Not much of a day for gardening, anyway,' Eleanor observed, as they walked across the car park. She looked up at the overcast sky and buttoned her jacket, feeling cold. There was nothing to break the wind as it swept low across the open acre of cars, exposed and bleak.

The glass doors moved apart as they reached them, and Eleanor stepped through with Marion.

'You'll be all right,' she insisted. 'You're not to die, not even to think about it, you hear me?'

Marion smiled. 'I'll do my best.'

'This won't last for ever.' But it was almost as if she were pleading with Marion, not reassuring her. Lightly, Marion touched her arm.

'See you tomorrow.' Then she turned and walked away.

In the afternoon, Eleanor worked in the cottage garden, wanting to do something physical and out of doors, in spite of the weather. Claire called at half-past four. 'I'm at Auntie Marion's,' she said. 'Will you come and get me after *Neighbours?*'

'You are a nuisance, Claire. Why didn't you get the school bus?'

'I walked down with Eilidh. Anyway, I'd still have had to walk up the lane, and my bag is mega-heavy. I had PE and cross country, remember?'

Eleanor sighed. 'Oh, all right. See you later.'

She went outdoors again, but had lost interest in gardening. If she had known Claire would be late she could have spent the whole afternoon with Gavin. He had gone into Inverness when she left him at half-past three. Eleanor put the fork and trowel back in the shed and the bag of prunings and dead leaves in the dustbin. Then she went indoors to get changed.

The last time Gavin had been home, at the end of the Easter holidays, she had spent almost the whole of the first week in increasing terror that she might be pregnant.

'What's wrong?' he kept asking, but got no real answer.

Then she found it was all right: the show of blood, the waves of relief. She was able to tell him then.

'God,' he said, 'that would have been a bit of a facer.' Eleanor, who had been annoyed with herself for over a week, now felt angry with him.

'I did try to tell you, about being careless.'

'Me?'

'Us then.'

'Takes two, Eleanor.' He drew back, frowning, distant. Eleanor sank again, under a different kind of relief. At first, it had been tinged with what – disappointment? Something of that. Not now. Foolish to think he would ever have wanted it, that it could have bound them together.

He was sitting up in bed, looking out of the window, his profile etched against the light, sharp and unsmiling.

'Right.' He turned and thrust off the bedclothes. 'Better get up. You want a cup of tea before you go?' Dressing quickly, he left her there, and disappeared into the kitchen. Eleanor could hear him filling the kettle, clattering mugs, whistling. For a little while she went on lying on the bed, growing colder. Then she got up.

But she had not the sense – or the experience – to know she should let this alone for now.

'What would you do,' she asked him. 'I mean, if I were really pregnant?'

'You're not,' he said, 'so it doesn't arise.'

'But—'

'We'll be careful,' he said. 'No more risks.'

'No,' she retorted. 'I'm doing something about that, at least. Seeing the doctor tomorrow.'

He looked startled. 'Oh. Right. What—' So she explained, and they discussed birth control, politely, for a few minutes.

Eleanor had put off doing anything till now. She knew the doctors too well; impossible to speak to Fergus or Andrew.

But she had gathered courage to see Mary Mackay, who was Marion's doctor.

'The idea horrifies you, doesn't it?' she said to Gavin, setting down her mug, the tea untasted. 'I thought at least you'd be sympathetic.'

If she were not careful, tears would come. Why am I on my own? she thought. I can't cope with this. She was angry with Ian for dying, for leaving her. This was not the life she had expected to have. And at forty, to want a man to stay because you were pregnant, to plead with him – she shuddered, and clutched the mug with both hands, not looking at him any more.

'Well, if it *had* happened, we'd have had to face it. Do something,' he admitted. Then: 'Sorry, I'm not dealing with this very well. Look, it's nothing to do with you, or how I feel about you.' He put a hand out and touched her face, tilting it up to meet his. 'My wife – I got married because my wife was pregnant. It was a mistake. Not a mistake I would ever repeat. I'll never marry again, you should realise that, Eleanor.' Unable to bear it, Eleanor began to cry. 'God, sorry. Come here. It's all right, it's all right.' He put his arms round her so that her face was buried in his rough jersey, his hands warm on the back of her neck, her shoulders.

Later, he said, 'I'm going to Aberdeen a day early, before I go back out. I'm seeing someone in the oil company I work for. About a job onshore.'

'Is that what you want?'

'Yes. And although I said that about marriage – well, we're not kids. We could be together anyway. Couldn't we? Give it a try, at least?'

She was confused, her faith in him shaken. And yet, yes, she did want this. A life of my own, she thought, and someone to care for me.

That had been over two weeks ago. Now he was newly home again, and she was full of hope. They were all right with each other, they were close, in bed and out of it. He had said, as he got into his car this afternoon, 'The job looks pretty likely. We can talk about it later.'

Driving through to Marion's house to fetch Claire, she thought about this, and began to believe it would all come right. Gavin would love her, they would be together, and Marion would get better.

Claire sat upstairs with Eilidh in her bedroom, watching television. They talked through it, waiting for *Neighbours*, not interested in what was on at the moment. Eilidh was on her bed, Claire on the floor, doing the children's jigsaws she had found under the bed in a box.

'She thinks I don't know,' Claire was saying. They were discussing Gavin.

'What, that they're *doing* it? Are they?'

'Well, she goes to see him, right, and she says to me, "Oh, I'll only be half an hour." Then it's, like, *two hours*. When she comes back she's bright red, kind of flustered.'

'But you said it was the *afternoon*?'

'I know. They're quite old for it, aren't they? My mum's forty, and he's older. Well, he looks older, in my opinion. She's really mad about him. I used to think people their age didn't get like that. It was only people our age. But it's not.'

'Maybe she'll get married to him.'

Clare made a face. 'Maybe.' She picked up a magazine and flicked through it.

'Would you mind, if she did?'

'I don't know. He goes away a lot, on the rigs. So I suppose I wouldn't see him that much. But it would be a bit pointless, I think, them living in the same house. Our house is so wee, and so is his. They're practically next door anyway, so why would we want to put all his furniture in our house? Or ours in his?'

'They could buy another house, a bigger one.' Eilidh

considered this. 'Mind, it would be a bit embarrassing them doing it if you were all living in the same house.'

'Oh my God, it would be *disgusting*.' Claire flung the magazine down. 'Yuk.' She began to laugh. 'I'd see him in his pyjamas, eh? Oh my *God*, that is so *gross*.'

They both laughed. Then Eilidh said, growing solemn again, 'But what about your dad? Would you not feel bad about him, if Auntie Eleanor got married to somebody else?'

'Well, Gavin couldn't be, like, my *dad*, could he? No way.' Claire tried to picture her father, but all she could see was Gavin's grinning face, his red hair. 'Sometimes I can hardly remember my dad. Well, no, I remember him, but I can't sort of think of his face, or his voice. Not really. I look at the photographs, that brings it back.'

'Do you believe in heaven?' Eilidh asked.

'Yeah. Sort of.' Claire tried to picture a place where you were happy all the time, with flowers, she supposed. Warm and hazy. Where her father wandered, or perhaps less improbably, Granny and Auntie Alice.

'I don't,' Eilidh said. 'I don't even believe in God. Neither does Ross. Kirsty does. She still goes to Sunday School.'

Claire sat back on her heels, nonplussed. She had not thought you could choose like that, just say, and mean it, *I don't believe*. The idea both frightened and attracted her. It was like a door opening, and nothing beyond, just empty space, no floor even. It made you giddy.

'But don't tell my mum,' Eilidh warned. 'It might upset her.'

Kirsty pushed the door open. 'Is *Neighbours* on yet?'

'In a minute.'

Kirsty came in and got down on the floor beside Claire. 'That's my jigsaw,' she said.

'It was Ross's first, then mine,' Eilidh reminded her.

'Well, then it was mine, and there's nobody younger than me, so it's still mine.' She broke up the picture and began again. 'I used to think this one was really difficult, when I was wee.' Expertly, she fitted the pieces together. 'Is Auntie Eleanor coming for you?'

'Yeah, at tea-time.'

'Can we ask her, I forgot last time?'

'What?'

'About the Wishing Tree. She said we could go and hang something up for Mummy.'

'OK.'

The theme music began, and they all got on Eilidh's bed to watch.

'Mind, Kirsty. Can you not sit on the floor? There's no room for you here.'

'No. I'll get a sore neck looking up the way.'

They squabbled, settled down, fell into silence.

But Kirsty, hearing Eleanor come in later, was first off the bed and downstairs. 'Can we go to the Wishing Tree, Auntie Eleanor?'

Eleanor still had the piece of lace in the dashboard compartment of her car, wrapped in tissue paper.

'All right,' she said, 'if your dad agrees. We could go straight after tea.'

'And then can we go and see Granny?'

'No, it would be too late. If you want to do that, it has to be another day.'

But Kirsty did not want to wait. 'No, let's go tonight.'

Later, Eleanor stood by the car while Kirsty solemnly tied the lace round a twig, and Eilidh and Claire gave instructions. Below their voices, water splashed softly onto stone. For the first time, Eleanor looked closely at what hung there. Some of the rags were no more than scraps of blue checked kitchen cloth; others were recognisable pieces of clothing. Someone had even hung a grubby pair of trainers near the back. What was recently attached still had colour, and flapped in the breeze. The older rags, stiff and unmoving, were uniformly grey. She had a pang of dismay that wishing for Marion might have anything to do with this place – or the piece of lace that had come from someone long dead, and whose death had caused her mother and father such distress. Still, it was a way of getting rid of the thing for good.

'Find a place for it by itself,' Eilidh insisted. 'Not beside all that manky stuff.'

The lace hung there, looking clean and fresh, and very small.

'I feel bad leaving it,' Claire said. 'It looks too nice. Where did you get it, Mum?'

'It's Marion's. She's had it for a long time.'

Kirsty stood back, looking at the tree. 'Will our bit get all dirty and hard like the rest?'

'Eventually.'

'That means the wish is over, it's come true, or whatever,' Eilidh explained.

'Is that right?' Kirsty looked to Eleanor for confirmation.

'Oh, well. I'm not sure. Have you made your wish?'

'No, I'm doing it now.' Kirsty shut her eyes, clenched her fists, wished.

Eleanor, turning back to the car, wished for Marion, tried not to wish for herself. You would need something else for that, she thought, not the tinker's bit of lace.

That night it rained, and she thought of the strip of lace dripping water onto the ground below. As she got up to draw the curtains and shut out the rainy night, the telephone rang. She expected it to be Gavin, who often called just before he came round, checking it was still all right, asking if she wanted him to bring a bottle of wine. But it was her father.

'Eleanor, Marion's not at home, Fergus tells me it's her night at the hospital. But I said to him I'd speak to you myself. Not to bother her. I wondered if maybe you could come down for a day.'

'What's wrong?' Mamie. Another death, she could not bear another death.

'Mamie's taken a tumble. Fell down the stairs and broke her hip. She's in Foresterhill.'

'Oh *no*. Will she be all right?'

'They're going to put in a pin. She's shaken up, of course. But they can mend the hip.'

'Oh dear. How did it happen?' Had she lain in the hall in pain, waiting for someone to come? Eleanor was distressed by this picture, and felt her throat tighten.

'By great good fortune, she knocked over the phone when she tumbled down, so she was able to reach it and dial for an ambulance.'

'Well, I don't know about good fortune,' Eleanor protested, 'but I'm glad she didn't have to lie a long time on her own.'

She did not want to go to Aberdeen. Gavin was at home for another week and a half. But of course, she had to.

'You want me to come and visit her?'

'Well, I'm sure she would appreciate that, but what it is, Eleanor, the reason she took a fall: she was going through Alice's things, it was high time, she'd been putting it off, she said. But anyway, she had a pile of clothes in her arms, no use to her, Alice was aye a beanpole, and something slipped onto the floor, and she tripped on it, came rattling down the stairs.'

'So she didn't manage to sort out the clothes, is that it?'

'Well, it's not just the clothes. She wondered – I wondered – it would set her mind at rest. Would you finish the job, Eleanor? Sort out what Alice left, the clothes and letters and whatnot. It's nae a job for a man.'

'But Mamie—'

'Mamie says to me, ask the girls. She says to take what you want yourselves. Alice had a nice locket, and a string of pearls; she wants you and Marion to have them. There's not much else – Alice didn't go in for jewellery. Anyway, I told Mamie I'd ask you. She was a bittie agitated about it.'

'I don't think Marion would be up to it yet. Maybe in a couple of weeks.' And Gavin would be away then, of course.

'Best get it over while Mamie's in the hospital,' he said. 'I can see it's distressing her.'

'All right.' Eleanor made up her mind. 'I'll come myself, and if there's anything I don't know what to do with, it can wait for Mamie. How about that?'

'Aye, that's grand. It's a load off my mind.'

'Give Mamie my love.'

'They're operating the morn. She'll be out for the count the rest of the day. But I'll look in anyway, in the evening.'

'I'll ring you tomorrow,' Eleanor promised. 'I have to sort out Claire, but I'll come as soon as I can.'

Fergus collected Marion next day. When Eleanor called in the evening to see her, she found her sister subdued, resting, but pleased to see her.

'Kirsty said you hung that bit of lace at the Clootie Well.'

'She was keen to do it.'

'I know. Thanks.'

'Listen, something's happened.' Eleanor told Marion about Mamie.

'Could you wait a couple of days?' Marion asked. 'I'd like to come. Just – the first few days are the worst. And I've got thrush again, and another crop of mouth ulcers. I feel foul, I really do. Thank God that's over. Well, I hope it is.'

'It will be.'

'Would you mind, if I came?'

'Mind? I'd love it. I won't know what to do with half the stuff, and it would be horrible to have to go through it on my own. But Dad obviously wants it done while Mamie's in hospital.' She cheered up at the thought of having Marion with her. 'I'll drive and everything. And we can stay at Pitcairn one night, come back next day.'

'Maybe at the weekend?'

But Claire would be away at least one night at the weekend. She wanted to spend it with Gavin.

'Leave it till Monday or Tuesday, eh? Give yourself a chance. I don't know how long Mamie's going to be in, but surely it'll be a week, at least?'

So this was what they agreed. Eleanor arranged for Claire to stay at Sarah's, and Fergus said he would take a day at home. The sisters would go down on Tuesday morning, and return Wednesday afternoon.

They had travelled the road to Aberdeen many times together, and in the last few years, often in sadness, it seemed to Marion. They could not know, of course, that when they came home again this time, everything would look different, the very landscape changed by new knowledge. The world would look different because it was different, altered for ever.

21

All his parents ever asked him about was school. School, Highers, university. Marion was finishing her degree, going on to Teacher Training next year. Eleanor was first year, doing English and Psychology. Both were still living at home, though sometimes they stayed in Aberdeen overnight at the aunts' house, or more often on the floor of someone's student flat. Marion was getting engaged at Christmas. She seemed very settled, his mother said. She approved of Fergus, because he was going to be a doctor. And Eleanor had given up that silly idea about Art School. She might become a teacher as well. They had no worries about the girls.

He supposed he would be a student too. But he would have to go somewhere else – Edinburgh, St Andrews. He really could not go on living at home. But the trouble was, he had to get the Highers first. It was nearly May, and he had done no work.

In the holidays and at weekends, he worked at the Mains, as he had done since he was fourteen. Sometimes, heaving bales of straw, or out with the tractor, he thought he would be happy enough doing this all his life. You could just do it: feel your muscles stretch and ache, suffer the cold wind, or the sun burning on the back of your neck, and not think about anything at all.

He hated school. He seemed, this year, to have got too big

for the desks and chairs, so that there was nowhere to put his long legs without entangling them in someone's schoolbag, or scraping the desk over the floor. He was always in trouble, not major trouble, nothing serious. But they got at him all the time, nag, nag. He was late, his work was untidy (or not done at all); he wasn't paying attention; he was disrupting the class. He had got too big, too restless, too old for school. Other boys he had grown up with were working now, earning. Look at Stan – apprenticed to his dad, learning joinery, saving for a motor bike. He had a steady girlfriend now, a tiny blonde girl called Irene, pert and possessive. But Stan was restless too. David knew that – they had seen each other several times lately.

When they went to the Academy, they had been put in different classes. Stan had resisted the place from the start, cheeking the teachers, skiving off. And yet, most of the time, he got away with it. He was popular: hard to discipline, but impossible to dislike. At primary school, David had been the leader, the one with ideas and schemes. Now Stanley had gathered different people round him; he had his own mates. David, intended for an academic career, university, was excluded. At first, he and Stanley still spent Saturdays together. By the end of first year, however, they had drifted away from each other.

Just after his seventeenth birthday, David took a whole day away from school. He had skived off before, of course; everyone did it sometimes. But only the last day of term, or missing double Maths at the end of Friday afternoon. Everyone did that – not often, but once or twice. This was different. He had got off the bus and walked up to the school gates with everyone else. There he had stopped. The others flowed past him, through the yard and up to the main pupil entrance. He went on standing there, just staring at the school. Ian Johnson turned and saw him, shouted something. David shouted back: 'Yeah, in a minute.' Then they had all disappeared somewhere inside the building, and a bell rang.

It had been raining, a mild misty April rain. They had been back two weeks since the end of the Easter holidays, but the weather was less like spring than ever. Now, David realised the rain had stopped. Above him, clouds parted and the sun glinted, vanished, glinted again, then was suddenly hot and bright in a clear blue space. On the railings drops of water glittered; just next to him a blackbird sang its clear notes, over and over, high in a tree that had its roots within the school grounds. Its leaves had just unfurled, deep green and shining with newness.

David thought of the dusty, stale-smelling classrooms, the drone of voices, the scrape of chairs, and the long hours indoors, doing boring things he hated. Then he turned and walked back through the side streets of the village, till he was on a country road again, heading for home. He had no idea what he was going to do. In a school blazer, shirt and tie, he was much too conspicuous to wander around Inverurie. He stopped by the side of the road, took off his blazer and tie and stuffed them into his schoolbag. Then he undid the top button of his shirt and rolled up his sleeves. The sky was entirely blue now, and the breeze hardly ruffled the long grass growing over the ditch. A glorious day. Looking round, David checked that there was nothing on the road, then he put his bag in the ditch. It was dry, muddy on the bottom maybe, but he set the bag on a large boulder. He brushed the disturbed grass over it again. Then he turned off the road and went up a farm track that edged the fields for a mile or so.

He still did not know where he was going. Later, he could come back down, pick up his bag, eat his sandwiches, and hitch a lift home. If anyone asked, he would say he had missed the bus into Aberdeen. They would not know he was supposed to be at school. He was over six feet, thin yet, but with a dark growth of beard already that made him look older than seventeen.

At the top of the hill, half hidden for most of the way by a group of Scotch pines, were farm buildings, and a house. He would skirt these, circle the field on his right, and meet up with the path that led back down into Inverurie. Pupils from the Academy ran cross-country over this land in the winter term, so he knew the layout: it was familiar territory. He would not go into Inverurie, but double back through the bottom field. That would be the worst bit – rough walking, but quite close to the road, so someone might see, and wonder what he was up to.

Thinking about this, he reached the top of the hill. Sitting on the farm gate, smoking, was Stanley. Stanley had been watching him for fifteen minutes or so, but because he was short-sighted, had only just realised who it was coming slowly up the track, catching long grasses in his right hand, whistling faintly.

They looked at each other in some surprise.

'Aye, aye,' Stanley said. 'Out for a walk?'

David grinned. 'Felt like stretching my legs.'

'You skive off?'

'What does it look like?'

'Want a fag?'

They both sat on the gate, smoking.

'What're you doing here, anyhow?' David asked.

'Oh, the auld man's in the hoose, seeing about a job. They're pittin in a loft conversion or something.' He shrugged. 'I said I'd wait oot here.'

'Do you like it?' David asked. 'Working for your dad?'

'It's a richt. I dinna mind the work, like. Lang as he stays off the booze.' Stanley looked sideways at David. 'Fit about yoursel? Stickin in at your books, eh?'

'As you can see.'

They both laughed. David put out his cigarette on the gate post, stabbing the cork tip till it twisted and frayed.

'See,' he said, 'they think I'll go to university like my sisters. Be an accountant or some bloody thing.'

'Be all right though, bein a student. Drink, parties, women.'

'Pity I've got to pass my Highers first.'

'Ach, you were aye clever at the school.'

'Not any more. Well, I don't care, really.'

'Aye, but the likes of you – you're nae going to be a joiner, are ye? Tradesman.'

'Nothing wrong with that.'

'What about your dad – will he nae get you into Shanks's place?'

David snorted. 'Catch me working for that capitalist!' He thought of Eddie Shanks's big red face, the way he slapped you on the back, making you cough, by way of greeting. His piggy eyes, his fat wife with her fancy house in Rubislaw Den, her big gold and pearl earrings, her daughters at Albyn School with accents far posher than their parents were ever going to manage. No, he would never work for Shanks.

'Your dad likes him a richt though?'

'He's a good boss,' his father had said. 'Lets you get on with the job, doesn't interfere. And he's generous.'

'They're only interested in making money,' David said. 'That's all that the whole business is *for*.'

'Well, if it comes till't,' Stanley confessed, 'it's all that bothers most folk.'

'So that's it, then,' David mocked. 'You're going to be a joiner and live in Aberdeenshire all your life.' He warmed to his picture of Stanley's future. 'Get married to Irene, have two kids, maybe your son will be a joiner too, right?' Stanley looked at the ground, not answering, so David went on: 'And you'll live in a council house, go to Majorca for your holidays, go down the pub on Friday night, read the *Press and Journal*, but never any books – and vote Conservative.'

'I will not vote bloody Conservative!'

David grinned. 'Knew that you would get you. Vote Labour then.' He nudged Stanley. 'But you see what I mean? Your life will stay the same, you won't go round the world, make any real difference, change anything.'

'And you're goin to?' Stanley turned, challenging him. 'You're goin to change the world? David Cairns, Prime Minister.' He shoved David so hard he slid off the gate. David shoved back, and somehow, not knowing how it had happened, they were wrestling on the ground. A blind and breathless struggle of pulled collars and fists and kicks.

'Here! Fit the bloody hell's goin on here? Get tae yer feet, the pair of ye!'

It was Stanley's father, leaning out of his van. The boys separated slowly and stood up, looking at each other. David's white school shirt and dark trousers were streaked brown and grey, and one shirt sleeve was torn at the shoulder seam. Stanley, in work jeans and jersey, did not look so bad.

Jimmy Robertson got out of his van. 'Davy Cairns, fit wey are you nae at the school?'

So much for no one knowing or noticing. David groaned. But Jimmy did not seem interested in the answer.

'Get in the van,' he said.

Stanley, climbing in the back with the tools, let David sit beside his father. They drove in silence for a few minutes.

'A fine mess you're in. Nae muckle ees takin ee back to the school, eh?'

'No. But I left my bag in the ditch at the side of the road. Near the phone box.'

'Oh aye.'

'I'd better . . . collect it.' Silence. But Stanley's father made for the Inverurie road, and stopped by the call box, so that David could retrieve his bag.

'I've got a job the other side of Pitcairn,' he said as David got back in the van. 'I'll drop you at the end of your road.'

'Thanks,' David muttered.

'So you've exams comin up syne?'

'Next month.'

'Then you'll be away to the college?'

He knows that, thought David irritably. He was worried now. Was Jimmy going to tell his parents?

'He'd rather get a job,' Stanley put in, from the rear of the van.

'Oh aye. Fit kinda job would ye like?'

'Prime—' Stanley began, then thought better of it.

'I wouldn't mind being out and about, like you,' David said, inspired. 'I hate sitting in school, I don't want to be stuck in a library or something.'

'You're good wi your hands, is that it?'

'Yes,' David said, having no idea really.

'I've a mate, Ronnie Farquhar, over at Kintore. He'll be looking for a likely lad, come the autumn.'

'Is he a joiner as well?'

'Plumber. Plumbing and heating.'

'Oh.'

'You think about it. Very respectable trade. No book learnin required.'

Was Jimmy making fun of him?

'No, he disna want to be a plumber,' Stanley put in, barely able to keep the laugh from his voice. 'He's goin to change the world.'

But all his father said was, 'Well, there's plenty needs changing.'

They stopped at the end of the road to Pitcairn House. David got out with his bag. 'Thanks,' he said. 'And I'll think about . . . what you said.'

Why not, he thought, shouldering his bag and setting off up the road. Better than nothing. Better than school. Learn a trade. Then, with a bit of cash in hand, take a year out, go to Europe. Canada, maybe.

On either side, the fields lay baking in the first hot day of the year. Sunlight flashed through the trees. The verges were lined with whin and broom, the broom still black, but the whin brilliant yellow, coconut-scenting the air. On such a day, anything seemed possible.

When he reached the stone pillars at the end of his driveway, he hesitated. His father would be at work, his mother – what? What did his mother do, now they were all grown up – housework? But Ruby still came to help with that, though only twice a week now. It was years since the troops of little girls had come for dancing lessons on Saturdays. And the garden was his father's really, though she filled tubs with geraniums in the summer, and harvested the vegetables.

Perhaps she would be out – he knew she did some sort of voluntary work at the hospital. He walked slowly round the side of the house. As he turned the corner, he saw his mother. She was standing on the drying green, a basket at her feet, hanging out washing. She lifted a sheet from the basket and flipped it neatly over the line, spreading it along, fixing the pegs. All her movements were economical, graceful. Not moving, holding his breath, David watched her. She pegged out a row of towels and pillow cases on the other half of the line. Then she bent to pick up the basket, but halfway changed her mind. She straightened again, and raised her arms smoothly so that they stretched out on either side. She wore a short-sleeved blouse, white with a blue pattern, and grey slacks. Lifting one arched foot to her knee, she rose on the ball of the other one. One arm swept up over her head, and then she moved. A sweeping round of arms, a turn of the body, a step, a leap, and she was off down the garden in a series of wide, springing movements. By the lilac trees she stopped, and her body sagged, the arms coming down. She turned. David flung himself back round the side of the house, so that she would not see him.

When she held her Saturday ballet classes, they had had

to keep out of the way, and behave. He had cleared off with Stanley, roaming the fields, or down the woods, till dinner-time. Now he leaned against the side of the house, breathing hard. He did not think he had ever seen his mother dance like that. There were things you did not know about your parents, secret things in the past, hidden thoughts. Was his mother sorry she had given up dancing, sorry she had given it up to be married and have children? The extraordinary novelty of this idea shook him, left him uncertain, afraid, and yet exhilarated. He realised he was proud of his mother, embarrassed and surprised, but proud. She had looked so young, and had moved like someone used all her life to dancing like this, to performance.

David hoisted his bag again, and went off to stay in the woods until it was time for him to be home from school.

After that, it was easy. He learned that if you use Basildon Bond, and write a very short note with no spelling mistakes, you can explain your absences very satisfactorily. No one checks up, if they think you have been ill. His Aunt Alice used to get migraines, which kept her in bed for at least a day. She did not get them now, but he remembered his mother saying she had 'struggled' with them, and that they had started long ago when she was seventeen. He decided that was what he would have too. He just had to be quiet in class the day after, and put his head in his hands now and again.

He stayed away more and more. During exams, it was easy to be missing. He sat his Highers as he was supposed to; he went along and opened his paper when everyone else did, sat listening to the soft scraping of pens, shuffles, sighs, and the quiet tread of the invigilators, pacing between rows. He wrote something, answered the questions, he supposed. Sometimes he sat for a long time staring at the wooden floor, growing familiar with the grain of the boards, the knot just by one leg of his desk.

'How did it go?' they asked. 'How did you get on?'

'Fine,' he said, 'it was OK.'

His Aunt Alice had been in hospital for a minor operation. She came out to stay at Pitcairn for a few days. It was odd seeing her without Mamie, but Mamie had gone to the funeral of Uncle Tom's mother who had died at the great age of ninety-five, and she was staying on to visit some of her old friends in Northumberland. Alice did not seem ill. She sat in the garden reading, or helped his father tidy the borders or tie up the peas. Marion was about to sit her final exams, and spent every evening in her bedroom, working. Eleanor had first-year exams, and was studying too. The house was full of quiet industry.

By the time Highers were over, David had got out of the way of going to school. Often, he did not even get on the school bus, but waited till it had passed, then went back along the lane to the woods. Sometimes, Martin Cleland came with him. Martin was the doctor's son, who was expected to get As in his Highers, and do medicine at Aberdeen. But he too had had enough of school. He was a follower, as Stanley had been when they were eight. However, he was not fearless like Stanley, and worried a lot about being caught. So David was mostly on his own. He stayed in the woods and read, or fell asleep. He was often very bored, but he had somehow got himself into this, and there did not seem to be any way to stop. The weather went on being hot and bright. If he had not worked at the Mains every weekend, if he had not anyway a brownish skin, he might have looked mysteriously tanned for someone still at school every day. Even so, he was bound to be found out.

One day Stanley came to find him. His father was on the booze again, he said. It would be next week before he was working again.

'I dinna ken why you're hidin awa in the woodies,' Stanley said. 'Fit's the point? Just tell them you're leavin school.'

'I'm supposed to stay another year.'

'Fit wey?'

'Well, I must've failed all these Highers for a start. So I'll have to resit them, I suppose.'

'You fancy doing that, then?'

At this idea, at the thought of staying another year in school, a great wave of weariness and nausea swept over David.

'No,' he said at last. 'No, I'm leaving.'

'Go on then. Just tell them.'

'I'm not going to be a plumber either, Stan,' David warned.

Stanley laughed. 'It's OK, I never thocht you were. Canna see you fittin lavvy pans, nae if you're goin to be the Prime Minister.'

They both laughed, thinking of the day they had rolled on the ground, fighting because David was going to change the world, and Stanley had mocked.

'Anyway,' David said, 'what about you?'

'Ach.' Stanley shrugged. 'As lang's the auld man keeps off the drink, we're OK.'

'You don't want to stay here either, do you?'

'Nae much choice now.'

'You have, you could—'

'No.'

At this change in tone, David looked up. 'What's wrong?'

'Irene's up the stick.'

David did not understand. Then he did. 'Christ, that's a bit of a problem.'

'You're nae kiddin. She hasna telt her ma yet, but fan she does—'

'What?'

'Weddin bells for Stan.'

'You're not eighteen yet, you can't get married.'

'Try tellin that to Irene's ma.'

They spent the morning together, then Stanley went home

to rouse his father. David sat on in the wood for a while. It was still hot, the air oppressive now with clouds massing, a threat of thunder. He got to his feet. Home, he thought. I'm going to tell them tonight. I'm leaving school.

As he came round the side of the house this time, he heard voices: his mother and Alice. Mostly Alice, which was unusual. Then he sensed that this was not just a conversation. The voices were quiet and controlled, but it was an argument. A quarrel. He hesitated, then moved round the corner. They were not there. He realised that they had just gone indoors, and he followed. From the edge of the yard, he could see them through the kitchen window, standing by the table, facing each other. They did not hear him, did not turn in his direction. It was like a dream: everything was moving slowly, he was in a bubble of time, space, their voices did not sound as they usually did.

Years later, he was to ask himself why he had been so slow to understand. But the things they were saying made no sense. They were arguing about someone they called 'the boy'. But he was the boy – who else could it be?

Alice said, 'He could bide with us when he's at the college.' She leaned forward, emphatic. 'It's time he knew, high time.'

'It would only do him harm, the way he is just now.' His mother sat down at the table. He could see the top of her dark head, bent, staring at the floor.

'Please.' It was as if he had never heard his aunt say this word before: *please*. It came hard from her, squeezed out.

'No.' His mother looked up again. 'I'm worried about him. I had a call from the school this morning.'

David's heart leapt, and he took an instinctive step back. But could not leave.

Silence. Then Alice said, sounding weary now, 'I'll not go against you and John. You've done your best for him. But sometime, I think he should know. It's not easy for me, to admit to my mistake – more than a mistake, looking back. But nowadays, young folk want to know everything; they want to know more than we did.'

'He'll have to be told, I do know that. I'm not daft, Alice, these things always come out. But not just now, not yet.'

Alice said something in answer to this, but her voice was low, and he could not hear. Then she went out of the kitchen. He could slink away now, as he had before, but somehow he had left it too late. Compelled, he went up to the open kitchen door, and stepped inside.

'What was all that about?'

Shocked, his mother started up, her hand to her breast, her skin blanching. He had never seen anyone change colour like that, so fast.

'David.' It came out in a whisper.

'Sorry – I skived off. I came home, I wanted to tell you – anyway, sorry, I'm going to leave school.'

Faith was shaking, but she took a deep breath, steadying herself. 'You gave me such a fright.'

'Sorry,' he said again. She seemed to recover, and to be aware, for the first time, of what he had said.

'I'm not surprised,' she said. 'When Mr Brodie phoned this morning, I knew what he was going to say before he came out with it. The state you come home, sometimes. I knew you hadn't been at school.'

He saw that she was preoccupied with something far greater than the question of whether he went to school or not. This – from a mother who had gone on and on about Highers, university, making something of himself.

'What were you and Auntie Alice talking about?'

She bit her lip, and looked away. 'I'll talk to you about that later. When Alice is away. Mamie's home tonight – she's going back to Duthie Terrace tomorrow.'

'Right.'

'I want you to keep it to yourself,' she went on. 'You're not to say anything to the girls, or to Dad.'

'What – about skiving off?'

'About what I will tell you.'

'But – are you going to speak to Dad about me leaving school?'

'Yes.'

It was not the first bargain his mother had made with him. But the childish negotiations over food, pocket money, staying out late – these were on a different scale. And there, she took no risk, had nothing to lose. This was different.

In bed that night, he puzzled over the words he had heard. Next day, he made no pretence of going to school.

'What's up with you?' Eleanor asked, standing in the doorway of his bedroom.

'I've got a headache.'

'No, you haven't. You're skiving. You've been skiving for weeks. Mum and Dad were talking about it last night after Auntie Alice had gone to bed. I hope you sat the Highers. Did you?'

'Go away.' He turned over, pulling the covers round him.

'You must have been a changeling,' Eleanor mocked. 'Here's Marion and me, working hard, being good girls, and look at you. What are you going to do instead? Instead of being good, and going to university, like they want you to.'

He sat up in bed. 'What's a changeling?' he asked. 'I used to know, but I've forgotten.'

'That's because you're thick,' Eleanor said, going out of the room, her mind on the day ahead, on Ian Cooper, who had asked her out, *her*. Three of her friends had been after him for ages.

'No, Eleanor, tell me. What is it?'

'What, a changeling? It's a baby the fairies leave in place of your real one. So it grows up a kind of fairy child, trouble all the way.' She waggled her fingers at him as she left with a swish of her long flowery skirt, a jingle of silver bangles.

David lay back, staring at the ceiling.

He got up after his father had gone to work, after the morning had ticked by, after lunch. Mamie had called to collect Alice. Downstairs, the house was very quiet. He found his mother sitting in the living room, the newspaper on her lap, the coffee cups still on the table by the window. She looked round as he came in.

'There you are,' she said.

'Sorry, I should have got up to see Auntie Mamie.'

'I told them you weren't well.'

'Right.'

He sat down on the chair opposite hers, and stretched out his legs. In his pyjama trousers and T-shirt, his hair on end, he looked rough, still bleary from sleep.

'You'd better get washed and dressed,' she said. 'Do you want something to eat?' She made as if to get up.

'I'm adopted, amn't I?'

His mother sat down on her chair again. Carefully, she folded the *Press and Journal* and laid it on the floor.

'No.'

'What then?'

'We never adopted you.'

'I'm right, though, eh? I'm not yours, I'm somebody else's. Where's my mother then, my father – are they dead or what?'

His mother looked shocked, her face whitening. 'No, no of course not. I thought – I thought you had guessed, that you knew that.'

'Guessed what? You and Alice were arguing. She wants me to know I'm adopted or whatever, right – and you don't. Is that it? What's it got to do with her?'

And then, as his mother covered her face for a moment with both hands, as she sighed, and then looked up at him, her face full of truth at last, he did guess. He did know.

Stanley came with him as far as Newcastle. The lifts were easy at first, and one lorry driver treated them to ham and eggs in a service station. He could see they were running away, not really headed anywhere in particular. But it was not his business, so he fed them, gave them a fag each with their mugs of tea, and eventually left them on the A9, just south of Newcastle. He was going into Sunderland, with his delivery.

There, Stanley lost his nerve.

'What, you really want to go back home? Back to working for your dad, getting married to Irene – all that?'

'Naw, but I've got tae tell them I'm OK. The old man'll be haein kittens. We've a big job startin Thursday, and he'll need to get somebody else in to gie him a hand.'

'Go on then,' David said. 'Fuck off back to Inverurie – just don't expect me to come with you.'

Stanley's sympathy for David had taken him halfway down the country, all the way out of Scotland, further than he had ever been in his life. But he was beginning to panic, so far from home. It was not just his dad and the job, anyway. There was Irene, and the baby. What did he look like, running out on her? But he did not want to say this to David.

For years he had been bound to David: the den in the garden, the private games, the long summer holiday weeks when he had been at Pitcairn much more than at home. And for all the years at secondary school when they had moved apart and taken up different friends, they were still joined: by childhood, secrecy, the flames of friendship still burning.

He too had watched the fire at the Mackies', from the tiny front garden of his house where he had stood with his father. Jimmy had just come back from the pub, and swayed a little, appalled but not sober enough to walk the mile and a half to the Mains, and give his help, as all the other men in the place had done. Bar one.

'I was drinking with yon tinker,' his father had said. 'He telt me his family's bidin at the Mains the nicht.' Then he had turned indoors, unsteady, heading for the whisky bottle he kept in the sideboard, leaving Stanley alone by the gate, sick at heart.

He was bound to David. That was why he had travelled so far. But perhaps there was only so far you *could* go. He had other ties now.

They stood by the side of the road, traffic roaring past, and in its wake, over and over, gusts of gritty wind. Even more now, David wanted to go on, to put as great a distance as he could between himself and the long cheating lie that all his life had turned out to be. But he also saw that no one else could share this. He turned to Stanley, looking skinny and frail in his combat jacket and jeans, the rucksack too heavy for him.

'Cheers,' David said. 'It's OK. You go home. I'll manage fine – send you a postcard.'

Stanley hesitated. Then he put out his hand, and David gripped it in his larger, stronger one.

'Aye. All right then. Keep in touch, eh? See you, Davy.' He crossed the dual carriageway by a pedestrian bridge arching overhead. Then, for a while, they stood on either side of the road, waiting for lifts in different directions. David got one first – a Jaguar with a couple in the front, going on holiday. He turned round as they drove on with him in the back, and waved at Stanley, who was too far off to see, and anyway, holding out his arm, thumb extended, watching the traffic.

David leaned back, and shut his eyes.

'Back-packing, are you?' the woman asked, turning round and offering him a toffee. 'You students – such wonderful long holidays.'

'Yes,' David said. 'It's great.'

22

Eleanor spent Sunday evening with Gavin.

'We'll be back on Wednesday night,' she said. 'I'll see you then.'

'I'll survive. In fact, I'm going out Wednesday.'

'Oh.'

'Guy I know works in Aberdeen now – he's up seeing his sister. We're having a drink. Don't worry,' he added. 'It's not another woman.'

'I didn't think it was.' She punched him with a cushion, joking, but thinking, Can I trust him, really?

'I'm cementing relationships,' he told her. 'For when I move to Aberdeen.'

'*Move?*'

'In six months, maybe. Not more.' He saw the look on her face. 'I told you, Eleanor, about the job.'

'Yes, but I thought you meant here.'

'That's not possible. What is there to do here? The office is in Aberdeen. That's where I'll be based.'

'But I thought – I thought you wanted . . .' She could not say it. Had she got this all wrong?

He put his arm round her. 'I was hoping you'd come with me. We could get a house, see how things went. But I thought, since it's months away, we'd have plenty of time to discuss it later. You're caught up in family stuff just now, I realise that.'

'Yes, but—'

'You don't want to.'

'No. Yes. I thought—'

She had thought, foolishly, she realised now, that he would work in Inverness, and they would somehow continue as they were, but planning perhaps to buy a bigger house together, years from now, when Claire had left home. Since Ian's death she had had only hazy notions of the future. This had been, for her, quite a clear vision.

'I can't leave here,' she said. 'Claire would hate to move. And she's doing Standard Grades next year. I couldn't disrupt her then.'

'You wouldn't have to move right away,' he suggested. 'I'd come up weekends, maybe till she'd finished her exams.'

More parting and reunion, she thought, only worse. He would not be safely on an oil rig, but in the city, working and living a separate life.

'There's Marion too.'

'But her treatment's finished, you said. In six months, she'll be a lot better. Believe me.'

She saw that he did not understand. She could not be so far away every time Marion had a scan, a test, if she needed more treatment; if the cancer came back. She had to live here; that would not change.

'I don't know,' she said. 'I don't know what to say.'

'Leave it,' he advised. 'There's no need to make any decisions just now.'

Eleanor did not sleep well that night, and got up tired to see Claire off to school. At half past eight, clearing away breakfast, she thought of calling David. Perhaps he would want to meet them in Aberdeen. There was nothing of Alice's he would want, surely, and he would soon have his £6,000, but he should at least be told what they were doing. But there was no reply from the flat.

'Yes, I tried him last night,' Marion said when Eleanor told her this. 'He must have been out all evening.'

When they reached Pitcairn, their father had also been trying to contact David. 'He must be away on business,' he decided. 'Now then, I'll get you the house keys.'

'How's Mamie?'

'Not so bad. They've had her up already, trying to walk.'

'It's a wonder she wasn't killed, falling downstairs,' Marion said.

'Plenty of padding,' their father joked, handing over the keys.

'We'll see you back here at tea-time, then, or are you coming to the house too?'

'No, no. I'll visit her, then just come home. But why don't you two have your tea at the house, then go up to the hospital a wee while afterwards? Save you driving all the way out here and back again.'

'All right – that's not a bad idea.' Eleanor was worried that any more driving around would tire Marion too much.

Their father set off for the hospital after they had had a sandwich lunch.

'How long do you think it will take us?' Marion asked as they washed up the plates and mugs.

'I don't know. Two hours?'

'Let's leave it then, go in about three.'

'Right – you have a liedown, till then.'

The sun was shining, so Marion sat at the back door on one of the old garden chairs, and read for an hour.

Alice's house smelt musty when they opened the front door. Sunlight lay across the hall, but upstairs the landing seemed dark. At the top, there was a bundle of clothes, roughly piled together.

'Look. She must have been carrying that lot when she tripped. I suppose Dad gathered them up.' Eleanor ran lightly upstairs, then at the top turned and looked back. Marion was leaning on the newel post. 'You go and sit in the living room.

I'll scout around, see what there is, and either bring it down or you can come up.'

'All right.' Here, Marion saw that the surfaces were dusty, but the room was neat, with nothing lying about except a copy of the *People's Friend* on the coffee-table, and Mamie's knitting bag, leaning against an armchair. Marion sat down, and waited for Eleanor.

Eleanor hardly knew where or how to begin. She went into Alice's bedroom. It was at the back of the house, cool and shadowy. Eleanor had not often been in the room before, though of course she had seen it, passing the open door on her way to the bathroom. Here were the familiar oak dressing-table and wardrobe, the green satin counterpane, the wallpaper with tiny violets and roses, the bedside table with its green-shaded lamp and alarm clock. Throughout the rest of the house every surface had its photographs, china shepherdesses, Hummel figures, glass animals, silver rose bowls. But perhaps they all belonged to Mamie. Here, there were no ornaments, and on the dressing-table, apart from Alice's tortoiseshell brush and comb, and a jar of Pond's Cold Cream, only one small photograph in a gilt frame. Eleanor picked it up. David, aged about twelve, in the garden at Pitcairn. He grinned out at Eleanor, hair tousled, in open-necked shirt and shorts. She looked round again, but there were no other photographs, nothing that was not functional and necessary. In the corner by the window stood an elegant little bureau, polished walnut, with two drawers. There were three books lying on top: a biography of Mary Wollstonecraft, a gardening manual, and a historical novel set during the Napoleonic Wars. The biography and the novel were from the library, and weeks overdue. Eleanor put them aside, so that her father could return them later.

The wardrobe door was open. There were still a few skirts and dresses hanging there, and on the floor, a roll of black plastic bags. Eleanor checked the dressing-table drawers: white slips, underwear, cotton pyjamas, stockings. She closed them, feeling awkward about touching these. But they would have to go, and there were plenty of charities to take them. So, the clothes were easy. She could fold them neatly, and tie up the bags. Before she did, she would just check through and see if there was anything she and Marion might want to have. Alice's clothes were good, if plain, and Eleanor could see herself wearing one of the grey or navy suit jackets with her jeans, or a long patterned skirt.

She crossed to the bureau and opened the flap, which squeaked as it moved. In the pigeon-holes, there were letters and other documents neatly tied with pink legal tape. In the centre was a tiny cupboard, locked, but without a key. Eleanor tried the desk key, but that was too big. She looked in all the pigeon-holes, taking out the contents and laying them on the leather-covered writing surface, faded red, edged with a gold border that had rubbed off in places. Gently, she raised the flap and opened the drawers. In the top one, writing paper, envelopes, engagement diaries for the last two or three years, a few pens and pencils. In the bottom drawer were photograph albums, some very old, and two jewellers' boxes, long and narrow. One held the locket, the other a single string of pearls. Eleanor took the boxes out and laid them on the desk with the papers. Then she slid the drawer shut. She would look at the albums later, with Marion. Then, as if something – someone – nudged her, she opened the box with the locket again and took it out. The locket was large and old-fashioned. Eleanor thought it had belonged to her grandmother, whom she barely remembered. She could not make out the initials entwined on the front. It was difficult to prise apart, but she finally managed to edge a fingernail under the catch and it flew open. Inside, two tiny photographs. Eleanor moved nearer to the window.

In one, a man from another age, with a moustache and a stiff collar, perhaps her grandfather. In the other, a young woman with piled-up hair and a high-necked dress. As Eleanor touched this tiny representation of someone she recalled only as an old woman with an apron and a querulous voice, who smelled of peppermints, it slipped out and fluttered to the floor. Eleanor was about to bend to pick it up, when she saw that there was another photograph behind – no wonder the top one was loose. A baby. Very young and new, in a shawl, with eyes shut. Alice? Gently, Eleanor touched the photograph of her grandfather, and it too slipped out of the oval frame. Behind this also, another photograph. A boy of six or seven, faint, but this time unmistakable. Eleanor's heart began to beat faster. This was an invasion, it did not feel right. Alice's room, her clothes, her jewellery, her dead parents. Her secrets.

Eleanor fitted the photographs back into the locket and laid it in its box. Then she pulled up the dressing-table stool and sat by the bureau, opening the pink-taped bundles one by one. She was doing no more than glance through, aware that she was looking for something, without knowing quite what it was. Even when she found it, opened up the sheet of paper, dry with age and disuse, tried to read it, make sense of the information it so coolly imparted: even then, she did not at first understand what she had discovered.

Downstairs, Marion had looked idly through the *People's Friend*, comforted by the way it remained unchanged since she had read it as a child, coming to visit her aunts. However, in a few minutes, the pages blurred, and she grew drowsy. Warmed by the sunlight spreading over carpet and chairs, she fell into a doze, her head resting on the cushions of Alice's high-backed armchair. She swam in and out of dreams, heard cattle lowing in the field behind Pitcairn, seemed to hear Kirsty and Eilidh talking together. Then her mother was there, in the kitchen not at Pitcairn but in Marion's own house. Sleeves pushed back, her apron on, rolling out pastry at Marion's pine table. Marion was annoyed that she could not make the pie herself, because she was too tired, but relieved that at last her mother had come to look after them all. 'It's David I worry about,' her mother was saying.

'Marion!'

She opened her eyes, tried to focus. Eleanor was in the room, Alice and Mamie's living room, holding up a sheet of paper, a form of some kind.

'I'm sorry, you were asleep. But Marion—' Eleanor's face was flushed, her eyes wide. Marion made an effort, and sat up.

'What's wrong?'

'This – look at this.'

'What is it?' Eleanor thrust the paper at her. Marion turned it the right way up, held it straight, worked out what it was. 'It's a birth certificate,' she said, feeling stupid and slow.

'It's David's.' Eleanor slumped on the other chair by the fireside, Mamie's smaller, softer chair.

Marion studied the certificate again, then looked up at Eleanor. 'It can't be. It's – good grief, Alice had a baby, years ago – that's what it tells us. She had a baby. What on earth . . .'

'It's David.'

'Well, the name is the same, but that could be a coincidence.'

'No, look at the date. There couldn't have been another baby.'

Marion looked. 'Oh God.'

'This can't be true, can it? Marion, tell me there's some other explanation.'

Marion shook her head. 'No,' she said. 'You're right. David John Cairns, born twenty-seventh April, Aberdeen Royal Maternity Hospital.'

'But the mother's name – it's not Mum. It's Alice.'

'And no father's name – there's no entry for that.'

'Then who—' Eleanor began.

'Well, who is there to ask, now?'

'Dad. Mamie.'

'We're going to have to ask. Aren't we?'

Eleanor did not know. They sat quite still, Marion holding the certificate.

'Look,' Marion said, after a moment. 'It was Dad who asked us to go through Alice's things.'

'And Mamie.'

'They knew fine we were going to find this.'

'You think . . .' Eleanor hesitated. 'They *wanted* us to find out?'

'Yes. Doesn't it look like that to you?'

'I don't know. I don't feel I know *anything* any more. The whole world seems to have got a big crack in it.'

'Are there a lot of other papers?' Marion asked.

'Well, yes, but I hadn't got far when I found this.'

'I'll come up,' Marion said, easing herself out of the chair.

'No, it's cold up there. I'll bring everything down, all the papers. There's only one wee cupboard thing in the bureau I can't get into. The key's missing. But I'll bring everything that was in the pigeon-holes.'

'Try the dressing table,' Marion suggested. 'Taped behind the mirror.'

'What?'

'For the other key.'

'Really?'

Marion was right: a tiny key was taped to the back of the dressing-table mirror. Eleanor prised it off, and used it to open the bureau cupboard. Inside were a couple of black and white photographs, and a letter. One of the photographs was of Alice, standing by a window, a shawled infant in her arms. But she did not look at the child she held so firmly; she stared at the camera, unsmiling. She was stiff and strange, like someone who had never held a child before. And yet, there was something uneasily familiar too, in her outline, her appearance. Eleanor put this behind the other photograph and studied it instead. A man, not young or handsome, but with a hard, vigorous face, a shock of dark hair, a high-bridged nose. It was a snapshot taken in the open air. He leaned on the parapet of a bridge; there were trees behind, and he wore slacks and a pullover over an open-necked shirt. He smiled, but fixedly, as if he had held the pose too long, and the casual grin for the camera had become rigid, humourless.

Eleanor gathered up everything in her arms: papers, photographs, letters, and took them downstairs. Together, she and Marion went through everything.

'You know,' Eleanor said as they began, 'Dad's the executor. Surely he should have gone through all this lot?'

'Not necessarily. There are no bank statements here, no cheque books, any of that stuff. He must have all of those. And the will.'

'That's right,' Eleanor agreed. 'He said there were shares and building society accounts, and there's no evidence of that here. This is all just personal stuff.'

'But he's been through these as well,' Marion pointed out. 'Or someone has. Perhaps Mamie.'

'How do you know?'

'The tape is wrinkled – look, as if the knot was somewhere else before.'

'Goodness, you're very observant.'

'Slow, that's all,' Marion smiled. 'I can't go at your speed.'

'It's like being a detective, isn't it?' Eleanor said. 'Except it's too . . . I don't know. I feel terribly anxious suddenly. I want more . . . proof.'

'What, that David is really Alice's son?'

'Did Mum and Dad adopt him?'

'Maybe. Or maybe he just came to live with us. He certainly

lived with us from when he was very, very tiny.' Marion thought of the baby taken from the pram, held out for her to see. *Your new brother.*

'Why didn't Alice keep him?'

'She was single. I suppose the guy made off.'

Eleanor held out the photograph of the man leaning on the bridge. 'I think this was him.'

'Goodness,' Marion said. 'I see what you mean.'

'David?'

'Oh yes.' Marion took the photograph from Eleanor. 'David's father, all right.'

Eleanor thrust the other photograph at Marion. 'It was in the locked cupboard along with this – Alice, with David, I assume.'

Marion took this photograph from Eleanor as well, and gazed at it in silence for a moment. Then she murmured, 'She's like – I don't know. It reminds me of something.'

'I know. I think it's just a family likeness – Dad and her. David as well, I suppose.'

'Maybe.'

'There was this letter too. I haven't opened it yet. It's to Alice at another address – Viewfield Road?'

'That was her flat, I think,' Marion said. 'Where she lived before Mamie came back to stay with her.'

Eleanor was sliding out a single sheet of paper. 'Eric,' she said. 'It's from someone called Eric.'

'What does it say?'

Eleanor's fingers trembled a little as she passed it over. Her eyes were filled with tears. 'Oh dear, oh Marion.'

Marion read it. 'Not a love letter then,' she said.

'What a sod. It was him then, this Eric, got her pregnant. Then left her.'

'But Eleanor . . .' Marion bit her lip, then went on: 'Eleanor, she was over forty by then. Forty-two, in fact. Not a young girl.'

'All the worse,' Eleanor said, knowing this, thinking Marion was too safe in marriage to understand.

'All these other letters.' Marion picked up a bundle of them. 'No love letters here, either? They're wartime ones. Some from Dad.'

'And women friends. And someone called Jack, or it could be Jackie, so that might be a woman too.' Eleanor peered at a signature. 'But they're just friendly letters all of them. Nothing romantic.'

'It must have been awful for her.' Marion took up the photograph of the man again.

'He doesn't look like an Eric,' Eleanor said.

'Maybe not, but this is him, David's father, isn't it?'

'Oh yes,' Eleanor agreed. 'Now I know, I can see it. The jawline, the hair . . . I bet he never settled anywhere either. Men like that – do so much damage.' She was thinking of Gavin, not sure if her tears were for Alice or for herself. But all her pity was for Alice, caught in an age when illegitimacy was a scandal, full of shame.

'I recognise this name.' Marion was still reading. 'It was someone she was in the WAAFs with – these letters and postcards are all from her. And letters from Mamie. One about Uncle Tom – look.' Marion sat back, one of Mamie's letters in her hand. 'Eleanor, when did Mamie move back to Aberdeen?'

'I'm not sure. Around the time David was born, I think.'

'We'll ask Dad. But I think it was before that. She came because Alice was pregnant, didn't she?'

'Yes,' Eleanor said. 'That's what you or I would do.'

'And they *were* like sisters,' Marion realised.

'There's an awful lot of unanswered questions here, though,' Eleanor pointed out.

'Look,' Marion suggested, 'it's going to take ages, if we go at this rate. Why don't we take all the papers and the jewellery—'

'Oh, the locket. I have to show you the locket,' Eleanor broke in. 'Wait a minute, I've left it upstairs.'

'Hang on – there are the clothes as well. We should sort out everything today that has to go to Oxfam or wherever. Then we can parcel up what we want to take back to Pitcairn to go through more slowly. Or take home, perhaps.'

'Yes, you're right. Do you want any of the clothes, Marion? She had very nice jackets and blouses, for someone of eighty.'

Marion laughed. 'Oh dear, it seems so weird, doesn't it?' She got to her feet. 'I'll make us a cup of tea, and you start on the clothes. I'll be up in a minute.'

In the kitchen, waiting for the kettle to boil, Marion thought of Alice and Mamie living here all these years while Alice's son was brought up by someone else. She wondered if Mamie had wanted to keep David with them. Who had made the decision? And her mother – Marion could not imagine how it had all happened. As if, she thought, when Ian died, Eleanor had a baby and I took that baby to live with me. Or no, if she had a baby now, and this Gavin disappeared . . . But this was so far beyond imagining that she gave it up, and made the tea, taking it up to Eleanor with a tin of chocolate biscuits.

So they worked on together, the sisters, packing up clothes, talking, laying aside a blouse or a jacket, but conscious that what mattered of Alice was lying on the living-room floor below, telling a different story from the cool bedroom, the plain clothes, the spinster's life.

The question now, of course, was whether David knew, and if he did not, how – or whether – they should tell him.

23

'Somehow,' Marion said, as they drove to the hospital later, 'when you find out something like this, however much of a shock it is, you feel, in a way, you've always known it.'

'I still can't imagine what we're going to say to Mamie,' Eleanor sighed. 'I mean, she's only just had a major operation, and she's quite frail.'

'We could wait, speak to Dad instead,' Marion suggested. 'But we'll see how Mamie is first.'

Mamie was sitting up in bed, pink with the heat in the ward, wearing a lacy nightdress. Her lipstick was slightly smeared, but the wearing of it was defiant and cheerful. Her hair stood up in a white fluff, and she apologised for it the minute they arrived.

'You canna keep yourself nice in hospital,' she complained. 'Look at me, I'm nae presentable. I winna get my hair washed e'er the morn.'

'You look great,' Eleanor said, bending to kiss the soft cheek, smelling illness, sourness, under a waft of flowery perfume. Indeed, she looked better than Marion who had sat down at once on one of the plastic chairs, white faced.

'We brought you some flowers and a magazine.' Eleanor laid them on the bed.

'Lovely, dear. Your dad was in this afternoon. He said you were coming.'

Eleanor and Marion glanced at each other. Then Eleanor went to fetch another chair. When she came back, Mamie said, 'You've been at the house today?'

'Yes, I hope it's all right with you. Dad said you wanted us to sort out Alice's things.'

'I've been putting it off, and that's the truth,' Mamie admitted. 'Eh dearie me, it's a sad business, getting rid of a body's belongings.' She patted the bed. 'And now look at me. What a silly auld woman, eh? Tumbled a the wey down the stairs.'

'You could have been killed,' Eleanor said.

'Ach I'm nae so easy to kill.' She chuckled and lifted the flowers to sniff at them. 'Oh, I aye liked freesias.' She laid them down again. 'Now then, did you go into the bureau?'

'Yes,' Eleanor said, 'we took everything out.'

'And what did you find?'

She knows, Marion thought, she knows what we found. She and Eleanor looked at each other again, not sure what to say.

'Ach, I telt your father. I said it was high time he said something. You were bound to find out by and by; indeed, if Alice had had her way, he'd have gone into it all when your mother died. But he wouldn't go against your mother's wishes. She couldn't persuade him to that.'

'Mamie, what happened?' Marion asked. 'We found David's birth certificate – it was an awful shock.'

'Of course it was. Daft, to keep it hidden all these years. Not that it was all your mother's doing. Alice was just as determined. But oh, I often thought, one wrong word – it was like walking a tightrope sometimes, but the trouble is, the langer a secret's kept, the mair difficult it is to let it out.' She looked sharply at Marion. 'Poor lass, it's been too much for you, I can see that. You're not up to hospital visiting. Away you go, the pair of you. Come in tomorrow afore you set off home. They'll let you in, I'll speak to the ward sister.'

'I'm sorry,' Eleanor began, 'we do have to go home tomorrow.' She would have liked to stay on, to question Mamie. She was sure it was Mamie who could best make it all clear, and she was afraid of upsetting her father, who would find it more difficult to talk. But Marion looked ill, and must be got back to Pitcairn, and bed.

As they prepared to leave, and Eleanor leaned down to kiss her aunt again, she could not help asking, 'Auntie Mamie, does David know?'

'Ah,' she said, and for the first time in their visit, looked old and weary, 'that I canna say. But you could maybe take a guess yourselves about that.'

'I'm sorry,' Marion said as Eleanor negotiated traffic, getting them out onto the Deeside road at last. 'We should have stayed and talked. But . . .'

'It's all right, you're worn out. No wonder. All these bloody secrets – it's exhausting.'

'I still can't believe it.'

'I know this is silly, but I've only just realised – David's not our brother.'

'Somehow,' Marion said, 'that's the least surprising thing about it.'

'Oh, Marion.'

'Well, he's always been different. Remember all that fuss about his Highers? He was perfectly well able to pass them. And the way he just ran off? I'll never forget those awful days when no one knew where he was. Well, weeks, really, before he got in touch. It was only because poor Stanley changed his mind at Newcastle and came back that we knew anything at all. He didn't just have to face his dad, and that dreadful Irene, it was our parents as well. I think a lot of Stanley for coming to tell Mum the way he did.'

'It was the year you got married,' Eleanor said.

'That's right – graduated in July, married in September. And not a word from David till just before the wedding. It was years before I could think about that without being *angry*. He absolutely ruined that summer. It should have been so lovely.' The anger was rising again, as she thought of it. 'And look at the mess he's made of his life since then.'

'It's not a mess – well, no more than mine is.' Eleanor still felt she and David were twinned, belonged together. Impossible to accept he could have known this unbelievable thing, without telling her he knew. Marion thinks I'm like her, she thought, but I'm not, I'm like David.

'Oh nonsense,' Marion said. '*Your* life's not a mess. You've had awful things happen – losing a baby, then Ian. But you've been brave and strong: made a life for yourself and Claire, managed on your own. I'm only concerned this Gavin isn't good enough for you. Another drifter like David. That's what I'm afraid of.'

The road was quiet; the car coasted. On either side there were trees, then fields. It was easy driving, but for Eleanor it was almost too much. Her hands gripped the wheel, and she leaned forward, tense.

'Do you think so?' she said. 'Do you really think I coped well?'

'Whereas David,' Marion went on, 'has drifted about from one place to another, had dozens of jobs, and moved from one woman to another as well, I'm pretty sure. I'm not altogether convinced he hasn't actually been in prison during one of his long absences.'

'Oh no, Marion.'

'Well.' Her sister fell silent, looking out of the window.

'He's still our cousin,' Eleanor said, after a moment.

'I wonder what his father was like, this Eric,' Marion mused.

'He looked quite a strong character, in the photograph.'

'He left her flat.'

'Maybe she wouldn't have him,' Eleanor suggested.

Marion laughed. 'Well, knowing Alice, that's certainly a possibility.'

'How did it all come about?' Eleanor wondered. 'I somehow can't picture it – the discussions they must have had. Was it Alice's idea, to give him up for adoption? Then Mum and Dad said they would have him?'

'I suppose it must have been something like that,' Marion nodded. 'Och, there's no point speculating. We've got to ask Dad.'

But they continued to speculate, all the way back to Pitcairn.

As they drew up in front of the house, Marion said, 'Are you going to say something?'

'Me?'

'Well, I will then. But what? It might come better from you.'

'Why?'

'You were the one who found it.' Marion shrugged. 'I just feel so awkward. Not the kind of thing it's easy to speak to your parents about.'

Eleanor switched off the engine, but neither made a move to get out of the car.

'He must know, anyway,' Eleanor pointed out. 'He was so keen for me to go through everything.'

Their father was watching television. He rose and switched it off as they came in. 'Sit yourselves down. How was she tonight?'

Eleanor hovered by the door as Marion went to an armchair near the fire. It was not cold, but their father chopped wood all year, and liked to keep the open fire going. And he, Marion realised, had always been the one to clear out and lay the fire in the morning, before he went to work. David used to watch, wanting to do it himself, wanting to be the one to strike the match, and light it. But by the time he was old enough to be allowed, he had lost interest, and would have nothing to do with it. He had given up, she saw now, playing with matches.

But this memory, like all the others, might have to be adjusted. He was not their brother.

'Do you want tea or coffee or something, Marion?' Eleanor asked.

'A cup of tea, if you can be bothered.'

'Dad?'

'Aye, fine. There's cake in the tin. Mamie made me take it from the house. She said it would go to waste.'

Left alone with her father, Marion was silent, gazing at the fire.

'How did you get on?' John Cairns leaned forward to take up the poker and stab at burning logs. They fell apart, a red-hot glow appearing between, and he placed another log on top.

'Oh, we've parcelled up all the clothes. Eleanor's taken the locket, and I have the pearls. Is that all right?'

'I'm sure it is. Mamie wanted you to have the things.'

An awkward silence fell between them. Then Eleanor came in with the tray. 'Kettle's nearly boiling,' she said. 'I'll bring the tea in a minute.' She laid the tray on the table by the window and went out again. Their father made a remark about the weather, and Marion agreed. There was silence again, till Eleanor came in.

The cake was dark and moist, full of fruit. And yet, none of them could eat it. They drank tea, all three conscious of the unspoken thing that was with them in the room.

'So,' their father said, setting down his mug, 'did you look in the bureau? I took out the bank books and so on, but I left everything else she had in there. There were photograph albums I thought you girls might like to have. They go back before Alice was born – they belonged to your grandparents.

You'll hardly mind on them, I dare say. But there's snaps of their life, when they had the smiddy. Did you recall your Granda Cairns was a blacksmith?'

'Yes, I think so.'

'And Mamie's mother and father, Alex and Rose. You'll maybe mind on them, Marion. They used to visit us when we first moved here.' He seemed to muse for a moment on these long-finished lives. 'Then Alex died, and she went into a home,' he began again.

'Dad,' Eleanor broke in, unable to go on with this. 'Dad, I've got to say it. You know anyway, don't you? We found David's birth certificate.'

John Cairns leaned back in his chair, one hand in front of his face, shielding his eyes. He rubbed them hard, then pushed his hand back over brow and scalp. 'Aye,' he said. 'It's bound to have been a shock to you. You didn't know, then? You had no inkling?'

'How could we?' Marion burst out. 'How could we possibly know?'

'I'm sorry,' he said. 'I'm very sorry about all of this.' His face looked grey. A surge of pity swept over Eleanor.

'Oh Dad,' she cried, 'why did no one tell us? We're not blaming you, it's not that.'

'Was it Alice?' Marion asked. 'Did she not want anyone to know?'

'Alice and your mother.' He managed a rueful smile. 'I couldn't go against the pair of them, now could I?' He took the poker to the fire again, spoiling it. 'And in the end, it was the right way to do it. We brought him up, he was our boy.'

'But you wanted us to know now, didn't you?' Marion prompted. 'Was that because Alice and Mum are both . . . gone?'

'Oh well, I'd no choice. With the will.'

'The will?'

I knew there was something, Marion thought.

'Alice has left the house to David.'

Eleanor frowned. 'But how could she do that? It's Mamie's house too.'

'No, it belonged to Alice. Mamie's to be allowed to live in it the rest of her life, but then it passes to David.'

'The house. The house in Duthie Crescent is David's.' Eleanor could not take this in. 'And he got £6,000 as well – like Marion and me?'

Their father looked uneasy. 'Quite a bit more than that. Legacies to Mamie and me, and you girls. The rest to David.' He sighed. 'Ach, wills cause nothing but ill-feeling. Mamie thinks you girls should have equal shares with David. She says she told Alice you were the ones came to visit, and did things for them, kept in touch, brought your bairns. Not David.'

'Oh well,' Marion said dryly, 'he is her son.'

'That's the way Alice thought of it.' Eleanor was nearest her father; he patted her knee. 'And you two will get this place when I'm gone. Nae that I've much money to leave. But with house prices they way they are, even this far out of Aberdeen, you'll have a tidy sum each.'

'I don't care about the money!' Eleanor burst out. 'It's the secret – it's not being told. I feel as if you and Mum were lying to us all our lives.'

'Oh dear me, now see what a hornet's nest this has stirred up. I saw how it would be.' And her father rose, unable to sit still. 'I tell you what, how about a dram? We could do with it.'

Marion would not have one, but he poured generous whiskies for Eleanor and himself. He downed half of his in the first swallow.

'That's more like it.'

'Oh, Dad.'

'I'm sorry, Eleanor. I'm sorry for the pair of you. But what could I do?'

'Nothing, knowing Mum, knowing Alice,' Marion admitted. 'It's all right, we're just feeling a bit stunned. And we want to know now how it happened, all that.'

'Oh, Mamie could tell you better than I could. At least how Alice came to have a bairn at that age, after being a single woman all her life. For she was never interested in men, that I could see. Though she was bonny enough as a young lass.'

'Dad,' Eleanor asked, 'Does David know?' A pause, while her father took another gulp of whisky.

'Yes,' he said. 'Not that we told him. We never intended to make him any different from the two of you. And to this day, I couldn't tell you exactly how he did come to know. But he does.'

'Does he know he's inherited her house, and Alice's money?' Marion asked.

'No, he's no idea of that. I've been phoning the number he gave me, but there's never a soul there.'

'Poor old David,' Marion said, half laughing, 'we should put out an SOS for him.'

'An ad in the paper,' Eleanor suggested. '*If David Cairns contacts his family, he will hear something to his advantage.*'

They both laughed, then stopped, looking guiltily at their father. But he seemed relieved, and smiled back. Some of the tension had gone.

'Tell us, then,' Eleanor prompted. 'Tell us what happened.'

So in the mild May evening, daylight fading behind the lilac trees, with the fire glowing, the room shadowy, their father talked, and the old story unfolded.

'The first we knew of it,' he began, 'was when Mamie came to us.'

Mamie was still living in Northumberland then. Uncle Tom had died the previous year, but Mamie lived on in the police house, since it was not yet wanted for anyone else. She worked in a draper's, and sold jumpers and cardigans she had knitted at home, through the shop. She had thought about coming back to Aberdeen, but she liked her village by the sea, and has good friends there.

'She wouldn't have come home at all, would she,' Marion guessed, 'if Alice hadn't got pregnant?'

'Who's to say? But Alice got in touch, and asked her to come up. "I need your help," she said. Mamie was never one to turn away anyone that needed her. Pity, your mother and I used to say, she never had bairns herself.'

When Mamie arrived, she saw at once that Alice was pregnant.

'She hadn't been near us in over a month,' John Cairns said. 'Kept saying she was busy at work.'

So it was Mamie who had come to tell John and Faith. Their house in Aberdeen was on the other side of the city from Alice's flat, two separate bus rides away. Mamie missed her second bus, and ended up walking the last two miles. She arrived to find Faith in the garden taking down her washing, with Marion on the swing, Eleanor toddling by her feet. It was a blustery October day, a good drying day, but a black cloud was rising from the horizon, so Faith wanted to get the clothes in and folded. She had not heard Mamie coming, and almost dropped the full basket she was holding when she turned. Mamie was not used to walking; even then, she was plump, and had arrived very out of breath. For a moment, neither of them spoke. Later, Mamie was to say, 'I hardly needed to say a word. She was very quick, your mother. She saw there was trouble.'

In the kitchen, the women talked. Frequently, the children interrupted, and Faith had to get up to fetch Eleanor's pot, or untie a knitted doll's bonnet for Marion – childish, mundane things. Mamie began to think of Alice's 'problem' as a baby, another life, someone who would call and cry and play like Marion and Eleanor.

'Stay for your tea,' Faith said. 'We'll get peace when the bairns are in bed.'

'No, I don't want to be out when Alice gets home from her work. She's in a bad way.'

'Upset?' Faith could not imagine this. Nothing seemed to distress Alice; she was too cool, dry.

'Well, yes. But not what you'd call – showing it.' Mamie tried to find the words. 'Buttoned-up. Angry.'

'Angry?'

'Aye, that's it. She just canna get ower this happening. I says to her, it happens to the best of women, we all make mistakes. Nature has her way, whiles. But she would do anything to change the way things are. If you get my meaning.'

'Oh no, Mamie. Surely not. But how . . . ?' They knew only respectable women and doctors. But they had heard of other kinds. However, Mamie had put her foot down, a rare thing.

'"I will help you all I can," I says to her. "I'll bring up the bairn myself. But I will not have anything to do with these backstreet craturs".'

Perhaps in the end, Alice had not known how to set about getting rid of her baby. Or her nerve had failed. But she had gone on as if it were possible to keep the secret for ever. She would talk to no one about it.

'But at work?' Eleanor asked her father. 'It was a scandal in those days. She was lucky they kept her on.'

'Ach, they couldn't in decency do anything else,' John scoffed. 'They had employed the fellow.'

'Eric?'

'Was that what he was called. I hadna minded. His surname was Foster, anyway.' He snorted. 'Fellow went off with more than Alice's good name, at any rate. Took a deal of money he wasn't entitled to as well. But in the end, Peter Simpson decided to hush it up. For Alice's sake, I whiles think. He was fond of Alice, in his way.'

'Why didn't he marry her, this Eric? Or was he really just some sort of criminal?' Marion wanted to know.

It had fallen into place. The old man at the funeral, her father's reference to the partner who had left. Eric was that partner; Eric was Alice's lover.

'That's what your mother asked: could she not get married? But Mamie said the fellow had left the town already. She was convinced he had a wife some other place. I couldn't say. Then, as I said, it was discovered he'd taken money out of the firm. Peter blamed himself for that. I think he felt he should have kept a closer eye, noticed something.'

'Was he prosecuted? Did you ever find him?' Eleanor asked.

'Peter and I did try to trace him,' her father said. 'At least to get some money for Alice, for the bairn. But she put a stop to that. She said she wouldn't take a penny from him anyway. Proud! She was a proud woman, by God.'

All the way through her pregnancy, Alice insisted that the baby was to be given up for adoption. Mamie tried to persuade her otherwise, offering to stay with Alice and look after the child.

'He'll want for nothing,' she had said.

'He'll want for a father,' Alice had retorted. 'Brought up by two old women – no, no. Better adopted. Plenty couples want babies.'

Then, when the child was born, she changed her mind. Eleanor and Marion, trying to imagine how this had come about, found themselves daunted, unable to fill in the gaps in their father's story. It was the gaps that mattered, Eleanor decided, but no one could tell them what Alice had been thinking. At any rate, she was no longer willing to give the child up to strangers. But she would not feed him, nor change him herself. As soon as she was home from the Maternity Hospital, she gave him over to Mamie.

Then Mamie changed too. She was forty-one; she realised

suddenly how demanding a baby would be. David cried. He cried most of the day and all night, it seemed to those two desperate women, Mamie pacing the floor, Alice heating Ovaltine for them both, to comfort them in the long night.

'What do you want to do?' Mamie had asked, and Alice replied, trying to talk above the baby's piercing screams, 'I don't know. But it seems wrong to give him away. How would we know they'd bring him up right?'

'Should we keep him ourselves?' But Mamie, jiggling the infant in her arms, so that he redoubled his efforts, screamed even louder, was now afraid of what would happen if Alice said yes.

'Then everyone would know he had no father!' Alice shouted. Then, for the first time, she broke down and began to cry. 'No father, no brothers and sisters – what kind of life could we give him?'

Mamie never forgot that night. Alice, with black thumb-print shadows under her dark eyes, huddled on her bed. Mamie walking up and down, up and down. Finally, exhausted, she laid the baby in the pram they had bought, and suddenly, with no subsiding cries, no warning, he fell asleep. They sat together in a silence that was even more terrifying than the noise which had preceded it, and wept together.

'In the end,' John Cairns told his daughters, 'your mother said we could take him. She was having no more children herself, for Eleanor had been a Caesarian section, and they told her then she shouldn't have another. But she knew I'd have liked a boy.' He saw the way Marion and Eleanor looked at each other.

'However,' he said, 'by that time, I had my two wee girls. I'd stopped minding.' Marion shook her head, smiling. 'Aye, lass, I had,' he insisted. 'I'm proud of my girls.' He cleared his throat, embarrassed. 'Well, your mother was only twenty-eight. Young. She said she would take him.'

'And was that all right with Alice and Mamie?' Marion asked.

'At the time, they were mightily relieved, I suspect. You never heard an infant bawl the way David did, those first weeks.' He shook his head, smiling. 'And yet, you know, he was only a few weeks old when he came to us, and he hadn't been here more than two or three days, when he settled. Your mother had him sleeping near through the night.' He sighed. 'So it was the best thing, eh?'

'So, did you go on to adopt him?' Eleanor wanted to know.

'We never saw the need. Maybe we put it off, left it too late. We were afraid of others interfering. It was a family concern. Your mother said to me, "He's better here, he'd be an only child otherwise." She had been an only one herself, and her mother very possessive. Very ambitious. Her mother wasn't best pleased when she married me, and gave up the dancing.'

Marion and Eleanor had heard this story before, and saw no need to go over it again.

'So there was no formal adoption?' Eleanor persisted.

'No.'

'But what about when he needed a birth certificate? I mean, why didn't you just tell him the truth from the start?'

'Neither Alice nor your mother would have it. They agreed on that. And you can get a short certificate that just has the name and date and place. Nothing about parents on it. That one is fine for most things.'

'So everyone agreed? Alice and Mum took the same view?'

'Oh well. As long as David was a wee boy, it was fine. Or it seemed to be. Alice never interfered.' Looking back, he thought this was both fair and true. But how little the words revealed. He would leave it to Mamie to tell the rest, he thought, finding it painful to go over the old ground. Women were better at this kind of thing.

After a year or so, he admitted, Faith had wanted to make the adoption legal. But Alice would not have this: she agreed that nothing would be said to David and she would not interfere, but she refused to give up her son altogether. Faith lay awake, worrying about it. In the end, this was what persuaded her when John wanted to buy Pitcairn rather than another house in town. They were too close, in Aberdeen; too many people knew them. Physically removed from the city, from Alice, David would be more their own. Even then, she went on worrying.

'If she changes her mind, and wants him back,' she said, 'could we do anything about it? Could we go to court, do you think?'

'Go to court!' He was horrified. This was his family; it would be impossible.

'No,' Faith agreed, 'but I'd like to think we were safe.'

And yet, David had caused her nothing but trouble, growing up, especially when he turned seventeen. That had been a bad time.

However, all through the childhood years, Alice had kept her word, and left it to Faith and John to bring up her son as they saw fit. Faith began to relax. As time went on, it became less and less likely that there would be any change. Alice wanted the best for him, she said. She would not tear him from their family now. She had not been happy about the move to Pitcairn, but later told John she realised it was the best thing for David.

'He can run wild,' she said. 'Boys have a lot of energy. He's safer out here, in the country.'

She sent cheques regularly, insisting on this contribution, and just as regularly Faith paid them into a separate building society account for David. When he went to university, it would help to see him through, she said, and would not touch it for clothes or toys or food. Alice bought his bicycles, a new one every time he outgrew (or outwore) the last. Faith did not like this, but she did not resist.

'Keep my name out of it,' Alice said. 'There's no need to say where the money came from.' Uneasily, with a sense almost of guilt, Faith gave in.

Keeping her distance, Alice had seemed content in her orderly single life. In the summer, she and Mamie went to Austria or Switzerland, once to the Italian lakes. They were active in the church; Mamie helped in an Oxfam shop; Alice chaired the Women's Guild, and sang in a choir. Alice went on working for Simpson and Dalgarno, taking the bus to the city centre in the morning, walking home at five to get exercise. Mamie kept house and cooked. They both gardened at the weekends. They led useful, busy lives.

'I still don't understand how she could do it,' Eleanor said. 'Did she never want David to know she was his mother? I couldn't bear that. It must have been awful.'

'It's a different world now, lass,' her father said. 'Alice hated the idea of anybody knowing she'd had a child out of wedlock. And the funny thing was, even people who knew, people she'd worked with, or at the church, seemed almost to forget. It was as if she had wiped out the past. Wiped it out.'

Eleanor thought of the locket, with its hidden photographs. 'I don't believe that. She hadn't wiped it out for *herself*.'

'You're right,' her father agreed. 'Because when David was seventeen, she suddenly took it into her head she wanted to tell him the truth.'

'No!' Marion exclaimed. 'Why, after all that time?'

'She had a cancer scare – a lump in her breast.' Marion and Eleanor looked at each other, saying nothing. 'Oh, she was luckier than you, it was nothing, not malignant. She had a wee op, she was fine. But she'd had a fright.'

Perhaps, Eleanor wondered, Alice had feared that if she

died, if the secret went on being kept, David would never know who his mother was. And she could not bear that. But Marion wasn't having this.

'Oh come on, Dad, he was *bound* to find out.'

'Oh aye,' her father admitted. 'Bound to. And did. Anyway, it was what you might call a bit of a tussle between your mother and Alice for a while.'

Faith had thought David was at a dangerous age; they were very worried about him.

'It'll do nothing but harm just now,' she insisted. 'Wait at least till his exams are over.'

Alice had finally agreed to this.

'And you know that story,' their father went on. 'David and his exams.'

'So did Alice agree never to say anything?'

'Well, that was the summer he went off to London and disappeared. When he finally got in touch, Alice and your mother were so relieved he was safe – that was the end of it. They agreed to say nothing. In a funny way, all that business brought them together.'

Privately, Alice might have blamed his upbringing; Faith his father, the unknowable genes. But both women wanted only the best for their difficult son.

Marion yawned, shivering a little. 'Oh dear, it's too much, all of this.'

'Time you went to bed.' Eleanor was watchful, her father thought, always watchful of Marion these days.

'You can speak to Mamie tomorrow,' he said. 'She'll tell you more.'

After Marion was in bed, Eleanor came into her room for half an hour. She sat on the bed, and they went on talking. But there could be no end to such a conversation. It would go on and on, for years to come.

'You should sleep now,' Eleanor said, getting up. 'Tomorrow, we really must try to get hold of David again. Maybe

I could find his partner. He had an unusual sort of name – what was it?'

'So strange, the whole thing,' Marion murmured, settling her pillows, lying down. She seemed young and childlike, her dark hair, her pale face, against the white pillows. Eleanor had a lurch of fear for her. *I don't have a brother now. All those years, I believed I had a brother.* She could not grasp this, that David was no longer their brother. But the idea made her want to cling to Marion even more.

Eleanor lay awake for a long time, unable to sleep. Once, falling into a floating half-consciousness, she thought she heard a baby cry, and started awake again. But it was only an owl, hooting in the trees. As she lay listening to it, there came into her mind a memory of the uproar in the night when Marion had fled to their parents' room shrieking about a ghost, a baby crying. Afterwards, she and Marion had cuddled up together in the same bed. Were they still sharing a room then – or had one crept along to be with the other? It must have been me, Eleanor thought drowsily, I was always the scaredy-cat, needing her. Marion's hair, tickling her face like feathers, the softness of her Winceyette pyjamas, their legs tangled together in the narrow bed.

What did she look like, the lady?

A bit like Auntie Alice.

Maybe it was a dream.

The crying wasn't. I heard the crying.

So where did the ghost come from, with her baby in her arms? I saw her too, Eleanor thought, in the garden at Pitcairn, years later. I thought it was the tinker woman, who died in the fire, clinging to her baby. *A bit like Auntie Alice.*

Eleanor turned over, and fell into sleep again, dreaming of Gavin, and that she was going to have his baby after all. When she woke, still believing this, her face was wet with tears. This dream had been so clear and present to her that she was scarcely aware now of having wakened in the night. Something had come to her then, some new idea. But she could not have said what it was.

24

Marion and Eleanor drove home next day, after calling in to see Mamie. She looked more tired than she had the evening before.

'They've had me on two sticks walking the length of that corridor,' she told them, and they were not sure if she was boasting or complaining. She was to be in hospital until the end of the week, then at a convalescent home on Deeside. She was looking forward to that: she had heard the food was good, and there was a visiting hairdresser, so she would get her hair set.

'Have you got hold of David?' she kept asking them. 'He'll want to come and see the house.' She switched between this and a story the nurse had told her. 'She's to be engaged at Christmas. "Why wait?" I says to her. "What have you to wait for at your age?"'

Marion and Eleanor looked at each other. What should they ask, if anything? It seemed more difficult, Mamie less approachable. Then she switched track again.

'Well, did you speak to your father?'

'Yes,' Eleanor said. She hesitated, and Marion stepped in.

'Aunt Mamie, did you meet him, this Eric – David's father?'

Mamie narrowed her eyes, thinking back. 'Aye, I did,' she nodded. 'But that was lang afore Alice was in trouble. By the time I got up to Aberdeen, he'd made himself scarce. But I'd been in Aberdeen a few months back, and we were having our lunch in Esslemont and Mackintosh. They had a nice restaurant, very reasonable.'

However forgetful she was now, Marion knew Mamie would be able to recall the whole menu, and was likely to describe it in detail. She tried to head her off. 'Did you see him in the office then? What was he like?'

'No, no, he came up to us in the restaurant. We were just finishing our first course – steak and kidney pie, I think. Alice just had the Welsh Rarebit, she never ate much in the middle of the day. Anyway, up he comes, and Alice has no choice but to introduce him to me. But you could see she didn't want to.'

'Why not?'

'Och, she was like that. Close.'

'Maybe there was something going on then?' Eleanor asked.

Mamie shook her head. 'I dinna think it. But he was a good-looking man, I'll grant you that.'

'Tidy,' Eleanor supplied. 'That's Claire's word.'

'Oh well, he was in a shirt and tie,' Mamie said, missing this. 'Everybody was smart in an office in those days. Not like the young ones now in their jeans.'

'Aunt Mamie,' Marion asked, 'is David like him?'

'Oh my, yes. Just as well he left the area. He couldn't have made out Davy wasn't his son if he'd stayed.' She paused. 'Oh, he was a waster. A rogue. He was wicked to Alice. A decent woman, he should have kent better.' Mamie was red with indignation, as if the years between had vanished, and the old wrongs were fresh as ever.

'I know he went off with money, Dad told us. But he must have had some good qualities,' Marion persisted.

'He was a charmer,' Mamie said. 'That's what he was.'

'Not *bad* though?' Eleanor asked, knowing what Marion

was trying to find out. 'A rogue, like you said, and probably scared off when she was pregnant, but not really a wicked person.'

But Mamie's gaze had wandered beyond them, down the length of the ward. She touched Eleanor's arm. 'There. That's her.'

'Who?'

'The wee nurse I telt you about. Ask to see her ring – it's awful bonny. She's got it on a chain round her neck while she's at work.'

Eleanor and Marion looked at each other. Mamie leaned back with a sigh.

'Ach, I'm fushionless the day. I'll be glad to get out of here. Did I tell you they're putting me out to Deeside? I'll get my hair done, that's a blessing.'

'That's good,' Marion said, rising from her chair. 'You'll be more rested there. We'd better leave you in peace.'

'Your dad will be wondering where you've got to.'

'No, we're going home now, Aunt Mamie.'

In turn, the sisters kissed Mamie's soft cheek, left her lying with her eyes shut.

'She's not so great today,' Marion said as they left.

'No wonder – it's been a shock.'

'The operation or all the secrets coming out at last?'

'Both.'

They did not talk much for the first part of the journey. It was as if they had reached a barrier that could not be taken down until they had seen David. They were weary of speculation, and felt the hollowness that comes with truth.

'All these lies,' Eleanor said. 'Over and over, for years and years.'

'Oh,' Marion sighed, 'let's talk about something else.'

At this, they both fell silent. Then Eleanor had to stop for traffic lights set up at roadworks, and the silence became too much for Marion.

'What about Gavin?' she asked. 'He's home just now, isn't he?'

'Yes.' The lights changed; the car moved on.

'Are you seeing him tonight, then?'

'He's getting a job in Aberdeen,' Eleanor said abruptly.

'Oh! Oh, I see. When?'

'Six months' time.'

'Right.' Another pause. 'So . . . what made him decide on that? Did his firm move him or something?'

'He's fed up going offshore.' Eleanor glanced sideways at Marion. 'But he's not abandoning me or anything. He wants me to go with him.'

'Aberdeen?'

'I know. I mean, it's impossible. I can't move down there.'

'Why not? Not that I want you to go,' Marion added hastily. 'Of course not.'

'Oh come on, Marion, I couldn't take Claire away. She's got standard grades next year, and she'd hate it anyway, a city, after all the freedom she's had here.'

'She might be quite grateful to you, when she's seventeen and wants to go clubbing.'

'Whatever – I can't go off and leave you.'

'Oh, Eleanor.' Marion was dismayed. 'You can't live your life round my illness. I'll be all right soon anyway, and I've got Fergus and the kids. You need to have a life of your own.'

'Look,' Eleanor said through gritted teeth, clenching the wheel, 'I want to stay here. It's my *home*.'

She is angry, Marion thought. What have I said?

'Eleanor.' She touched her sister's arm, stiff with tension. 'Look, it's all right. I want you to do whatever will make you happy. I don't want to be putting any pressure on. You've been so good to me these last horrible months. I don't know what I'd have done without you.'

Silence. But Eleanor's fingers unclenched, the knuckles no

longer white. How difficult it all is, Marion thought. We have lost our brother; now we are frightened of losing each other. There was more than one way for such a loss to happen.

They stopped at Baxter's to eat, shortly after two. Here, in the quiet restaurant with its wooden tables and smells of tinned game soup and baking pancakes, they lapsed with relief into one of their ordinary conversations. They talked about their children. Briefly, there might have been nothing else for them to discuss, no views to exchange except those they had aired a dozen times before, scarcely listening to each other, content. The rest of the journey, after this, did not seem so bad.

Eleanor took Marion home, then went to collect Claire from Sarah's house.

'Come in,' Andrea said. 'I've had an awful day clearing out the loft, so I could do with a cup of tea. Would you like one? How was your aunt?'

Eleanor had meant to go straight home and see Gavin as soon as she could, for an hour or so at least, before he went out with his friend in the evening. But Andrea's welcome, the thought of the sunny conservatory at the back of the house, where they could sit and talk about ordinary things, were all at once irresistible.

'You mustn't run after him, that's the one bit of advice I'll give you,' Marion had said, and because they were comfortable again by the time she offered this, Eleanor had not resented it.

'Thank you,' she said to Andrea. 'I'd love that.'

What Eleanor longed to tell Andrea, of course, were the things she had learned in the last two days. What a fertile source of conversation (and gossip) for months to come. But it was no good, she could not say anything. They talked instead about their daughters, about the summer holidays.

'I think I might actually take a proper holiday this year,' Eleanor said, thinking of this just as the words came out. 'My aunt left me some money. I could take Claire somewhere exotic.' She laughed. 'Only trouble is, she'd want half her class with her as well.'

'Oh, they can't live without their pals,' Andrea said easily.

The late afternoon sun shone warmly through glass. Andrea had opened the door and several windows, but they both grew lazy with the heat, reluctant to move. Eventually, Eleanor stirred herself, and Andrea went to call Claire.

'I know I've only been away a couple of days,' Eleanor said as they drove back down the lane to the cottage, 'but for some reason, it feels like weeks.' She knew the reason, of course, but could not tell Claire yet. She and Marion had discussed telling their children. Should they do it at all, and if so, when?

'I will speak to Fergus,' Marion had said in the end. 'He's good at helping me sort things out.'

As they drew up at the cottage, Gavin appeared at his front door and waved. He came straight across, before Eleanor had even emerged from the car.

'Hi,' she said, pleased to see him, reassured. He must have been looking out for her. But he took her aside as Claire bent to fuss with Jim and Edie's cat.

'Eleanor.' He held her arm, meaning to tell her something without Claire hearing.

'How are you?' She would talk to him about David, she thought. If Marion could ask Fergus, surely she could speak to Gavin?

'Your brother's here.'

'What?'

'I wasn't sure at first, but Edie recognised him. He was banging at your door, shouting your name.'

'David? When was this?'

'Last night. He turned up about . . . oh God, ten o'clock? I heard the shouting and came out. Edie was peering round her curtains. When she saw me she came out too. Then she tells me it's your brother.'

'But where is he now?'

'I gave him the spare key. I hope that's OK. Then I got him in. I'd have offered him a drink, but to tell you the truth, he'd had a bucketful already.'

'He's still here then?'

'I was just thinking I'd go in again, see how he's doing, when I saw your car.'

'How had he got here?'

'I've no idea. Train, maybe? Anyway, he seems to have got as far as Dingwall, gone to the pub, come out guttered after a couple of hours, headed out the Strathpeffer road. I don't know – he could have hitched, or maybe just walked, though the shape he was in . . .'

Eleanor started for her door. 'I'd better go and see him.' She hesitated. 'Sorry, you're going out tonight, aren't you?'

'Yes, but I won't be late. Call me if you want. Or I'll give you a knock when I get back. Check you're OK.'

'Gavin, you said he was drunk. But have you seen him today? Is he all right?'

'Sure. I went in and made him some coffee and toast this morning. He's all right, apart from his face, of course. And there must be other bruises; he's stiffened up a bit today.'

'His face?'

'Can I go in?' Claire asked. 'Where's the key, Mum?'

'Just a minute – hang on.'

Gavin shook his head, reluctant to say more with Claire listening, hopping with impatience. The cat was stretched out on the path, and they stepped over it to reach the front door. Distracted, Eleanor said, 'Has he had an accident or something?'

'You could call it that.' He nodded at Claire. 'Hi, have a good time at Sarah's? The two of you hit the high spots last night?'

Claire looked at him coldly. 'We had homework,' she said. 'It was a school night.'

'Oops!' He grimaced, then grinned at both of them, squeezing Eleanor's arm. 'I'll see you later. Here—' He picked up her bag and took it to the front door, opening it, depositing the bag in the hall. Then he went back to his own house. Eleanor became aware that Edie was at her window, signalling wildly.

'Claire, hang on. I think Edie wants to speak to us.'

But Claire was on her way indoors. In a moment, she was back, her face puzzled, white. 'Mam – Uncle David's on the sofa and his face is all swollen and purple. He looks awful, his mouth has a big cut and – is that what Gavin was telling you?'

Edie was at her door now, head bobbing with anxiety.

'It's all right,' Eleanor reassured her. 'Gavin's told me. I'm sorry David disturbed you.'

'Dear, dear, poor laddie, I hope they catch whoever it was. Wicked, to do such a thing. It must have been a big fellow, to go for your brother, or maybe it was a few of them, eh? He's tall, your brother, isn't he? I says to Jim, "They're a tall family, look at her dad, but of course Marion's not so tall" . . .'

Eleanor broke in, afraid this might go on for an hour or so. 'Sorry, Edie, I'd better go and see him.'

'Oh yes, yes, I'll put a wee drop of soup through later for you.' And she hurried indoors.

'Oh God,' Eleanor said, 'what a time we're having. What next?'

'Why, what else has happened?' Claire was following her into the living-room.

David had been asleep stretched out on the sofa, but Claire's appearance must have disturbed him. He was sitting up, easing his legs over so that he could put his feet on the floor. 'Eleanor,' he said. 'Thank God.' His voice was thick, the words slurred.

Since she had seen him last, the world had shifted. He was not her brother, but he was not rootless and impoverished either. He had money and a house. This new knowledge had removed him from her. This was what she had been thinking all the way home, whenever she and Marion had fallen silent. And yet now, as he came towards her, all she felt was shock, pity, disbelief. His face!

'Walked into a door,' he said, trying to smile, but not managing. To smile, to talk, hurt too much. The blackened eye half-shut, the blood-crusted cut on his lip, the swollen cheek and rising purple bruises – they were so bad, his face was altogether changed.

'Don't hug me,' he mumbled, as Eleanor put out her arms. 'Sorry, it's just I think a couple of ribs might be broken.'

'Sit down,' she said. 'I'll ring the doctor. Or we'll go to Casualty. This is awful – what happened?'

'No, no doctors. No hospital. I'll be all right. Really. Bas'lly I jus' want to sleep.'

'I'll get Fergus. What am I thinking about – Fergus will come.'

'*No!*' He put his hand to his face. 'Oh God. Look, it'll get better . . . I only need a bit of time. I lost a tooth, but it's at the back. Had a huge filling anyway. Taste of blood in my mouth. But that's the worst of it. They don't strap up ribs now.' He spoke all of this slowly, finding it hard to get the words out. Then he caught sight of Claire, hovering in the doorway, wide-eyed, and tried to smile at her, raised a hand instead. 'Hi.'

A little later, Edie brought the promised soup, liquid-ised. David drank it through a wide straw cut in half that Claire found in the kitchen drawer, left over from one of her parties, a long time ago. Edie went up in Eleanor's estimation. She had realised he would not be able to eat.

'It's very kind of you,' Eleanor said, showing Edie out,

almost tearful with gratitude, too shocked to keep calm any more.

Edie patted her arm. 'Now, now, he'll be a lot better in the morning. You get the doctor to come and take a look. Dr Munro will come, eh?'

'Yes,' Eleanor said, too weary to explain anything. 'Goodnight, Edie, thank you.'

'No trouble, no trouble. You just give me a knock if you need anything else. A wee drop brandy, if you have such a thing, give him that.'

But Eleanor knew better than to give David brandy. She and Claire made up the sofa bed, and David got into it when he had had as much of the soup as he could manage. Eleanor helped him take his shoes and jersey off. He could not bend easily, or raise his arms above his head. 'Thank you, thank you,' he murmured each time she did something for him. 'What it is to have sisters. Should have kept away from all other women, eh?'

'So that's it,' she said.

'What's it?' Claire asked when they were downstairs again. 'Nothing.'

'Somebody beat him up, didn't they?'

'Yes, that's what it looks like.'

'Will the police get them?'

'I doubt it.'

'That's not fair. Poor Uncle David.'

Not your uncle, Eleanor thought. Second cousin, something like that. Not your uncle. A liar, possibly a thief, certainly an adulterer. Like his father.

What a mess, she fretted as she got into her own bed at last, dazed with tiredness and repeated shocks. As she fell asleep the road raced towards her again, cars sped past, swerved, and she braked, hurtled into wakefulness. For a few minutes she lay listening, but there was no sound from Claire, only the faint creak of her bed as she turned over, nothing from

David. She would call Marion in the morning, not too early. Early was bad for Marion, but she improved when she had been up for a couple of hours.

My sister, she thought, drifting into sleep again, my brother. Not my brother.

25

In the morning, the swelling on David's face had gone down a little. He did not look so bad, though perhaps, Eleanor thought, it was just that she was less shocked by it. When Claire had gone to school, she looked in on him. He was awake, but drowsy. 'Did you sleep?' she asked.

'On and off. Bloody sore and stiff, though.'

'I'll get you some more paracetemol. Cup of tea?'

He nodded.

While he was still in bed, she telephoned the surgery and asked if Fergus could call her back when he was free. He rang a few minutes later.

'Eleanor? It's Fergus, is something wrong?' He was thinking of Marion, of their father, Eleanor realised. Briefly, she explained about David.

'He hasn't told me what happened – well, it's really hard for him to speak, the way he is. It looks as if he's been badly beaten up. Punched in the face and ribs – kicked too, maybe. What should I do?'

'Nothing much you can do. Any bones broken?'

'I don't think so.'

'I'll look in around lunch-time, check him over. In the meantime, make sure any open cuts are clean, give him paracetemol for the pain, get him to rest.'

'Right.'

'Are you all right? The pair of you have had enough shocks, without this.'

Eleanor was touched. 'I'm OK. I was going to ring Marion – maybe I'll leave it for a while.'

'She wasn't great this morning – I made her stay in bed. Why don't I tell her when I go home at dinner-time, after I've seen David?'

'All right. See you later.'

When she put her head round the spare-room door again, David was asleep. Shortly after eleven, she heard him get up and go into the bathroom. He came downstairs after this, dressed in the jeans and sweatshirt he had worn the previous night. They looked crumpled and grubby, and the sweatshirt had a dark stain down the front.

'Will I run you a bath? It might help the stiffness.'

'Yeah. OK.' He lowered himself on to a kitchen chair.

'Do you want something to eat?'

He seemed to sag in the chair. 'What? Oh, I don't mind.'

'I rang Fergus. He's coming over on his way home at lunch-time.'

David shrugged, not answering this.

'Look I'll go and start the bath, then I'll cook you some scrambled eggs.' She paused by the door. 'Oh, Davy.'

He managed to lift a corner of his mouth, the less damaged corner, in an attempt at a smile. 'I'm fine. Don't you worry.'

'Have you any other clothes? Did you bring a bag?'

'In the hall, I think.'

'I'll soak these, then. Is that blood?'

He looked down. 'I suppose so.'

She swirled hot water in the bath, adding salts, wondering what had happened. He thinks he has to tell me something, but oh, the things I have to tell him. All at once, she was longing to talk, and draw him close again, this bruised stranger. What do I care, she thought, if your mother was not who we thought, your father no one we ever saw. You're still David –

you grew up with us. She turned the taps off, and stood up, giddy, relieved.

He had a long bath and emerged looking better: still unshaven, but his hair wet and shining, and in clean clothes. Eleanor had unpacked his bag, ironed the shirt she found there, and the spare jeans. There was not much else; he had left in a hurry.

At half-past twelve, Fergus came in, and David submitted to be examined.

'He's all right – cracked ribs, I suspect,' Fergus said as he left. 'You could take him into Accident and Emergency – let them decide if he should go in, or if X-rays are needed.'

'He won't go.'

'Oh well, time's the great healer, as they say, so we'll just have to trust to that. But if he gets feverish, or complains of headaches, dizziness, let me know. Otherwise, advice as before.'

'So . . . you're going to tell Marion?'

'Yes. Will I say you'll be in touch?'

'If I can leave David, I'll go over this afternoon.'

By the front door, Fergus paused. 'Has he said anything yet about how it happened?'

'No.'

'Ah well, no doubt we'll hear in due course.'

As he drove off, Gavin appeared in his doorway. 'Hi, how's things?'

'Come in,' Eleanor called. 'It's too cold to stand out here.' In her narrow hallway his hand curved round her neck, and they kissed. Eleanor moved away, flustered at the thought of David in the living room. 'David's in there,' she whispered.

'How you doing?' Gavin went in at once and sat down. Eleanor hovered by the door.

'We've got this pot of soup Edie gave me,' she said. 'Do you both want some?'

So they all had soup, and David dunked his bread in it,

unable to eat it dry. It was easy, with Gavin there, much easier than it had ever been with Ian, in all the years they had been married. He and David had set each other's hackles up, like dogs, circled each other, managed only an uneasy truce. But Gavin talked, drew Eleanor in, was openly curious about David, but did not probe. David seemed to relax and was brighter.

'Would you stay a while?' Eleanor asked, as Gavin helped her wash up. 'I want to go to Marion's, but I don't like leaving him.'

'Sure. No problem.'

'Later, maybe we could talk.'

'Come over this evening.'

Marion was looking out for Eleanor. She had got up just before Fergus and the girls came in at lunch-time. Ross was on study leave now, and lying on the sofa watching television with her when Eleanor arrived.

'I thought your Highers started in a week?'

Ross grinned, and got to his feet. 'Been revising Maths all morning.'

'Put the kettle on,' Marion asked him. 'Are you going up to your room again?'

'Yeah.' He drifted off.

'Never mind tea,' Eleanor said.

'Och, I don't want it either. Tastes like dish-water just now. But all our lives seem to be punctuated by cups of tea. It marks the crises, I suppose.'

'It's not as if it helps,' Eleanor smiled. 'Probably what we really need is a stiff drink. That's what men do, not make tea.'

'Well, David anyway.' Marion sounded tart.

'You're awful white – are you OK?'

'Well, I would be if I didn't have to take all these tablets.' Marion went to turn off the television. 'That's better. Goodness, look at me, in front of the TV in the middle of the day.'

She settled herself again in the chair. 'Anyway, what's all this about David?'

Eleanor told the story again, filling in some of the gaps Fergus had left.

'Did you tell him about Alice?'

'It didn't seem the right time, and anyway, he can hardly speak.'

'Oh well. No hurry, I suppose.'

They fell silent, Eleanor thinking of David, Marion of how the card had come through that morning with the date and time of her scan. *Your blood count is low,* Mary Mackay had told her the day before, when she had been down at the surgery, talking it over, getting another prescription, the results of blood tests.

'You're not really bothered about David, are you?' Eleanor broke in on her thoughts.

'What? Oh, well, of course I'm sorry he's hurt. But I dare say he brought it on himself.' She saw Eleanor's face. 'Sorry, I'm preoccupied. By boring things – my blood count, the scan – all that.'

'When *is* the scan? Have they given you a date yet?'

Marion told her. 'Not long, I suppose,' she added. 'Though it feels long.'

'But then, if everything's all right,' Eleanor said, trying to reassure, 'that will be the end of it.'

'Well, they'll go on doing scans, even if the treatment stops now.'

'Go on doing them?'

'Just to check up. Every three months, I think, then every six. Then once a year. I don't know how long for.'

'But it won't come back,' Eleanor said, dismayed. Was there no end to it then? She imagined, only too vividly, the anxiety before and after each scan, the renewed tension and fear. Another wait.

'They have to check,' Marion shrugged.

'Yes, yes I see that.'

'Anyway,' Marion was brisk, changing the subject, 'I should make an effort. Think about other people for a change.'

'Not if you – oh, damn David and all this stuff – the past.'

'Och, I'm sorry, Eleanor. I didn't mean to be like this. Cancer . . . it changes you, I think. I know I won't always feel ill, feel like this, but I find it difficult just now to concentrate on anything else.'

She had come to realise, over the last few weeks, that cancer was what informed her world. Illness, the threat of it, the fear that in the end, she might die. But it was not what preoccupied anyone else, apart, perhaps, from Fergus. Even her children – their lives continued unchanged. She could see they were concerned: Eilidh, she thought, was the one most affected. But she and Fergus had taken pains to keep everything the same, make as little of this whole business as they could. So even Eilidh, sensitive as she was, did not have this at the centre of her life. And that was right, the way it should be. But Marion, knowing this, knowing how alone she was, felt both isolated and impatient. If what you are facing is your own mortality, what does anything else matter? But perhaps this cold, unhappy separation from everyone else was partly the effect of the drugs, of being perpetually tired and aching. Any kind of connection with other people had become difficult, and she was less and less inclined to make an effort.

Driving home later, Eleanor was depressed by how distant Marion had been. There was no one she could turn to: Marion remote, David unable to speak, locked in some misery he would not share, and Gavin planning to leave for Aberdeen, whether or not she went with him. I want to go on believing David is my brother, she thought, resenting the dangerous past that loomed between them now.

When she got home, David was cheerful; he and Gavin were talking about music, having discovered they liked the same things. Claire was home, but upstairs playing a different kind of music.

'Uncle David and Gavin are getting on all right,' she informed her mother, when Eleanor looked in. Claire was lying on her stomach on the bed, doing French homework.

'Sit up at your desk,' Eleanor told her. 'That's what we got it for. No wonder your writing is so messy.'

'Um,' Claire said, but did not move.

In the evening Eleanor left Claire and David in front of the television, and went over to Gavin's cottage.

'Let's go to bed,' he said. 'Sex first, talking after.'

She was glad enough to agree. Sex was easy, you didn't have to think. But in bed, she was tense.

'You're not with me here, are you?' Gavin asked after he had made all the moves that usually worked so well, but this time were not getting much response.

'Sorry.'

'What is it – this brother of yours? Has he told you yet who beat him up?'

'No, there hasn't really been a chance.'

Gavin sat up and pulled the pillows straight behind him. 'Snuggle up.' She lay in the crook of his arm, held close, breathing in the smell of him that was now familiar as her own, and yet still intoxicating.

'It's not giving away any secrets,' he said, 'if I tell you that there's a woman behind it.'

'Oh, I guessed that. Did he talk to you?'

'Not a lot. Married woman, I gathered.'

'I sort of guessed that too. But goodness knows who actually attacked him – not the woman, surely?'

Gavin laughed. 'Some woman, eh? No, that's a bit of the story he hasn't revealed yet. But don't worry about him. He'll recover, go home, leave this lady alone in future – if he's any sense.'

Eleanor sighed, and went on leaning on Gavin. Did David have a home to go back to now? Twenty-three Duthie Crescent, she realised, but it was absurd to think of David in the house that in every corner was Alice's, Mamie's, with their flowered wallpaper and china ornaments, and good, solid furniture.

'You OK?' he asked.

'Yes. It's just – there's more to David than this. More to know.'

'What?'

'Och, I'll tell you sometime. Never mind just now.' Did Gavin count, for her, in the way Fergus did for Marion? 'The thing is,' she began, sitting up in bed, 'David's not really my – our – brother. There's been this big family secret—'

'He's the by-blow, is he?' Gavin looked amused.

'Well, you know I told you about . . .' As Eleanor began to explain, she realised how little Gavin knew. He had not met any of the people she was talking about – only David, who did not even look like himself just now, and Marion very briefly. But you had to start somewhere, she decided. He had to know all this, if they were to be together.

But all Gavin said when she had finished was, 'Oh, all families have their dark secrets – nobody bothers nowadays. I had an uncle who turned out to be my cousin. That generation was fixated on legitimacy, on sex being legal – all that. Who cares, now?'

'I care,' Eleanor said. 'Our sort of family still cares. And it's not the legal thing, though that does make a difference – property, inheritance. I never even thought of it before. But the point is – it's a huge thing in our family. Family's so important.'

'Far too important, in my view,' he said coolly.

Eleanor thought of what Marion meant to her, and David, yes David too, always, always. *Not my brother, still my brother.*

She sank back beside Gavin. Idly, he began stroking her breasts, tugging the nipples to make them stand out. She moved away, out of his reach.

'Gavin, if I got cancer, and had to have one of my breasts removed, would you still want me? Would you still like making love to me?'

'What on earth brought that on?'

'Well?'

'Is Marion worse, is that it?'

Eleanor flung off the covers and stood up, trembling, by the side of the bed. I don't know him, she thought, I hardly know him. 'Where are my clothes? I think I should go home.'

Gavin watched her scrabble for her underwear, start to dress. Then he got up too. 'Eleanor.'

She was crying. How she despised herself, crying for nothing, when Marion was so brave. 'No, leave me. I'm going home. What's the *point*, Gavin? We're miles apart, we don't think in the same way at all. You're going to Aberdeen anyway, and you know I can't do that – you *know*. What's the sense in it? Why are we bothering?'

'For Christ's sake, that might not even happen. And you know I want you to come with me. It's up to you.'

'I don't know that,' she said, still crying, unable to hook up her bra, the catches not meeting, her fingers in the way. She gave up and flung it on the floor, grabbing her T-shirt instead.

'Look, calm down, this is ridiculous. I don't know why you're in such a state, but it's nothing to do with me.'

'No, you're right, nothing. Nothing.' All she could do was stand there, half-naked, crying, crying. He came and put his arms round her, his body warm against her cold skin, sheltering her, stroking her hair.

They got back into bed. Somehow, she was in bed again, and he was all over her, there was no way of stopping this time, and she did not care, she wanted it, oblivion, the powerful rhythms of desire, fulfilment.

'Now then,' he said later, much later, as they lay beached, exhausted. 'Now then, that's better.'

And for a time, it was.

26

Eleanor had imagined that when David was better, and able to speak without pain, she would drive him over to Marion's house and they would talk, all three of them. That would draw them close again, all misunderstandings cleared up. They would reassure him that he was still as dear to them as ever, that it made no difference who his mother was. Or father. And he would say – but here, Eleanor's imagination faltered. What would he say? He had known, and he had lied to them. Perhaps for years. Even if he told them who had attacked him, even if he told them some story about how he had found out Alice was his mother, how would they know it was the truth – any of it?

She lay awake in bed, longing to go and sleep with Gavin, but unable to because now she must stay with David even if Claire went elsewhere for the night. She must stay – and what? Guard him?

However, the talking did not work out neatly like this anyway. By the next day, David was so much better that she had stopped feeling sorry for him. She talked to her father on the telephone, and he said he would come up and see them when David was fit to listen to what he had to say about Alice, and the house. Marion did not come. 'What's the point in rushing things?' she said when Eleanor called. 'We've waited years, let's wait a bit longer. He's got to be able to explain himself.'

David appeared about ten, and made coffee and toast with more mess than Eleanor would have thought possible: breadboard and table littered with crumbs, coffee grounds spilt by the kettle, a pool of water dripping onto the floor. She wiped up after him, feeling irritated.

'What about work?' she asked. 'Have you rung your partner – what's his name? – to let him know what's happened?'

David looked up from the newspaper. 'Not a lot of point,' he said.

'Why not?'

'He was the guy that hammered me.'

'What? *He* attacked you?'

'Not personally. But then he never did anything himself he could get some other sucker to do. He has mates who're not averse to a bit of violence.'

'But what on earth *for*? This is awful. I'd no idea you were mixed up with people like that.'

David snorted, unable to manage a laugh yet. 'Well, he did have a grievance.'

'A grievance?' Eleanor sat down opposite him at the table.

'Found me in bed with his bird. Well, not in bed, on the floor actually. But you get the picture.'

Eleanor went red. Only a few months ago, she would not have understood this. Why take risks for sex? Now she knew that you would, knew just how you could.

'This was Sophie, is that right? Sophie who was so sympathetic?'

'Yeah. That's it.'

'But to beat you up like that – get someone *else* to do it – that's completely over the top. It's criminal, David. You could have him prosecuted.'

David shook his head. 'Let's just call it a lesson learned, eh?'

'What about Sophie, is she all right? He didn't—'

'I don't know. Left in a bit of a rush, shall we say. Didn't stop to enquire.'

'But aren't you worried about her? You could phone. Or I'll do it for you, if you like.'

'Eleanor.' He put his hand over hers, restlessly poking about among the crumbs on the table. 'They're not the kind of people you could ever understand, or connect with. And Sophie's all right, believe me. I'm well out of it.'

Still his large warm hand covered hers. The skinned knuckles (he had fought back, anyway), the crooked middle finger he had broken playing rugby at fifteen. His hand was as familiar as her own. *My brother's hand. Not my brother's hand.*

'David,' she said, 'there's something I've got to tell you.'

'This about Gavin?'

'No.'

'It's OK – high time you had a fella.'

'David, we went to Alice's house; we went through all her things, Marion and me. We tried to reach you, we all tried, Dad as well. But in the end, we had to go ahead on our own.'

Slowly he withdrew his hand. 'And?'

'We found your birth certificate.'

'Oh yes?'

'Dad said . . . Dad said you knew.'

'Yeah. Sure.' His eyes opaque, his mouth in a tight line.

'Why didn't you tell us, Marion and me? Why on earth didn't you say? How long have you known about it?'

'Since I was seventeen.'

Outraged, stunned, Eleanor pushed back her chair and stood up. '*Seventeen?* Twenty *years?*'

His eyes darkened, and he flushed. 'Why d'you think I buggered off that summer before the Higher results came out?'

'Ran away,' she said. 'You ran away.' Breathless, she sat down again. 'Tell me, David, *please.*'

So he did. And yet, even now, it hurt to call it up again.

'I'd been restless all year, fed up with school, wanting out,' he said. 'But after that I just couldn't stay at all. Couldn't face anybody. And I had no place any more, no family. I certainly never wanted to see Alice, sort of confront her. God. The embarrassment. When you're seventeen, that's the worst feeling you can have. Well, no. But you can't face that, when you *are* feeling the worst thing.'

'Betrayed?' Eleanor asked.

'Shut out. I didn't belong.'

'But you did, *you do*.' How could she ever have thought that he did not?

'No. Faith was not my mother.' The secret self, glimpsed in the dancer on the grass, silent and graceful. He had been both mystified and proud: his mother someone special, magical. To find she was not his mother, no blood relation at all – that had been the worst thing.

'What about Dad? Not knowing who your real father was, that must have been worse.'

'Actually, it wasn't. Awful, yes, but Dad was a pal, you know. Just the same to me, really. There wasn't any other person on the edge somewhere, hovering, waiting to be my father. Like Alice. And, I don't know if you can understand this, how could you? He was still my uncle, still my family. Faith wasn't. That was what – that was the core of it. Anyway, I don't think Mum – Faith – told Dad I knew. Not for a while, anyway. She was scared it was her fault I'd gone off. It was. It *was* her fault! Hers and Alice's.'

'My God,' Eleanor said. 'All those secrets.'

'You had them too, of course,' he reminded her.

'Not from you.'

'It would have been much better for you if I'd stayed away,' he said, raising his shoulders, his bruised mouth attempting a smile. 'Never hooked myself on to you and Ian. Not been there when Ian died. Much better.'

'Oh no, I needed you, I'd have been so alone—'

'If I hadn't been there, you'd have gone to him, called the doctor sooner. I was the one persuaded you not to.'

Eleanor pressed her hands to her head. 'I don't remember that.'

'All you remember is guilt. But it was never your fault. Ian didn't like me – we both played on that. Him and me. You were in the middle, to and fro between us. He was to blame for that, and so was I. But not you.'

'But—'

'Eleanor, you *tried* to go upstairs, but you'd had far too much to drink, more than you could handle. I knew that, and I kept giving you more. So when I persuaded you to leave Ian alone, you did. You were relieved – he'd been cold to you ever since I arrived.'

'Had he?'

David spoke slowly, each word given weight. 'He never liked me. He was jealous.'

Eleanor did not answer. For a few moments, they sat in silence, Eleanor staring at the floor. There was something she had to ask, but the words stuck in her throat. 'Ian,' she tried. 'Ian didn't know though, did he? That you were not my brother?'

'What do you think?'

'Well, how could he, if I didn't know?'

David shrugged. 'That wasn't the point. He was jealous. You were easier with me, happier.'

He did care, then, Eleanor thought. He did mind. And the pain of this, the desolation of it, squeezed so hard in her chest she was breathless again.

David got up and went to put his dishes in the sink. 'Anyway,' he said, 'you should be glad I'm not your brother after all. I'm nothing but trouble. Marion is right – wherever I am, disaster strikes. I used to think it was my bad judgement, but of course it's not that at all. It's bred in me, something destructive there from the start.'

She looked up at him, but could not say a word.

'Other people come to harm because of me,' he said, sitting down opposite her again. 'Look at Stanley, poor kid.'

'Oh come on, David, it can hardly be anything to do with you that he's in prison.'

'It was something to do with me, when we were kids.'

'What was?'

'You remember the fire at the Mackies'?'

'Of course I do.'

'Mum – Faith – she thought I started it.'

'Oh *no*. That's ridiculous.' But she remembered her father speaking of it, after Faith's death. *He was home long before it started.* 'You couldn't have done – she never thought that. She was just frightened – you were late home, weren't you. They couldn't find you and Stanley. It wasn't *your* fault.'

'No, I didn't start the bloody fire. I wasn't in the barn, we didn't go to the Mackies'. Or I don't think we did. But now, years later, I'm not sure of anything. How can you be? Your childhood goes into a kind of blur; the years and the adventures that were so clear, sort of merge. Don't they? What do you remember?'

'That glow in the sky – being at the window with Marion. You were there, mad with excitement, running from one window to another. You'd have been frightened, if you'd had anything to do with it.'

'Would I? We did have matches, you know. We did light fires. We did give some to those kids. The tinker's kids.'

Eleanor was holding her breath. She let it out in a slow sigh. 'Oh, then *they* . . .'

'God knows. They didn't have a forensic science team going over the place next day, did they? Not in those days. The father got the blame – he smoked.' He leaned back folding his arms, looking at Eleanor, watching her reaction. 'So did we. We all smoked. That was really why we wanted matches. Stan nicked his father's cigarettes. That was long before Jimmy got the scare with his lung, went on to a pipe. Much good it did him, when he was pickled in alcohol anyway. We nicked his ciggies, the tinker's kids nicked their dad's, when he was drunk and wouldn't notice, wouldn't leather them.'

'You remember all that,' Eleanor said, 'so you must remember what happened that night.'

David shook his head. 'Not really. But the point is, I'm still responsible. Whatever happened. *Responsible!* That's not really the word for me, is it?'

'All that – it's got nothing to do with whose son you are.'

'No?' He cast around for his cigarettes, lit one. 'Sorry, can I smoke it in here? I need it.'

'Yes, sure.' She breathed in his smoke.

David turned the lit cigarette in his fingers, watching it burn. 'Marion's right,' he said. 'I'm a curse – I wreak havoc for other people. I was right to leave; it's better if I keep away.'

He was dramatising, she thought, annoyed with him, and yet uneasy. 'Didn't you think how awful it was for us, not knowing where you were?'

David shrugged, and drew on his cigarette. 'I used to think, you know, that I would look for my father one day. My real father.'

'And did you?'

'No.'

'But you knew who he was?' Do I have to tell him this? Eleanor wondered. Please God, don't let me have to tell anybody anything any more.

'Oh yeah, Mum said. *Faith.*' He shrugged, half-laughing at himself. 'So I decided if he was such a jerk I didn't want to meet him anyway. Except maybe to spit in his eye.'

'Oh, David.'

'After all, if I'm such a liability, it must be because of him, eh? His legacy.'

'But Mum and Dad are your *real* parents, they brought you up.' She bit her lip. 'I'll never get used to this, never.'

'That I'm not your true blood brother?'

'Any of it. The lying. Years and years of it. Mum and Dad, and Alice and Mamie. Then you.' She took a deep breath. 'And then you come and tell me that when Ian had that heart attack, it wasn't the way I remember it. You have a different version. But why should I believe yours? You've been lying to me since you were seventeen. Not just about jobs, girlfriends, what you're up to all the time. About *who you are*.'

David looked down, not answering.

'So tell me,' she pleaded, in tears now, 'why should what you say about anything be the truth? How could anyone tell, anyway? You don't even remember what you've done. What you're guilty of.' He was blurred by tears; she could not see him any more. 'There just isn't any truth,' she said, and got up, tearing off a square of kitchen paper, blowing her nose.

'I'm sorry,' he said. 'I know I should have talked to you and Marion. You especially.'

'Well, why didn't you?'

'Och, I don't know, Eleanor. There was Dad, keeping quiet because Mum wanted him to. Even after Mum's funeral – Alice came to him then and said he'd got to tell me. So of course, Dad said, "David knows, Alice. He's known since he left school".'

'Oh God. What did she say to that?'

'Something like, obviously if I'd wanted to, I would have gone to her before now. Something about being punished for it. God knows. Anyhow, the money kept on coming.'

'What money?'

David told her about those stilted conversations with his father, as the arrangements Alice had made to pay for what she called his 'upkeep' were explained.

'Your mother wants me to go over this with you,' he had said, bringing out the building society book, the records they had kept.

'Which one? Which mother?' he had asked. ('I was nine-teen,' he told Eleanor now, 'and still sore as hell.') His father, confused, embarrassed, said, 'I meant Faith.'

'So that was it,' David shrugged. 'There was always money when I needed it. In my many . . . crises.'

'Did you never . . .' Eleanor hesitated. 'Did you never speak to Alice about it directly, nor she to you?'

'No.'

'You never even . . . acknowledged it?'

He did not answer this directly. 'I was angry and sore, and guilty too, for going off and upsetting them all. The silence just sort of got stronger. In the end, it was impossible to break it. And the truth – I never wanted it to be the truth. I wanted to pretend Faith – well, I wanted to go on believing what I'd believed when I was a kid.' He smiled, mocking himself. 'But I went on taking the money, of course.'

'And now she's dead, and you've got *all* her money,' Eleanor said, but wonderingly, not thinking for the moment how this would sound to David.

He scraped his chair back violently. 'Say that again?'

'Oh God. Dad was trying to reach you as well, you know. When you're a bit better he's going to come and talk to you. About this.'

'About *what*?'

'Alice left you her house, her money.'

'She can't have done.' He was white.

'Well, she has. I mean, Mamie's all right, she's to live in the house till she dies, or whatever. But you own it, and there's money. I don't know how much, but Dad says – David, are you all right?'

'Christ.'

'What's wrong?'

'Come on, I can't *take* it. I can't take the house, the money – a fucking penny of it.'

'Why not? It's yours, she was your mother. She wanted you to have it.'

'I never had the guts, the *guts* even to speak to her. I can't take it.'

She had never seen him like this. 'David . . .'

'Christ, Eleanor, sorry, I've got to get out of here.'

'You can't, you're not well.'

He looked round wildly, snatched at his jersey hanging on the back of a chair, and pulled it over his head, wincing as it caught on his face. 'Got to get out. Don't worry. Just fresh air, that's all. A walk.'

'Don't go far – let me come too.'

'*No!* Just leave me, *leave* me, Eleanor. Please.'

She let him go. This is no good, she thought, tears falling again. This is no good at all. Everything's just coming to pieces, our whole family. Eventually, she stopped crying in this hopeless fashion, blew her nose again, and went to the telephone to call her father. She would ask him to come now. He was the one who had to deal with this, and speak to David.

He was a long time coming to the telephone. He's in the garden, Eleanor thought, I'll have to try later. But then, just as she was about to replace the receiver, he answered.

'Dad, are you OK? Were you outside?'

'No, no. Just takes me a while to get through.'

'Look, I'm sorry, but I told David about Alice's house – there wasn't any way I couldn't. We've been talking and talking. Could you come now, do you think? Could you come up as soon as you can? He's saying he won't take the money or the house. He's really upset about it.'

'Well, I would lass, but there's a problem.'

'What's wrong?'

'You'll mind I sprained my ankle at Christmas?' Christmas? Eleanor could hardly remember it. 'It seems I've done it again. Must have left a weakness, I don't know. I slipped coming down the stepladder.'

'What on earth were you doing on a stepladder? Are you all right?'

'Aye, aye, but I'd to get the doctor in, and I'm all strapped up. I've to have an X-ray. There's an ambulance comes round for the old folk, and it'll pick me up, take me in to the hospital. I canna drive, you see.'

'Oh *Dad*. Oh dear. Could we bring David down to you then? I just feel it's all got to be sorted out.'

'Aye, lass. You do that.'

'Are you managing? Are you all right?'

'Oh, Ruby's coming in. She's very good, Ruby.'

'We'll come down then, in a day or so.'

'You could visit Mamie. I'm nae able, with this foot of mine.'

'Right then. I'll speak to David.'

But first she would tell Marion.

'What do you think?' she asked her sister. 'I'm right, amn't I? It should be Dad that speaks to him.' Silence. What have I said? Eleanor wondered. Am I all wrong here, all wrong again?

'I'm coming too.' Marion's voice was firmer than Eleanor had heard it for months. 'You and me and David, the three of us. We have to speak to Dad together, and Mamie too, probably.'

Eleanor let out a breath of relief. 'Are you sure? Oh Marion, what a relief. Are you sure you can manage?'

'Yes. I'm not dead yet. And I don't intend to die.'

'No, I didn't mean—'

'It's all right. I'm all right. Well, no, I'm not, I feel foul, but I can't let my life just slip past like this. I've got to fight for it. So I'm coming with you.'

David had gone up the hill, and was sitting on a boulder near the farm gate where Eleanor herself had often paused to catch her breath, and hold the view like a great painting in her arms. Below them, the shining firth, the gentle rise of the Black Isle beyond, little huddles of houses set in fertile land, green and golden with spring growth. On the water, the white specks that were oyster-catchers or shelduck, too far to see which, gently bobbing. Water mirrored sky, glinting blue and grey.

'My view,' Eleanor said, reaching him a little out of breath, relieved to see that all he was doing was sitting smoking, and gazing out over hillside, woods and firth, to the place beyond. 'I love it up here.'

'I can see why,' he said, not looking at her yet.

'Are you all right?'

'Sure.'

'Dad's sprained his ankle again, quite badly. But I said we wanted to see him, and as he obviously can't come here . . .'

'What?'

'Well, we could go to Pitcairn. Marion says she'll come too. The three of us. To talk to Dad.' David put out his cigarette, and buried the stub, but he did not speak. 'Move over,' Eleanor told him. 'There's room for two on that boulder.'

They sat in silence together, as a flock of grey-lag geese rose from the water, their clacking a distant chorus, watched them wheel and turn and alight again, as the clouds shifted and broke, and the sun came and went, altering the light moment by moment.

'You're still my brother,' Eleanor said.

He laughed. 'Let's not bother with the facts, eh?'

She flushed. 'Shut up. Why are you making fun of me?'

'I'm not. Sorry.'

'I thought I was pregnant, you know,' she said abruptly, the words out almost before she knew she was going to say them. 'I thought I was having a baby, with Gavin. Then I thought he would leave, maybe even go back to his – to the woman he was with before. I was still unsure of him, it was all a bit unreal. I realised I could easily end up having a baby on my own. And before I knew all this, all this about Alice, I thought, Well, I'll ask David. He can come and help me, stay with me.'

'Ask me?'

'Yes. I thought, If I can't have Gavin, if I have to go through this on my own, David will come. To help me bring up the child.'

For several long minutes David did not speak. Eleanor kept looking at the firth, and waited. Then he put his arm round her and squeezed, tight.

'You know something? That's the nicest thing anybody's ever said to me.' He shook his head, almost laughing, but she saw the glitter of tears on his lashes, blinked away. 'Oh God, Eleanor, what a fate for any kid. Me as its guardian.'

'Well,' Eleanor persisted, 'that's what I would have wanted.'

'You're not then? Not pregnant?'

Eleanor smiled. 'No, I'm safe. You're safe.'

'I'd have quite liked it,' he smiled, putting his arm round her a little cautiously, conscious of his aching ribs. 'A reason to hang around. Defy the curse.'

'You don't need a reason.' Eleanor turned to him, touching his bruised face. 'You've got us.'

'Ah.' Still smiling, he moved his head to kiss the palm of her hand. 'My sisters.'

'That's right.'

'OK then, sister Eleanor,' he said, breezy again, grinning at her. 'Tell me about this Gavin who's too feeble to hang around for his own kid.'

'I never said that!'

'Really? Your turn, Eleanor, your turn to talk.'

In the open air, the truth spread out all around them, unexplored terrain, and yet familiar, familiar as her skin, and David's, Eleanor realised she could say anything now, anything, and it would be all right. This may not last, she thought, but right now, we can say anything.

'Tell me,' David said again. 'Tell me all about it.'

27

'I'm going to Pitcairn for a day or two,' Marion told Fergus, when he came home on the evening of the day this was decided. She had not seen him since he had left her in bed at eight o'clock.

'What for?'

'Dad has sprained his ankle.'

'Ah.'

Marion was putting knives and forks on the table for their evening meal.

'Is it ready?' he asked. 'Will I shout for the kids?'

'In a minute.' She turned to the cooker and tested the potatoes. 'Two minutes.'

'I'll get changed then.' But as he reached the door, she called him back. He had known there was more. He watched her sit down at the table, slowly, as if something hurt.

'Eleanor says David's refusing to have anything to do with Alice's house or her money.'

'Is that what the visit's about? I doubt there's anything you can do.'

'Well, the three of us are going down. Eleanor and David and me.'

'You're the mediators, you and Eleanor?'

'You're laughing at me.'

'No, indeed.' He sat down opposite her. 'You've enough to cope with. And David should be resting.'

'I know, but . . .'

'It's been a shock, this business. You need a bit of time to adjust to it.'

Marion nodded. 'Yes, we do. But in a strange way, it's not so bad for me. I don't mind as much as Eleanor does. I even feel warmer towards David, because of it. And you know, I think I need something to focus on that's nothing to do with cancer, with my own body.'

'Well, as long as you take care. Don't go overdoing things. Eleanor will be driving?'

'She'll have to.'

'Good.'

They sat in silence for a moment, then he patted her folded hands. 'Not long now.'

'No, not long now.'

But they knew this was not true. Not long till the scan, the result, not much longer till the next treatment, or, with luck, the next scan, the next good result. Longer till the one after. Time stretched out, like a road hidden by darkness, with many turnings.

'The potatoes must be done,' she said. 'Give the kids a shout, before you get changed.'

The same evening, Eleanor went in to tell Gavin what was happening.

'How long will you be away?'

'Two days, not more.'

'Right.'

'Gavin.'

'It's OK. You've got family stuff to sort out.'

'Yes. Look, it's best kept till I get back, but we do need to talk properly, don't we?'

'Sure, if you want to.' He smiled at her, untroubled, friendly.

'Gavin?'

'Mm?' He leaned back in his chair, watching her. Eleanor stood awkwardly in the middle of the room. She wanted to ask what she had never asked before, with him. There had never been any need, of course. But he seemed more distant now, separated from her by all the things that had stood in the way when she first met him: his past and hers, different lives. *I want him close again.* She did not know the words to use.

'Could we . . . before I go home . . . could we go to bed?'

He laughed. 'God, from your expression, I thought you were about to ask something really impossible!'

'Like what?' She was on his knee now, his arms round her, her voice muffled against his chest.

'Would I marry you, some awful thing like that.'

'Oh,' she cried, 'what does that matter?' What she wanted was the comfort of his body, fitting all the length of hers, the smell and taste and touch of him, the marriage of flesh. I am drunk on sex, she thought, as he moved inside, moved with her. Here at least, there was no need to make any sense of what might come, or of the confused past, to know or think of anything beyond the bed that cradled them like a tiny craft on a great ocean, the sea engulfing, yet keeping them safe.

'It's a risk, of course,' Marion said.

They were on their way to Pitcairn, and had stopped at Brodie's for soup. Usually, this was too soon, just outside Forres, but it had been after eleven by the time they set out.

'What's a risk?' David asked, bringing napkins and cutlery to their table.

'Throwing her lot in with Gavin.'

'So are you going to?'

They were both looking at her. Eleanor felt exasperated, but touched by so much concern. 'I can't. I've told you – there's Claire, and Marion, and my whole life.'

'Claire will be fine,' Marion soothed.

'*I'll* watch out for Marion – right?' David picked up his

soup spoon, waving it for emphasis. 'I'll live in your cottage, so you can keep it to come back to if things don't work out.'

Marion shook her head. 'You amaze me, David Cairns.'

'The Amazing David Cairns, and his even more amazing dancing – what?'

'Seagulls,' Eleanor offered, seeing a couple swoop down into the garden of the restaurant, and snatch up pieces of bread.

David grinned. 'Indiscretions, is what I thought.' He tapped the table next to Marion's plate. 'Eat your soup,' he urged. 'Do you good.'

Marion smiled. 'I do try. Everything tastes the same, though. Like a sort of wallpaper paste.' But she made an effort, and managed a few spoonfuls.

They were in the conservatory extension of the restaurant, under glass, and the doors to the garden stood open. Now and again a cool gust of wind shivered past them, but the sun was out, and they were bathed in warmth.

'Too hot for soup,' Marion sighed, apologising, pushing away her half-empty dish.

'What do you want instead? Ice cream?'

'No. Nothing, David. Really.'

'Coffee then?'

'I'll have coffee,' Eleanor said.

Marion shook her head. 'Maybe a glass of water?'

'Sure.' David went back to the counter to queue again.

'What are we doing?' Marion leaned across the table towards Eleanor.

'What?'

'I mean, why are we going to Pitcairn?'

'Well, to talk to Dad.'

'About Alice?'

Eleanor was silent, gazing out at the garden where a family was arranging itself at one of the picnic tables, tucking the children into chairs, taking plates of food from their trays. They were all talking at once.

'I don't know,' she said eventually. 'I suppose we want to understand better what really happened. But we have to persuade David to accept what Alice left him – the house, the money.'

'Have you spoken to him about that again?'

'The house? Not really – he was so upset about it.'

'But he agreed to come?'

'Yes. But he feels bad about it, I know he does.'

They both turned to look at David. He was discussing the merits of the home baking on offer with the girl behind the counter, oblivious of the queue behind him. The girl was pointing to cakes and biscuits in turn, looking up at David, smiling and answering him. David seemed to make his choice, joking about it, and the girl laughed, picking up what he wanted with her tongs, handing over plates.

'For goodness sake,' Marion sighed. 'I said I didn't want anything to eat.'

'He's trying to look after you,' Eleanor pointed out. 'You're still losing weight.'

'Ach.' Marion was impatient. Then she softened. 'I'm sorry, you're right. He does mean well, for once.' She turned back to Eleanor. 'His face is a lot better. What about the man who set his heavies on him? He's not going back to work for him?'

'Not a chance.' Eleanor was quite certain. 'I think he means it about staying on here, you know. He feels closer to us now, it's easier for him to do it.'

'Now we all know about Alice?'

Eleanor looked back at David. He had just paid at the till, and was lifting his full tray to bring it to their table. 'It can't have been easy, carrying that sort of secret on his own. No wonder he kept going off.' She still found it hard to forgive the silence, the deception he had kept up all through a time when she had thought they were close. But she was trying to understand.

'He won't stay now either,' Marion predicted. 'You'll see. He's not in the habit of it, even when there's no secret to keep.'

'You don't want him to.' But Eleanor smiled, making a joke of this. 'You still think he's trouble.'

'Well, he is. Och, maybe illness makes you fanciful, as well as feeble.' Marion turned her head to look at David, who had paused with the tray to speak to a small child in his way, whose mother gathered her up, apologised, answered David when he commented on the child. What does it amount to, she thought, the damage he seems to have done? A dog dying one Christmas, a car accident that was not his fault, a heart attack he certainly could not have caused, Eleanor in tow with some man who's only going to break her heart – and me? No, no, none of it had anything to do with David. And yet . . .

'Here we are. Thought you might like a biscuit or something. The girl says the shortbread's good.' David began to empty the tray, putting out two plates with large wedges of shortbread, and one with a chunk of something that had a heavy layer of peanuts embedded in toffee. 'I fancied this,' he went on, 'but one of you can have it if you like.' He sat down to find both his sisters laughing at him, and grinned, rueful. 'Oh well.'

Eleanor picked up her coffee cup. 'It's all right, you can keep the peanut thing.'

'I can't eat all of this,' Marion began, then caught Eleanor's eye. 'But thank you. I'll have half, and you can take the rest.'

How careful we all are of each other, Eleanor thought, breaking her piece of shortbread in pieces, the coating of sugar gritty on her fingers.

'What will you do,' Marion asked David, 'if you stay on in the Highlands?'

'Oh, I'm going to stay.' Briskly, he stirred sugar into his coffee. 'There's this guy I know in the States – an old mate – and he's involved in an industrial exchange scheme: people from one country go and do the same job in another for six months or a year. They get new experience, give their expertise to other people. Scientists do it, businessmen, even farmers. He thought I could handle this end of it. It's been going in the Central Belt for ages. In fact, I was thinking of packing in the internet thing and doing some work for Jay in Edinburgh. But this will be better – really innovative – to bring it to the Highlands.' He seemed to become aware of silence, of Eleanor and Marion looking at each other, not at him. 'It's OK, Jay's a really decent guy – no worries there.' He took a large bite of his peanut and toffee slice, and beamed at them.

'Well,' Eleanor said, 'it sounds interesting.'

'It's a question of making contacts,' David went on. 'So I thought I'd get a job here for a while, maybe do some consultancy work, just till I get to know my way around.' He turned to Eleanor. 'Could be some work for you in it, if you're still here. Or even in Aberdeen.'

For a moment, Eleanor saw herself in a suit, making business contacts, flying regularly to the States.

'But where's the money in it?' Marion asked. 'I mean, is this Jay going to pay you?'

'Well, it's commission. I get a fee for every exchange I fix up.'

'I see.' Eleanor let go of the woman in the suit, with her mobile phone and lap-top. She tapped away on high-heeled shoes, fictional, impossible.

David studied the last piece of his peanut slice. 'Anyway, I thought I'd give it a go.'

'So you're not going to live in Alice's house?' Marion asked. Someone has to say it, she thought. We can't pussyfoot around, end up having some sort of scene at Pitcairn. It's not fair on Dad, or on Mamie.

David flushed. 'It's Mamie's home,' he said. 'What do you take me for? You're not suggesting I live there *with* her? That really would be a crazy idea.' In there, somewhere, was the admission that all his ideas had some degree of craziness, but Marion knew better than to pick him up on that just now.

Eleanor was thinking of what their father had told them. She wanted to say, 'Mamie walked up and down with you in her arms all night. You screamed and screamed, but she was the one who mothered you, when Alice couldn't – or would not'.

'No,' she said to David, 'of course you couldn't do that. You want to be independent. But at least it will be yours one day. It's a kind of security, isn't it?'

'I wouldn't know what to do with security, after all these years. When Mamie . . . when it's eventually mine, I'll sell it, divide the money up amongst all your kids.' His face had closed, and Eleanor felt afraid, as if he were still divided from them, by secrets they could never know. Sharing the knowledge of his birth had seemed to unite them, but that might not last. It could take him away again.

'Never mind about it just now,' she said gently, touching his arm. 'Mamie will go on for years, and it's her home, as you said.'

The tight line of David's mouth relaxed. 'Yes,' he said. 'That's not going to change.'

'What about the money? You know there's some money as well?'

'Yes.' David turned to Marion as she spoke. 'Come on,' he said, 'you must know how easily I could get through that.'

'Yes. That's what I'm afraid of.'

He shrugged. 'You'll have to keep me right, then. Take charge of it or something.'

'Give you enough to live on, but not enough to squander on hopeless business ventures?'

Anxiously, Eleanor looked from David to Marion, back to David. But they were both smiling.

'Yeah,' he agreed. 'Something like that.'

They lapsed into silence, Eleanor finishing her coffee, Marion pushing away her plate with its half-eaten piece of shortbread. After a moment, David said, 'Better get going, eh?'

They gathered their things together. Then David turned to stand in front of them, spreading his hands wide: 'I mean it, about the house. It's in Aberdeen, it'll be worth a fair bit. It would give your kids a nice sum each – for uni, or a deposit on a flat, to take them back-packing round the world – whatever. If I do that, I'll feel I've done *something* good. You know?'

'Yes,' Marion said. 'We know.'

Eleanor's eyes filled with tears, and she turned away, so that they would not see. What can I do, she thought, that will be something good? In atonement. For she knew what David meant, better than Marion ever could.

Slowly, they walked through the shop that was laid out between the restaurant and the entrance, pointing things out to each other, Marion pausing by a clothes rack, David at the shelves of gourmet food, Eleanor by the pile of wicker baskets, all shapes and sizes, at the door. When one stopped, they all did. Why, it's like happiness, Eleanor realised, this sort of bubble we are in. It could not of course be happiness: here was Marion with cancer, David an alcoholic – more or less – and Eleanor herself, with her diminished but permanent parcel of guilt, in love with someone who would never marry her. Worse, all their lives, they had been deceived. Fundamental truths had dissolved in the space of an afternoon; nothing was the way they had believed it to be. But David, who did know the truth, had been half-destroyed by it. How, then, could the lightness, the sweetness of the afternoon be anything other than an illusory peace. They were like ordinary people, breaking their journey.

But perhaps, Eleanor thought, as David held the door open for Marion and her to pass through, out into the sunshine, this is all that happiness is.

The place was busy; they had had to park at the far end of the grounds among the trees. Halfway there, Marion realised they had bought nothing to take to their father.

'Get him some of that whisky-flavoured marmalade,' David suggested, 'thus combining the two foods he always seems to have in supply.'

'I'll go back,' Marion said. 'I'm more likely to find something sensible.'

'Are you sure?' Eleanor hovered anxiously.

Marion, fighting irritation, said only, 'I'm fine, Eleanor. I'll go.' She turned and walked back to the shop.

At first, when she came out again, she could not see Eleanor and David. Then there they were – near the car, standing close together, talking. They were beneath the trees, in shade, but Eleanor's hair gleamed for a moment in a shaft of sunlight as she moved. David, much taller, loomed over her. He waved his hands around illustrating a point, as he talked. But to Marion, for a few seconds, it looked as if he were casting a spell. She stopped, and something that was nothing to do with illness, or treatment, made her catch her breath. *What if he stays? What if he really does stay, this time?*

John Cairns sat on the bench at his back door, looking down the garden. There was so much to do at this time of year, and look at him. Foot strapped up, hobbling on crutches. Irritated, he kicked with his good leg at one of the crutches leaning beside him on the bench, and it crashed to the ground. 'Ach!' With a grunt, he bent down to retrieve it. Then glanced at his watch. They had said they would arrive some time in the middle of the afternoon. Almost without being aware of it, he was listening for the car.

When was the last time he had had just the three of them

in the house? Not since they were young, and all still living at home. He closed his eyes, hearing his wife's voice, his young wife, who had rested her dark head on his shoulder – though she was so small she scarcely reached it, leaned rather on his arm – and said, 'We'll take him, John, we can give him a good home.'

But that had not been here at Pitcairn. It was in their much smaller house in Aberdeen she had said that, their daughters tiny, Eleanor not much more than a baby herself. His memory was playing him false. It was harder, these days, to get the memories clear in his head, separate out one thing from another. But he did remember what she had said: 'As long as she doesn't change her mind. That's all I worry about.'

'It can't be an easy thing for her,' he had warned, 'giving up her bairn.'

'Oh,' Faith shuddered. 'To lose a bairn, that must be the worst thing in the world.' But she was thinking of herself as she spoke, not Alice.

Inexorably, his thoughts travelled back to the fire at the Mackies', to the tinker quine who had died with her baby. *The worst thing in the world.* They had gone through that too, in a way, the summer David disappeared. He rubbed his hand over his face, reluctant to let the memory in, so painful it still was, and hearing Faith's voice in his head as she wept in his arms at night, angry and frightened.

'Do you know something?' she had said, sitting up in bed, blowing her nose, defying the tears. He did not want to hear, but knew he must.

'We've been over it,' he began.

'I used to dream Alice had come back for him. When he was a baby, little, I used to dream she had stolen him back. Once, I even thought . . .' She shook her head. 'But now – now I almost wish she had.'

'You don't mean that, you don't mean it,' he soothed, his arms round her as she leaned on his chest, breathing hard, trying not to cry in case she woke the girls. Anxiety was like a stone in his chest, immovable. He was helpless; they could do nothing. Worse than anything had been the way she cried, his wife who rarely wept, and never did again, like that.

Never, he thought, looking up to see a cloud covering the sun, darkening the shadows among the bushes, between the lilac trees. The scent of the lacy cones of blossom travelled up the garden towards him, heavy and sweet. For a moment, he fancied he saw her again. Oh, not the tinker, not her but his wife, tiny and quick-moving, her feet scarcely touching the ground. He leaned back and rubbed his eyes. When he looked again, the garden was empty, the only movement a blackbird, flying up between the trees.

No, no, he scolded himself. There were no ghosts here at Pitcairn. It was all in the imagination. Then he turned, tilting his head, listening. He thought he heard Eleanor's car, the sound of it on the drive, his children coming home.

Epilogue)

Across the fields from the Mains of Pitcairn, moving slowly in windless air, came the hot smells of charred wood, burnt straw, and something else, not so natural, or clean. They came in a haze of what was no longer smoke, but an invisible vapour that settled on paths and trees with a fine dusting of ash. You could not see it now, but it caught in your throat when you breathed in. At the farm, the air still quivered above the ruins of the barn, but that may have been no more than the heat of the afternoon, which was even heavier and more intense than the previous day.

At the far end of the garden at Pitcairn, under the apple trees, it was cooler, and you could hardly smell smoke any more. Eleanor sat with her back to one of the tree trunks, laying her selection of leaves in a circle. At Pitcairn today, she counted, there were four grown-ups, three children and two cats. One cat was their own, young and skittish; the other was an elderly tabby from the Mains, that spent more than half its time here. Eleanor had a leaf for each member of the family. She included the tabby cat. It rolled over on its back next to her, the fur on its stomach the colour of honey, and stretched out a paw to touch one of the leaves. There were only four so far, because it took Eleanor so long to choose the best one for each person.

Her father's was a horse-chestnut leaf, from the tree at the end of the drive. It had five fingers: one for each member of the family at Pitcairn (not counting cats, this time) because he looked after all of them. Her mother's was a pair of sycamore wings, like a tiny dancer.

Hearing her name, Eleanor paused and looked up. She was at the end of the path near the apple trees, out of everyone's sight. Her mother was calling.

'I'm here!'

Faith was standing on the path, a few yards away. 'Aunt Alice wants to take some snaps with her new camera.'

'Do I have to come? I'm busy.'

'It won't take long.'

'My leaves might blow away.'

Faith turned to go back up the path towards the house. 'Hurry up,' she said. 'We're all waiting for you.'

Reluctantly, Eleanor rose and left her game.

They were by the bench at the back door. As Faith reappeared, Alice raised her camera and pressed the button: *click*.

'Oh,' Faith said. 'I haven't even brushed my hair.'

Mamie had her compact out, and was peering into the little mirror. Eleanor's father was sitting on the bench waiting, with Marion next to him, nursing her doll.

'I'm wanting back to my runner beans,' he said. 'I was in the middle of tying them up.'

'Where's David?' Alice asked. 'I thought he was here a minute ago.'

David was discovered in a tree, and made to come down. Eventually, Alice had them all arranged: adults on the bench, children kneeling in front. As soon as the first photograph was taken, John Cairns was off, back down to his vegetable plot.

'I'll take one of just the bairns,' Alice said.

'We'd better hurry up then,' Faith warned. 'Look at these black clouds.'

As he worked, John could hear the women talking. The sharp rise of Faith's voice told him David was being awkward, and he sighed. Then they must have gone indoors, for it went quiet. A few minutes later Eleanor strolled past the fence that bordered the vegetable garden, singing to herself and waving a bunch of leaves.

Later, as he hoed round the carrots, he felt a drop of two of rain in the sultry air, and was glad to see Faith appearing at the gate.

'Am I getting a fly cup?' he asked her, resting his hoe. 'I could do with one, it's thirsty work the day. I felt a spit of rain a minute ago – we'll get a thunder clap soon.'

'I've the kettle on,' Faith said, coming up to him. 'John – there's an awful thing happened.'

'What's that?' But he could tell from her face, from the steady way she walked, that there was no crisis over one of the children. When David fell from the horse-chestnut and cracked his head, she had come flying down the garden, white and breathless.

'Sheila Mackie's been in.'

'Ah. How is she?'

'Och, you know Sheila. Never any self-pity.' Her face was grave.

'It's a terrible blow, all their hay harvest gone, and—' John began. Faith reached out a hand and plucked a twig from his sleeve. 'Is there something else?' he asked.

'Yes.'

He waited, then she looked up full into his face.

'There were two bodies found,' she said. 'Dead in the fire – they must have been trapped.' He gripped her arm, as if to steady her, but really for himself. 'The tinker and her baby,' she went on. 'That young woman who came to the door yesterday. Sheila said Dan had turned them away in the end, he was scared the man would smoke in the barn. But they must have gone in anyway.'

'Good God,' he said, his grip on her arm slackening as they moved a little apart, no longer looking at each other, but at the brown earth below, cracked and dry in the heat.

'What did David say?' he asked at last.

'I told you. They were nowhere near the Mains. Nowhere near,' she repeated.

'I hope to God they werena. I couldna bear it if for one minute I thought . . .'

She raised her hand and laid it on his lips, pressing gently, silencing him. 'The other bairns are all right,' she said. 'The two wee boys were out of the place.' Her voice sharpened. 'And her man was found in a ditch with an empty bottle this morning. They think he left a cigarette end in the barn before he went out, and it smouldered away . . .' She stood back, watching her husband's face lighten.

'Davy and Stanley – you think they were playing with these loons?'

'That's what I think. Davy is scared to say, he knows he was supposed to be home long since, not supposed to be with these laddies at all. But they were raking away somewhere, down the woods as usual. Forgot the time.'

'Aye, that's what it will have been.' He paused. 'It'll upset the bairns if we tell them.'

'They'll hear it anyway, bound to.' She patted his arm. 'But we'll not talk of it in this house.'

In the distance, the first rumble of thunder growled like a beast stirring beneath the horizon, so low did the black clouds there seem.

'Come in,' Faith said. 'It's away to rain at last.'

'Right.' But when she had gone, he stood for several long minutes, leaning on his hoe, gazing at the earth.

Down by the apple trees, Eleanor laid out her leaves again, this time in a circle. The cat had gone, and she was alone. Often on Sundays, she and Marion played together all day, and sometimes David joined in, because Sunday was the one day Violet and Stanley were not allowed to come. Violet went to her aunt's house in Aberdeen for dinner, and Stanley went to his Granny's house straight after Sunday school. He looked a different boy, in white shirt and pressed shorts, his hair shiny with Brylcreem, and smoothed flat. Sometimes he did turn up at tea-time, and was allowed to stay for an hour. However, today he and Davy were in awful trouble for coming home so late the night before, so she did not think Stanley would reappear for a while.

The hot, heavy weather had made everyone irritable, and they had all fallen out soon after the aunts came at dinner-time. Eleanor had been glad to be alone, but now she was bored. The leaf game was silly; she couldn't be bothered with it any more. What was she going to *do* anyway, now she had one for everybody? The air seemed to press in on her, stifling. She had heard thunder once or twice, but it was still so far away it did not frighten her. Then, all at once, the branches overhead moved in a new flurry of breeze, and a few drops of rain pattered through, softly at first, then faster and harder, knocking leaves sideways, stinging on her arms and legs. Someone was coming along the path, someone she felt rather than heard. Turning, she saw through the trees a dark figure carrying a bundle. For a moment, she thought it was the tinker lady, who was camping by the woods yesterday. Somewhere, a cry that was thin as the wind, echoed in the darkening air.

Then she saw it was Aunt Alice, come to bring her indoors, Aunt Alice carrying her jacket and an umbrella, so that she would not get soaked running up the long garden to the back door. Suddenly, making her jump, the tabby shot past her, its tail stiff and horizontal, mewing with disgust at the rain, making for shelter.

'Come away, Eleanor,' Aunt Alice said. 'There's going to

be a real downpour.' She handed Eleanor her jacket, and spread the black umbrella over them both. 'Ready?'

The rain was sweeping across the garden in torrents now. Eleanor kept close to Aunt Alice, and they began to run, both of them laughing, because they were soaked through in a minute.

'There now,' Alice said, shaking her brolly out of the back door as Eleanor ran past her into the kitchen. 'Is that everybody?'

'No,' Faith said. 'Goodness knows where David is.' Outside, the rain poured down, a grey curtain veiling the garden.

'He'll be in his camp,' Marion said. 'He's got a camp behind the henhouse.'

Across the sky, a yellow glitter of lightning. Instinctively, they all stepped back, and John began to close the door. Faith took his arm, and held it.

'David,' she said, But Alice was stepping out already, her umbrella whipping open, catching in the wind, her skirt twisting round her legs.

'I'll go,' she said, and plunged outside again.

'I hope the lightning won't get her,' Marion said, and Eleanor, in fright, burst into tears.

'Don't be daft,' her mother said. Everyone else laughed, but Faith was unsmiling. Standing by the door, she waited for Alice to bring David in.

Down under the apple trees, a gust of wind swept up Eleanor's circle of leaves, and whirled them into the air. The beech leaf she had found for David, that was lightest of all, blew up and over the wall, out into the field and away.